THE AMERICAN

This is a work of fiction. Characters, locations, entities, and events are either products of the author's imagination or are used fictitiously; any resemblance to actual characters, locations, entities, and events are entirely coincidental.

First published in the United States by Grimweir Publishing.

For inquiries, please contact Grimweir Publishing, LLC, 8800 W. 116th Circle, #6161, Broomfield, Colorado 80021, U.S.A.

THE AMERICAN

by Indy River

for my children

PROLOGUE

DIARY OF MING—FINAL ENTRY

I don't think anyone heard me. Not when I said they should stop ten years ago because people would get hurt. Not when I begged them to stop nine years ago, so no one else would be. Not when I screamed so loudly eight years ago when they told me you were dead. And not on the nights since when I've cried myself to sleep because our son made a gesture or expression that reminded me so much of you.

You would be proud of him, even more than you already were. He's such a good boy, such a bright light. He always seeks happiness and accepts joy wherever he finds it. His mind is so sharp, like yours. He loves puzzles like you did—he cannot resist them. But we both feel your absence, even though he was too young to remember.

I did not want your death to be in vain. When no one here would listen, I tried to tell someone else. Not the government or police, for fear of the ties our employer may have with them. Instead, I bided my time and then risked everything to tell an outsider. But the outsider did not listen, either, since I did not have proof of my words. Then, for a long time, I tried for a time to do nothing, for our son's sake. I am all he has left. But I know the meaning of the legends on the walls too well, and it is getting worse. Now they have set a meeting. This means that more people will die. I am afraid that it will not be the occasional one or two that they can cover up. It will be many.

I cannot do nothing. I must get the proof required. I must get someone to listen. I must try. I will honor your death and our son's life. Before it is too late for everyone.

PART 1
American Tourist

1

I tore out the door and down the walkway, attempting a beeline for the two dragon-topped stone pillars marking the property's entry. Torpedoes of cold rain stung my eyes, and I tried to shield my face with one hand and squint through the darkness while running. It wasn't easy, and was made even harder by the fact that I was making the trek in thin, cotton ankle socks. The soles of my feet let me know the moment they left the hard, stone-paved walkway and hit the bumpy, rough gravel road. (*Holy*...!) Unfortunately, I didn't have time for pain, so my wince and gasp had to be sucked down as I kept moving.

This all would have been difficult enough for someone making a mad dash, but these were only secondary concerns. My biggest, most alarming hindrance was clinging to my left hand: the kid. I was dragging along a young boy I barely knew, who didn't get what was going on. I couldn't explain it to him because he didn't speak English. And I didn't speak Chinese.

This was all my fault. Some stupid, thrill-seeking, rebellious streak in me had decided to rear its ugly head out of nowhere.

And I'd let it.

A deafening clap of thunder boomed into a long roll. Too late, I realized the sound of the thunder-roll had combined with the growl of a car's engine. Whirling, I saw headlights coming from the direction of Zhuang Dian's parking lot, bearing down on us hard and fast. I leaped off the side of the road, pulling the kid behind the pillar with me.

Headlight beams hit the spot where we'd been standing less than a second before. I did not feel thrill-seeking or rebellious at all anymore. A sleek, black sedan raced past. As it did, a flash of lightning illuminated the car's interior. The man on the passenger side turned his head. I recognized him. My stomach gave an unpleasant turn. Fortunately, we were in the shadows.

Unfortunately, in that same instant, he seemed to look straight at me, despite the darkness. His eyes narrowed.

Shit!

But the car kept going, racing down the mountain.

My breaths came in rapid, shallow gulps. *It's too dark. There's no way he could have seen us, even with the lightning. We're still safe.* I thought the words to convince myself we hadn't been followed.

Yet.

I hurried back onto the road and pulled the kid with me. We pressed down the mountain as fast as his ten-year-old legs would allow. Or maybe it was as quickly as his ten-year-old stubbornness would allow because the kid kept lagging like he didn't grasp the "time is of the essence" concept—which, of course, he didn't. I couldn't really be mad at him for either stubbornness or for having kid-legs. Besides, it would take up too much time and energy to stop and try to explain things to him, and I had to use everything in me to keep dragging him.

Ten-year-olds are not light.

He also kept trying to speak to me, but I kept shooshing him by talking over him with a cheerful, "Come on! You're doing great!" and giving a bright smile that I didn't feel, so it probably came out like a scary grimace each time. Which likely made him more reluctant because then I had to drag him harder.

My hands were frozen. I was sure my soaked feet would go numb before we reached the village. With my cell phone still up in my room at the monastery—not to mention my passport, wallet, and all my other belongings—the coffee shop's computer was my only hope for communication.

Provided the coffee shop was open. It *had* to be. I needed the computer to reach Qing.

I'd seen the town plenty of times on my daily runs, though I'd only been to the coffee shop once before, on a walk. Xiǎozhèn was a mile and a half down the mountain, over a rutted, dirt road. Between dragging the kid and trying to avoid sharp rocks poking through my socks, my normally-twenty-minute run was taking us twice that.

I tried to calculate how long it would take until someone figured out it had been me in that room and that I'd left the grounds. But my mind raced past that to the realization that, at some point, they would go through my things. They would find out that Qing was the one-and-only person I knew in this entire country. I ignored the pain in my feet and picked up my pace.

If I *hadn't* interfered in this poor kid's life, if I could've just *overlooked* the fact that he was a little tired and hungry, then neither of us would be in this mess. What did I even know about kids? *Zip!* I'd come here to find myself, and now the only place I might find myself was dead! How the hell had I gotten myself into this?

THIRTY MINUTES EARLIER...

If I fall from here, I could die.

I didn't have a death wish, but a strange thrill ignited inside me at this thought. Ignoring the faint warning in my brain, I wiggled up onto the crenelated gap, feeling its sun-warmed, weathered stone against my palms. Then I sat in a cross-legged position, with my palms upturned and my thumb and index fingers touching. *Calmess. Serenity. Ohmmmmm.* A strong breeze blew through my long hair, cooling my scalp from the earlier afternoon yoga session. This was what I'd really wanted. I started to relax.

Until a few sweaty strands whipped into my eye.

Ouch! I shouldn't have left my ponytail band in my room.

I tucked my hair behind my ears. Deep breath. *Find your center.*

The invisible waterfall—the one I'd only glimpsed from the sunken gardens behind the castle—sloshed in the background.

Like a water-main break.

Omg, what is wrong with me?

And what if I do *get caught out here?*

I thought of Lo Wen and glanced over my shoulder at the door. Not that there was anywhere I could hide out here on the turret if he did catch me. Last week the ever-lurking monk had found me wandering the halls of the castle-turned-monastery. He'd dragged me, prison-guard style, twisting my arm behind my back, to the sculpting class I was supposed to have been in. My shoulder had been sore for two days. I wasn't sure if he was pissed that I'd ditched the class or because I'd been wandering around alone. Either way, it made me think twice about sneaking out here again today.

But I'd needed the view.

I looked down at the massive steppe on which the ancient castle sat, like a series of interconnected, oversized pagodas fronted by a Great-Wall-of-China-with-turrets. A hundred feet down, the line of workers exited the monastery from some door beyond a bend in the road I couldn't see. It was just like the other times I'd come out here: my secret, bird's-eye window to another life. They were going home to their loved ones, where they belonged.

I wish I belonged somewhere. Even just in my own skin.

Some three thousand feet down the slope from the workers, the muddy, brown waters of the Yangtze slithered around the base of the mountain. I wondered how many thousands of people had peed in the world's third-longest river. Then I shook my head, reminding myself that I'd risked coming out here to get my nature-Zen on and to stave off homesickness. Not to be gloomy. I tried to re-focus on my breathing.

Beyond the manhandling, Lo Wen and the rest of the monks gave me the creeps. There was something very off with them. But, dammit, I'd forked over big bucks for this "retreat for Westerners" on the edge of BFE-sub-Himalayan wilderness, and instead of finding myself, I was even more lost than when I'd started. In fact, I felt utterly isolated: I was the only one who'd come solo, the only person who spoke English as a first language, and, at twenty-nine, I was the only guest who wasn't a Lipitor prescription away from a retirement club membership.

And this turret was the only place I could get the incredible view that reminded me of home. Even if I'd had to steal a key to get out here.

The breeze blew with a new, chilling edge. I lifted my gaze and scanned the horizon. To my right, the sun was beginning its descent behind the distant Hengduan Mountains. But to my left, dark clouds boiled behind the nearer white caps of the Jade Dragon Snow Mountain range. A storm was moving in.

I gave up trying to meditate, slouched against the side of the battlement wall, and played with my sneaker laces, which I hadn't bothered to re-tie after yoga class.

A sabbatical in China had seemed like a good idea a few months ago. I was already coming here for Qing's wedding, but I'd added this pre-wedding, six-week retreat. The hasty addition came on the heels of my latest humiliation. I'd had to get away. My cheeks heated all over, just remembering.

I would have left Zhuang Dian if I could. Unfortunately, I didn't have the money or other resources to deviate from my itinerary. I'd learned prior to my first trip to China (okay, my first trip anywhere outside the U.S.), that their government was very sticky about foreigners officially registering their whereabouts, either with their hotels or with the local police. The penalty for not doing so was prison. Not to mention my almost-nonexistent Mandarin skills would render me functionally incapacitated within at least a 50-mile radius. And the Zhuang Dian Monastery didn't give refunds. I'd all but drained my main savings account to pay for this trip. I couldn't just take off and go somewhere else. Not unless I was willing to break my emergency-only credit card rule, and I wasn't ready to do that. (This wasn't an emergency; I could do this). And not without magically learning to speak Chinese overnight.

I had to stick it out two more weeks until Qing's wedding. Then I'd be done with this place.

Just-friends. That's all Qing and I are. I repeated the mantra to myself, not counting the time he'd visited the U.S. the summer before my senior year of high school, and we'd kissed. *Best friends*, I told myself. *And Nori is fabulous.*

So, of course, I would be there for him at his wedding—correction, his and Nori's wedding. I had a few hotels lined up for that portion of my China visit, plus a bit of sightseeing. But for the next two weeks, I was stuck here at the monastery. My money, my time. Might as well make the most of it.

I shifted against the wall, my left leg dangling over the side, and began flexing my toes, causing my sneaker to repeatedly slap my heel with a satisfying *thwop*.

Looking at the mountains from this vantage point, as I had the handful of times I'd snuck out here, reminded me of Golden, Colorado, where I'd grown up. Home.

Thwop. Thwop. Thwop.

I sighed and blew a loose tendril of hair off my face. This was nothing more than a lie, a façade achieved with a stolen key. After a month at the monastery, the extent of my self-discovery only served to reinforce the colossal mess I'd made of my life.

Tears pricked my eyes. I guess what I'd really come out here for was a pity party. *Table for one, please.*

I tore my gaze from the mountains. A hundred feet below, the last of the workers finished their trek along the exterior of the monastery wall, shuffling single file, hunched over. Did they rue their lives, as I did mine, or did the glory of the Yunnan landscape tip the balance of their scales to happiness?

Thwop. Thwop. Thwop.

A biting wind picked up, stinging my nose and eyes. The temperature dropped. I shivered. Blinking away tears, I stopped thwopping my shoe, closed my eyes, and took a deep breath to center myself. *You are a leaf in the wind. Namaste.*

Thunder clapped too close for comfort. My eyes sprang open. The distant black clouds were now practically on top of me, and large raindrops pelted my cheeks. Attempting to restore my inner peace was one thing, but I couldn't meditate my way through a bona fide thunderstorm wearing a thin, fuchsia hoodie and black yoga pants. *Don't think they meant a leaf in* that *kind of wind!*

I swiveled my butt around in the crenelated gap, in a hurry to get indoors. As I pulled up my leg, my untied left shoe scraped against the side of the wall, came loose, and fell off.

Wind penetrated through the fabric of my sock.

That did not *just happen.*

My gut clenched. I leaned forward and peered down in time to see my shoe, a tiny white speck, bounce on the ground and land to the side of the trail.

Crap! I'd have to run out to retrieve it before the rain completely soaked it. And before anyone else found it and wondered how it got there. *Stupid, stupid, stupid!*

I shimmied down and hurried across the turret. On the way, my bare sock landed in a small puddle. *Of course!* I grabbed my mandatory black, hooded robe, which I'd ditched the second I got out here, and squish-tiptoed down the spiral staircase, pulling on the robe as I went.

I reached the second floor, exited the stairway, and turned down the cool, limestone-walled corridor. Everything was quiet. A sense of guilt crept up with the vague recollection of having heard the gong chime however-many minutes ago. I was late for dinner. *Oops.* Lo Wen's angry face flashed in my mind. Maybe the reason I couldn't find myself here was that the hairs on the back of my neck kept standing up.

Shake it off, Morrison. You've got two more weeks to go before the wedding. And you've already spent the money. Focus on the positives. You can do this.

It felt weird having just one shoe on, so I pulled the other off. Then I remembered the turret door: I'd forgotten to lock it! If they found out, they might get suspicious and start questioning guests. Maybe even search them until they discovered who had a key. *Wonder what that penalty would be?* I rolled my shoulders. Half of me wanted to run back up and lock it; the other half thought I should try to sneak into dinner.

Harsh, low voices caught my attention. Two monks stood in a shadowed corner, their heads bowed deep in discussion, bodies rigid, fists clenched at their sides. I recognized one as my gardening class instructor. Both men turned to look at me. *So much for sneaking into dinner.* The men scowled like they thought I'd been eavesdropping on purpose, even though everyone knew I didn't speak Chinese. I wondered how strange I looked, walking down the hall in socks, carrying a single tennis shoe, leaving a wet sock-print behind. Disquiet unsettled my stomach. Nodding in apology, hoping I'd find a chance to lock the door later, I hurried on.

An eerie hush had settled on the castle. I paused at the top of the main stairs. It was too quiet. I tried to shake off the sense of wrongness. Then I heard the echo of a small, sad sigh coming from the next corridor. It sounded like a child.

I knew I should keep my nose down and mind my own business. After all, I was a guest at the monastery; this was the monks' home, not mine. I should just go down to dinner and stay out of trouble.

Or run outside to find my other shoe.

But something about the sigh was pitiful, helpless—a child in distress.

The strange thrill sensation I'd had on the turret returned: this was something I needed to do. After a quick glance over my shoulder to make sure the two monks weren't watching, I followed the sound.

2

Turning away from the broad, main staircase, the one I should've taken down to the dining room, I made a left down the other wing. As I rounded the corner, sure enough, I saw the silhouette of a child sitting on a bench at the far end of the hall.

"Li?"

He looked up at the sound of my voice. Li smiled at me as I approached, but it seemed forced. He looked exhausted. I smiled back, hoping I was able to hide my concern. I sat on the bench next to him.

"Why are you still here?" I asked the question more to myself since Li spoke no English.

Li was the ten-year-old son of Ming, the monastery's maid, with whom I'd formed a friendly acquaintanceship. I always smiled at Ming and said hi when I saw her. After a few weeks, I'd noticed I was the only one who did this, which I thought was weird, not to mention rude, on the part of the other guests. But to each, their own. Ming spoke some English, so we'd chatted a bit. I was pretty sure she knew about my "borrowed" key, but she hadn't said anything. Normally, Li walked to the monastery after school, hung out and had a snack, and then he and Ming left by four. Now it was after six.

Where was his mother?

As though he'd understood my question, Li pointed at the ceiling and said, "*Māmā*."

"Ming is upstairs?" I asked, mirroring his action.

Li nodded.

Okay. Sign language. I pointed to my watch. "How long?"

Li took my wrist and studied the watch. I wondered whether he understood Arabic numerals since the Chinese used different characters for their numbers. Li held up three fingers.

"Three minutes?"

Li nodded. Okay, three minutes wasn't so bad. But then he took my wrist again and pointed to the three in the hour position. Again, he held up three fingers. Suddenly I got it.

"Three *hours*!" I gasped. Li had been sitting here for three hours! I remembered when I was ten and how interminably long one hour of sitting seemed. I couldn't imagine *three* for a kid that age. Empathy for the little guy flooded me. Ignoring the voice in the back of my head that said I was getting involved where I didn't belong, and the thought of Lurking Lo Wen, I stood and held out my hand.

"Come on, Li." I set down my lone, right sneaker on the bench and pointed at the ceiling with my other hand. "Let's go find your mama." Li took my hand, nodding. Any doubts I had were erased by the relief in his weary eyes.

A stone spiral staircase nearby led from the main level all the way up to the turret. It was the twin of the one I'd dashed down earlier. Li led me all the way up, up, up the stairs to the top level of the castle, the fifth floor, stopping before the door.

The fifth floor was off-limits to guests. I knew from my previous explorations of the castle that its doors were always locked. Same story now, when I jiggled the knob. Figuring the monks' quarters were up there, and having no desire to invade anyone's privacy, I'd never tried my key. I'd only ever used it for the view from the turret. But now, with Li's hopeful face looking up at me, I reached into my pocket.

I hesitated with the key in mid-air, wondering if I was being too bold and whether this might get me into real trouble, like breaking-and-entering-type stuff.

Shit or get off the pot, Morrison.

I inhaled, inserted the key in the lock, and hoped that it would work. It twisted, and I tried the knob. *Click!*

Li and I padded down the dimly lit corridor. Intricate, ancient-looking stone and wood carvings loomed up the sides of the high walls. The feeling I'd had earlier of wrongness began to grow. Grotesque dragons, birds, tigers, and monkeys leered at us in the dim lighting. Clearly, Happy Panda take-out did not come from this corner of the globe.

I noticed a human infant who recurred in the carvings, a boy. But he didn't look like any cute-and-cuddly bundle-of-joy I'd ever seen. He scowled. He looked fierce and cold—a warrior-baby. I shivered and squeezed Li's hand.

As we continued, the doors and walls became progressively more ornate until we came to the middle of the corridor. The wall on the left opened up to a balcony, which overlooked the great hall, four floors below. On the right, opposite the terrace, a massive, jewel-encrusted double door rose the full height of the wall. The painting on the door depicted two angry dragons, one white, one silver, locked in battle. The warrior-baby stood with one foot on the head of each dragon. Swans, swimming in a red lake, bowed before him. *Like a bloodthirsty emperor's room*, I thought, cringing.

I looked at Li. He wasn't paying attention to the picture but had taken a step toward the doors and cocked his head. I stepped forward, too, and listened. Voices. But before I could open the heavy-looking doors for a quick look, Li tugged me back the way we'd come, his eyes wide.

"Li, where…?" I stopped, afraid my words might echo off all of the stone surrounding us. I didn't want to get caught up here.

Li took us to the last door we'd passed and turned the knob, revealing a darkened room. He broke away and dashed across the threshold. "*Li*!" I whispered. I headed in after him. My eyes adjusted to the last vestiges of daylight coming through the windows, ahead of the worst of the storm.

Li ran toward a figure sitting in a chair facing a door in the left wall. *Ming*. Li's mother looked tense with hands fisted in her lap, head bowed, and eyes closed in concentration. Then her eyes flew open in alarm, and she whirled toward the direction of Li's footsteps. Leaping to her feet, Ming caught her son as he barreled headfirst into her stomach. He wrapped his arms around her waist. She smiled down at him and smoothed her fingers through his hair, kissing his forehead.

I glanced around. We were in a kitchen that looked like it was straight out of a Home Depot ad. I frowned, trying to reconcile the modern appliances with the rest of what I'd seen of the ancient palace. Ming leaned to whisper in Li's ear and shook a finger at him. Tension radiated from her.

"Ming—" I began but stopped, silenced by a sharp look and a finger to her lips. Ming shook her head and pointed at the far door. It was slightly ajar. A swath of light cut a path into the kitchen. I could hear voices on the other side. Curious, I took a few steps and listened. The voices rose in anger.

"You promised us sole access to that mine!" a man shouted. He had an American accent. East Coast, like my father. It was the first time I'd heard anyone who sounded remotely like home in four weeks. Despite the man's anger, curiosity drew me forward. Another man spoke, saying something in what I assumed was Mandarin, but his tone didn't match the hostility of the American's. Then a third male voice, also in Mandarin, authoritative and angry: a Chinese commander.

The second voice—the neutral one—spoke again, this time in Chinese-accented English. He was obviously a translator.

"The terms have changed. We have another buyer interested whose offer is double yours."

"*Another* buyer? I thought you said *I* was the first you approached about this! No one was to know until I made my offer! That was the deal! Who is it?" the American demanded. "It's Pathos, isn't it?"

The name Pathos rang a bell, but I couldn't place it.

The translator did his thing. There was a pause.

Ming put her hand on my arm, and I realized I shouldn't be eavesdropping. But I couldn't make my feet move. Not just yet.

"I knew it!" the American said. He sounded smug, though still angry. "That's all Pathos can give you, though. He doesn't have my facilities. You know that, right?"

A translation, another pause. Then the American man sighed; he sounded resigned. "How much?"

I was fascinated. Having been in the room dozens of times when the account execs were negotiating with clients at the ad agency, I knew a thing or two about "the game." Also, I found it intriguing that they were talking about mines. I'd learned in my pre-trip research that China had one of the richest mineral deposits in the world. Perhaps if the monastery had some sort of valuable element under its grounds, mining could be a way for the monks to supplement their retreat income. *Interesting.* And exclusive access to a mine was probably a pricey proposition, so they were most likely talking at least a couple million dollars. And a chance to beat out Pathos… why was his name familiar?

The translator spoke to the Chinese commander. Brief pain shot through my arm. Startled, I ripped my attention away from the conversation. Ming had pinched me! She pointed at Li and then at the door leading from the kitchen to the hallway. It was clear she wanted me to take Li and leave the room.

Okay, okay.

Though I was still terribly curious about the negotiation, Ming was right. I shouldn't be listening in. I shouldn't even be here. It was weird for a maid to pinch a guest, especially friendly, humble Ming, so maybe this was an even bigger deal than I realized. And, in truth, Ming was the only one authorized to be in here. I gave a conciliatory nod and took a step back.

But the men's voices carried.

"All we ask is our original price, plus three hundred," I heard the translator say.

"*Three hundred!?!*" the American shouted.

Even as I took another step away, my attention slid back. The American had sounded like he was about to spontaneously combust, and *that* delighted me to no end. One of my ad agency's account execs, Smitty, was famous for his overly animated business discussions. He used aggressive tactics to close deals, to great effect, though outside the board room, he was the nicest guy in the world—everybody's favorite uncle-type. I'd bet money that the American businessman, with an accent like my father's, was putting on a show, like Smitty. I totally wished I could see this.

Just then, Ming became distracted by Li. She left my side and crossed the room. Feeling a bit like an errant child but also feeling the return of the dangerous thrill-sensation, I took the opportunity and tiptoed a few steps back toward the door.

Through the sliver of an opening, I could see the room beyond. It shimmered with tapestries lining the walls in gold and crimson. A chandelier, dripping with colorful Chinese lanterns, hung over a massive, black lacquered table. The American sat at one end. He looked about mid-to-late-30s, with mousy-brown hair, a goatee, and an expensive suit. He wasn't bad-looking, but his overall expression was peeved. He looked entitled; a typical American brat. Suddenly, he didn't seem at all like Smitty or my father. I instinctively didn't like him. A huge blond guy in a navy suit stood a few feet behind him. The blond didn't seem like a business associate. More like a bodyguard.

A sense of unease ghosted through me.

I ran my gaze down the glossy tabletop until I came to the center chair. The translator. He was an Asian man with sparse hair combed neatly over a balding pate and eyebrows puckered in worry. He looked away from the American and at the Chinese commander. The commander was just out of sight from my angle, at the other end of the table.

The translator turned back toward the American. "That is our offer. If you do not like it, we can go elsewhere."

I heard the barely-whispered sounds of Ming speaking to Li somewhere behind me.

The American pursed his lips and glared. "Fine. But I want proof."

Proof? Proof of what? I looked at the translator, wishing I could see the Chinese commander. But something made me relieved I was invisible to the people inside.

I was aware of Ming's grip on my arm again, this time giving it a serious yank. I nodded. I knew on some innate level that the men on the other side of the door were hardened and cold. Predators.

But it was like walking in on two people in bed: I couldn't tear my eyes away.

The translator responded: "We will give you proof of our plume, but first, we want to see the money."

"No!" The American jumped to his feet. I jumped, too, and Ming stopped yanking my arm but kept her hand in place. "I traveled *across the world* with a viable offer because you said you've got a massive plume of *cad-too*, but all I've gotten is three hours of this song and dance *shit*! Either you show me proof *now*, or I'm walking!"

I heard the scrape of a chair sliding back. The commander's face rose into view in the reflection on the glossy tabletop. It was Tulku Yat-sen Xun. Not a Chinese commander at all, but the chief monk, the lama, at the monastery. I hadn't met him personally, but there was a huge portrait of him in the great hall.

My heart rate picked up. Everything about this scene was a contradiction, from the modern kitchen in the ancient monastery to the harsh parley between a Tibetan monk and a Wall Street businessman. And an apparently loving mother leaving her young son alone, exhausted, and hungry so she could sit by herself in a room, in the dark, waiting on cleanup duty. And for what? No one was even drinking coffee in there. Or tea, or whatever.

Suddenly I wished I'd never seen Yat-sen Xun's face—or heard any of the conversation.

I started to back away, and Ming released her grip on my arm. The lama gave a curt nod. Another black-robed monk flitted to the center of the table, behind the translator. In a single, graceful movement, the monk whipped the translator's head to the side.

A faint snap sounded.

The monk lowered the translator gently to the table like a lover with his bride.

The gasp froze in my throat. My stomach clenched. I stared dumbly at the comb-over on top of the translator's head.

Yat-sen Xun spoke in stilted English. "I wish you had not named substance, as agreed, in presence of translator." His tone was even, measured, emotionless.

Get. Out. Now!

Reason took over, forcing my leaden legs to back away from the door. *Bend the knee, push the quadriceps back, place the toes down. Now the other foot.*

Suddenly, Ming cried out, "*Jué!*" and dashed across the room behind me.

Whirling, I saw the light pouring out of the open refrigerator and Li digging around inside. The poor kid was probably starving. Ming pushed her son aside, rearranged the contents, and closed the door quickly and quietly.

But the movement inside the other room had ceased.

"Ming?" Yat-sen Xun called out. "*Nǐ shì nàli ma?*"

I looked at the door to the conference room, then back at Ming. Ming's eyes were huge with fear. She put her finger to her lips, indicating for me and Li to remain silent. I looked back at the door.

"*Shì*," Ming answered. Her voice was dry.

"*Lái zhèbiān!*" Yat-sen Xun commanded.

"*Nuò, zūnzhě,*" Ming squeaked.

I stared at the door and backed away, knowing someone was about to come through and find Li and me. Ming was the only one who was supposed to be here. I heard a low rustle and turned to see Ming forcing Li to quickly put on his backpack. She threw me one more desperate look, then pointed at the door to the hallway… at Li… and back at me. Terror ringed her stare. I could feel her urgency—she was afraid to go into the room where a man had just been murdered—but my shock at what had just happened to the translator made me slow to understand what Ming was trying to say. She couldn't mean…

Then it clicked. Ming wasn't supposed to be in here, either.

Blood drained from my cheeks. I knew then that the translator would only be the first fatality of that business negotiation.

I felt faint. I crossed to Ming and reached to clasp Li's hand.

With a last, meaningful gaze in her son's eyes and a nod toward me that told him to go with me, Ming kissed Li's forehead. Then she crossed to the conference room door and walked through to meet the lama, shutting the door behind her.

I clapped a hand to my mouth. It was all I could do to stifle the sob. I forced myself to focus on the surreal yet very real danger of the moment, pulling Li toward the hall, unable to look at his face to see whether he knew what had just happened—what was happening—for fear that I would lose it. Instead, I hustled him down the hall.

Speed walking. Past the warrior-baby, past the grotesque animal carvings. He went along, but I could feel reluctance in his slack grip on my palm and his slower pace. I knew it was only his mother's last-second nonverbal "orders" that kept him compliant with me. For now.

I half-dragged him down the hall while trying to figure out how much trouble—how much *danger*—we could be in.

I would have been missed at dinner. Eventually, someone from the staff would come looking for me. I could return to my room and make up an excuse. Say that I was journaling and lost track of time.

But my gardening instructor and the other monk had seen me in the hall and therefore knew I hadn't been in my room. Plus, word of me missing at dinner could easily make its way through the ranks. Yat-sen Xun could hear about it.

Shit! I *had* to get back to my room—my cell phone was up there! We hustled faster.

I opened the door at the top of the spiral stairs but peeked back for one last glance. Li turned with me. At that moment door to the conference room opened, and we saw the American businessman being hustled out by his large, blond bodyguard. The bodyguard held a gun. He looked left and right, pausing to glance at us. For a fraction of a second, the bodyguard assessed us coldly. I instinctively pushed Li behind me. The bodyguard seemed to decide that we weren't a threat. He turned the opposite direction and hurried his boss down the hall. They were in a rush.

My heart thumped like a racehorse. The door to the kitchen began to swing open. Make that a racehorse at the Kentucky Derby. Angry male voices shouted in Mandarin.

I didn't wait to see who it was this time and urged Li to start down the stairs. I turned and spared a precious second to pull out the key and lock the door, hoping it would slow down the monks. Then I ran down the stairs behind Li. They hadn't seen me, I was sure. Yet they'd all come running. They must have suspected that someone else had been there in the room with Ming.

Li wasn't moving as fast as I'd have liked. I glanced down at him. What was I going to do with this kid? The first thing that flashed through my head was to deposit him back on the bench where I'd found him. I'd had no idea this was what I was leading him into, or myself, for that matter. And WTF, anyway? What was Ming doing up there in the first place, in the dark? And what was "cad-too" that people were getting killed over it? *Holy crap!* Maybe I could just put Li back on the bench, and we could pretend that I'd never come along, never gotten involved. That Li had just been waiting down there this whole time. Someone from the staff would come looking for him eventually, right? They'd take care of him, now that his mother was dead, right?

Then again, "someone from the staff" had just killed her.

A gong sounded throughout the castle. Dinner was over. In-between gong chimes, I heard muffled shouts from the top of the stairs. Someone rattled the door I'd just locked. I urged Li to move faster.

My mind raced. I couldn't leave him on the bench. I wasn't sure how much he'd seen, since he'd been across the room, but the words had been easy to make out. The men had been talking loudly. Li would probably have recognized the lama's voice. And whatever I'd heard in English, I was sure Li had heard something similar in Mandarin. Even if the boy didn't know it, the little bit he'd heard could get him in trouble. Hell, we'd *both* just overheard something that Yat-sen Xun deemed proprietary, and I'd just been an eyewitness to a murder. No, *two* murders!

I was even more screwed than Li. I needed to figure something out. Fast.

We were on the second floor, where my lone shoe was on the bench. I was going to have to be quick to retrieve it. But Li pulled back, forcing me to a standstill. He started to speak.

Shouts came from above: "Who is there? Stop! *Arrêter! Zhùshǒu!*" Cries not muffled by the door. *Crap! Screw the shoe!* I knew at that moment I wouldn't be able to make it back up to my room, either. *Shit, shit, shit!* My cell phone, my passport, my purse—*everything*, all of my belongings, were up in that room.

But they were coming.

Squeezing Li's hand hard, I pulled him along at a run down the last flight to the main floor.

Footsteps echoed above, slapping the cold, hard stone. Coming down the stairs. Fast. We were being hunted.

We reached the main floor. I pulled up the deep hood of my robe and led Li toward the group of people leaving the dining hall.

But I felt another tug from the boy and whirled around to face him—really face him—for the first time since we'd left the kitchen. I had no time to compose my features and was certain he could read the fear in my face. His brows lifted; his almond eyes were full of confusion.

"*Wǒ de māmā zài nǎlǐ ma?*" he asked.

The one word I understood was enough to know what Li wanted. *Māmā.* But there wasn't any way for me to explain things to this poor child. The footsteps echoed closer. I shook my head and put a finger to my lips. I willed Li to comprehend the urgency in my eyes. In a burst of adrenaline, I dragged the ten-year-old into the throng.

Wading to the center of the crowd, I followed along to the central foyer, where the main group broke apart, each person going to their evening activity. I was supposed to be working on my sculpture tonight. Li drew a few stares, a young schoolkid with a backpack, but, like me, half of the crowd had their hoods up, so no one could tell it was me with him. Plus, he wasn't protesting at the moment, so at least it wouldn't look like I was kidnapping him or something. When we got close enough, I made a purposeful beeline for the front doors: not too fast, not too slow, as though I was doing exactly what I was supposed to be doing.

None of the other retreat guests had seemed to be paying any attention as they ambled through the main hall, but I was sure they'd notice now that I was struggling to pull the monster-size front door to go out. While it was storming. Wearing only socks.

I got the door open. A gust of wind sent my black robes billowing out behind me. It blew the deep hood off my head. I swore mentally as rain stung my eyes, and my face was exposed to the floodlight in the entryway. Anyone looking would see that it was me.

This is not *how a Zen-yoga-find-yourself retreat is supposed to work!*

The image flashed in my mind like lightning. The translator's neck being twisted to the side. I could see it happening again as though I was still in that room. Just as I could hear the sickening snap that had accompanied it, despite the hiss-clatter of the rain. My stomach recoiled, and the next thought pounced in as though it had been waiting:

Did the same thing happen to Ming? Or did they torture her first?

I cried out loud and clapped a hand to my mouth, trying desperately to blot out the picture.

I pulled Li across the threshold, spun, and pulled the door back shut with one hand, yanked my hood back up, and began hustling us down the walkway as fast as I could.

Focus, Morrison! You didn't know any better, and all you can do now is go forward. You have to go forward. Your life depends on it, and so does Li's!

3

"Oswald Kelso?"

Through barroom murmurings and the torrents of rain on the corrugated metal roof, the uncertain male voice carried through the air, loud enough so that the person to whom the name belonged pricked his ears. Keeping his eyes on his poker game, he zeroed in on the conversation between the speaker and the bartender. They were using Naxi, the language of an indigenous people of the same name, rather than Mandarin, but he could still make out a few words here and there.

Something about a meeting.

Kelso was here for a meeting that should have started forty-five minutes ago. Adrenaline surged through his body and simmered in his muscles, ready for the job. None of the Chinese men at his table seemed to notice anything different about his mood, and he wouldn't have expected them to. He'd mastered his emotions long ago. Anything more substantial than amusement or displeasure had been buried. Permanently. He tossed a few *yuan* into the pot, meeting the up in ante, and passed the play.

"Oswald… Kelso?" the speaker called into the room.

Without yet answering, Kelso glanced up from his cards. The speaker was a drenched young man dressed in a t-shirt and threadbare cargo pants. He stood near the bar as though leery of stepping farther into the room. Kelso couldn't blame him.

He'd chosen this bar because it was situated southeast of the historic section of Old Lijiang, away from the more frequented shops, temples, and tea gardens.

Intrepid tourists with less money to spend sometimes discovered it. Unfortunately, tonight's rain had kept people hanging around for longer than they probably would have stayed otherwise. And Kelso didn't want a crowd for his meeting.

The reek of Chinese sweat—a mixture of tea, cabbages, and vinegar—hovered in the air. Cracked, unframed posters from old Chinese movies such as *Legend of Tianyun Mountain*, *Farewell My Concubine*, and *Crouching Tiger, Hidden Dragon* curled from the walls. The posters were probably a weak attempt to sway tourists' attention from the unsavory locals gathered at the establishment.

Kelso studied the young Naxi as the man's gaze darted among the variety of patrons. *What's your angle? Are you nervous? Do you know that half the people in this room are thieves and murderers?*

A private, sarcastic chuckle accompanied his afterthought:

Just like me.

Then he noticed a folded piece of paper in the Naxi's hand. This couldn't be good. He stared, making deliberate eye contact until the man trotted over, holding up the note. Kelso nodded, and the man extended his empty palm.

Right. Money. Kelso pulled a fifty *yuan* note from his stack. The Naxi looked at it and kept his palm open.

All-too-familiar resentment left a taste like turned milk in Kelso's mouth. *That's right: bribe me with the note you've already been paid to deliver. Get as much of the pie as you can. It's all about what's in it for you.* Scowling, he pulled another fifty and slapped it down.

The Naxi hesitated, his palm still open.

Enough.

Kelso put his cards face-down on the table and stood. His well-muscled, six-six frame towered over the messenger. The other men froze, watching.

The Naxi's eyes went wide. He stuffed the two fifty *yuan* notes in his pocket, handed over the paper, and scurried out of the bar. Still standing, Kelso unfolded the note. It was written in English:

Deal's off. Monks unable to produce essential raw material. Leaving town.

Keeping his expression unreadable, Kelso pocketed the note, scooped up his pile of renminbi, and nodded at the other players.

"*Wǎn'ān.*" Good night.

He ducked out the door into the rain.

Twelve fucking months.

That's how long Kelso had been stuck in the underdeveloped armpit that was Yunnan, China. He was supposed to find the substance and get it back to the people he worked for. That's why they were paying him. But he was chasing a ghost. He would go back to his rental house, email his employers, and convince them it was a bust. He was sick of China, sick of his job, and sick of being Oswald Kelso. He wanted to go home.

Home.

As he thought it, the word rang hollow in his chest. He would go back and check in with people who had no clue what he did for a living, what his life was like.

Not that it mattered. After what had happened, priorities had had to be rearranged. Actions had consequences. Attachments were not for him.

In the storm's deluge, his clothes stuck to him like a clumsy second skin. Water trickled down into uncomfortable places. He ignored it and continued to trudge.

Yeah, he'd go home. And then he'd turn around and leave again.

In a strange way, the little area around Lijiang had become more like a home than his own had felt like in a long time. He'd been here for a year—longer than he'd ever been anywhere. There were even a couple of locals he enjoyed hanging out with. To his amusement, they referred to him as their friend. It made him wistful. They only thought he was their friend because they didn't know him. They were good people.

He shrugged. Time to cut his losses and move on.

He was still in the less-than-desirable section of town, and none of the lights were on. The power must have gone out again. He could barely see where he planted his feet, let alone where unsavory individuals might be skulking. They'd have a hard time seeing him, too, he reasoned. And there weren't many people out in the rain.

Usually, it wasn't this bad. Usually, the jobs were quicker and much more lucrative. The people he worked for had wanted to use someone else this time because Kelso stuck out like a sore thumb in this neck of the woods. Well, given his size, he stood out in a crowd most places, but in the heart of rural Asia, he was even more of an anomaly. But he spoke the language, had more than enough experience and training, and he'd liked the idea of the challenge. He'd just had to come up with a good enough cover. And he had.

He hadn't known he'd be stuck here forever, though.

Kelso thought he heard an odd pattern of rain splashing near him. His muscles automatically tensed. A lightning flash revealed a broken gutter on a house. He shook his head at the ordinariness of it but moved to the side, away from the middle of the road.

After following a string of dead-ends, tonight was the first time he'd seen a dim torch in the endless, gray tunnel that was this job—shit, that was his *life*. But that torch had been extinguished.

It was almost an accident, really. Eight months ago, when none of his initial information had panned out, Kelso had put out feelers to his own private network. Then, three weeks ago, when he'd long since given up hope and had exhausted every other resource at his disposal, something took. *Finally.* One of his private-network sources had been able to set up a meeting with a guy who said he could deliver explosive devices that had nuclear-destructive capabilities and minimal radiation. After eleven months of nothing, Kelso was doubtful. But the punch-without-the-radiation sounded like the right stuff: Cadmium-201, the substance he was after. Maybe he could get it through the weapons dealer.

Problem was, he had no idea who the dealer was. Tonight was supposed to have been the first meeting. The guy was smart to have used a messenger back there rather than send a text that could be traced. You had to be careful in this business. After living this way for so long, Kelso was constantly alert, always at the ready. He wondered, though, if he'd become complacent over the past twelve boring months. It'd been a long time since he'd killed anyone, and on this job, that's what complacency would get you. Dead.

Footsteps sounded behind him, slightly louder splashes in the rain. The hairs on the back of his neck prickled. Kelso whirled to check his six. Nothing.

Maybe he wasn't complacent. Maybe his autopilot was on overdrive.

He passed out of the city's seedy section and neared the edge of historic Old Town. The tourists were all inside, but, despite the ferocious storm, the power remained on. For now, at least. He used the reflections from the shop windows to check behind him—still nothing.

If the meeting *had* happened tonight, Kelso would have listened to what the guy had to say, and then he would get him to talk about his supplier. Kelso could always get people to talk, one way or another. Then he wouldn't need the dealer anymore. Why go through a middleman when you can have the supplier?

Cadmium-201 was a fantasy substance, really. In addition to the huge impact that just a small amount of it made, and the fact that it didn't put off radiation, Cadmium-201 didn't need a primary incendiary. All it needed was to heat up. The production of Cadmium-201, however, was an expensive, time-consuming, and hazardous process. The three known labs in the world that had tried had given up.

But, if there was some way it could be made safely and correctly, it was powerful enough that countries would clamor for it. A terrorist organization could put even a small amount of it to effective use, and that's all Kelso needed for now. Just a tiny amount.

Arriving at the bar an hour early, he'd managed to wrangle his way into a five-card stud game in a corner. He'd waited. Watched.

All for nothing.

Monks? Really? There were dozens of monasteries in the region, but few were large enough to have housed the type of laboratory necessary to manufacture the substance. Kelso had already checked them all out, anyway. There was nothing. Not in any warehouse, airplane hangar, office building, or rural farmhouse. And certainly not in any monk-house. There was no Cadmium-201 manufacturing facility anywhere in northwestern Yunnan. The dealer must have been scammed into even taking a meeting with monks in the first place. The guy was probably being set up.

Unless…!

Kelso experienced the familiar sensation of his emotions vanishing, draining out of him, as though ice had replaced the warm blood in his veins. Nothing remained but the essential, highly capable machine. A cold smile curled his lips.

Of course.

Unless he was the one who'd been set up.

Checking again for a tail, he picked up his pace. Something was up. He could feel it. Through the driving rain, he hurried up the streets and across town.

4

Soaked and shivering, we made it to the coffee shop. My first instinct was to flip off my hood, but I thought better of it in case the shop had cameras. I knew from my post-college days as a cashier at Target that entryways and cash registers were prime locations for security cameras. I needed to hide my face. I also made a point to keep Li behind me, hiding his face, too, as we entered.

I resisted checking back over my shoulder for the millionth time to see if we were being followed. I thought of the American businessman, who'd turned his head in my direction as his bodyguard drove through the monastery's entryway. What would stop him from calling Yat-sen Xun and telling him where I was?

Don't be ridiculous! He didn't know who you were. You could have been any retreat guest out for a walk.

With a kid. In a thunderstorm.

Besides, the American man was pretty pissed at Yat-sen Xun. Why would he call him? Also, he hadn't seen me. Right?

He didn't see you. He didn't see you!

But I knew in my heart that he had. In the brief flash of lightning, he'd seen my face, just as clearly as I'd seen his. And his bodyguard had seen me too, back up in the castle, even if only in the shadows. It was more a question of whether or not they'd relay the info to Yat-sen Xun.

Oh, please, no!

American businessman aside, I wondered how soon the monks, themselves, would complete their own search and figure out I was missing. And how soon they'd start looking off-grounds for me. Having nothing on my feet but wet socks had probably made me conspicuous enough already. (I'd tracked mud into the coffee shop. *Greaaaat.*)

I noted with relief that the shop only had a few customers, all of whom seemed oblivious to anything but their own thoughts. A young couple gazed dreamily at each other across a table, their fingers from one hand interlaced, their other hands grasping their respective, matching, foamy drinks. Near them, a man hunched over a laptop, his back to the door. Three teenage girls chatted animatedly.

But the right side of the shop was vacant. There, an electric space heater designed to look like a fireplace blasted away. Too hot for the other customers, I thought, almost hot enough for Li and me. The poor kid looked as bone-cold as I felt. I settled him next to the heat with his face away from the door and counter.

"*Māmā?*" he asked.

Once again, I shooshed him, though more gently than I'd done for the past forty-five minutes. Confusion and worry haunted his face. I stroked his cheek. I wished there was a way to explain to him what was happening, but I couldn't risk finding a translator here.

Instead, I did the only thing I could think to do for my new charge. Digging past my black robe to my hoodie, I unzipped the left pocket and slid my hand in. It had to be here, one of the emergency five-dollar bills I always carried. It had been a while since I'd worn this top, but almost immediately, my fingers touched paper. I pulled out a washed-and-dried Lincoln. *Paydirt!*

"Li, I'll get you something to eat. Stay here." I gestured with my palm flat, parallel to the table, on "stay here" so he'd understand. Then I squished the short distance to the counter in my wet socks and searched the display, looking for something remotely healthy to feed a child. Away from the fire, I shivered. My toes were numb. Maybe I should get him some hot chocolate.

Someone small bumped into my side. I turned, and Li squirmed in front of me.

"Hey! Thought I told you to stay at the table?"

Alarm shot through me at the idea of him being exposed to the shop-cameras. I tried to steer him back around, but he wiggled out of my grasp, looked straight at the barista—who suddenly, conveniently, appeared behind the counter—and pointed at one of the ginormous chocolate chip cookies on display.

"*Zhè ge!*" he declared. Then he looked at me as though daring me to deny him a cookie, like I'd denied him his mother.

Or maybe it was just my guilt making me think that's what was going through his head.

I gave in, partly from contrition and partly because it was the path of least resistance. We had to hurry. This small town was the first stop of any kind down the mountain. Once the monks figured out I was missing, it would only be a matter of time before they came here.

I handed over the five-dollar bill. The barista rolled her eyes and frowned at the American currency. Still, she'd apparently dealt with tourists before because she accepted it, giving Li the cookie and giving me my change in *renminbi*.

We returned to the table near the space heater. Li began to eat. Slowly at first, then large bites as his appetite kicked in.

I ignored a thousand pin-prickles in my fingers, set the change on the table, and made my way to the shop's free computer terminal. The need to get us out of here far outweighed my physical discomfort.

The storm sent a clattering salvo against the window in front of me. Gritting my teeth, I shook my head. I hated to ask Qing to come out in this weather—let alone involve him in this at all. There *had* to be another way!

Then the image of Ming's last hollow stare replayed in my head: the eyes of a woman resigned to death. My brain coupled the image with the *snap* of the translator's neck being broken. I flinched.

I *knew* too much, even if I didn't know what it meant. Yat-sen Xun, the American businessman, and a mine. Whatever *cad-too* was, it was bad news.

And they knew someone else had been in that room. *They knew.*

No, I had no other choice. I had to contact Qing.

I stared at the computer terminal and hated myself. By involving him, I would be putting his life in danger, too. If this mess was as big as I feared, the monks might track him down. They could uncover my email or just assume Qing had deleted it, and I'd told him everything I knew. They might kill him for something as small as knowing that word I'd heard "cad-too," just like they'd killed the translator. My best friend was supposed to be getting married, not murdered!

Unfortunately, I didn't know anyone else in China.

Another thought occurred to me: maybe there was a way to keep him out of it and still get myself and Li to safety. Logging on, I created a new e-mail account. I sent Qing a message explaining where I was but avoided telling him why:

> *Qing – I'm typing this from the computer at the coffee shop in the village (don't know how to spell the name, but it's the one right down the mountain from Zhuang Dian). I know I'm not using my normal account, but I believe I am in danger. Please come and get me! Also, I don't have my cell phone. And also: wear something to hide your face from the security cameras. But first, AFTER READING THIS E-MAIL, YOU MUST DELETE IT. Don't even reply to it. In a few minutes, you'll receive another message from me, from my normal e-mail account. Subject line: "Sorry." It is imperative that you do NOT open this second e-mail, the one from my regular account. Please hurry! Moo.*

"Moo" was an inside joke between us. I knew that if Qing had any doubts that this cryptic message was from me, the last word, Moo, would prove it was me.

I reread what I'd written and hit send. Then I logged on to my regular account. A month's worth of e-mails began flooding my inbox. I didn't have time to look at them. Lightning flashed; thunder boomed. The lights in the shop flickered. *No!* The power had to stay on. My fingers flew as I typed the second e-mail to Qing.

> *I'm sorry, but I won't be able to make it to your wedding. I have to leave the country immediately due to unforeseen circumstances. I'm sorry. Give my love to Nori.*
>
> - *Kelly*

There. That had to work. If anyone checked Qing's emails from me, they'd assume I was already on my way out of the country. And if he left it marked as unread, they'd assume that he knew nothing about it. I hit "send" and quickly deleted the coffee shop computer's history. Then I checked out the window again. Nothing.

Yet.

But they were coming.

I logged off and returned to Li. He'd finished the cookie and leaned forward in his chair, arms crossed on the table with his head down, a picture of exhaustion in soaked school clothes and a wet backpack. I tried to ease the backpack's straps so he could relax more easily. Sleepy though he was, Li resisted. I relented.

"Okay, it's okay," I soothed, rubbing his shoulders with my palms to indicate that I was leaving his backpack in place, then a quick stroke-and-smooth of his hair. I wanted him to settle down, not tense up. I fought the pang that threatened to overwhelm me, knowing this little boy still didn't understand what had happened. He'd acquiesced to the bizarre, furtive trek to the town, but he'd kept asking for his mother—*Māmā*. I pulled him into a sideways hug against my damp, black robe and stroked his wet hair again. My heart sagged under the weight of what I would soon have to tell him.

A chill shivered through my body, and my half-white fingers reminded me they hurt from lack of blood flow. *Stupid, Raynaud's.* I'd had the condition forever. Releasing Li, I held my hands out to the electric blaze, massaging blood back into my fingers.

Precious minutes ticked by. I was a foreigner, now illegally unregistered, in a country where I didn't speak the language. Sooner or later, someone would catch up to us. Either Qing would make it to the shop first, or the death-monks would. If Qing checked his e-mail, followed my directions, and left immediately, I guessed it would take him about a half-hour to get to the coffee shop from his place. That was a pretty big *if*. I had to correctly hedge my bets on how long we could afford to wait here.

When my hands were pink again, I slid them deep into my hoodie pockets to keep them warm but was surprised when my fingers touched metal in both pockets. I pulled out the stolen, antique-looking turret key from the pocket on the right and a flattened, bent nickel from the left. I'd forgotten about the turret key. I'd need to ditch that soon. Setting it on the table next to the *renminbi*-change, I turned my attention to the nickel.

"So that's where you went," I murmured. It had been in the same pocket as my forgotten five-dollar bill. I sat back in my chair and flipped the nickel over and under my middle finger, rolling it between my index and thumb, feeling the curved narrowing of the blunt edge in the flattened bend as it pressed against the pads of my digits. Now that I'd used the five-dollar bill and received change in *renminbi*, the bent nickel was the only piece of American currency I had left. In fact, it dawned on me, this misshapen piece of metal was the only tie I had to home at all. I might never recover my belongings from the monastery.

The door-jingle made me jump.

It was just the lovers leaving the shop.

I exhaled, shoved the bent nickel in my pocket, and checked my watch. Eight o'clock. Had it really only been two hours since I'd stood on the turret, gazing at the mountains, and brooding over my problems while ignoring the warning signs right in front of me? Apparently, the hostile monks had been making the hairs on the back of my neck stand up for a reason.

The shop's power flickered off, leaving us in pitch blackness again. I tensed. It was off for a while, this time. A voice, presumably the coffee shop manager, said something in Chinese. I held my breath. No one in the shop made any sudden movements; the rest of the patrons seemed relaxed. Probably, he'd said something about the power outage. I exhaled a quiet sigh of relief.

The bells over the coffee shop's door jingled again.

The sound of rain lashing onto the floor.

The swish of fabric against the doorframe.

I tensed again and, without thinking, moved silently to a crouch behind Li.

In the next flash of lightning, I saw two figures near the front door. They wore black robes, just like mine, but I knew these were not retreat guests. My pulse raced.

I ran my right palm in quick, hard rubs on Li's arm to wake him. He stirred. While the figures were still crossing the threshold, I grabbed Li's hand and pulled him toward the emergency exit at the back of the shop. With the power out, the alarm didn't sound, but the door creaked. Crap! I pulled Li into the rain, down the alley, around the corner, and back to the sidewalk, hurrying us away from the shop.

And smack into a tall Chinese man wearing a black trench coat and sunglasses.

The man recovered quickly and stabilized his umbrella in the split second before seeing me, and recognition lit his features. Before I had time to react, he grabbed my arm. I froze.

5

Li stiffened beside me and stared back at the sunglasses-wearing man. The man frowned. Still grasping my arm, he divided his attention between me, Li, and my sock-shod feet, which had instantly become numb again in the cold rain. Despite his umbrella, water droplets beaded on the spiky ends of his bangs due to the relentless storm.

"*What* is going on?" he demanded in perfect English, yelling above the sound of the rain. He gave up trying to stay dry and used his umbrella hand to lift his shades.

Relief flooded through me.

Qing had gone from being pleasant-looking in high school to very handsome by the time he'd graduated college. Over the last decade, his lanky body had filled out with sinewy muscle, and he'd ditched his glasses for contact lenses. Not only that, but he was truly a nice person—one of the good guys. I'd often wondered what it would be like to be in love with someone like that. Nori was a lucky woman.

I glanced nervously back over my shoulder at the shop. "I can explain," I began. But the urgency to get-the-heck-out-of-Dodge was too great. "But not here," I added in a quieter tone.

"Yes here," Qing answered, though he took my cue and kept his volume down, too. He released my arm and massaged the back of his neck—a sign he was stressed out.

"No. It's not safe," I persisted. "We have to leave first."

"Cow," Qing leaned in and whispered, "What are you doing with this child? Who is he?"

"I'll tell you in the car," I whispered back. I clenched Li's hand and started walking away from the shop.

"Are we kidnapping him?"

"What?" I stopped and looked back at Qing in shock to see if he was kidding. "No!"

Qing's face relaxed at once, in complete trust. "Well, okay then."

I started walking again. I didn't even know if I was going in the right direction. We just needed to get away from the monks.

"Uh," Qing said. I stopped and turned around again. Qing still hadn't moved. He glanced at my feet, "You're not wearing shoes."

"I'm aware of that," I spat out, glancing again over Qing's shoulder. The monks would be out here any second!

"Why—?"

"Long story. I'll explain—"

"In the car. Got it. Okay, let's go."

We hustled through the storm, a half-block down to Qing's car. The rain came in such torrents that I didn't bother getting into the front seat but just climbed in the back with Li as a unit. I buckled our seatbelts, my hands shaking as much from cold as from fear. Qing eased the car carefully out of his parking space and onto the road. He paused to let another driver cut in front of him.

"Don't be polite, Qing! Not now!" Clearly, Driving Miss Daisy here didn't understand the need for speed.

Then again, I hadn't explained anything to him yet.

We pulled abreast of the coffee shop. Qing braked for an old woman crossing the street with a shopping cart.

You've got to be kidding! I gave a gasp of disbelief at the delay and turned to look at the shop. Its power was back on.

One of the monks hurried out the front door. He whipped his gaze up and down the block. His companion dashed up from around the corner. He shook his head no, and the first monk gestured wildly. Fear seized me. I was right: they'd heard the back door squeak and, once they realized I'd been there, they'd followed.

Just then, the first monk glanced up at Qing's car. In the shop's front light, I recognized him immediately. It was Lo Wen, my evil yoga instructor.

Unfortunately, he recognized me, too.

Uh-oh.

He gave a cruel smile of triumph and started toward the car.

"Go, Qing! Go!" I screamed.

Qing wasn't paying any attention to the monks. He was waiting for the old lady, who was still crossing the road.

"What's wrong?" Qing asked, starting to twist around from the driver's seat.

"Don't look! Just drive!"

"Okay!" He put his foot on the gas, swerved around the old lady, narrowly missing her, and surged forward. "I'm driving!"

I stared in horror as Lo Wen and his companion broke into a run. They almost collided with the old woman. It slowed them down, and Qing gained distance.

"Keep going!" I shouted. I didn't stop looking out the back window until the monks were well out of sight.

Qing raced through the streets of the mountain village. If only I hadn't decided to interfere in Li's life, I wouldn't be in this mess! And neither would Li. If I'd left him where he was, on the bench back in the monastery's hallway where his mother had put him, Ming would probably still be alive.

It's my fault that Ming is dead.

An awful, sickening wave of guilt washed over me.

"Kelly, where are we going?" Qing's voice interrupted my thoughts. "Do you want to stay at my place until the wedding?"

"No." I had thought this much through. "I have to get out of the country somehow."

"You want to go to the airport?"

"I have no money—"

"I can help you out."

"—and I don't have any form of ID. Thanks, though. I think maybe I have to go to Beijing. I have to get to the American Embassy."

"Beijing!" Qing cried. "That's almost twenty-six hundred kilometers away!" I did the conversion in my head: almost seventeen hundred miles.

"I know, but—"

"Cow, maybe you should tell me what's going on. *Now.*"

I hesitated. Now that it had come to it, I wasn't sure how to handle this. My initial relief at seeing Qing was tempered by the uncertainty of how much it was safe to tell him.

"I'm waiting," Qing said. He looked as though he was trying to be patient, but I could tell he was worried. Qing had always had good instincts. Unfortunately, what I revealed could ruin both his and Nori's futures.

"Are we far away from the coffee shop?"

"Yes...?"

"Are we being followed?"

Qing peered into both his rearview and side-view mirrors. "No. Now talk."

But I had made a decision. No one else was going to be hurt on my account.

"No."

Qing slammed on the brakes. My body jerked forward against the seat belt, then bounced back against the seat. Startled, I glanced up to find him staring at me in the rearview mirror. He looked taken aback. My stomach clenched even more. I realized I was being unreasonable. I had to tell him something. Not too much. Just enough to explain but not get him killed.

Rain made soft pops on the roof of the car.

"Okay, look, Qing. I saw something tonight. Something bad." I searched for the correct wording. "And I overheard a conversation I shouldn't have. We both did." I indicated Li. "He heard it in Chinese. I heard it in English."

After a pause, I added, "His mother was there too."

"And where is she now?"

We exchanged glances in the rearview mirror. I shook my head. Qing's eyes grew wide.

"You're telling me she's...?"

I nodded. Qing made his lips into an "O" and blew out his breath. "Oh, man," he uttered softly. He started driving again. "Where were you when this happened? What were you even doing in the town? Did you get stuck there this afternoon and thought you could ride out the storm? And what happened to your shoes?"

With a sense of relief, I realized that Qing automatically assumed that this hadn't happened at the monastery. Good. His ignorance would protect him.

"I can't say anymore, Q. I don't want you involved any deeper."

Qing glared at me and shook his head, but he didn't say anything and kept driving. After a few minutes, he asked, "Does he know?" Meaning Li, about his mother.

"I don't think so."

"What about his father?"

"I don't think he has one." Ming had told me once that it was just the two of them, just her and Li.

"And all of this has to do with that whole double e-mail thing you sent me?"

"Yes. You didn't open the other one, did you?"

"You said not to."

"Good. If they ever do decide to question you about me, you can claim ignorance."

"Who's 'they?'"

I pressed my lips together stubbornly. Qing issued an annoyed huff.

We zigzagged down a few narrow streets closely packed with identical two-story stone houses. Eventually, Qing pulled up next to one, got out, and opened the back door for Li.

"Everything looks the same here," I said. I opened my own door, stood, and stared up, shading my eyes from the raindrops. "Where are we? This looks just like the picture of your parents' house."

"It is my parents' house. Their old one, at least."

"But you can't—"

Qing said something in Chinese to Li. He held out his hand, coaxing the ten-year-old out of the car. To my surprise, Li took Qing's hand and went with him.

"Qing, we *really* shouldn't be here!" I emphasized.

Qing looked across the roof of the car. Exasperation lined his face. I had taxed his hospitality very close to its limit. Right before his wedding. He still didn't understand how much danger we were in.

"Cow, if we're going to go on a road trip, one of us has to have supplies," he pointed out. He was already walking Li toward the front door.

I watched, torn, as they walked away from me. Li looked back, confused, and I gave in. "Okay, I'm coming," I groaned, running to catch up. "But we have to make this quick!"

6

Yat-sen Xun waited in his conference room. He stood perfectly still with his head bowed in thought. His grizzled, white beard made a long, narrow V down the front of his black robes. Zhuang Dian was in lockdown. The guests had been told that someone had become seriously ill. They had all been quarantined to their rooms "until the cause could be identified." The real reason for the quarantine was so the monks could determine if all of the guests could be accounted for. A box containing a sample of Yat-sen Xun's most powerful secret was missing. Someone had fled the grounds with it. Possibly a retreat guest. Definitely someone who had been sent to steal it.

His failure to produce the substance at the meeting had been devastating. The eager businessman had been furious. He'd accused Yat-sen Xun of running a scam. Yat-sen Xun had been humiliated and enraged to be taken as a weak player on the world stage. Amid the turmoil, the American businessman's bodyguard had quickly ushered his boss out of the room and away from the monastery. The business deal, so critical to the success of his plans, was lost, perhaps forever. More importantly, if whoever had taken the sample was the same person who had spied on the meeting, then the information alone could put both Yat-sen Xun and his plans in grave jeopardy.

He would find his box.

And the one who'd taken it would pay.

Across the room, Ding Li-Liang sat at the long table, hunched over a laptop computer. The laptop emitted a series of low beeps.

"You are certain the box has left the grounds?" Yat-sen Xun asked. He spoke in Mongolian, the language of his ancestors, the ones who had ruled the Yuan Dynasty over seven hundred years ago.

"Yes, Tulku," the monk answered.

The laptop emitted more low beeps and then a sudden, single high beep. The monk quickly clicked some keys.

Yat-sen Xun crossed the room, clamped his hand on Ding Li-Liang's shoulder, and peered at the laptop screen. "Have you found it?"

"No, Tulku," Ding Li-Liang answered. "It was a false alert. We cannot get an idea of the location until the person carrying the box ceases movement for a while. Further, the storm, cell phones, or other signals may interfere with our transmitter's frequency. It is the first time we have had to test it at this range."

Suspicion interlaced Yat-sen Xun's thoughts. He had begun to suspect Ding Li-Liang and another monk, Deng Hu, the last two of the original monks from the order, were not loyal, and he had beun to doubt their words of late. Unfortunately, they were too valuable for him to dispose of. His frustration mounted. He dug his long nails into the fabric of Ding Li-Liang's robes. The monk flinched in pain.

The door burst open. Lo Wen and another monk bowed as they entered. Rain dripped from their black robes.

Yat-sen Xun released Ding Li-Liang's shoulder, stepped forward, and inhaled, returning to a state of calm. Whether Ding Li-Liang was untrue or not, there were other ways to locate the box.

"Tulku," Lo Wen said. He and the other monk bowed their heads. "We went to Xiǎozhèn. A western woman, dressed in robes like ours had been in the coffee shop. She bought something and paid with American currency. She departed moments before we arrived. We saw her fleeing in a car, but she was not the driver. I am certain I recognized her. I caught her roaming the corridors alone only a week ago."

Yat-sen Xun's gaze drifted to the distance. He nodded. Out of all the current retreat guests, only one had been American. And it had been a woman. Was she, indeed, missing from the monastery? Was she the one who had stolen his box?

His breathing increased ever-so-slightly. It was imperative that he find the person who had stolen his box before he—or *she*, he reminded himself—gave it to whomever they worked for.

"Also, she left this behind on a table." Lo Wen held up a key, which Yat-sen

Xun recognized immediately. The implications brought an acid taste to his tongue. Was it possible…?

The door burst open again. Two more monks entered.

"We have completed our check of the rooms. A guest is missing. An American woman named Kelly Morrison. She appears to have left all of her things in her room, as though her departure was unplanned." He held out a cell phone. "Her last communication was a text message earlier today to a local man, Yang Qing."

Yat-sen Xun took the phone and read the message: *Getting my nirvana on. Hugs! See you soon!*

"It could be a code," one of the monks suggested.

"But the fact that the phone is not with her is good, is it not?" another asked. "Perhaps she departed in haste and is ill-prepared. Perhaps it was she whom we chased down the steps."

"We did not chase her far enough."

"We did not know we were searching for one of our own guests at the time."

"We assumed the person we were chasing had gone down to—"

"We cannot afford assumptions!" Yat-sen Xun snapped. He turned to the second pair. "Find this man, her contact, Yang Qing." He glanced at the first pair, who still appeared anxious.

"Tulku?" Lo Wen asked. "We are not certain what this means, but the worker at the coffee shop also reported that the Western woman was traveling with a young schoolboy. He wore a uniform like the children in town."

Yat-sen Xun frowned. The maid, Ming, had a son who usually met his mother here, at the monastery, after school. He had not even considered the boy's whereabouts. Though in hindsight, the boy would probably have been at Zhuang Dian today. But why would the American woman have taken him?

Then again, he thought, if the boy was with her, it would make her that much easier to find.

Yat-sen Xun smiled.

"Wait!" He stopped the second pair, who'd been about to depart to locate Yang Qing. "Do not go anywhere. Call the police instead."

7

There's something I haven't had a chance to do yet. Come here, you." Qing pulled me into a hug. With a sigh of relief and gratitude, I wrapped my arms around his warmth. He smelled like tea and garden vegetables, stirring memories of my childhood. *Our* childhood. Even if we hadn't met in person until we were teen-agers, we'd still known each other since we were kids. He smelled like home and contentment. Like my best friend, Qing.

Love.

Friendship.

Nothing more. Nothing less.

It was enough. Right now, it was exactly what I needed.

Well, that, and a time machine. Or an escape pod.

"Qing, I'm so sorry about this—"

"Shhh! It's good to see you again. Even if everything else about this reunion sucks." He kissed the top of my head and released me. He hung his trench coat on a hook and turned to Li, saying something in Mandarin. He motioned for the boy to follow.

As much as I wanted to keep running, it was a relief to momentarily get out of the rain. Mr. and Mrs. Yang had recently moved to a swanky apartment building in the newer, more cosmopolitan section of Lijiang. Qing had stayed behind in the family home on the outskirts of the historic Old Town area until his wedding. Then he and Nori were moving to Shanghai, where they would both be working in the financial district. The old Yang house would be furnished and rented out to tourists. For now, it had been overtaken by large, open cardboard boxes.

Across the room, a packaging tape dispenser lay on the coffee table in front of the low sofa. A messy stack of flat cardboard teetered next to it. I yanked my wet, black robe over my head, balled it up, and dropped it on a flattened box. I wanted to ditch the robe, but if anyone found it anywhere near Qing, even in his trash, it would make it obvious he was helping me. Soon, though, I would chuck it.

Qing kicked empty boxes out of his way, wading through the living room toward the small kitchen. He hoisted Li onto a counter stool, pulled several burrito-sized eggrolls out of the freezer, and popped them in the microwave.

Still standing in the living room, I stared in horror.

"You're making dinner? Now? We have to get out of here!"

"I'm hungry."

Qing pulled three bottles of juice from his fridge and set them near Li. The boy looked at Qing, Qing nodded, and Li snapped the top off one, slurping with a vengeance. Qing pulled three plates out of a nearby box.

"He's hungry too. Aren't you?" he asked.

"No! I'm—"

The microwave dinged. Qing and Li began to eat. My stomach growled. Having been too wrapped up in shady-business-deal-slash-fatalities, I'd missed dinner. But here, everything seemed so quiet. Normal. Maybe it was safe to take just a teensy break?

Chicken and ginger scented tendrils wafted through the apartment—my salivary glands practically forced me to the kitchen. Before I knew it, I'd devoured two whole eggrolls and downed a bottle of juice. A few minutes later, I tidied the kitchen, making sure to eliminate any trace of either my or Li's presence.

Qing ambled around, searching through rooms, rummaging through drawers and under furniture. Occasionally he put things on the countertop in the kitchen, forming a pile.

"What are you doing?"

"I'm packing for our road trip. Here." He handed me clean socks and a pair of slightly worn sneakers.

"Thank you!" I gushed, like he'd just handed me gold. I immediately sat down, stripped off my muddy socks, and then waved my feet to air-dry them. "Nori's?" I asked, indicating the "gold."

“No. My sister’s.” He made a face. “Two fewer things I have to send her when I finish packing this place up.”

I grimaced in sympathy, knowing about his less-than-fun relationship with his “evil” sister, but I privately thanked her for being a slacker and gave a sigh of relief as I put on the clean socks. The sneakers were only a half-size too big—not bad, especially under these circumstances. I laced them tightly.

Qing returned to the living room to search for more items for the road trip. He kicked aside an empty box with a hollow *thunk*, which seemed to amuse him. He said something I didn’t understand, and suddenly Li ran over to Qing. The boy grinned from ear to ear as Qing slid a large, empty box across the tile floor to him. Li kicked it back, a small giggle escaping his throat. His eyes danced with glee, and he focused on the box. Qing returned the box, but at an angle that forced Li to run across the room, and he almost didn’t make it in time.

I smiled. *Box-soccer.* Then I took the opportunity of their distraction to use the bathroom. Brown eyes stared back at me in shock as I caught my reflection in the mirror. My wet, shoulder-length brown hair was drying in limp, stringy clumps around my head, like a defeated medusa. Lines of dirt streaked down my pale cheeks. At least I didn’t have makeup on. I hadn’t worn any since beginning the retreat. It felt weird to be out in public without it but right now, smeared eye-makeup would have made me look even worse. It was incredible that Qing hadn’t said anything about how scary I looked. He really was a good friend.

I washed my face quickly, then found a brush and worked tangles out in brisk strokes until my hair was slicked back smooth. There. No time for perfection, but it was better than before.

I finished up in the bathroom in time to see Li score a goal against Qing. Qing regarded the severely dented box and sagged his body in a dramatic defeat posture. Li smiled timidly until Qing popped back upright with a broad grin. He held up his hand. The boy jumped for the high-five and erupted in a belly laugh.

I couldn’t help but smile, too. I’d never heard Li laugh. The sound was awesome. Then a sobering thought popped in my head. I wondered whether Li would ever be able to laugh like this again once I told him about his mother. Maybe I could put that off.

Like, forever.

No, obviously, I had to tell him. In fact, maybe it was good that we'd come to Qing's apartment. I could explain it to him here, privately, let him have a minute to mourn in peace before we'd have to be on the move again.

I set the brush I'd used on the counter with the pile Qing had made.

"Li," I began softly.

I was interrupted by a heavy pounding at the door.

Qing and I froze. Li followed suit. A voice called from the other side of the door. Qing translated in a dry whisper.

"It's the police. They said they received word that I was harboring an unregistered foreigner."

We exchanged horrified expressions. Yat-sen Xun's men hadn't needed to follow me. All they'd had to do was call the police. By law, all foreigners who weren't staying at hotels in China were required to register with the local police. It was a very strict rule. The monastery's program qualified as a form of registry, but I'd left Zhuang Dian—at least I was sure that's what they'd told the police.

The penalty for both Qing and me would be imprisonment.

More pounding, more words. Qing translated again.

"Also, you're wanted for kidnapping."

My hands flew to my mouth. I remembered the key I'd left behind at the coffee shop. The key would link me to the monastery, from which point it would be easy to prove that Li was not my ward and had no legal reason to be with me.

"Oh, Qing, I'm so sorry!" I whispered. "I never should have involved you!"

I considered making Qing promise to get Li to safety and then turning myself over to local authorities. Then again, I'd read stories of people rotting for months, sometimes years, in Chinese prisons, waiting for a court date and a chance to explain themselves. I wondered if I was selfless enough to move my legs to the front door and open it and how long I could put off that decision.

But Qing was already turning off lights, and waving for Li and me to follow him though the kitchen. I grabbed the last evidence of our presence at Qing's house: my black robe and Li's backpack. Then I seized Li's hand and dashed after Qing.

Heavy thuds on the front door. The voices were yelling now. Qing snatched a messenger bag off a chair and swept the pile he'd made from the countertop into the bag. Li and I tailed him through the kitchen and up the back stairs.

Dodging into a bedroom, past a computer with a stock-market-ticker screen saver, Qing opened a window, sat on the sill, and swung his legs around and out. Ducking under the frame, he disappeared out the second-floor window into the pitch-black night. The pounding stopped. Qing's hands reappeared through the window.

I pressed my hand on Li's back, guiding the boy forward as I slipped his backpack on him. Li shrugged it on but stopped in his tracks, resisting moving forward. He turned. His brows were knit with the same confusion as when we'd been running down the stairs at the monastery.

Empathy filled me, but our situation hadn't become any less urgent.

"Come on, Li," I gestured with my hands, waiting.

A heavy sound thundered through the house from the first floor. *Bam!*

The police had given up waiting for someone to answer the door.

They were breaking through. *Bam!*

Li still didn't move. He *needed* to move. *Bam!*

"Look, it's okay. I'll go first."

I sat on the sill, pivoted, ducked, and grabbed Qing's outstretched hand for balance. I found my footing on the sloped ledge of the roof that covered the first-floor's patio. Handing the black robe to Qing, I turned back for Li.

"See? Come on, you can do it!" I encouraged. *Bam!*

The sound of wood splintering.

"*Māmā?*" Li asked, and with his expression, I realized Li thought we were going to go to his mother. *Bam! Splinter!* Voices.

My heart breaking, I did the only thing I could.

"Yes," I lied, hating myself. "*Māmā.*" I held out my hands.

Fortunately, Li couldn't see the knot of self-loathing in my stomach. He smiled, clasped my palms, and almost flew out the window into my arms.

8

Ignoring the rain pouring onto his back, Oswald Kelso approached his rental house with caution. He'd spent the past hour hunting down his source, the guy who'd set up the meeting, on Kelso's end.

The guy had known nothing.

Kelso was assured of that fact by his highly effective methods of persuasion. Not only did his source not know the name of either the arms dealer or the dealer's contact, but he didn't even know where to find the dealer's contact. Had never met him until three weeks ago and hadn't seen him since.

Brilliant.

The only way to get to the bottom of this now was the hard way. Which, he thought with a bit of a cruel thrill, was the reason Oswald Kelso existed in the first place. He edged toward his front door.

He'd checked his cell phone for alerts from his security system, but there hadn't been any. There was the chance that it *was* a legitimately canceled meeting. If it had just been a set-up, most likely, they wouldn't have bothered to send a messenger.

Then again, you could never be too careful.

And the stuff about "monks" was wonky. Kelso's internal security alert stayed on red.

The lights were off, as he'd left them. The alarm hadn't been tripped. That was good. On the other hand, if this *had* been a set-up, he was dealing with a pro—someone who'd have been able to get past all that. He slid a Heckler & Koch USP from the back of his pants and twisted the doorknob. Anticipation curled through his veins. He wanted to find someone inside. He was ready.

Throwing the door wide, he flattened himself against the outer wall, listening. There were no sounds from within of someone having been startled. But the storm could mask that.

Alright, then. Maybe it's time to die.

His lips curled at the thought. Whipping around the doorframe, gun-first, he entered.

9

We lay hidden in the dark against the long, even rows of half-round tiles on Qing's rooftop. My starting-to-dry clothes had immediately re-soaked. What had previously been a downpour had lessened to "regular" rain, but it was still wet, and I was cold all over again.

Damp rooftop dirt grimed my hands and cheek. I slid my hand beneath Li's backpack and grasped his school sweater—the only part of his clothes that wasn't wet—to make sure the ten-year-old was stable and didn't fall. Qing stuffed my black robe into his messenger bag, then slid the window shut and hoisted himself to the shadows of the upper roof, next to Li and me.

Below us, a boom sounded. The police had broken through the front door. Through the roof tiles, I thought I could hear the muted sounds of Qing's moving boxes being kicked aside, doors to rooms, closets, and cupboards being opened and slammed shut.

They were ransacking my best friend's house because of me. I'd stuck my nose where it didn't belong, and now people were dead. And I'd involved Qing.

A grating sound: the window directly below us was sliding open. A man's coarse breath wheezed inches beneath us. I was afraid my knocking heart would thump against the roof tiles and give us away. I knew the policeman was looking out, and I just *knew* he was wondering if Li and I had been in Qing's apartment. Wondering if we'd escaped this way, through the window. Wondering if we'd gone up to the roof.

Maybe he would wonder enough that he would climb out and look on the upper ledge.

Just then, another policeman called something out from inside. I didn't know what he'd said, but the man below us answered and shut the window. They continued talking, but even if I'd understood the language, the sound had become too muffled. The voices became distant. I thought I heard car doors shut, but everything blended with the storm. Then it was quiet again—just the rain. Fear seized me, along with the thought that the police were headed out to get a ladder.

A hand tugged on my leg. Qing was motioning for us to get up and move. I understood: the police would come back.

Qing bent down. He produced three long bamboo poles from a hidden recess in one of the eaves. He handed one to me and one to Li. I gave him a quizzical stare.

"Why do you have poles on your roof?" I whispered.

"Laundry," he whispered back as though that was an explanation. "Come on, let's go."

Qing took the third pole, planted it on the street below, and sailed over to the next rooftop. My jaw dropped in disbelief, and I felt my stomach lurch. I'd never pole-vaulted in my life. Now, I had to be successful on the first try, on rain-slicked surfaces. I didn't think I could do it.

Before I could whisper in protest, however, Li landed lightly next to Qing. I gasped in surprise. Qing waved his arm for me to hurry.

Come on, Morrison, don't be a pansy-ass! If a ten-year-old can do it, so can you.

I finished berating myself. With a deep breath and my heart pounding, I stepped, planted, and soared. My feet made an awkward plunk. The momentum forced me down onto my hands, and I dropped the pole. Qing made a grab and caught it. To my amazement, I'd made it.

The rooftops were close enough together that we could go house to house without too much difficulty. As we jumped, I was afraid the roof tiles would come loose and go clattering to the street below. But the ancient Chinese architecture held firm, and, thanks to the rain, none of the locals were outdoors to witness this strange activity. I worried whether anyone could hear the noise on their rooftops. But Qing kept going, and I was forced to hurry to keep up with him and Li.

We traveled south, then around the outskirts of Old Lijiang. The rain became a drizzle and then stopped. The clouds parted. All of the houses looked the same in the moonlight, a sea of ribbed waves undulating across the horizon. Farther away, I caught glimpses between the rooftops to the streets below, where lights shimmered off waterways that linked through the town. Sporadic peals of laughter floated in the night, now that the weather had cleared up enough for tourists to begin spilling back out into the streets.

Eventually, Qing motioned, palm out, for us to stop on one of the rooftops. He put a finger to his lips. He seemed tense, nervous. I froze and listened.

"What is it?"

Qing didn't answer. He handed me his bamboo pole, lay on his belly, and lowered his head past the edge, studying something. After a minute, he reached his hands around the lip of the soffit and flipped forward, disappearing below. I heard a soft plop.

"Qing?" I whispered. Placing both of our poles horizontally in the upturned eaves, I lay on my belly and peeked my head over the edge to see a small, second-floor patio.

Li slid his pole into the eve, lay down next to me, and looked down, too. Even though we'd all just spent the past thirty minutes jumping safely across these roofs, I still felt the need to work my left hand under Li's backpack and grab the boy's sweater to make sure he was secure on the slope. Qing rapped quietly on the patio's sliding door.

"Oz?" he called in a raised whisper. "Ozzie?"

10

A thorough search of his rental house had yielded nothing. Everything was as he'd left it, which meant no one had been there. But it also meant that the meeting-that-wasn't hadn't been a setup. There was a real arms dealer out there who really had failed to obtain the substance.

Which really meant that there was no hope of finding a Cadmium-201 manufacturing plant anywhere in China. Though how monks played into the picture, he had no idea.

And he didn't care anymore.

Deflated and bitter, he e-mailed his employers to explain the futility of the situation, hit send, stripped off his wet clothes, and stepped in the shower. If they sent him back a negative response, he was considering telling them to go fuck themselves and then living in hiding the rest of his life.

Just as he turned off the water, he heard a tapping sound. It was coming from the patio door. On the second floor.

Throwing on a robe, he grabbed his gun from the dresser and padded into the hall. The tapping came again. This time it was accompanied by the voice of one of the locals he'd known for about a year, Yang Qing. The guy was getting married and had even invited him to the wedding. He'd accepted to be nice, but all along, he'd planned to cancel at the last minute. He wanted to be home by then.

But now, here was Qing, knocking on his patio door at ten o'clock.

His patio door on the second floor.

It was turning into a strange night.

On instinct, he stashed his pistol and crossed to the door.

11

Where are we?" I looked at Qing upside-down from the rooftop. "Whose house is this?"

Qing put his finger to his lips and waved his arm, motioning for Li and me to pull our heads up. Just as we did, I heard the patio door sliding open.

"Qing? What are you doing out here, mate?" an Australian-accented man's surprised voice asked. I noted that he'd pronounced Qing's name with the "ch" sound at the beginning, instead of "k," as I'd always done. I knew it was correct, but it sounded weird.

"Hi, Oz. Sorry to bother you like this," Qing apologized.

"No worries. What's up?"

"I… a friend of mine… is in some difficulties, and I need to borrow your car to get… uh… my friend… to… um… I need to borrow your car."

He was fishing for the right words. I was grateful that Qing wasn't divulging any more than necessary to this stranger. Not that Qing knew much more than he'd just revealed.

"This 'friend.' Is it your fiancée? Nori? Is everything alright with her?"

"It's not Nori."

"Okay. Right, then. Something wrong with your car?"

"My car is… out of commission at the moment." The police were watching it.

"Sure, you can borrow mine." The Australian sounded suspicious. "How long do you need it?"

"No longer than two weeks. Probably less."

"Two weeks! Mmmm. Okay, Qing-o. So, where is this friend of yours, anyway?"

"Nearby. I apologize that I can't say more. If this is too much trouble, we can… Oz? What are you doing?"

I heard the alarm in Qing's voice. Suddenly a large hand shot up next to Li. It touched a roof tile, but as Li wriggled closer to me to get away from it, the hand grabbed Li's arm and yanked him downward with a tremendous tug. Li squealed. I was still holding his shirt under his backpack, and though I tried to keep us steady, the man was too strong.

We both tumbled off the roof, airborne, falling. I shrieked. A split second later, my fall was arrested by powerful arms.

My shriek turned to a surprised gasp. I stared at the largest, most gorgeous man I'd ever seen. I mean, Qing was attractive, but this guy was off the charts. His rugged jawline, piercing blue eyes, and chiseled lips were inches from my face. My left hand had wound up braced against part of his hard, broad chest that was bare beneath a soft, blue terrycloth bathrobe, and his scent reminded me of summer afternoons hiking on the forested paths of Estes Park when I was growing up. He held Li in his massive right arm, me in his left, my feet dangling a foot off the patio floor. Though he seemed shocked that he'd just pulled two people off his roof, he didn't drop either of us.

The man studied Li, who was clearly terrified, and the man's expression softened. Setting Li down, he looked at me. As his gaze met mine, something deep and smoldering suddenly sparked in his cobalt eyes. To my embarrassment, my breasts swelled in instant arousal against the man's muscled chest.

Then, for a second, I saw him—who he really was—in his eyes. It was one of those moments where you instinctively feel connected with someone on a deeper level. A sense of familiarity, that *Hey, you*, just for a split second. My heart beat faster.

Then his look changed. His expression flickered through a rapid succession of surprise, annoyance, and finally calculating intelligence—*a tiger*, I thought of the last—before those looks were gone, leaving nothing on his face but relaxed curiosity. He lowered me to my feet, releasing his grip on my torso.

I staggered back a few steps, wondering if I'd imagined all of those emotions coming from him. Especially the one that had made my pulse race. *Wake up, Morrison! You can't afford to be stupid right now.* I stepped over to position myself in front of Li. This man, no matter how good he looked or smelled, or whatever may or may not have just passed between us, was still a stranger.

"So," he said, not taking his eyes off mine, "you must be the friend."

I didn't respond. I stared back at him, still reeling from all the near-death events of my evening, leading up to literally falling into the arms of this hunky Aussie. The Aussie, after my lack of response, was now frowning at Qing, casting occasional glances back in my direction. I understood the confusion he must be feeling. The interest he'd already piqued in me continued to replay in my head. I felt myself warming to him but wondered whether it just had to do with his exterior trappings. I couldn't trust someone just because he was good-looking. Okay, *really* good-looking in this case, but it set off all of my hard-learned, carefully placed internal alarms.

Don't go there, Morrison. Remember your track record. If you're attracted to him, he's not trustworthy. Just go with that. You can't afford to trust anyone right now!

Still, Qing had brought us here, and I trusted *him* at least.

"Let me guess, Qing," the man was saying, "she's wanted by whom? The police?"

Maybe I couldn't trust him, but I definitely empathized with his bewilderment. The Aussie raked his fingers through his damp brown hair.

Qing sighed. "I'm sorry. It was a mistake to come here. We should go. May we use your front…?" But the man turned away from Qing, his curiosity focused on Li now.

"And if you're the friend," he pointed at me, "then who's this little bloke?" He walked around me and crouched down next to Li.

I felt Li's weight press against my back. He was frightened and exhausted. I pivoted around and pulled him into a hug, ignoring the man.

"Ssshh," I soothed, kissing the top of Li's head.

"*Māmā,*" Li whispered, almost a moan.

He drooped against me, his arms hanging limply at his sides. At that moment, the culmination of all of my own fatigue, frustration, terror, guilt, and sadness overwhelmed me. In the child's one word, my heart broke. Tears filled my eyes.

"Oh Li," I whispered back into his hair, "I'm so sorry, so sorry." I looked up at Qing. "I *have* to tell him," I begged.

Qing understood. "Yes," he agreed. "But not out here." He glanced around at the dark night. "May we borrow your living room for a few moments, Oz? Then we'll split."

"Sure," the man agreed slowly.

He led us through the sliding glass door into a small, upstairs living room. I sat Li down on a low sofa, ignoring that he was wet as a rag, and knelt in front of him on the tile floor. Qing sat next to Li, and the man-whom-Qing-knew-well-enough-that-he'd-brought-us-here stood somewhere off to the side.

"Li," I began, "do you remember when we went to see your mother earlier tonight?" Qing translated, and the boy nodded. "Do you remember the conversation we heard from that other room? When the men argued?" Li nodded again. "Well, that was something we shouldn't have heard. You must not tell anyone what we heard until I tell you it's okay." Qing translated, and Li asked him a question.

"He wants to know whether he can tell me," Qing explained.

"No." I shook my head. "Even though Qing is my *best friend*," I grabbed Qing's hand for emphasis as I said those words, "you can't even tell him." Another exchange between Qing and Li.

"Why not?" Qing asked for Li.

I sighed. Now it got tricky. I didn't think Li had seen what had happened to the translator since he'd been somewhere across the room. However, I didn't know what he understood from what he'd overheard in Chinese.

No. I couldn't allow him the luxury of being shielded. He needed to know how serious his own situation was. He needed to know the truth. Unfortunately, that meant all of it. My jaw tightened against the words I didn't want to say, but I pushed forward, made myself keep speaking.

"Because it's too dangerous," I said. "Li, a man in that room got killed tonight because of what he heard. The same information *we* heard. Our lives are in danger, Li, and I don't want anyone else's to be."

After Qing explained, Li asked another question in Mandarin, but I saw the dawn of understanding in the boy's eyes, the growing fear, and the last flicker of hope. And I understood when he said the word *māmā*. Qing didn't need to translate. My stomach recoiled, and my eyes burned. But before I could look away, Li's eyes met my gaze.

I nodded.

Rivers poured down the boy's cheeks. A wail escaped his throat. His pain seared me. I pulled him into my arms, my own eyes flooding. "I'm so sorry, I'm so sorry," I whispered over and over. Grief wracked his jerking body. I wanted to explain to him how his mother was a hero. How she'd wanted so desperately for Li to live that she'd handed him over to a relative stranger and then given up her own life to protect him. How I had known all of this in that one exchange of glances. And how Ming's final expression would haunt me forever.

Devoid of the ability, I just held him, letting his tears run with mine. I didn't know why Ming had been in that room, and it bothered me. But right now, the only thing that mattered was her child.

"Your mother loved you so much, Li," I whispered. Qing translated quietly. His eyes were wet, too.

Li's body convulsed. I held him and let him cry. After several minutes he sobbed out a question, but he was still crying so hard that Qing had to ask him to repeat it.

"He wants to know if he hadn't taken the box, would his mother still be alive?" Qing said.

Confused, I pulled back from Li and looked at him. I blinked back my tears. What hadn't he understood about what I'd said? Wiping my eyes, I pushed him back by his shoulders to arm's length, then cupped his face and thumbed away wetness from beneath his eyes.

"No, sweetie," I soothed. "What box? Your mommy heard something she shouldn't have. Just like you and me. There was no box."

Qing translated. But Li nodded his head vigorously, his red-rimmed eyes defiant.

"*Shì*," he insisted.

He threw off all of the hands that comforted him and shook his arms out of his backpack. He pulled it around to his lap, unzipped it, rummaged around, and produced a small, black, lacquered square about the size of a Rubik's cube. I took it in my hands and studied it. It was lighter than it looked, weighing less than a pound. I turned it in my hands. The wooden carving of a baby warrior holding a sword adorned one side of the cube. It was the same baby-warrior image I'd seen on the doors of the emperor's room at the monastery. On the side opposite the baby was a swan, and dragon figures sat on each side between them. A starburst shape adorned the fifth side, and the sixth contained a simple, flat square.

"What is this, Li? Where did you get it?"

Qing spoke a few words, Li responded. Qing asked him something else. Then something else. A sense of unease grew in my chest. Qing was doing more than translating. He was learning too much.

"Qing!" I warned, wishing I'd somehow been able to ask Li about this in private.

"He says he took it out of the refrigerator when he was looking for something to eat. That's when his mother yelled at him, took the box away, and put it back in the fridge. But Li was pissed that his mom still had to work. So when the lama called for her, and she was distracted, he took the box back out again and shoved it in his backpack. Then he says his mom went to the other room." Qing's brow furrowed. "The lama? This happened at the monastery? Are you saying Yat-sen Xun committed murder?"

Fear and the need to protect my friend rose in my chest. "Drop it, Qing," I said firmly. "We're not discussing this any further."

I looked back at the box and thought about that moment at Zhuang Dian. Ming had heard everything I'd heard; surely, she'd understood the severity of what had been going on. In fact, I'd begun to think Ming was most likely in that room to intentionally listen in on the same conversation Li and I had accidentally overheard. But was this box somehow tied to all of it? Was there something about this box that was so important—or so dangerous?—that her instinct for self-preservation had been overridden by her need to protect her son? She'd yelled at him, exposing herself to the men in the room, and Li, oblivious to the oppressive, adult emotions at play, had asserted his ten-year-old-ness and snuck the box into his backpack. What *was* this thing?

"Looks like a puzzle box," came a comment next to my ear.

I jumped. I'd forgotten all about Qing's friend, in whose home we'd landed, a man whose name I still didn't even know. He'd changed into khaki shorts and a white polo shirt and was crouched down next to me, studying the box with intense curiosity.

"Mind if I have a look?" His tone was amiable, but when he reached for it, I snatched the box from Li and bounced to my feet.

"Yes, I do mind," I said in alarm. "Look, Mister… Oz…?"

"Just Oz is fine."

He stood up, offering his hand with a dazzling smile. I felt my resolve waver. Damn, he was good-looking.

"Your name really is Oz? I thought that was just Qing's nickname because you're…" I glanced at Qing uncertainly.

"That's all anyone ever calls him around here," Qing shrugged.

My jaw dropped. A new wave of fear seized me. "Our *lives* are in danger, and you brought us to the house of someone you don't even *know*?"

12

This had to be some sort of game.

When he'd come out of the shower and heard the knock on his patio door, his instincts had gone right back up on high alert. Qing was grimy, he was acting cagey, and he'd kept shooting nervous glances at the roof. Not too hard to figure out Qing's "friend" was up there. Though it was a bit of a surprise when he'd reached his arm up and hauled down, not one person, but two—neither of whom seemed fight-ready. With what he'd seen in his life, he was fully prepared to be ambushed, even by someone he'd previously pegged as a decent bloke, like Qing. Plus, as in-shape as Qing was, there was no way the bastard could've taken him on his own, and Qing would've known that. Hence the need for the "friend," right?

Instead, he'd hauled down a Chinese boy and Caucasian woman, both streaked with rooftop soot, like Qing, but even grimier and wetter than him. The boy was probably around nine or ten, and he'd looked scared. Couldn't blame the little tyke. *That* made sense.

But the woman? Despite the dirt, for a fleeting second, he'd been taken by the complete vulnerability in her large, cocoa-colored eyes. An instinctive desire to protect her—to keep his arm wrapped tightly around her—had swept through him. He'd had to suppress a sudden urge to kiss her.

Oi, she's good! Interesting game. What's your angle, sweetheart? What kind of scam are you running, and how did you get poor Qing-o involved? And how does the kid figure in?

There had to be a catch. The woman was afraid, but she wasn't scared of *him.* She didn't trust him, but that wasn't the same as fear.

Didn't matter. He didn't want any part of whatever mess Qing had gotten himself into.

He'd begun to doubt his resolution, however, a few moments later, when she'd told the kid about his mom. Everything about her tone and body language rang with authenticity. Either she was an exceptional pro—and exceptionally cruel for what she was telling the kid—or she was telling the truth. And if she *was* telling the truth…

He'd squashed a wave of compassion before it could rise. Natural curiosity had made him wonder where they'd been and what sort of scene they'd come across that had turned so ugly. But, he'd reminded himself again, he didn't need to get involved. He was done with this place, done with China. Time to get a move on.

It was difficult, though, to watch the boy, Li, being told his mother was dead.

Probably a good time to put on something more than this bathrobe.

Going quickly and quietly to his room, he'd opened his dresser and pondered the woman further. She looked to be several years younger than him—maybe closer to Qing's age. She spoke with an accent that made her either American or Canadian, and she'd referred to Qing as her best friend. Qing had mentioned an American friend who was like a sister to him, but this couldn't be her. This was not a girl who gave off a vibe of "sister." In fact, even with the dirt…

Damn! He forced away the thought wreaking havoc in his brain and other body parts. It had been a while, but now was not the time. Besides, she'd come here with Qing. Maybe, despite Qing's about-to-be-married status, he had some sort of claim on her. The thought bothered him. Shoving his feet into sandals, he'd sauntered back to the tragic scene in his living room.

Just in time to hear the entirety of Qing's dialogue with the kid about why his mom might have died. And the kid's guilt about a stolen box.

From a monastery.

Whoa… what!?

The torch in his dark tunnel instantly re-lit. For the second time that night, monks had come up on the wrong side of the story. First with the note about his canceled meeting with the dealer, and now this. It was too much of a coincidence. Everything went back on full alert. Who *was* this girl? And what was this box? Was it possible it was somehow important? Was the kid right?

His thoughts returned to the woman.

And the game.

She was somehow involved in the Cadmium-201 meeting he was supposed to have had earlier tonight. She had to be. And she must suspect the same thing he did about the box. That's why she hadn't let him even touch it. Now she was feigning caution, pretending she was worried when she yelled at Qing that they were "at the house of someone Qing didn't even know."

Right.

What she was *really* doing was digging for information about him, using Qing—someone he knew and trusted—as a buffer to get him to let his guard down.

He admired her cunning.

"You don't have to know someone's name to know who they are, Cow," Qing was protesting at the moment. "Besides, I didn't mean for you two to meet tonight. I was just going to see if I could borrow his car and ask him a few questions."

It puzzled him when Qing called her "Cow." This girl, though dirty at the moment, was neither fat nor ugly. But she was fishing for his identity. *'Someone Qing didn't even know.' Right. Well-played. And how well does he know* you, *Miss Cow?*

Alright, then. He might have to kill her later, but if that's how she wanted it to go down, then okay. Game on.

He was sick of being Oswald Kelso, anyway.

He had the sensation of approaching a blind turn and knowing something was on the other side. Numbed by a year of nothingness in a life that was already empty, he didn't care if whatever was on the other side of that turn was good or bad. It was *something.* And it was big. He could feel that, too. Grinning to himself, he rushed toward the turn. On the exterior, his demeanor remained relaxed, but every nerve in his body tingled with reckless excitement.

I'll show you mine…?

"If it makes you feel better, my name is Durango Trunk," he said, wiping out a year's worth of cover in the voluntary blink of an eye.

Reckless.

Deadly.

Exhilarating.

Now, sweetheart, let's find out who you *are.*

The woman appeared to be processing the knowledge of his name, and she seemed conflicted. She arched an eyebrow and opened her mouth as if to speak. Then changed her mind, knit her brows, and closed her mouth in a bit of a frowny-pout, her lower lip jutting out just slightly more. He caught himself staring at her lips, aware of his sudden rise in body temperature. Oh, she was good. She *had* to know the effect she had on heterosexual males. His long, boring, empty year had just become *very* interesting. The woman opened her mouth again. This time she spoke.

"Mister Trunk, I—."

"Just Durango is fine. Or some of my friends call me—"

"*Mister* Trunk…" she began in a clipped tone, then pressed her lips together and bowed her head as though collecting herself. Was she acting? Or was she really under this much stress? "Durango," she continued in a softer tone, "I'm sorry you've been dragged into this, but two people are *dead* because of what Li and I have seen and heard, and now we're in danger. If this box does have anything to do with it… well, it's better if you don't find out, isn't it? I won't put anyone else at risk if I can help it. In fact, if you're willing to give me your car, Durango, I could make it to the embassy alone, with Li."

Ah, there it was: she was trying to make her exit. He was unclear, though, as to why she wanted to bring the kid along. The woman turned to Qing.

"And *you* could go home, Q. You could pretend that you were never there earlier, that you never saw me. You could walk home to your apartment from here, right? And if you're questioned, you could just say you were visiting *him*." She pointed at Durango.

Durango chuckled to himself, exhilarated by the start of the game. *Oh no, sweetheart, there's was no way you're getting out of here. Not with that box, not without me.* Fortunately, he wasn't the only one who didn't like the idea of letting her get away so easily.

"That's a long trip, Cow," Qing said, frowning. "And you don't speak Chinese."

"Yeah, I agree with Qing," Durango chimed in, taking his opening. "You're going to try to go where? All the way to the American embassy? Er, you are American, not Canadian, Miss, er, Cow?"

"It's Kelly," the woman sputtered, color rising in her dirt-streaked cheeks. "Kelly Morrison. And, yes, the American embassy."

Wait…! What the—?

This time he had to make a conscious effort to keep the surprise off his face.

"You're Kelly," he said. "Huh."

Well, that changed things. Kelly was the name of Qing's American friend. The one he'd known for years. Was it *possible* she was just an innocent tourist, here for Qing's wedding, and had stumbled into all of this by accident?

No. There was no way. Even if she *was* innocent, he couldn't let her go anywhere. He needed to get a closer look at that box, and he needed to know what she'd seen and heard. But the coincidence was just too convenient. She'd shown up on *his* roof, on the very night that his meeting… No, she had to be a plant. Maybe her relationship with Qing had been an opportunity for plausible cover.

She might be taking advantage of her friendship with Qing, but so could he.

Time to set the rules of the game. *His* rules. His game.

"Well, at any rate, you'd never make it," he continued. "Not if the police are looking for you here. They'll already have your face plastered up at all the likely stops: airports, railway stations, bus stops, and everywhere along the way to Beijing. There's a closer consulate in Chengdu, but that's probably the first place they'd think you'd go."

"What am I supposed to do, then? Stay here like a sitting duck?"

The girl appeared frustrated. She glared at the floor, frowning, and tapped her foot. Then she did something strange. Crossing to Li's backpack on the floor near the sofa, she returned the box to it, zipped it up, and handed it to Li, who was still seated. Why was she giving the box back to the boy?

Li dragged his arms through the straps. The kid looked clagged out.

"Please tell him that the box had nothing to do with his mother and that it's not his fault," she said, addressing Qing but keeping her eyes evenly on Li.

Qing translated, and Li nodded at Kelly. Another tear rolled down his cheek. He wiped it away with his sleeve, and Kelly held out her hand to him. He took it, and she pulled him to standing.

"Come on, sweetie," she said, starting for the door.

Oh no, sweetheart, you're not getting away from me.

13

Wait a minute," Durango said, his blue eyes wide, "where do you think you're going?"

"We're getting out of your hair," I sighed.

"You're not in my hair."

"It's an expression. Maybe an American one. It just means—" And then I saw the bemused look on his face. He'd understood the first time. "Oh, right," I muttered. Of course, he'd understood. "Sorry. Think I lost my sense of humor a few hours ago."

My shoulders sagged. My whole body felt heavy. I didn't have the energy for banter right now, and Li's legs were already beginning to give out. I was worried I'd have to carry him, and I didn't know if I could do it. Just then, he stumbled forward, away from me. I tried to catch him, but Durango was quicker.

"I gotcha, mate." He caught the ten-year-old and cradled him as though Li were only a toddler. Li didn't resist. In fact, he seemed to relax in the big man's arms. My surprise gave way to warm fuzzies at Durango's easy tenderness toward the little boy.

"Let's put the little tyke down in a proper bed," Durango said. "What do you say?"

It was on the tip of my tongue to say okay. But then my mind revolted, unable to shake the events of the night and the urgency of getting to safety. I tried to ignore the part of me that wanted to rely on this gorgeous specimen of a Y-chromosome for hospitality. Or for anything. Attraction, in my experience, only led to abandonment. Staying here with the Australian Adonis—remaining stationary and not continuing to run—none of this seemed like a smart idea for various reasons. But in my brief hesitation, the decision was made for me.

"Thank you, but—" I started to say at the same time Qing said, "I'll meet you in the kitchen." He headed toward the stairs. Durango nodded and started leaving the room.

Wait, what?

I blinked. I was outnumbered, and I'd just been overruled.

I bit my tongue, instinctively wanting to remain polite and not get in an argument with Qing in front of Durango, but I scowled at my friend's back as he disappeared down the stairs. I felt irritated at him for not supporting me in fleeing out the door.

For not feeling the same sense of urgency I felt.

For bringing me here to Durango's house and letting me feel this cruel, pointless tease of desire. As if I didn't have enough tension already.

But some small corner of my brain realized that exhaustion was making me unreasonable. I should trust Qing and our friendship. I should accept the kindness of Qing's friend and say thank you.

I sighed, turned my attention back to the Greek god carrying Li, and followed them down a short hallway. We entered a bedroom. I gathered, from the blue bathrobe on a chair—the one he'd been wearing earlier—that this was his room. I hurried around to the other side of the queen-sized bed and helped extricate Li from his backpack once more. The bed was still made, I noted. I felt a little less awkward to know that at least we hadn't woken Durango when we'd dropped down on his house. The huge man laid the boy down gently and covered him with a blanket. Li immediately twisted to his side, bent his knees into a fetal position, and burrowed his face into a pillow. He took a deep breath and visibly relaxed into sleep. Setting the backpack on the floor next to the bed, I kissed Li on his head and exited back into the hall. Durango shut the door behind us.

"Thank you," I said solemnly.

"No worries," he shrugged, turning the corner and heading downstairs.

"We'll be gone as soon as possible," I reassured him, trailing behind. Durango grunted something in response that sounded like, "We'll see," but I didn't quite catch it, and we were already down the stairs.

We passed a laundry closet and a formal dining room. An even layer of dust muted the dining table's surface, making the room seem unused. In the dim light, something glinted on one of the chair cushions. I automatically turned my head to look, but Durango was walking quickly, so I turned my head back and kept pace.

We arrived in the kitchen. Qing was already pouring tea at the small table, and I pulled up a chair. The tea was too hot to drink, but I gratefully wrapped my perpetually cold fingers around the cup to warm my hands and help remove some of the Raynaud's pin prickles.

Durango rifled through a stack of books on a shelf until he found the one he wanted, an atlas. He plopped down at the table and began flipping through pages, simultaneously pulling up a website on a small laptop.

"So, you're Kelly," he said without looking up from the book. It was the second time he'd said that. Before I could ask why he kept repeating it, he followed up with, "You and my soon-to-be *un*-bachelor friend here go back a long way, don't you?"

"Yeah, we do," I said, still wondering how Qing knew this Australian man. I'd never even heard Qing mention him before, and I was confident that I was better friends with Qing than Durango could possibly be. "We've been friends since we were kids. We started out as pen pals back in the fourth grade. I was nine. He'd just turned eleven. But that was forever ago."

I smiled at Qing, reached over, and squeezed his hand.

"Twenty years," Qing nodded, squeezing back.

"So, how do *you* two know each other?" I asked, trying to keep my tone sweet but hearing the words come out laced with suspicion. No matter how good a judge of character Qing was, something still didn't sit right with me about the fact that he hadn't even known Durango's real name.

"Facebook," Qing replied.

I frowned. "But you don't have Facebook in China."

"Not legally, we don't. But I got a new VPN service a while back and decided to risk it. The world is a big place, and if I'm going to make it in finance, I need to know what's going on out there."

I blinked and sat up straighter, trying to mask a mounting sense of displacement.

"Yeah, he friended me about… a year ago, was it?" Durango tore his eyes away from the atlas to give Qing an innocent cock of his head.

"About fourteen months," Qing nodded again. "Right when I got the VPN."

Shocked, I stared at Qing.

"You have a Facebook page?"

Qing looked bewildered. "Yes?"

"But how come *I* didn't know about it? I mean not that you have to tell me everything, but…. You're on Facebook?"

Part of the floor had dropped out from underneath me. My best friend had a whole life I didn't know anything about. I saw Durango's lips twitch, though he kept his eyes on the atlas.

"Yes, but you're not on Facebook," Qing pointed out, still perplexed.

"Well, I *know*, but—"

"Remember when we had that conversation a few years ago, and you said you didn't want to waste your time with it because your life wasn't interesting enough to write about, and you were happy to keep up with the friends you *wanted* to keep up with by phone, text, and e-mail?"

"Vaguely." I didn't actually remember having that conversation with Qing, but he'd nailed my stance on social networking for the most part, so I didn't doubt I'd said it. I was on Instagram and LinkedIn, but I kept those more professional-level.

"Then why do you care if I'm on Facebook or not?"

"It's not that I care whether you have a page. It's just that I didn't know you *did*. I thought you felt the same as me about it. It's just weird, that's all."

I frowned at the table. Part of my world had shifted, and now I was the one, rather than this Aussie newcomer, who didn't know Qing as well as I'd thought. Sitting back in the chair, I brought the tea to my lips, sipped it, and scalded my tongue.

"So you met on Facebook."

"Yes," Qing said. He didn't elaborate. I looked up. He was giving me an "are you gonna make a federal case about it" look. I rolled my eyes. *Seriously?* I was allowed to feel briefly out of sorts. Especially after the evening I'd just had.

After an awkward pause, Durango broke the silence.

"*Any*way, in addition to my house being conveniently located for your escape,

I suspect that one of the other reasons Qing-o may have brought you here is because of my professional expertise. Am I right?"

"Your professional expertise?" I asked, returning to the immediacy of the situation. I looked up, right into those intense, cobalt eyes. I caught my breath.

"He's a tour guide," Qing explained. "Yeah, Oz, it occurred to me that there might be another way than what I was thinking."

I looked at Qing, then back to Durango. "Another way to Beijing? Or to the closer place in Chengdu?"

"No," Durango answered, "another way out of the country."

I raised an eyebrow. "What do you mean? How?"

Durango rotated the map, so it was facing up between Qing and me.

"We're here." He pointed to Lijiang City. "And Beijing is all the way over here." He put another finger far northeast across the map. "That's a lot of Chinese police—and maybe a few Tibetan monks?—to have to deal with. It strikes me that it would be a whole lot easier to go from here," again, he indicated Lijiang, "to here instead." This time he put his other finger a few inches away to the west. The map was a different color there, but the page ended.

"Where's that?" I asked.

"Really? That's what you think we should do?" Qing asked in surprise.

Durango nodded and flipped a few pages forward in the atlas, pointing to the upper right of the new page. "Yup, this is the way to go. Assam. In the chicken neck of India."

"Wait a minute." I pointed to the map. "This is China, this is India, but what's this in the middle?"

"Myanmar," Qing said with disgust. "Or Burma, as your two's countries would say. You want us to go through there?" He frowned at Durango.

"Why not?" Durango asked. "It's the fastest route. Besides, there's no way we're going to go up and through the Himalayas."

"Myanmar's a cesspool. They are in continual political unrest, not to mention the drugs, human trafficking, child prostitution. They'd love these two." Qing nodded his head toward me and jerked his thumb upward, indicating the bedroom where Li slept. I'd never seen Qing indignant like this before. "I didn't realize before that there was an American Consulate in Chengdu. Let's try for that," he insisted.

But Durango shook his head. "Most of the illegal substance and human rights violations you mentioned goes on farther south in Burma, near the borders with Laos and Thailand. And Chengdu is the first place the police and the monks will think she's gone. If she's really scared for her life, she'll do well to avoid that route because you'd better believe they'll be looking for their chance to get her on the way there. The last place they'll think to look is India, by way of Burma. Chengdu might be a bit faster, but this way is safer. Even if Burma has its problems, she's not wanted there, and neither is Li. Plus, Assam has an international airport in Guwahati. We can get her back on her own turf the quickest this way. But it's her choice."

Her own turf. The words echoed in my head. *Home.* Purple mountains, red rocks, aspen trees, my parents…

Qing, however, had jumped onto another of Durango's words.

"'*We* can get her back?'" he repeated. "Wait a minute. Oz, I didn't mean for you to have to do this."

"I've got some downtime," Durango shrugged.

Qing knit his brows. "What would you charge for this kind of… trip, excursion?"

"Nothing. I'm volunteering."

"No, Oz. I didn't mean for you to get dragged into this. Seriously, what would you charge?"

Durango pursed his lips. There was a pause as he exhaled.

"I don't know. It would depend on which way we went, of course, but it wouldn't be much. We'll work something out."

Hope rose in my chest. Maybe it was because, like me, Durango was from a westernized country—except that he spoke his English with a delicious accent.

Maybe it was because his entire being radiated confidence so potent that it bolstered my spirits.

Maybe it was because of the spark of life that lit his cobalt eyes—and that millisecond on the patio when I'd caught a glimpse of the tiger behind them.

Maybe it was just because he was so darned *hawt.*

Whatever the reason, I couldn't avoid the fact that, despite my issues with men and relationships, I still liked the thought of being able to spend more time around him.

"Cow?" Qing asked, snapping me back to reality. "What do you want to do? Do you want to go this route, through *Myanmar*, over to India? Or would you rather stay here, in just one country, where you at least already have a visa, and head for the consulate?"

It was apparent, from the way he sneered the name Myanmar, what Qing wanted to do. This was his homeland, and he had very definitive thoughts on the subject of Burma. He glanced at the website Durango had pulled up and whipped the laptop around so that it faced me.

It was the page for the U.S. Embassy's branch in Chengdu. I took one look at the screen and felt my stomach lurch. The happy thoughts drained from my soul.

On the website's front page was a photo of the U.S. Ambassador to China shaking hands with the same, sallow-faced, brown-bearded American businessman I'd seen in the room with Yat-sen Xun tonight.

I would never forget that face.

The same man I'd seen driving away from the monastery.

As I looked at the picture, I remembered that moment, and I knew—I *knew*—he'd seen me, too.

Beneath the photo was a caption. The man was Nathaniel Richardson, a high-stakes venture capitalist. My pulse quickened. Nathaniel Richardson had money, he had connections in both China and the U.S., and he was willing to work with people who killed to get what they wanted. And *I'd* just ruined a big-ass business deal for him.

Something clicked. The other name I'd heard suddenly made sense too. Richardson had been upset with Yat-sen Xun because there was another bidder for this cad-too stuff. *"Another buyer? Who is it? It's Pathos, isn't it? I knew it!"* Pathos. He'd meant Alexander Pathos—a terrifyingly powerful Egyptian business mogul who openly despised the U.S. and was suspected of having links to terrorist groups.

There was no way I was waltzing straight back into either of their worlds.

All bets were off.

Qing and Durango both waited for my answer. They couldn't know about Richardson. I hid my fear by quickly flipping through the website, pretending I was reading something about it. Qing thought it would be safer and easier to go to Chengdu. Durango sounded sure about taking us all to India.

But I had an idea of my own.

"I think I ought to sleep on it if that's okay," I said. The men looked surprised, but they agreed.

I rose from the table, pushed in my chair, hugged Qing, thanked Durango, and retreated upstairs to the room where Li was sleeping. Lifting an extra pillow from the bed, I gave Li's shoulder a soft squeeze, put the pillow on the floor, and curled up on the carpet. Since Durango had expressed an interest in the box, I also hugged Li's backpack to my chest. I allowed my heavy lids to close—just for a short time, I promised myself. I wasn't going to take any chances. No one else was going to get hurt.

14

"So, Qing-o," Durango said as he put away the atlas and closed his laptop, "you and your friend have had quite a night."

"It was mostly her. Her and Li." Qing brought the mugs to the sink and washed them. "*I* was at home trying to think of a way to get out of packing boxes when she sent me a strange e-mail from a new account she'd just created, saying she was in danger and to please come to pick her up from a coffee shop."

"She didn't use her regular email?"

"No. It was weird. Then she sent me another email from her main account—look, it's complicated, but she told me later that she was trying to give me plausible deniability." Qing shook his head.

Clever girl, Durango thought, his suspicions about her strengthening.

"So," he said, "you had your own car at that point when you went to get her, and now, for some reason, you don't have it?"

"Yeah. She wanted me to try to drive her and Li straight to the embassy—we'd thought the closest one was in Beijing—but I went back to my parents' house first. We needed supplies for that kind of road trip, and I didn't get the gist of her sitch. I still don't get it all. She didn't want to give me any deets. She's been hella tight-lipped. But when I got even an inkling of what she'd gone through, I felt terrible. *I'm* the one who talked her into going to Zhuang Dian in the first place."

Zhuang Dian: the name of the monastery.

Durango latched onto the piece of information. He remembered the place was up on a mountain, about ninety minutes north of Lijiang. He wondered what else Qing knew.

"And what exactly *has* she gone through? I mean, besides seeing the two murders. And if she's not the murderer, why are the police after her?"

"Kidnapping and being an unregistered foreigner—neither is accurate, but apparently that's what they've been told by whoever's after her. As far as the rest of it, it's been like dragging an ox to try and get anything out of her. At first, I thought it was because she was traumatized. But now I think she believes she's protecting me by keeping me in the dark."

"But *why* were they killed—Li's mum and the other bloke? Level with me, mate. What are we up against?"

Qing shrugged. "Monks and cops. You know as much as I do, dude."

Dude. Qing's Americanized English always made him chuckle.

Durango was an expert at reading people—his life had depended on the skill more than once—and he knew Qing was a clean, by-the-book kind of fellow. He was telling the truth. Qing clearly didn't know anything more about the context of his friend's plight.

"So, you took Kelly and Li back to your parents' place, and then what happened?"

"About twenty minutes after we got there, the *wǔjǐng* were pounding on the door. We went out an upstairs window and used my mother's old bamboo laundry rods to jump across the rooftops."

"Laundry rods?"

"Yeah. The long poles she used to hang between us and the neighbor's house for the big stuff like rugs and blankets. Didn't your mother ever use things like that? Why am I the only one whose mom used laundry rods? Anyway, I used to sneak out that way at night when I was young. Until my sister found out and told on me." He scowled.

"So…" Durango needed to make sure Qing was in the present, "you're running from the police, and your first thought was to come here?"

"No. My first thought was An-Man, a block away from my house. He has a decent car, but then I remembered he's out of town."

"Oh, right. He's at that… what is it? A chicken convention?"

"Agricultural seminar."

"That's what I said."

"So, my next thought was Kang, but, well… Kang."

"That friend you brought to the bar a few times? The one with the glasses?" Durango made O's with his fingers to indicate thick, coke-bottle spectacles.

Qing nodded.

"Yeah," Durango agreed, "that bloke'd probably be so flustered to have an actual female in his apartment, he'd just stare at her chest for five minutes and then have to spend the rest of the night in the bathroom."

"Exactly. But *your* face also kept popping into my head. I'd already started leading us south into Old Town, and the more I thought about it, the more it seemed like a good idea. Even if your car wasn't available, you know the area as well as anyone. Maybe better, because of what you do. Plus, even though I never intended to ask you to come with us—I was only going to ask for your car and maybe help with ideas and directions—I did think it might make her feel better if she met you."

"Why's that?"

Qing took a breath and knit his brow. "Tonight, I saw Cow freaked out like I've never seen her. But this is also as single-minded as she's ever been. Everything she's doing is coming straight from her core. For a very long time, she's been led to believe that it's not enough for her to just be herself. She's been second-guessing herself for many years. But right now, she's trusting her own instincts. Which is hard for her but good. That's why it's good that she met you. You're very self-assured. You have a stable presence. Your energy is good for her. She responded to it. You calmed her." Qing cocked his head to the side and met his gaze evenly. "Even if it was hard to tell," he added with a grin.

"Thanks," Durango mumbled. Receiving compliments was not his strong suit, especially when they came from decent people who thought he was one of them.

They went upstairs. Durango pulled a pillow and a blanket from a closet and tossed them at Qing. "You get the sofa out here. I'll take the one in the other room." He nodded toward the closed door at the far end of the hall. He turned to leave, then turned back. It had niggled in his mind all night, and he had to know.

"You're protective of her, aren't you?"

"I've known her most of my life. She's like a sister to me."

"*Like* a sister. But have you and she ever…?" He quirked an eyebrow, smirked.

"No," Qing replied.

That wasn't what he'd expected. Durango felt his insides instantly become lighter. He smiled. Then Qing narrowed his eyes and frowned.

"Why did you want to know?"

"No reason," Durango said, still smiling. "Just curious."

"*No*," Qing said. "Don't even *think* about it, Oz. She's off-limits."

"Sure. Whatever you say. She's *your* friend."

"I mean it!" Qing glared at him. "She's been through enough. If you hurt her, I'd have to… hunt you down and kill you!"

Durango gave an amused chuckle. Qing would never be able to touch him, but his bravado was sweet.

As if he sensed the impossibility of his words, Qing rolled his eyes at the bigger man.

"You know: Chinese family honor and all that shit. But seriously, Oz, you don't have to do this. She's not your responsibility. Look, we'll crash here for the night, and in the morning, I'll borrow Kang's car and get them to Chengdu—"

"Whoa, mate. Thought you were going to let *her* make that decision," Durango interrupted. He'd pushed too far with the personal and needed to steer the game back on course. "Really, mate, it's fine. Look, business is slow right now, and I really do want to help you and your friend. I feel bad for the little guy, and she seems like a nice girl."

Nice girl. Yeah, right. The cloyingly platonic words did not at all describe the awareness she sent to his system, but he hoped they would be enough to neutralize Qing's defensiveness.

Qing narrowed his eyes again. He rubbed the back of his neck.

"I'll be on my best behavior." Durango held up his hands. "Come on, mate. Let me do this. It'll be fun. Like a road trip before your wedding. You'll be back in a few days, and then you can get everything else in order before Nori starts to worry."

"Your best behavior?"

"Yes."

"You swear? On Waltzing Matilda's grave?"

"Absolutely." It was all Durango could do not to laugh at the basis of Qing's oath. "Everything's going to be grand. Burma's beautiful this time of year."

"Or Chengdu, if that's what she decides."

"Or Chengdu. You're right. It's her decision. Now, you look stuffed. Get some shut-eye. This is going to be fun!" He grinned.

A slow smile of relief spread across Qing's face. "Thanks, Oz."

"No worries, mate! I'll see you in the morning."

Durango walked down the short hall, out of Qing's view, and past the room housing Kelly and Li. He took a key out of his pocket and unlocked the door at the far end. Locking it again behind himself, Qing set his laptop onto a docking station and parked himself at the desk. He clicked through screens that showed various live-camera angles of the house. He stopped when he got to the master bedroom. The boy was still asleep on the bed, and Qing's friend was sleeping on the floor. Her arms were linked through the boy's backpack. Damn. It would be hard to get at the box. Yeah, she knew what she was doing, alright.

Keeping the bedroom image in a corner of his screen, he sent an e-mail to his employer:

Situation has changed, need to explore new angle.

Then he logged onto an encrypted website and requested an urgent, full-scale background check on Kelly Morrison. He entered the little information he had to help narrow the field. White female. Average height. Brown hair, brown eyes. American citizen. Currently wanted by police in Yunnan, China. Last point of registration: Zhuang Dian Monastery.

As soon as he'd finished, he began his own search on her. Within an hour, he'd dug up basics: Kelly Anne Morrison, born September 22, almost thirty years ago. She'd held a driver's license in the State of Minnesota for seven years and before that had held one in Colorado consistently since she was sixteen. Her current residence was listed as a third-floor apartment in downtown Minneapolis.

Kelly Anne Morrison had held varying low-level positions—receptionist, executive secretary, executive assistant, and her latest, production assistant—at L&L Media, an advertising firm, over the course of her time in Minnesota. None seemed to match up to the Bachelor of Science in Strategic Communications she'd received from the University of Colorado in Boulder. She was far too intelligent from what he'd seen to not be worthy of a higher position. Maybe the ad agency was a cover. Maybe the positions he was looking at were fake.

If her passport records were to be believed, this was her first trip out of the United States. She had no criminal record. A few speeding tickets from her time in Colorado, and one incident where it appeared she'd crashed a motorbike, but there were no other police reports involving her. And she didn't have a Facebook page. It looked like the bio of an ordinary person.

The reports he'd requested began coming in. Most of what they told him were overlaps of what he'd just found out. The ad agency was real, not a fake. There was, however, one thing that stood out. Despite the lower-level positions she'd held and the fact that she had traveled all the way here to China, the two credit cards that were issued in her name both held a zero balance. Something didn't feel right about that. He sent out another e-mail:

Dig deeper.

A reply came back almost immediately:

She looks clean. How much more do you need?

He typed back:

Everything. And fast. Looks can be deceiving.

Then he went to check on a few things.

Qing was asleep on the sofa. Durango crept to the bookshelf on the far wall. He reached his hand past a row of bestsellers, in both English and Mandarin, which he'd picked up over the past year. Drawing out his Heckler & Koch from behind them, he returned the gun to his office.

Then he stole into the master bedroom.

The boy slept soundly. Perhaps his child-brain had managed to block the stressful events, and his growing body's demand for rest had temporarily overridden the horror of his loss.

The same could not be said for the woman. When Durango crept to the other side of the bed, where she was asleep on the floor, she gasped.

He retreated a few steps, thinking she'd seen him. But she moaned and rolled to her other side and seemed to go back to sleep. He tiptoed forward again and peeked. She still clutched the backpack. He frowned. He could remove it by force, but there was no point. In addition to needing to examine the box, he couldn't let her go until he knew what she'd seen and heard. But he needed to find out without arousing too much suspicion. She wasn't going anywhere without him. He had time.

He studied her as she slept, curled fetal position around Li's backpack. Her brown hair clung in damp strands to her pale cheeks, and her eyebrows were knit, as though even in sleep, she was worried.

Durango had no doubt that Qing and Kelly had known each other as long as Qing said they had. Qing had a nice group of friends; presumably, he was a good judge of character. But everything about this girl was just too big of a coincidence: the monastery, the murders, his own canceled meeting that same night, and that strange box. Coincidences like this didn't exist, no matter what the initial background reports said.

Kelly Anne Morrison. What are you hiding?

Nothing about this girl made sense. She must have somehow gotten Qing to think her trip to the monastery was all his idea. And then she'd gotten Li to take the box. But once she had it, what was the point of continuing to care for the boy?

And then there was Qing. Durango couldn't understand why Kelly wouldn't have taken the box and fled alone. Why involve Qing?

She looks clean, they'd said. Were the reports right? Was it possible she was just an ordinary citizen?

Her body quivered; she was shivering. Her thin, pink zip-up and black pants were probably still damp from earlier. He went to the closet and took out a spare blanket.

Crossing back toward her, he stopped himself. What did it matter if she were cold? Was he allowing himself to have empathy for her?

No. The journey ahead would be difficult. They would go through Burma to India. He intended to control the route by any means necessary, but it wouldn't help if she took ill along the way.

Durango draped the blanket over her, watched for a few more seconds until she stopped shivering, and then left the room. Whatever the results of the background check, he was going to need all of his wits about him. Returning to his office, he stretched out on the sofa and closed his eyes.

The sky was still pitch black when he woke at five a.m. The rain had stopped. He checked his e-mail. All reports that could be done in such a short time were in.

They'd combed through databases on federal, state, and local levels. This was definitely her first trip out of the United States. She'd never been arrested, married, or in the military and hadn't registered to vote since living in Minnesota. She filed taxes annually, and it seemed that one of the reasons she was able to make ends meet is because she shared her fifth-floor apartment with a roommate, someone named Kim.

Male or female? he wondered.

They'd gone through her academic records back through grammar school. She had passing marks, though there were drops in her science and math scores in the eleventh and twelfth grades. She'd been on her high school's ski team for four years. Yeah, he could see that: she looked athletic, and she'd grown up surrounded by the Rocky Mountains. By the time she went to the University of Colorado, her grades had picked up—she'd graduated with a respectable 3.3-grade point average.

They'd produced her medical records. She was listed as five-foot-seven inches, one hundred twenty pounds, and was in overall good health. She'd injured her leg in a skiing accident when she was sixteen but had fully recovered. There was one mention of something called Raynaud's disease but nothing else about it elsewhere.

She'd never been pregnant. She received annual flu shots, physicals, gynecological exams, and was not on medication of any kind, including birth control, which made him wonder about her sex life.

And while Kelly Morrison may not have been on Facebook, she was definitely still present on social media. An Instagram account that seemed to belong to her contained photos of rooms and places, including a half dozen recent scenic shots taken in Yunnan. She had a good eye for the camera.

She, herself, wasn't in any of her own photos, but she'd been tagged in several of her other friends' accounts. Over the past year alone, her name came up in conjunction with having been in four of her friends' wedding parties. In at least a dozen of her friends' pictures, she wore glossy dresses—presumably the four wedding parties from the past year—and she was stunning. Her smile in every one of those photos, candid or posed, was genuine.

And now she's here for Qing's wedding.

He chuckled—yet another wedding she had to attend this year. Then the reality of it struck him: she really *was* here for Qing's wedding. And she'd gone to the monastery—on holiday—ahead of it.

The summary pinged in his inbox. He read it, even though he already knew what it said before he opened it. It was just as they'd surmised earlier. Kelly Morrison was clean. She was nobody—a regular, ordinary, innocent person.

He thought about this with a growing sense of wonder.

She's not ordinary, though, is she? What kind of regular person goes on holiday, sees two murders, has to go on the run herself—while sheltering a child who's not even hers—and then refuses to tell the story to her best friend because she's thought ahead that it might get him hurt? She's got more heart than a lot of blokes I know.

He clicked the master bedroom's camera to full-size on the monitor and watched her sleep, plans re-forming in his mind. It didn't change the overall scheme of things. He still needed to know what she knew: what she'd seen and what she'd heard. He needed to get a closer look at the box. But he was going to have to be careful around her in different ways. He didn't kill innocents if he didn't have to. Now that he was reasonably sure she wasn't playing a game, it was even more imperative that he not tip his hand about his motives. Or about his employer. He would have to handle her with a more delicate touch.

Well, it wasn't like he didn't know his way around women.

It might be a problem, though, that he'd already told her his real name.

It was almost six. Durango downsized the camera screen of the master bedroom and rummaged through a drawer. Using a photo of her that he cropped from one of her friends' photos, he dummied up a page and laminated it into a passport. Not knowing her linguistic abilities, he made it a U.S. Passport. Satisfied, he made a phone call and put in an order for an early-morning delivery with a local service. Then he went to shower and shave in the hall bathroom. It was going to be an interesting next few days.

When he returned, he checked for any more messages. There were none. He pulled up the master bedroom camera screen again.

The room was empty.

Kelly and Li were gone.

Fuck!

15

Sleep was evasive. I'd have questioned that I'd slept at all, but at some point during the night, someone—probably Qing—had put a blanket on me.

I'd tried to sleep lightly, but I kept drifting off out of sheer, physical fatigue, and then I'd wake with a start and a gasp—once I think I heard myself scream—always the same picture in my head: the translator's neck being snapped. This image was coupled with the bottomless dread I'd felt seeing the knowing in Ming's face and always followed by guilt.

Guilt that maybe I could have tried to do something to save Ming, but instead, I'd run.

Guilt that if I'd left well enough alone, Li wouldn't have found the box, which had caused Ming to yell at him, which had led to her discovery.

Guilt that Ming might still be alive, and Li might still have his mother if only I hadn't gotten involved.

The sense of guilt felt like a monastery robe, but one that sat heavily on my limbs and, instead of fabric, it was made out of human bones that snapped and crackled every time I moved, and then my mind would replay the conference room scene once more. I became desperate to outrun this feeling.

The sleep-wake-guilt cycle continued until the room's wooden shutters were backlit by the early morning sky. By then, my plan had become firm. I wouldn't allow anyone else to be hurt by this.

I got up, folded the blanket, and rummaged through Li's backpack. Taking a piece of paper from one of his notebooks, I jotted down a few sentences.

Qing, I'm so sorry I dragged you into my mess. Please forgive me. Durango, thank you for your hospitality. I will pay you both back as soon as I am able. All of it! -- K

Opening the bedroom door, I peeked out. There was a bathroom attached to the bedroom Li and I had used, and there was a second bathroom across the hallway. To my left was another closed door—a second bedroom, most likely. To the right was the living room, where Qing was asleep on the sofa, and off of that was the patio on which we'd descended last night. Durango was nowhere to be seen, but the house was quiet. He was probably sleeping in the other bedroom. Hopefully, he wasn't awake downstairs.

I ducked my head back in the bedroom. Rummaging through the dresser, I found a long-sleeved navy polo shirt with the words "Mackay Cutters" in maroon on the front and a picture of a football. I also found a black baseball cap with a dragon on it. Unzipping my lightweight hoodie, I stuffed it in Li's backpack and donned the polo. It smelled like woods and sunshine.

Colorado. Home. Durango. I shook my head in self-reproach against the disturbing knowledge that I loved the tour guide's scent.

I had to roll up the sleeves to stop my arms from disappearing in the large shirt, and the hem landed halfway down my thighs, but the dark color was decidedly less conspicuous than my hot pink hoodie had been. Then I stuffed my hair inside the cap and checked my reflection in the mirror on the closet door. Not perfect, but it cut a different profile from before.

I woke Li. He started to protest but quickly acclimated to his unfamiliar surroundings and heeded the finger I pressed to my lips. Then realization hit his features. His eyes filled. I held him close while he sobbed quietly for a few minutes.

When he was able to compose himself, I pointed to the bedroom's adjoining bathroom so he could freshen up. Li's outfit remained the same, partly because he already blended in with every other schoolboy in this area and partly because Durango's clothes, which swam on me, would swallow Li whole.

We stole out into the living room. I silently transferred some of the food items and some cash from Qing's messenger bag into Li's backpack. I also placed the note on a side table near my sleeping friend.

Tiptoeing downstairs with Li, I checked for Durango. There were no signs of anyone being awake yet. I scooped up the atlas from the kitchen table and shoved that in the messenger bag, too. I needed one more thing: the car keys. Hoping they weren't in one of the bedrooms or stuck in the sofa cushions, I hunted through the obvious areas—near the house's front door, on countertops, side tables—and then remembered the glint I'd seen on one of the chairs in the dusty dining room.

Paydirt! But what a weird place to keep car keys.

We eased out the carved wooden front door. Mercifully, it didn't creak as I shut it behind us.

The sky was light gray; the sun hadn't yet broken the horizon. Mist ghosted across the cobblestones as it rose from the myriad waterways that traversed Lijiang. Silent, ancient streets, devoid of their tourist populace and local hosts, beckoned with storied shadows. Vehicles were prohibited in the historic section of town, meaning Durango would have had to park somewhere away from his house. The question was: where?

I shouldered Li's backpack—now much heavier than it had been—and surveyed the streets. I hadn't a clue which way to go. But Li was from around here. I looked down at him, held up the car keys, motioned with my hands as though I was holding a steering wheel, and then shrugged.

Li nodded. He took my hand and led me through the empty streets. A few of the local shops were beginning to open. A market owner hung lines of eggs bound together by some sort of grass rope. A woman readied a fruit stand. But no one paid any attention to Li or me. We walked for twenty minutes. We went up a hill, rounded a corner, and came to a street. Across the street was a parking lot.

The sky was already pink. We strode briskly, purposefully, to the lot. The first rays of sunshine reflected off the cars. I shielded my eyes and held up the keyless remote, pushing the lock button. It beeped forward and to the left. We waded between vehicles to get to the correct row. But as we turned, I froze.

Two cars away, leaning against the hood of an olive-green SUV, with his arms folded across his broad chest, stood Durango. He was clean-shaven, his short brown hair combed, and he cut an elegantly casual profile in tan sports pants, brown hiking boots, and a light blue, button-down shirt with the sleeves rolled up to the elbows. His smile was grim, and his eyes didn't twinkle.

I gulped and tightened my grip on Li's hand. I'd been so *certain* Durango had been asleep behind that other door. The fear of being caught by him had to be set aside for now, though, because the stakes of being caught by the others after us were too great. Ignoring the mystery of how Durango had known where we were headed and how he'd arrived here before us, I set my jaw.

"Right, then," he said. "Did you decide which way you wanted to go?"

"Yes."

"And?"

I straightened to my full height, pulled my shoulders back, and stood my ground. Decision made. I met Durango's gaze evenly. "We're going to go the way that won't put anyone else at risk."

Durango pushed off the car, arms still crossed, and stood to *his* full height. He strode forward until he was close enough that I was forced to tilt my head up. He towered above me. I felt myself shrink and tried to maintain composure by keeping my breath steady and expression fixed. I refused to step back. Inside, however, my pulse raced. The man was a walking pheromone machine. *Day-um!*

"And how were you going to do that? You don't speak the language." His voice was flat. I couldn't read his mood. Was he pissed? Probably. I'd been about to steal his car.

"Li does," I answered, feeling my defenses go up. My main motivation had been to protect innocent people, like him. "And we made it this far, didn't we?"

"You made it a few blocks. Bravo. What were you going to do when you reached the border? Does Li speak Burmese or Assamese?"

"I don't know, but I'm sure that between English and Mandarin, we can figure it out. We—"

"Aha!" Durango interrupted. "So, you *have* decided to follow my route!" He smirked.

I gaped at him, realizing the trap I'd just walked into. My fluster only seemed to amuse him more. His eyes were twinkling again. His smirk deepened to a lopsided grin, which did fluttery things to my insides. This made me even more frustrated.

"This isn't a *joke* or some kind of… tour guide excursion!" I spluttered. "You need to believe me when I tell you this is *deadly* serious!"

My whole body had become rigid, and I squeezed Li's hand too tightly before thinking to ease up. Durango's expression became sober at once, though his eyes still twinkled.

"Oh, I believe you. I know you're serious."

"Look, if you don't want us taking your car, I get it. I'm sorry. It just seemed like the easiest thing to do. But you're right: it was wrong of me." I held out the keys with my free hand.

Instead of taking them from me, though, he gently grasped my shoulders. "Kelly, *you* need to believe *me* when I tell you that I know this terrain and these people. I can get you there safely. Both of you."

He gazed into my eyes, pleading with me, willing me to trust him. It would be so easy to let down my guard with this man. My arm dropped to my side as I began to relax, falling under his sway. I did trust him.

But then he added two words.

The exact two wrong words.

"I promise."

****

SEVEN YEARS AGO…

"You'd have to move here. Would that be a problem?" Percy Loomis's hazel eyes studied me with more interest than I'd realized a potential employer would have in a relatively recent college graduate.

"Um, no, of course not, Mr. Loomis." I smiled and shook my head, searching for proper wording in my first professional interview that seemed to be going anywhere. Receptionist wasn't my first choice. I'd thought I was interviewing for a copywriter position when I'd flown to the Twin Cities for the day. But he'd offered me this, and I should probably take it. Maybe a year of fruitless searching had made me a little over-eager.

"We always look to promote from within before going outside the agency." His voice was seductive, soothing. This was a foot in the door in my field of choice, advertising, as opposed to the cashier job at Target, which had kept me afloat, albeit while living at my parents' house, for the past thirteen months since graduation.

"I mean, as long as I knew I'd be able to advance?"

"I promise." A cocky, self-assured smile broke his lips.

He leaned forward, reached across the corner of the conference room table, and gave my hand an intimate squeeze. *I promise.* His smile deepened.

I gulped, feeling my cheeks get hot, knowing I was blushing. This handsome, professional *advertising executive* was interested in hiring me. And maybe also in something more. I smiled back.

"Does that mean I'll be seeing you soon?" he asked.

I could hear my mother's voice in my head, telling me that I should live at home for a while longer. I could feel the disapproval of my mother's eyes, even from a thousand miles away, watching me succumb to Percy Loomis's flirting.

But Mom wasn't offering me a job. And Mom didn't get to live my life for me. The heady rush of perceived maturity and adulthood made me giddy. I'd be able to move out of my parents' house—I'd have to—and I'd be living in a new state, a new time zone, on my way up in the world. *I promise.* It was an adventure!

"I can be ready to start in a month, Mr. Loomis. Maybe less."

"Exquisite. And call me Percy."

****

Handsome, slick, jerk.

I swore I'd never again let myself be humiliated by an empty promiser. And now, as those words oozed out of Durango Trunk's chiseled lips I was acutely aware of his touch, his scent, and my body's hyper-magnetic response to him, as though he was my own personal North Pole

My muscles tensed all over again. I scowled, becoming vaguely aware of a tug on my hand.

"Cow-li?" a small voice said.

Li was trying to pry his fingers from my death grip. It broke my dark reverie.

"Sorry, Li," I said, letting go of his hand.

"If you don't trust me now, then trust your friend," Durango hastened to add. He was still grasping my shoulders, and I had the fleeting notion that he was holding me prisoner. "You do trust Qing, don't you?"

"Of course." Unlike last night, I made no attempt to keep the wariness out of my tone.

"Good. Because he brought you to me for a reason. He knows I can get you where you need to go."

I shook my head. "Qing doesn't want to go your way."

"But you do."

"Well, it sounded like a better option," I admitted. "But…"

Understanding dawned in his eyes. "Oh, I get it. You don't want to offend Qing by choosing my route over his. Is that it?"

I shrugged and looked at the ground. "That's part of it," I mumbled. I wasn't going to tell him about Nathaniel Richardson and the photo of him buddied-up with the American ambassador at the Chengdu consulate.

Durango chuckled, giving my shoulders a squeeze and my visor a tug before releasing me and taking a step back. Then he turned to Li and spoke something in Mandarin. Li nodded.

"Well, he's hungry, and so am I," Durango said. "Come on. Let's get back to my place for brekkie before we hit the road, shall we?"

He took Li's hand and started through the rows of vehicles, walking with a gait that ever-so-slightly favored his right leg. Li ambled along with no signs of doubt. I suddenly grasped the significance of what had just happened. My eyebrows shot up. I hurried after them.

"You speak Chinese?"

"I live here, don't I?"

It was obvious, but I hadn't considered it. Durango had understood the conversation between Qing and Li last night! And he'd have the ability to question Li if he ever got the boy alone. In fact, they were chatting as they walked right now!

"You're not asking him about…?" I blurted out.

Durango glanced over his shoulder. "No worries!"

He grinned and gave me a wink. The action both reassured me and told me that he would do whatever he wanted—not good.

Then he said something else to Li, and the boy laughed. They continued talking. I hoped Li would listen to what I'd told him via Qing last night, about not telling *anyone* what we knew.

We returned to the house. Qing sauntered down the stairs. His hair was a mess, as though he'd just woken. He looked surprised to see us coming through the front door.

"You went on a walk without me? Nice hat, Cow. Hey, Oz, there was a knock on the door a few minutes ago. Were you expecting someone? I didn't answer."

"Oi! Did it come already?" Durango doubled back outside the front door and returned with three parcels. "Delivery. If I don't answer, they know to put it in my bench box. Here, this one's for you, you, and you." he tossed one at each of us.

"What's this?" I asked.

"Thought you could use a change of clothes, each of you. Not that you don't look far better in that shirt than I ever did." He winked at me with that lopsided smirk of his, and my cheeks grew warm. "By the way," he pointed at my head, "the baseball hat was a mistake."

"You're mad that I took it. I'm sorry." I pulled it off and handed it to him.

"Er, no, that's not what I meant." He took the cap. "It's just that people think hats hide them, but they don't. They draw attention. Well, I'll let you get to it." Turning abruptly, he headed for the kitchen and clanged out a couple of pans.

"You can use the bathroom in the bedroom you slept in," Qing said. "Li and I can take turns in the other one."

I retreated upstairs. I'd been too concerned with waking people to take a shower earlier, though I'd really wanted one. Stripping, I hand-washed my underwear and bra in the sink, rolled them in a towel to remove excess water, and hung them to dry. I stepped in the shower, sudsed up my hair, and scoured every inch of my body. The shower rinsed off not only the dirt from last night's rain, mud, and rooftop-jumping but also soothed the edges of my fatigue. I turned off the water and sighed.

Wrapped in a towel, I found a small blow dryer and happily used it on my hair and undergarments before I finally peeked in the package. Inside were a pair of khaki, drawstring cargo pants, a white tank top, and a light blue oxford shirt. I chuckled. I left the oxford open over the tank top, knotting it at the waist above the cargos, but I rolled the sleeves just like Durango had done on his shirt. The effect was the same: The Durango Uniform. The thought made me giggle.

"We match," I announced, striding into the kitchen.

Durango turned from the stove to glance at me. His eyes lit, and all of a sudden, that strange, intense connection I'd felt when he'd caught me off the roof the night before surged between us.

"That's the idea," he mumbled, turning back to flip a pancake.

And then it was gone.

I knit my brows. I was as confused about the energy shift I'd just felt as I was about Durango's clothing choice for me.

"You made us match on purpose? Why?"

Li was already at the table, working on a stack of pancakes, scrambled eggs, and bacon. He wore a gray zip-up hoodie over a Pokémon t-shirt and navy cargo pants. Not the Durango Uniform.

"You two look like tourists," Qing commented, entering the room behind me. I turned. He was wearing his glasses. His contacts had probably been disposables. He ran a hand over the top of his spiky black hair, flinging water droplets at me.

Laughing, I ducked from the water. Then I saw that Qing was wearing a long-sleeved brown t-shirt and jeans. Also not the Durango Uniform.

It dawned on me, then, why Durango had put me in this outfit. Together, Li and I had stood out like pair of white socks on an Italian mobster. But in a group with Durango and Qing, we blended in. Anyone observing would assume that Durango and I were one set, and Qing and Li were another.

"Hey, Cow, by the way, I forgot to tell you last night: your e-mail trick worked. That's what the police were doing when they were in my apartment. They read the e-mail you sent—the one you told me not to open—and they think I was out when it came in and that I might not know where you are. I called Nori to sort of let her know what's up, and she's already started covering for me. She texted me this morning. They called her, and she told them I was in Tokyo with her. I told her to tell them one of the neighbors who was watching the house for my family must have used the computer and left the lights on."

"Oh, Qing, I'm so relieved!" I sighed. "At least you're safe. Sort of. Nori rocks!"

"Yeah, she does, doesn't she?" Qing beamed.

Durango brought another stack of pancakes over to the table and sat down next to Li. Qing and I joined them. I picked at some eggs and mulled the situation over in my head.

Appearances were one thing. Qing and Li could pass as brothers, or maybe uncle and nephew. No one would question the two of them together. The other assumption would probably be that Durango and I were a couple. Maybe for our purposes, that was fine. We just needed to keep up the pretense for a short time; let people think what they wanted.

But I'd already started to think harder about it. Sure, he looked like an Adonis, he smelled amazing, and when he smiled, I thought my heart would fly away. But there was something about him that didn't sit right with me. It was almost as if he was too perfect, too willing to risk his life for a woman and a boy he didn't know. Why was that? Also, how had he known where to find Li and me this morning? Or that we'd left at all?

It hit me as I skewered the same chunk of eggs for the fourteenth time: the note!

Of course! That was how he'd known. He'd read the note I'd put on the side table before I'd left, and he'd figured it all out. He'd probably already been just about to leave his room, and we were lucky not to have run into him as we'd left. And he probably knew a shortcut to get to the parking lot. Come to think of it, Li had seemed to take me on a bit of a roundabout way down a side street or two. But Durango had read the note, and that's how he knew. And maybe the reason he was willing to risk his life for a couple of strangers was that he was just one of the good guys.

An altruistic hunk.

I popped the eggs in my mouth and exhaled an audible, dreamy sigh of relief.

"Is everything okay?" Qing asked.

"Yes." I smiled at him. "Everything is just fine." I sighed again.

Durango raised his eyebrows and gave my plate a dubious stare. "She must really like my cooking."

16

The first day of our journey to India would be the shortest. It was also supposed to be the easiest. After breakfast, Durango loaded us each with backpacks, supplies, and gear, and we made the trek back to the SUV.

Qing tried to keep up a conversation, but my ability to maintain social graces was slipping. I couldn't focus on what he was saying. The weight of the past day and my present, furtive situation pressed in, demanding my attention. And my walk back through Lijiang for the second time that morning, this time with my arms full of supplies, felt surreal.

As Qing kept talking, I remembered our conversation that had led me to the monastery in the first place. It was the day I'd stormed home after learning I hadn't gotten the promotion. Knowing it was only six a.m. in China, I'd Skyped him anyway. He'd answered on the fourth ring.

****

THREE MONTHS AGO…

"Hey, Cow. Sss'up?" Qing's voice was thick with sleep. He slid into camera range on the monitor, his dark hair clumped together at odd angles. He yawned and blinked. Suddenly my needs felt selfish.

"Crap. Sorry. I'll catch you another time." I worked to keep my voice steady, so he wouldn't feel bad about going back to bed. In the room behind him, the lump of bedcovers moved. A beautiful, ivory-skinned woman sat up. She held a sheet to her bare chest. *Crap!*

"*Zhě shì nàli ma?*" she asked. Qing moved aside. The woman peered across the room at the screen, and her face lit up. She waved. "Hi, Kelly!" Even this early in the morning, Nori's hair was perfect—a silky-straight, jet-black bob.

"Hi, Nori," I answered, trying to match brightness in my own tone, knowing I'd failed. "Qing, I had no idea Nori was there right now. I didn't mean to interrupt you guys. I'll call another—"

"S'okay. You're fine." He waved me off. "I'm gonna have to get used to getting up this early when we move to Shanghai in a few months, anyway." A smile eased onto his lips, and he gave his Japanese fiancée a meaningful gaze.

Behind him, Nori pulled the sheet all the way around herself and scooted out of bed. She crossed to Qing and glanced at me on the monitor. Her brows knit in sympathy.

Turning to Qing, she gave him a concerned frown, twisting her lips to the side. Then she kissed him on the head and left the room. Qing pulled on glasses instead of the contacts he usually wore. He frowned then, too.

"Kelly, you've been crying! What happened?"

Between Nori's hurry to leave us alone and Qing's switch from my nickname to my real name, I knew I looked as devastated as I felt. The realization caused my resolve at bravado to waver. My lower lip trembled.

"I didn't get it."

"You didn't get… Oh! The copywriter position? Again? You're kidding! How many…?"

"Five."

"You've been turned down *five times* for a basic copywriter position—even though you have the degree, and they've actually *used* some of your ideas, *and* you've been at that place for six years?"

"Almost seven."

"Who'd they give it to?"

"They hired some kid from New York." The sting of betrayal rose in my chest again, and my eyes burned. "Percy called him 'cutting edge.' He's fresh out of college, he wore a purple suit with a lime green tie to the interview, and he has a portfolio scented to smell like New Car. I mean, seriously!"

"I'm sorry."

"But the worst part"—I sniffed— "is that they didn't even have the decency to tell me I didn't get it." I flicked away two large tears. "I had to find out when they trotted him out in front of everyone and announced he was the new hire!"

"No!"

"Yeah. But I stuck up for myself this time. You'd have been proud of me. I marched straight into Percy's office and asked why I didn't get it." I picked up a paperclip and began flipping it between my fingers, trying to use it as a distraction against the urge to bawl my eyes out.

"Good for you! What did he say?"

My chin quivered, but I had to get it out. "*First* he said, 'Well, the photographers would kill me if I took away their best organizer.'" I mimicked a male voice. "And *then* he goes, 'Besides, I believe you've already given this department the best you had to give.'" The end of that sentence came out as a squeak, and I clapped a hand to my mouth, fighting the fresh round of tears. I didn't explain the full nuance of my boss's slight, but Qing was already steamed.

"*Douchebag!*" he muttered in a flawless Midwestern accent. It still gave me a surge of pride every time he used American slang. I'd played a minor role, coaching him on his English abilities over the years, and now he was on the brink of an exciting new life. I was happy for him. Even if my own life was going nowhere.

The stark contrast hit me, and the truth of what I was really upset about stood front-and-center.

"They're only ever going to see me as a support-staff nobody, aren't they?" I inhaled and blurted out the rest, "And maybe that's all I'll ever be good enough for. Maybe I'm just disposable!" I stopped flipping the paperclip, gave up trying not to cry, and let the rivers flow.

"You mean *he* will only see you that way." Qing scowled. "What an asswipe! All he's ever done is treat you like… You deserve so much better, Cow. That guy is such a dickhead. I don't understand the hold he has on you. Why do you stay at that place?"

Because once upon a time, I thought there was something more for me there.

I'd never admitted to Qing that one of the reasons I'd left Colorado in the first place was because my handsome boss had flirted with me in the interview.

And then…

No, it was too humiliating to say out loud, let alone relive in my own memories. I'd thought it was just *me*. But after what had happened today—*I believe you've already given this department the best you had to give*—I knew that Percy had only ever seen me as something he could throw away, like garbage. I felt so small and insignificant. Disposable.

Like trash.

I sucked in a staccato breath, wiped my fingers under my eyes, and tried to smile at Qing. "I gotta eat and pay rent. It's a job."

Qing frowned. "Well, then maybe you not getting the promotion is for the best."

"What do you mean?"

"Everything happens for a reason. Maybe this is a sign. You need to get out of there. You are porridge in a bowl of mouse droppings."

I knit my brows through my tears.

"Sorry, that didn't translate to English very well. You're better than that place," he clarified. "In fact, you need to get out of that state. It's been toxic for you ever since you moved there."

"I know, but what am I going to do? I can't quit! As much as I'd like to move home to Colorado, this is a tough economy to find a job. Especially in advertising. My savings would run out in, like, six months. And I *don't* want to go back to retail land." I'd been a cashier for thirteen months after graduation until I'd been able to land the job with L&L Media. To think, back then, I'd been happy to move to Minnesota.

I started flipping the paperclip again.

"You have a college degree," Qing said. "You could teach English. You did a great job with me."

"My degree is in advertising, not education. And I didn't teach you English, just how to speak it. And it only worked because you're such a brainiac—you sound more American than half the people in Minneapolis. But even if I *could* scrounge up an entire class of smart Chinese people, where would I live? I *can't* move back in with my parents!"

"It's not so bad moving back into your parents' house." He grinned and gestured at the space behind him.

I rolled my eyes. "That's only because your parents don't live there anymore."

"True. Or my sister." He shuddered. I smiled a little through my tears. "But you keep throwing up walls, Cow. You can't do *this*; you can't do *that*. You're trapping yourself. You're miserable, but you won't make changes. What do you *want*?"

"I...." I flipped the paperclip faster. What *did* I want? Well, I wanted to remember where I'd left my bent nickel; the paperclip felt all wrong.

But Qing's question wasn't about *that*. All I could think about, though, was what I *didn't* want.

"I...." The harder I tried to come up with an answer, the faster I flipped the paperclip. "I...." Until I abruptly stopped and threw it down on the desk in disgust.

"I don't know anymore!" I wailed. "You're right. I *am* miserable! It's freaking *cold* here all the time. I will *never* appreciate the Sven-and-Ole mentality. I live with the Mixologist of the Damned and her starving-magician boyfriend and their pet *snake*. I haven't been on a date in, like, a year and a half, and I'm stuck in a job that's never going to go *anywhere*! I'm almost *thirty* with *nothing* to show for it! I don't know what I want, I don't know what I like, I don't even know who I *am* anymore!" I rolled my eyes, then slammed my elbows on the desk, raked my hands into my hair, and stared at Qing through watered vision.

Qing sat back, cocking his head to the side. He pursed his lips.

"Hey, guess what?" he said.

"What?"

"Nori and I set a date." A corner of his mouth twisted up.

"You did?" I blinked, emerging from my own trauma. "That's wonderful! Oh, Qing, I'm so happy for you! When is it?"

"September 18th."

"That's less than four months from now."

"Yeah, we finally agreed on it last night. We decided to time it between when my job here ends and the one in Shanghai starts. That way, Nori doesn't have to move twice. We're going to send out formal invitations closer to the date, but there are a few people who might have to know earlier to make travel arrangements. Like Nori's family in Japan. And you?" He raised his brows and grinned like a kid asking for candy. "I mean, I know I'm basically asking you to spend your thirtieth birthday in a foreign country, but—"

"Oh, Qing, of *course* I'll be there! You *know* I've already set the plane fare aside. I'll have to get a passport and apply for a visa. Oh my gosh! You're getting married! I'm going to China!" My genuine grin for my friend's happiness was so huge it almost made my cheeks hurt. We held each other's stares for a moment that spanned the nineteen years we'd known each other. My eyes began to water for reasons other than my current life situation.

"Hey, do you still have that brochure I e-mailed you?" he asked.

"What?" I asked, grateful for the distraction. "The monastery that used to be a castle? The one with the find-yourself retreat program?"

"Yeah. The one near here."

"Um, honey, I don't have *that* much money set aside. It would take up like two-thirds of my savings."

"If you don't know what you want from life, what are you saving your money for?"

"Plus, I'd have to take all of that time off from work."

"*Qióng zé biàn, biàn zé tōng*. If you're stuck, you need to change something to make new opportunities. Good—that one translated better."

I opened my mouth to protest, but nothing came out. I closed my mouth and thought about Qing's words. Then I thought about my life and fumed. Seven years of slaving away at the ad agency had gotten me nowhere. Not to mention that the cramped apartment near Nicolette Mall—in fact, nothing about my time in Minnesota—had ever conjured up the word "home." Qing was right: something had to change. I snapped to attention.

"You know what? Screw it. You're right. I need a sabbatical." I began Googling. "Heh. Bet Mr. Purplepants college-kid has never been to a Tibetan monastery in China. Who's on the cutting edge *now*?"

I clicked my mouse with renewed vigor as vindictive thoughts ran rampant.

A certain new copywriter running back to New York with his tail between his legs. Percy eating crow and offering me the position.

At one-and-a-half times my current salary.

In the corner of my screen, Qing said something like, "Don't worry about Purplepants or your dickhead boss or anyone else. Just get *yourself* in order. Find peace for *you*."

"Uh-huh. Thanks, Q," I murmured.

"Anytime, Cow," he yawned. "And while you're surfing, remember to get me a really great wedding present."

I was too busy clicking on airfare to respond. One day I would watch Percy's face crumple like a car wreck when I left Minnesota, taking a few of his clients with me. I would go to China, and I would figure out exactly who I was supposed to be. Then I would get my life back.

****

I would've thought twice if I'd known it would turn out like this.

The hand-cramps I was getting from lugging the overly-large bag I'd been tasked with carrying were nothing compared to my fear of the situation. Suddenly revenge and redemption didn't sound all that appealing. I'd settle for getting the heck out of Dodge with my life intact. And Li's life.

And now Qing's.

PART 2
American Fugitive

17

We arrived at Durango's olive-green SUV. My biceps ached by the time we loaded on everything we'd carried. I flexed and massaged my palms and sank gratefully into the rear passenger seat.

Day one: from Lijiang to Pianmazhen, a town two miles from the Burmese border. A nine-hour drive, but on a toll road. To avoid any appearance of the wrong two people being together, Qing drove, with Li in the front passenger seat, since China didn't have a front seat age limit. Durango and I sat in the back.

Qing and Li prattled on in Chinese. I noted how well Li seemed to be doing, all things considered, and how well he seemed to be getting along with Qing. Then again, Qing was pretty easy to get along with. The scenery of the Yunnan Basin unfolded out the window as we headed south.

"Have you ever been this way before?" Durango asked.

"No." I shook my head.

"Well, if you look on the right, to our west, those are the Cangshan Mountains, and to the east, on our left, you'll see several small river villages."

I tried to listen politely while Durango did his tour guide thing. I figured it must be natural for him. He seemed relaxed and at ease. I wished I could feel the same way. I knew the SUV's tinted windows made it impossible for anyone to see into the car from outside, but that didn't stop the gnawing in my stomach, which had nothing to do with breakfast.

To calm myself, I dug around in the pockets of my cargo pants until I found the bent nickel, which I'd transferred from my pink hoodie. Using my thumb, I flipped it from the crack between my pinky and ring finger, over and over, to the crack between my middle and index finger, then back. Around, over, under, again. I'd misplaced it for several months, but the memory of the movement was imprinted in my muscles. Right hand, then left hand. I focused on this activity, even though I didn't need to. It was a distraction, and it reminded me of home.

I liked to wonder what could have caused such a deformity. My dad and I had been walking along the train tracks the day we'd found it. I used to believe it'd been run over by a giant, speeding freight engine. Later I'd thought that such an event would have flattened it completely, and you could still read the printing date on it, 1962, and you could still sort of make out the picture of Thomas Jefferson on the one side, and his house, Monticello, on the other. We'd found it on the day I'd given myself a hack-job of a haircut with my new, red safety scissors. Mom had gone ballistic, shrieking; Dad had taken me out for a stroll in the park near the abandoned train tracks. I was four.

****

"So," my father had said after we'd been walking a while, "I see you cut your hair."

"I did it all by myself!" I'd replied proudly. "With my new scissors!"

"All by yourself! I see." He nodded. "Do you like it?"

I hadn't actually looked in the mirror. I'd just reached up and snip-snip-snipped. It had felt good, but I hadn't seen it for myself.

"Can I see it?" I asked. "Do I look beautiful?"

And then my dad said, "Princess, you are always beautiful, no matter what."

The way he'd said those words, I knew he'd meant them, and I reveled in the warm glow of my dad's praise. That moment had felt magical. Just then, I'd looked back to the railroad tracks, and I'd spied the nickel.

"Oh, look, Daddy! A penny!"

****

I realized Durango was staring intently at me.

"Sorry," I mumbled. He'd stopped talking—probably because he saw I wasn't listening. Or even looking out the window.

"You really should take a gander at this." Durango nudged my arm. "Erhai Lake. It's beautiful, and all the way at its southern tip is Dali. Dali's sort of like Lijiang, in that it's got an Old Town section with pagodas, temples, and traditional Chinese architecture… You're really not interested, are you?"

"I'm sorry," I repeated quietly. "It's not that. I'm just really—"

Just then, the car slowed. Qing pulled up to the first toll booth. I froze, closing my palm around the deformed coin so that the flattened bend dug into my palm.

I shrank back against the seat as though I could camouflage into it. My eyes bored a hole into the tan skin behind Qing's right ear as I tried not to stare past him.

Don't make eye contact with the toll booth worker. Don't make eye contact with the toll booth worker.

The pulse in my neck throbbed. I tried to breathe small, inconspicuous breaths.

Qing, oblivious to my terror, handed over a few *jiao*, waved, and drove forward, rolling up his window. The toll booth worker hadn't even looked into the car past Qing. I held my breath as we merged back onto the main road, but nothing happened. No sirens, no one trying to stop us. The car just kept moving forward.

"That's it?" I squeaked in a low voice so Qing wouldn't hear.

"What's it?" Durango asked, keeping his voice quiet too.

"We made it through the toll booth. Will they all be this easy?"

"Today, yes, most likely," he nodded.

I pushed my thumb into my fist, massaging the edge of the coin, and forced myself to inhale, letting his words sink in. Today was enough for now—deep breaths.

I opened my hand and began flipping again.

"You're that scared? That's why you haven't been looking out the window?"

I stopped flipping and clenched my fists in my lap. I felt embarrassed that I seemed to be the only one who wasn't able to be calm.

"Maybe if *you'd* seen someone killed in cold blood and knew you were next, you'd understand!" I snapped.

My words and tone were harsher than I'd meant them to be. I'd been rude. Qing's eyes met mine in the rearview mirror. He looked concerned.

I winced in apology at Qing and glanced up at Durango for the first time since I got in the car. His blue eyes were expressionless, but his jaw seemed tense.

"Not," I added in a contrite tone, "that I would wish this on you. Or anyone. I'm sorry. I'm not usually so anti-social."

"No worries." He cocked a brow in curiosity, and his demeanor relaxed. "You know, I haven't been entirely secluded from the world my whole life. Would it help to talk about it?"

"No. It's bad enough that there are two of us." I nodded at Li. "And *he's* already lost more than…" My voice trailed off at the memory of the last look on Ming's face.

Love. That's what love looks like. She made the ultimate sacrifice.

Because of me.

Guilt reminded me of its awful presence. I closed my eyes. "No. You don't know what you're offering. But thank you."

I turned my head toward the window and fought back the tears. I wanted to dissolve and was surprised I hadn't already given in to the overwhelming emotional load of everything that had happened. The physical exhaustion. And the heaviness of what I'd helped cause. It's what I would've done in the past. But there was a new voice in my head right now, a new thought.

Giving up won't get you anywhere. You've got to help Li, and you've got to save yourself. Play it through. Keep going.

And with it came that strange, new thrill. It electrified and frightened me.

18

We headed west, away from Dali, past little villages nestled in the foothills of mountains broccolied with greenery, past a mix of greens, pinks, reds, and oranges rising up on both sides. I remembered something from my pre-trip research about Yunnan Province being home to over fifteen thousand different types of plants, over two thousand of which were endemic. Western Yunnan, through which we drove, was home to most of those. It was arguably one of the most gorgeous places in the world. But after my outburst at poor Durango earlier, I sat in silence, wishing the landscape was the reason I was brooding out the window.

We stopped in a small town, refueled, and used the facilities. I stretched my legs and encouraged Li to do the same. Lunch was a quick pick up from the convenience store. We had to keep moving.

After lunch, Li was antsy. I shook off my mood and leaned forward to teach him to play dots and boxes on a piece of his notebook paper on the console. I focused on the game with Li, but the colors of the landscape blurred past our windows, becoming the rich hues that had been on the lanterns and tapestries in the Zhuang Dian conference room, a scene not yet half as far from my mind as I'd have liked. Each time I converted a section of dots into a box, I was reminded of the box in Li's backpack, the toy he'd wanted to play with.

It seemed strange that the box had been in the monastery's refrigerator. Was there anything special about it? Or was it just a box—and now a strange, sad souvenir of the loss of Li's mother?

My ears popped as we continued down to lower elevations, following tributaries that would eventually meet up with the Lancang River. Finally, we crossed a mountain valley that carried the Lancang itself, one of the world's longest rivers. It passed through six countries in Southeast Asia until it diversified through Vietnam into the South China Sea. Here, though, the part of the Lancang I saw was little more than a muddy brown expanse, one more obstacle to overcome on the path to safety. By this time, Li was a dot-and-box pro, and, having grown bored of defeating me, he worked on beating Durango.

We left the toll road, paralleled the Lancang north for a while, then turned northwest back into the mountains. We drove until we crossed the Nu Jiang, another of the world's largest rivers. At that point, we made a sharp turn west, climbing a snaking road that made insane twists as it rode up and down the crests of the mountains, at times going through and over clouds. At certain points, we lost or gained over a half-mile of elevation in a matter of minutes. I thought my ears would explode from popping so much, and Li sat with his head between his legs, obviously in some pain. But by evening, we'd reached our destination.

Pianmazhen was a small town about two miles from the border with Burma. After stretching and refueling again, Durango directed us to a restaurant to eat. A sea of dark eyes met us when we entered. Sensing distaste that bordered on hostility, I backed away.

"What?" Qing asked.

I jerked my head at Durango. "He and I are the only *white people* in this place," I whispered. "Everyone's staring at us."

"Yeah, they don't get many foreigners through here," Durango agreed. He gave the hostess a magnanimous grin, held up four fingers, and followed her to a table. When we'd all sat down with our menus, Qing leaned toward Durango.

"Why's that?" Qing asked quietly. "Why don't foreigners come here?"

"Qing, why don't you order, mate. This menu's in Naxi or something," Durango said, ignoring Qing's query.

Qing glanced down. "I think it's Lisu, which is… hmmm," he studied the words. "Yeah, it's close enough to Yi. I can read it. Fine."

I felt the familiar surge of admiration for Qing's linguistic abilities. Not only could my friend speak Mandarin and English flawlessly, but he could punt his way around a small handful of regional Chinese languages, too. He described the choices to us, and we figured out what we each wanted.

"Now, don't avoid the question," Qing said, picking up right where he'd left off. "Why don't they get many foreigners through here?"

"Well," Durango said, lowering his voice, "the only land crossing allowed between non-Chinese or non-Burmese people is down at Ruili."

"What?!" Qing almost yelled. His nostrils twitched. I noticed Durango's quick glance at the other patrons, probably to see if anyone had paid attention. I put a hand gently on Qing's arm.

"You didn't know? About the crossing?" I asked in a whisper.

"No. Did *you* know?" Qing asked in shock, lowering his volume.

"Of course not. But you live here."

"Hey, China's a big country, and I've never had a reason to go to *Myanmar* before." He scoffed the name, as he'd done the night before.

"So, we need to go to this Ruili place," I said. I was unable to grasp why Qing seemed upset.

"No!" Qing said, disgusted. "We've gone the wrong direction for that. You got a magical trap door in your car, Oz, for you two to hide in and get across? Maybe the seats have a trick spring?"

"Naw," Durango sat back. "But it's not a bad idea."

Qing snorted his derision and opened his mouth for a retort, but the waitress came. Qing quickly ordered for everyone, and when she was gone, Durango continued.

"Not many foreigners come through here, but some do. The ones who know how to make a cobber out of a conch."

"Huh?"

"You know, a backhander…?"

Qing and I were both blank-faced. Durango sighed. "Oh, all right." He leaned in and dropped his voice. "You know," he rubbed his thumb and index fingers together, "a bribe."

Qing wrinkled his brow. "You think it's that easy? Have you done this before?" he whispered. Waves of tension rippled out from him.

I shifted uncomfortably, remembering Durango's earlier comment about "not having been entirely secluded from the world" and wondered what, exactly, that had meant. Even Li, who could have no idea of the English conversation, had picked up on the tension at the table. He raised his eyebrows and ping-ponged his gaze back and forth between the two men.

"Once or twice," Durango said. "When it was necessary."

My internal red flag warning went off. *Who* was *this man?* However, instead of mirroring my alarm, Qing actually seemed calmed by Durango's somber attitude.

"And given the current situation, it's necessary, isn't it?" It was more of a statement than a question. "Oz, I'm sorry. I know you know what you're doing." He sat back and massaged the back of his neck with a sigh of resignation.

What—just like that?

Qing's trust in this Australian man baffled me, especially after Durango's admission in the car. Qing had heard that part of our conversation. Apparently, it hadn't fazed him.

"S'okay, mate." Durango reached over and slugged Qing's shoulder. "You're getting married soon. This is a lot to deal with on top of that. But I promise: soon this will all be back of Bourke, these two will be safe, and you'll be together with Nori." At the thought of Nori, a smile lifted the corners of Qing's mouth.

I bit my lip. I was still uneasy. Even though Qing trusted Durango, I wasn't sure I should let my own guard down.

Then again, Qing is an excellent judge of character.

I rolled the tension out of my shoulders and tried to relax, too. The food came, and the restaurant's casual ambiance took over. We dug in.

But midway through the meal, Durango stiffened, making eye contact with Qing. Qing sat up, with his mouth set in a straight line. I looked from Qing to Durango. What silent language were they speaking to each other with their frowning stares?

Movement caught my attention. A woman across the restaurant was speaking to the waitress, pointing at our table. She seemed upset about something. The waitress tried to calm the woman, but other patrons were beginning to stare. I looked back to Qing.

"That woman thinks she recognizes you and Li from the news, which she saw at her sister's house in Luzhangzhen yesterday," Qing muttered.

"The news? We made the news? What do we do?" I whispered back. Fear prickled the hairs on the back of my neck.

Durango immediately took charge. "Just act natural, finish your meal, then take Li to the bathroom," he directed. Okay, I could do that. Then he muttered something in Mandarin to Li, who also nodded.

I'd already eaten most of my bridge noodles, so I pushed the rest around in the bowl with my spoon. The waitress began to approach. Out of the corner of my eye, I saw Qing swipe Li's chopsticks out of his hand, replacing them with a fork.

The waitress arrived and said something to us. I caught a word or two—enough to know she was speaking Mandarin—but I had no idea what she said. I was surprised, however, to see Durango also giving a vacant look, as if he didn't understand, either. Qing responded to the waitress, who eyed us suspiciously. Durango nudged me under the table, and I remembered his other directive.

"Let's take you to the potty." I stood up and reached for Li's hand.

"It's pah-ty time!" Li answered, grinning and giving me a thumbs-up.

He scooted out after me and took my hand. I had no idea that Li could say anything in English, let alone an American catchphrase. It was all I could do to keep the shock off my face and bite back a laugh.

We made our way to the restrooms. Qing continued to speak with the waitress, and I really did have to go, so I parted ways with Li at the bathroom doors. When I emerged two minutes later, Durango was waiting in the hallway with Li.

"Qing is already in the car. Let's go. And act offended."

I started walking and let out a great huff near the front door. For good measure, I tossed my hair as I opened it and made for the SUV.

It had begun to rain. This time, Li sat in back next to me, and Durango sat up front, with Qing driving again. Once we were all inside and back on the road, I spoke up.

"Okay, now how exactly did we get out of *that*?"

Durango chuckled. "Qing explained to the waitress that he was our tour guide and we were just here to show our adopted son his homeland. He 'translated' everything the waitress said to me, and I asked to speak to the manager. I let him know we were greatly insulted to have been treated so rudely by this establishment. The manager couldn't stop apologizing. He yelled at the waitress and wrote off our meal *and* the irate customer's. Told her to go home and stop watching so much TV. That put a cork in her."

"That was quick thinking," I said. Then I realized: "You've done this before, also?"

"I've been in a tight spot or two."

Durango was too nonchalant. He looked out the rain-streaked window. But as I stared at his perfect profile, contemplating what sorts of other dangerous situations he could have been in, a kernel of wonder and gratitude began to override my suspicions.

Could this guy really be for real? Gorgeous and *one of the good guys?*

We pulled up to the main road.

"We can't stay in Pianmazhen, like you planned," Qing pointed out. "If that woman is persistent, she might call the police to report a possible sighting. Or someone else could recognize us."

"Agreed," Durango commented. "Turn left here." We started back down the twisty mountain road.

"We're going back?"

"Nope, just a little farther north. This is Plan B."

19

We followed the road for two hours, then turned north at the Nu River. It was late, and Li was once again worn out. His fatigue echoed my own. His head began to droop, nodding to the *squeak-swish* of the wipers. I, too, could feel their hypnotic lure. Even Qing had fallen unusually quiet, and his shoulders sagged. Only Durango seemed alert.

We drove through another small village. I considered reaching in the back to grab Li's backpack and give it to him to use as a pillow, but just then, Durango told Qing to turn down a street, then around another corner, and into a parking lot. We stopped in front of a long, low building, a motel. My spirit sighed with relief at the thought of sleep. But was it safe to stop?

"Stay put," Durango ordered. He got out of the car. A few long minutes later, he was back, motioning for us. We unloaded our backpacks, dodged through the rain, and followed him to a door. From under the soffit, I could see a few pinpricks of light from the village to the west. Everything else was pitch-black. Durango held out a key to me.

"You're in there," he said, pointing to an adjacent door, "and we'll be in here if you need anything."

"I get my own room?"

"Yeah, I thought you might want a bit of privacy," Durango shrugged, adding his dazzling grin.

"Er, thanks," I smiled back.

What a gentleman! I sighed in my head. *Although…*

"Actually, before I crash, there's something I need from Li's backpack."

"Sure, what do you need? I'll get it for you," Durango said, reaching for the ten-year-old. But I was faster.

"That's okay. I'll get it." Li was already facing away from me, so his backpack was right there. I opened it and shoved my whole arm in.

"You need something of Li's?" Qing asked.

"Nope," I said, producing a wadded-up ball of hot pink fabric, "something of mine. I get cold."

"It's true," Qing said to Durango. "She's a human meat locker."

"Thanks, Qing."

"You're welcome."

I turned on my heel and fitted the key into the door, muttering about teaching English to smart-ass pen pals. Entering, I flipped on a switch.

The room was only slightly larger than the glorified closet I'd had at the monastery, and the only reason it was bigger was that it had a small bathroom. But once I was safe in the room, I locked the door and pulled the curtains shut. Then I unrolled my pink hoodie on the bed to reveal the box I'd smuggled out of Li's backpack.

Finally! I sprawled on my stomach across the bed to examine it.

The black lacquered sides betrayed traces of the wood grain beneath and showed more wear around the edges, as though the box was very old and had been held or carried a lot over its years. Was it a child's toy? I peered closer at the intricate, raised carvings on each of the sides. They were wood-colored, but their crevasses shimmered faintly in the hotel room's dim lighting, making me think they had originally been painted with gold leaf. The high-relief images seemed to have been sculpted directly from the cube and appeared seamless with each of its faces.

Though beautiful, the box bothered me. Durango had said it looked like a puzzle box. If that were true, what would be the point of keeping it in a refrigerator, where Li said he'd found it? Also, there would have to be some way to open it. On the other hand, if it wasn't a puzzle box, what was it? I felt along the cube's edges for some sort of crack or crevice. There was nothing. The box didn't appear to have any sort of opening. I spun it in my fingers, musing. Was it possible it was nothing more than a decorative cube? An *objet d'art*?

That had been in the refrigerator? Ugh!

The fridge was a major sticking point, but, unable to figure anything out, I gave up and took a hot shower. Dressing for bed in my undies and tank top, I folded the rest of my clothes neatly and placed them on the edge of the tub. Then I turned off the overhead room light and clicked on the nightstand lamp. Climbing under the sheets, I examined the cube once more, rotating it one way: dragon, swans, dragon, baby. Or maybe it was supposed to be rotated the other way: dragon, square, dragon, starburst. Or maybe there was no right or wrong way to rotate it at all.

I was getting nowhere. My lids were heavy. Clicking off the lamp, I stubbornly held onto the box in the dark, running the pads of my fingers along its smooth, cool surfaces and around the edges of the carvings, trying to feel its secrets by touch.

Sleep was too persistent.

20

He knew the conference room chandelier continued to glow red, even though he'd retired to the solitude of his personal chambers. With each passing minute, it grew increasingly difficult to settle his nerves and quell the sense that one or more forces were working against him. He struck a match and lit an incense stick, laying it across a tray to burn. Then he inhaled a deep, calming breath of the ylang ylang and cedar vapors.

He'd had his followers comb the town at the base of the mountain, but once he'd involved the police, he'd been certain of a quick resolution. He was on the right path. He would get his box back, and the police would take the girl into custody. His men would have easy access to her then.

Yat-sen Xun had explained to the police that the boy's mother worked at the monastery and was sick with worry. He had not offered to allow them to speak with her, and they had not asked. They trusted Yat-sen Xun; his word was good enough. They would recover both the kidnapped child and his stolen artifact.

But, he reflected, the police had looked at security cameras from the coffee shop. They could not confirm that it was her, Kelly Morrison, on the video. Nor were they sure of the boy's identity. The girl had been clever to conceal both her face and the boy's.

The police had broken into the home of Yang Qing, the local man to whom she'd sent the mysterious text message. He was not there. They had even gone so far as to contact his fiancée in Tokyo, who'd said that Yang Qing was with *her* in Japan. This morning the fiancée had sent the police a video of the two of them, holding a copy of today's *Asahi Shimbun*, the main Japanese newspaper.

Yang Qing was not with Kelly Morrison. She had a different accomplice.

The police had reported that there was one security image from the coffee shop that might be useful—an oddly-shaped coin the woman had carried. They'd been able to zoom in and enlarge it, but Yat-sen Xun hadn't recognized it. It looked like a misshapen piece of American currency.

Beyond that, the police had alerted all official stations and major travel stops, providing them with her photo and information. They were on the lookout for Kelly Morrison and the boy she was traveling with. They assured Yat-sen Xun she would not get far.

However, after the first few crucial hours, Yat-sen Xun's tepid faith in the *wǔ-jǐng* had drained away. It had been twenty-six hours since the substance had been removed from refrigeration. Too much time was passing. He needed to get it back soon to continue to conceal his secret until he was ready to let the world know about it.

He took another deep breath of incense vapors to regain composure.

His gaze fell upon the series of twenty-seven porcelain tiles that hung on his wall. They were miniature replicas he'd had made of the ancient tapestries which had been handed down to him through his family. His grandparents had said that the reason there were twenty-seven tapestries was that three and nine were both lucky numbers in the Mongol tradition. Therefore three groups of nine were exceedingly lucky. Together, these twenty-seven images told the mythologies of his ancestry.

However, Yat-sen Xun's father had taught him that the stories were more than myths: they were legends that told truths. One day Yat-sen Xun had realized that these weren't just truths about the past; they were a map to his future. He knew it could be no coincidence that he, himself, was the twenty-seventh generation descendent of Kublai Khan. This castle was his birthright. He had no qualms about what he'd had to do to reclaim it. His destiny was preordained.

One of the first things Yat-sen Xun had done when he'd become tulku was to have the twenty-seven tapestries, along with a plaque telling the story that each one illustrated, hung throughout the castle. He'd had each plaque printed in a dozen languages, so all who visited could know the glory of his heritage. He was mere steps away from assuming his true power.

But first, he had to deal with these unusual and unforeseen obstacles. Why now, he wondered, when his truth was so close to being revealed?

He had a sudden thought: perhaps the deities who had opposed his ancestors were conspiring against him. Yes, he could feel it. They did not want to see a Mongol return to power, particularly the direct descendant of Kublai Khan. Perhaps their spirits had even been able to influence someone hiding under his own roof. He thought of Ding Li-Liang. His blood began to boil, despite the calming incense.

The fabric of Yat-sen Xun's patience with Ding Li-Liang had frayed through. Ding Li-Liang should have been able to track the box sooner. Surely Kelly Morrison had either ceased movement, or she had been in an area where they could pick up a signal at *some* point in the past twenty-six hours!

Maybe Ding Li-Liang had finished serving his purposes. Perhaps Deng Hu was the only one of the previous monks that Yat-sen Xun needed. Besides, Deng Hu was old and frail. He would be easier to control without Ding Li-Liang to help him.

Yat-sen Xun left his chambers and entered the conference room swiftly, decision made.

Ding Li-Liang looked up from his computer.

"I have found it, Tulku. It has stopped moving."

21

Li was out almost immediately, but Qing was jittery. Durango spread out a map, and they discussed the route they would take early the next morning to get across into Burma. Afterward, Qing pulled out his cell phone.

"I'm going to call Nori and let her know I'm okay," he said.

"How much are you going to tell her?" Durango asked. "Or, how much have you already told her?"

"I talked to her before we left, and she's covering for me. Her little brother is one of the best graphic designers in Japan. He doctored up a video, and they've convinced the *wŭjĭng* here that I'm there, with them. But I couldn't tell her where we were going because I didn't know then, myself."

"You trust her brother?"

Qing looked offended. "Totes—he's family."

"Good. It's probably better that you keep Nori in the dark on our location. For now, at least."

"Okay. By the way, this morning when we talked, she was *really* glad to hear you were coming with us—like you being here meant we'd all be safer or something. What is it with you, dude? You have this, like, *effect* on women. I mean, Cow, I can understand. She's single and fragile. But my own fiancée? Seriously? With you around, it's like I forgot to take my man-pills, and you took double."

Durango laughed. "What are you yabbering about, mate? You're one of the manliest men in all of China."

"I know, right?"

Qing flexed both of his well-toned biceps.

Durango looked down at Qing and nonchalantly squeezed a fist. His arm bulged, straining against the fabric of his rolled-up shirtsleeve.

Qing scowled at him. "Show-off." He turned away and began dialing.

"Mate," Durango chuckled, "it's not your fault you weren't born Down Under. Tell Nori I said hello."

He listened at first, giving Qing a hand signal once when he got too close to revealing anything about where they were. Qing nodded, understanding, and eventually, their conversation shifted to the wedding.

He stopped paying close attention. Banter with Qing was fun, but the easygoing tour guide-buddy-thing was only a façade. The real object of his interest was elsewhere. Taking off his shoes, he lay down on the other bed, pretending to go to sleep, just in case Qing wanted to chat when he got off the phone. He needed Qing to go to sleep.

He *really* needed to check out the box in Li's backpack.

Qing cooed back and forth over the line for over an hour. His voice hushed to a melodic whisper, a blend of Mandarin and Japanese, his lovers' language with Nori.

Rain continued a steady patter on the motel's roof. The combination would have been enough to lull anyone else into a coma. But Durango's blood simmered with anticipation. He waited.

Finally, Qing hung up, used the bathroom, and soon his breathing patterns were steady. It was well after midnight.

Durango sat up. He pulled a penlight out of his pocket and found Li's backpack. Aiming the beam inside, he silently rummaged around.

The box was missing.

His pulse picked up. Had he been wrong? Had it been moved to one of the other packs? No. Understanding dawned. She'd taken it when she'd pulled out her pink jacket.

He grinned. *Clever girl.*

Then his grin faded. What if, even with all of the background work sourced, it still hadn't been deep enough?

She couldn't run away with it, he reasoned. He still had the car keys.

Unless she called for backup.

He wracked his brain, trying to think whether he'd heard any activity that might have indicated she'd left—doors opening or closing, a vehicle's motor idling—but he couldn't remember. He'd been too focused on Qing.

Damn it! If the background check was wrong, she's probably long gone with it by now!

Easing out of the room, he crept next door. The shades were drawn. He tried the handle. The door was locked. He pulled the extra room key out of his pocket, inserted it into the keyhole, and held his breath.

The door swung with a low creak. Light from the motel's parking lot cut a swath through the open frame, giving him enough illumination to see the room. She was there.

Kelly was on the bed, covers up to her chin, her arms flung to the sides. In her right hand, she held the box. It was unopened. She was sound asleep.

He exhaled in relief.

Maybe the background check had been correct, after all. Perhaps she was, as he'd begun to believe, *this* genuine. Maybe she was guarding the box so that, if it *was* something the monks were after, no one else could be hurt.

He approached the bed and reached for it. At that moment, she stirred and rolled to her side, clutching the box to her chest.

As though even in sleep, she guards it, he thought.

He drew his hand back.

Later. He would have to get the box later. He still had time.

He was still controlling the game.

Closing the door silently, he ensured it was locked and went back to his room. He lay back on the bed and closed his eyes, drifting to a state of half-sleep. At the slightest inconsistency, he would be fully alert.

Which was why, when the black-clad figure crawled through the window three hours later, Durango was already in position behind him.

The man headed straight for Li. He never made it.

Durango's arm went around the man's neck. The man reached back and flipped Durango forward, over his shoulder, onto the floor. His dark eyes remained expressionless as he bent to deliver a spear hand to Durango's esophagus. Durango grabbed the man's wrist. At the same time, he clenched his abdominals and swung his legs up, locking his feet around the man's neck. He drove his legs down. The man's body sailed over Durango, and his head smashed into the floor. Durango crunched up, leaped to a crouch, and powered his knuckles into the man's neck. He felt the crack as his fist collapsed the man's trachea and broke a cervical bone. The man lay still.

Qing woke up. "Oz? What's going on?"

"We had a visitor," Durango grunted.

Qing registered the body on the floor, Durango hunched over him. His eyes grew wide.

"A visitor? You think that woman at the restaurant called the police, and they alerted the monks?"

"That's what I'm thinking," Durango said.

He checked the man's pulse. Nothing. Good.

"But sometimes yobbos like this travel in pairs."

Qing gulped and jumped out of bed. "Kelly!"

Durango was already standing. He blocked Qing with an arm.

"Stay with Li. Get ready to go."

He was out the door.

22

Something made a scraping sound. I woke, lying on my left side with my back to the door and window. The clock on the nightstand read 4:30 a.m. The room was dark except for a vertical sliver of light on the wall opposite me, as though either the door was open or the curtains were parted.

A frisson of alarm sounded in my still sleep-fogged mind.

I knew I'd locked the door, and I thought I'd pulled the curtains all the way shut when I'd entered the room. I was pretty sure I had.

It took a full second for me to process other things that were off, too. The rain pattered louder than it should have. It wasn't filtered through a glass pane. That must have been the scraping sound I'd heard: someone had opened the window. I strained for more sounds and heard nothing. Suddenly I was afraid to turn and look.

You have to look. It could be Qing or Durango or Li. Of course, it must be. No one else knows we're here. What if it's poor little Li, and he needs you? You have to be brave. Turn and look!

I turned in time to see a sleek, dark silhouette already kneeling on my bed, arms outstretched toward my neck. *That* wasn't Li! I screamed, flung my bedcovers at him, and twisted violently in the opposite direction. A snarl told me the covers had surprised him. I fell off the bed onto the floor and scrambled to get my feet under me. A surge of adrenaline helped me leap to the bathroom door. But before I could get all the way into the bathroom, the man seized my arm.

I held onto the doorframe with my free hand, but he was too strong. The man yanked my arm hard, and I lost my grip on the doorframe. He grabbed me from behind, his gloved hand clenched around my throat. I clawed uselessly at his steel vice, gasping for air. As little as I'd understood from the conversation I'd overheard at the monastery, it was still too much.

"*Where is it?*" he whispered into my ear in Chinese-accented English. The man paused in his squeezing.

Rough fabric from the mask that covered his face pressed against my cheek. He was about to kill me. I knew it. His breath reeked of decaying fish, despite his mask. But where was *what*? As though he'd read my mind, the man clarified.

"*Where is box?*"

His grip on my neck tightened, the texture of his glove grated against my skin, and I realized, fully, that the box Li had found in the monastery refrigerator was no toy.

The man pushed one of his fingers up, under my chin, on the soft part of my lower palate behind the bone, causing tremendous, dull pain. Already struggling to breathe, I began to gag on my tongue. If I told him where the box was, he would kill me. If I didn't, he would probably still kill me and find the box anyway.

"No!" I exhaled out. I shook my head as much as his firm grip would allow. *Screw you!* He wasn't getting any help from me. My refusal made him angrier.

"*Where is box?*" he demanded again.

He loosened his grip on my neck but grabbed my right arm, twisting it up behind my back. My gasp for air became a scream, blinding me to anything but immediate pain.

"Bed!" I choked out. "On the bed!" I couldn't help it, even though I knew I'd just sealed my own fate.

He released my arm. *Relief!* I fell forward, grabbing the bathroom doorframe for support. But in the next instant, instead of going over to the bed, he clamped both of his hands around my neck from behind. His thumbs pushed against the base of my skull, and his fingers squeezed my trachea, hard. I raked uselessly at his steel grip and launched my bare heels backward, kicking air instead of my attacker.

No! No! No!

The strangled gurgling of my own airway sounded distant and foreign.

I heard a snap. *No!* Please *no! I don't want to die!*

The man's hands loosened from my neck, and I crumpled to the floor. *No!*

But I was coughing.

Why can I cough?

My heart raced. I wondered how long it took to die after your neck was broken. Suddenly it occurred to me that the man had decided to play with me—to torture me as he killed me. Something large plopped down behind me, and my muscles sprang to life. Still coughing, I struggled to my hands and knees.

At which point, I knew my neck wasn't broken.

Looking over my shoulder, I saw the masked man on the floor. A hulking figure stepped over him.

Animal instinct took over, fight-or-flight. *Flight!* I pivoted, landing on my butt, and back-crawled as fast as I could. The figure grabbed my arm. I kept kicking my feet backward, trying to get away, and simultaneously tried to pry my arm out of his grasp. He pulled me to my feet.

"Are you okay, Kelly?"

My back hit the wall, my breath coming in short, quick gasps. It was Durango's voice, Durango's scent. *What?* My instincts warred between terror and safety. He flicked a switch, and light from the bathroom illuminated the space. Durango's face. *Durango!* I was still breathing hard. He scowled and lightly touched my neck.

"Almost didn't make it in time," he said.

Still steadying my breathing, I stared at Durango, then at the man on the floor, processing what had just happened. The man's head was twisted off to the side at an unnatural angle, and his hands were splayed out in front of him. In my head, I knew he was dead and that Durango had killed him. But staring at those hands, I could feel them again on my neck: squeezing... pain... unable to breathe. I began to shake.

"Kelly." Durango lightly clasped my shoulders, turning me toward him and away from the man on the floor. "It's okay now. You're all right."

I could hear his words, but all I could see was the black silhouette on my bed and feel his fingers crushing the breath out of me. Durango clasped my arms.

"Look at me, Kells," he commanded. "Breathe."

Ghost faces of the translator and Ming flitted through my mind. I swayed.

23

She was in shock. A natural reaction, since she'd almost had the life crushed out of her. Finger-marks pinked her neck. He almost hadn't made it in time. The knowledge obliterated any lingering thoughts that she might be some sort of voluntary player in this game. Her gaze was still unfocused.

"Kells!" he commanded again.

It was like before when they were in the car, and he'd been asking about how Ming had died. He was trying to pry information from her about what she'd heard at the monastery—anything about Cadmium 201, please?—but gently. Gentle was not his normal M.O.

To his surprise, she'd refused to say anything. Not even a hint. He remembered her impassioned response: *Maybe if* you'd *seen someone killed in cold blood and knew you were next, you'd understand!* She'd managed a polite smile, but he'd seen the pain in her face. He understood it: she'd witnessed death for the first time. Yet, she resisted releasing her burden to anyone. Even him.

That part he didn't understand. It was as though she was protecting him with the same tenacity she used to protect Qing. It didn't make sense. Nothing about this girl made sense. Why would she try to protect him? *Him*, of all people! She didn't even know him, for starters.

He'd given an indifferent shrug and turned to look out his window. When he'd glanced back, he saw she was fighting tears. What she'd been through the night before, seeing a murder and being hunted like prey, were not common occurrences in her world. She wasn't acting. He'd resisted the impulse to reach over and give her shoulder a reassuring squeeze. Instead, he forced his attention back out the window.

Focus on the task at hand, mate.

That was less than twenty-four hours ago.

Now here he was again, with this woman faced with what was, for her, an utterly insane situation. He could see her visibly struggling to reconcile her own, continuing existence against the death of previously living beings around her. Even the life of this monk, who'd been trying to kill her.

She was wearing nothing but pink satin underwear and the white, body-hugging tank top. No bra.

He had an urge to wrap his arms around her and protect her—she was so frail—along with a mounting desire to do other things to her…

He shut down the line of thought, but he couldn't stop the pang, a slight twist in the corner of his heart, and he ignored the auto-command in his head to push it away, too. He couldn't *not* have empathy for her. She hadn't asked for any of this.

She still wasn't meeting his gaze. Her breathing was shallow. The twinge in his heart twisted again, signaling alarm to his brain. Shock was overriding her system. Then her knees buckled. Her head drooped, and he grabbed her arms and held her steady. He needed her to come back.

"Look at me, Kells!" he repeated.

Releasing her left arm, he grasped her chin between his thumb and the crook of his index finger. Gently, he tilted her face up toward his. "*Breathe*." He stared into her eyes and willed her to follow his order.

She took a deep, stuttered breath. Her brown eyes came into focus, and he felt some of the tension ease from his shoulders. She took another breath, less faltering.

"Are you back with me?" he asked. She nodded. More tension eased. "Atta girl!" He sighed. His task would've been more difficult had she gone into full-blown shock and fainted or something. He pulled her into an unexpected hug, surprising both of them, but released her quickly.

"It's over for now, but we have to get a move on," he said.

She was still shaking, but she managed to take deep breaths.

"Come on," he urged. "Get your things together. We've got to go. Now."

Her brows knit, and she frowned, conflicted. However, she pulled herself together in the next few seconds and then ducked into the bathroom to get dressed.

"How did you know?" she asked.

Durango felt himself breathe another sigh of relief at the fact that she was talking. That was good—the marks on her neck hadn't bruised deeply enough to cause vocal cord damage. He also wondered if she knew that he could've heard her perfectly fine, even if she hadn't left the bathroom door open a crack. But he didn't mind the view of her reflection in the bathroom mirror, so he didn't bring up that point.

"We had one of those in our room, too," he answered.

"One of those?" She poked her head out of the bathroom. He jerked his head toward the dead man. She gasped. "Qing! Li!"

"They're fine," he reassured her. Then he chuckled. "I don't think Li ever even woke up."

She sighed in relief and slid on her cargo pants.

"The real question," he continued, "is how did they know we were here? *And*, Miss Morrison, how big is this thing that you and your young friend have gotten yourselves into?"

"Oh, so *now* you believe me?" She'd raised her volume. Yup, her vocal cords were definitely intact. "I *told* you this was big and serious. And *Qing* told you the police raided his apartment—which is why we came to you in the first place. Then, a few hours ago, we practically had to run from a restaurant because we were spotted by someone who recognized us from the evening news. But that wasn't enough for you? Oh, but now that *ninja assassins* have come for Li and me and..."

She stopped, ending the sentence on a sudden hesitation, followed by a huff, midway through buttoning her shirt.

But he picked up on her gaffe.

"They've come for you and Li, and who?" he asked. "Or *what*?"

"What?" she asked, feigning obliviousness. Yeah, right.

She retreated back into the bathroom to finish getting dressed. He took the opportunity to look around for the box. A cursory check of the tangled sheets and bedspread yielded nothing. Maybe she'd stashed it in a drawer? He heard the toilet flush and used that, followed by the sound of running water while she presumably washed her hands, to quickly check the nightstand and dresser. No, it didn't seem to be in any of those, either.

Well, she'd taken it out of Li's backpack on the pretense of looking for her pink hoodie, so he located the hoodie. He sensed the pause in her activities in the bathroom, heard her sharp intake of breath, and knew she'd realized what he was doing.

He was holding up the pink jacket, dangling it from his hooked index finger when she rushed out to the bedroom. She stopped short, then approached him and reached for it. But he took a step back. He cocked an eyebrow.

"Finish your sentence," he said. She knit her brows innocently. He shook his head. She didn't get to play dumb. She knew exactly what he meant. "Naw, don't give me that. The assassins came here for you, and Li, *and*?"

Her shoulders slumped in defeat. "*Fine*." Her lower lip plumped forward in a pout, and he had to quell the impulse to grab her, kiss her, and bite that lip.

She walked forward. For a second, he thought maybe she had the same idea. But she swerved around him and climbed on the bed in a way that said she meant business, not pleasure. She fished around under the covers, then crawled up to the headboard and moved the pillows aside. She dove her hand between the mattress and headboard, moved her arm around some more, and pulled back. Sitting on her heels, she held up the box.

"This. They came here for me, and Li, and this. He asked me where it was before he started to..." She touched her neck, indicating the dead man on the floor, then looked away and swallowed hard. "Well, before you got here."

"Did you tell him?"

Taken aback, she looked straight at him and then glowered. *Yes*, her look said.

He raised a disapproving eyebrow.

She scowled back. "Apparently, I don't tolerate pain very well."

"What did he do?"

"Twisted my arm. Literally. And the whole choke-y thing. What? That wouldn't have been enough to make you crack? Fine, I'm a wimp."

"That's not what I'm thinking."

"Then what?"

"You need some serious self-defense training."

"Yeah, it's on my to-do list," she mumbled, rolling her eyes, "They offered yoga classes at Zhuang Dian, not karate."

"For the record, ninjas and karate are both Japanese. I think our visitors were some variation of Shaolin monks, which is a style of wushu fighting, and they were using *jiǎoli* techniques." He heard the completely irrelevant words coming out of his mouth, but for some reason, he'd felt the need to demonstrate his advanced knowledge of martial arts to her. Fortunately, he caught himself and stopped before he acted too much like a pretentious know-it-all—if he hadn't already. "In the meantime," he added, "why don't you let me carry that thing." He held out his hand for the box. This time she was the one who pulled back.

"No way!" She sidled backward, off the mattress, to the floor, putting the bed between them. "You haven't seen what I've seen and heard what I've heard. I'm already a target. If you have this, you'll be one too. I'm minimizing my damage radius as much as possible. So, thanks, but no thanks."

And there it was: undeniable proof that she really and truly was trying to protect him. *Him*. The pang twisted until it was almost an actual physical pain. This girl had the heart of a lion.

"Besides," she added, her voice softening, "I'm pretty sure you've already gone above and beyond your normal tour guide duties tonight. Thank you for that—for saving me."

Her big, brown eyes warmed with sincere gratitude, and his chest expanded with the echoes of a sensation he barely remembered: pride. He'd done something good tonight. The recognition made his cheeks warm. He pushed away the whole, awkward feeling.

Don't go getting a big head just because she's looking at you like that…

But something lingered. Hope.

"Come on," he said, turning away. "The boys are waiting next door."

24

It was five a.m. and still dark when we met in the parking lot. The rain had stopped, leaving the air muggy and thick. I bear-hugged Qing and Li before we all loaded up into the SUV. Durango drove. He and Qing conversed in low tones in the front seat. Li sat in the back next to me again.

"Did you get enough sleep last night, sweetie?" I stroked his hair.

Li looked up at me, smiled, and gave a thumbs up. "No worries!"

"Oh. You're learning American English *and* Australian English. Brilliant. You'll be tri-lingual in no time." I messed up his hair. He laughed and swatted my hand away.

"Today's the tricky part," Durango announced. He pulled to the side of the deserted road, put the car in park, and got out.

I frowned, puzzled. We'd only been driving for about five minutes, though the sky was beginning to lighten. Qing got out, too, and began helping Durango unload the back of the SUV. I looked at Li, cocked my head to the side, and held up my hands. *What's going on?* He held up his hands, shrugged, said something in Chinese, and then got out, too. I followed suit. Water splashed and babbled nearby.

"Where are we?" I asked.

"We're at the Timing River, just upstream from where it empties into the Nu," Durango answered. A mechanical whir groaned in the distance.

"What's that noise?"

"Sounds like another dam," Qing said with a note of disgust.

"You've got something against dams?" I asked. I thought of the one that bolstered the riverbank behind the monastery. It prevented the beautiful sunken gardens from being decimated in the rainy season. But that dam was just a wall. It didn't make any mechanical noise, like the one we were currently hearing.

"They've been trying to harness hydroelectricity in China," Qing explained, "but in the process, they're changing the ecosystems. Stuff that never used to get flooded floods now, and water is low where it never used to be."

"I thought hydroelectricity was clean energy?"

"It's a big controversy, is what it is. But in my opinion, they're an eyesore, an earsore, and they're building too many of them." He helped Durango lug a large, tan, folded-up piece of durable-looking fabric and an air compressor to the edge of the bank. Durango unfolded the fabric, started the air compressor, and began inflating a raft. Qing hauled more gear from the SUV.

"We're going across the border by boat?"

"You are," Qing answered. "Li and I will take the car back around to Pianma and meet you on the other side."

"How long do you think it will take?" I grabbed a pack and brought it over. Qing looked at Durango.

Durango tied something onto the back of the raft. "If all goes well, a few hours—for them. We should make it over that far ridge by sometime tomorrow. But, sorry, no cell phone or radio communication allowed until we make it well out of this country."

I would be away from Qing for a full day. I would be alone with Durango.

"But how will we know if they've made it okay? Or vice versa?" The pulse point below my jaw began to thrum, and my breathing started to become shallow. I felt responsible for Li, and the thought of being separated from him for such a critical part of our journey worried me.

"We won't know until we get there," Durango said. "They could be monitoring for communication signals. Sorry."

I shot my gaze to Qing, who was buckling Li into the front seat. Everything inside me was suddenly against this.

But I knew Durango understood this part of the world better than any of us. And I had no other options. There was no turning back.

Qing walked around the car, saluted, and opened his door. "See you on the other side."

The double entendre was too much. A hollow sound escaped the back of my throat. Tears pricked my eyes. I threw myself into his arms. He hugged back tightly. His Qing-scent of tea and garden vegetables filled my nostrils. A hot tear slid down my cheek and dissolved into the fabric of his shirt.

"It's going to be okay, Cow. We'll be fine, and you'll be safe with Oz."

"Promise me something, Q," I said into his shoulder.

"What?"

I pulled out of his embrace to look him squarely in the eye. "If something happens to me—"

"Nothing's going to happen." He thumbed away the remaining wetness under my eyes with a resolute look in his own. I couldn't tell if he was being brave or solicitous. Probably both.

"But if it *does*, I need you to take care of Li. Get him to safety. And don't let him *ever* tell *anyone* about that night—about what he heard or about the box he found. Never. Promise me."

Qing stifled a sigh. I knew he was exasperated with me. I was testing the strands of our friendship to the extreme. He shook his head and shrugged.

"I promise I'll try," he said. "But nothing's going to happen. This time tomorrow, you'll be telling me I was right." He released me and did a high-pitched voice: "'Oh, Qing, you were right, and I was wrong. You're the smartest person I know! And the handsomest, most generous, most caring individual—'"

"Yeah, okay, your highness. *And* the most clairvoyant. I forgot who I was talking to." I rolled my eyes and stepped back from the car. But I could feel a smile lifting the corners of my mouth. Qing got in, started the engine, and rolled down the window.

"You're a lot of work, Cow. You better have gotten me a really good wedding present."

"What, me coming all the way to China wasn't enough of a gift?"

Qing chuckled. This time I sighed. I'd better cut those friendship strands some slack.

"Fine," I said. "I got you and Nori the juicer."

Qing's eyes lit up. "The Fresh Squeezer 5000? With the double-power magnetized centrifuge?"

I did my best TV announcer: "Juices apples, oranges, carrots, even wheatgrass!"

"Cool!" He glowed in a daydream for a moment. "Okay, maybe you're not so bad. Awesome! The juicer! Thanks, Cow!"

He drove off, grinning. I waved. Li waved back and then turned in conversation with Qing. The car and the sound of its motor faded until they were gone around a green hill.

"Ready to shove off?" Durango called from the river.

No.

"Yes," I called back. I forced my feet to take me to the boat.

There's no turning back. You have *to go forward. Be brave. Get it over with.*

At least I was being led by someone who knew the area and was obviously more than capable of taking care of us both.

He stood in the water, barefoot, with his pants rolled up. I took off my socks and shoes and tossed them into the inflatable raft with his. Rolling up my cargos, I bit my tongue and plunged my feet into the gelid current. I tried to focus on the smooth rocks that kneaded my soles rather than the momentary pain from the shock of cold. We pulled the raft into deeper water and jumped in. I sat in front and steadied it with a paddle, preventing us from drifting. Durango started the motor. With the sun rising behind us, we started upstream.

After a few minutes, Durango snorted behind me. "A juicer? Really?"

"The Fresh Squeezer 5000." I nodded with self-importance. I squared my shoulders and thrust my chin in the air, turning away to hide my smirk. I felt the raft shake ever so slightly and knew it wasn't the current doing that. He was laughing.

"It's what he wanted," I said, turning around. "Why? What did you get them?"

A pause. "It's a surprise," he said.

"A surprise? From me?" I thought about that for a second before realizing, "You haven't shopped yet, have you?" More of a statement, really. I knew I was right. He didn't answer. "You know, they're registered at IKEA," I added helpfully.

"Good to know," he intoned.

Okay, I'll shut up now. I hunched my shoulders and turned to face the front of the boat, embarrassed that I might've crossed some boundary of being pushy rather than helpful.

We traveled in silence. I watched the reflection of the rising sun on the flowing water in front of us. It turned scarlet, vermillion, and golden as it danced, finally turning white as the corona broke from the horizon completely. Upstream was a slow way to travel, I thought, but decidedly quicker than hiking would have been.

The warm, azure, September sky overlooked magical walls of color along the hilly river banks. Moss-covered pine and oak canopies gave way to leafy fern and bamboo undergrowth, beneath which flowered a dazzling array of color. Flowers sprang up in small clusters from every sun-dappled nook and cranny in rocks and trees. They splashed the emerald hillsides in shades ranging from pale pink to fuchsia, lavender to royal purple, buttery yellow to deep golden, with occasional pops of tangerine and baby blue. It was hard to believe my life was in danger when I was surrounded by such beauty. The vista, coupled with Durango's calming presence—even if he was annoyed with me—helped me relax. This was much better than driving.

Eventually, we hit shallower water and had to get out and portage. I plunged my bare feet into the icy, mountain-fed stream, so we could carry the raft across the shoal. The water stabbed my feet and ankles. Shooting pain radiated through my body for a few seconds until I adjusted.

Ahh. Life with Raynaud's.

It wasn't something I ever complained about, not even to my doctor. It was a genetic nuisance, not life-threatening. I dealt with it. I clenched my jaw, focused on the scenery, and soldiered on, dragging the front of the boat until the river deepened again.

25

She was innocent, but she had information he needed. This bothered him, and now he had to weigh how much. He was going to have to get it out of her one way or another. The problem was, to do it the nice way—by pretending to have a conversation with her—he was going to have to ask her about herself, possibly supplying information about himself in return.

And he'd already almost slipped up with the wedding gift thing.

He hadn't planned to go to Qing's wedding, and therefore hadn't even considered getting him a gift. But the thought of the juicer, and the way she'd said it, had struck him as ridiculous. Home juicers were possibly the most over-rated, underused inventions ever. The amount of fruit it took to create a decent glass of juice—not to mention the fact that there were all kinds of parts that needed to be cleaned—made them expensively inefficient, not to mention exceedingly messy. Juice creation should be left to professionals, period.

And *nobody* in their right mind wanted to ingest wheatgrass. *Ugh!*

But because these were personal opinions of his, derived from his intimate knowledge of the fruit industry, because of who he was—or who he'd been once upon a time—he'd clammed up rather than explain something that might give away his identity.

Then, when she'd tried to give a helpful suggestion, he'd behaved in a way that was both rude and sullen, with the unintended effect of her thinking that *she* was the one who'd been rude. He could tell she'd been embarrassed, and he felt bad about it.

This conversation-thing wasn't going to be easy.

But he had a job to do. And she was part of it, like it or not. Better to get on with it. He really didn't want to have to force the information out of an innocent the hard way. He would start small with the easy stuff. Then build her trust from there.

They'd just climbed back in the raft from the first portage. The outboard motor hummed into deeper water. The sun was bright, and Kelly seemed to be enjoying the scenery.

"So, I noticed you pronounce Qing's name differently," he said.

"Because I say it 'King,' instead of 'Ching.'" She nodded. "Yeah, that goes back to when we were teenagers, and we first started Skyping. We realized we were both saying each other's names wrong, but he kind of liked that I'd accidentally given him royalty status. So, it stuck."

"And how had he been pronouncing yours?"

"He was saying, 'Cow-li,' like Li does. Hence…" She grinned.

Ah. He smiled back. So that's why Qing called her "Cow." Made much more sense than some sort of bovine physical comparison. He tried to picture her as a teenager: a younger version of the natural beauty in front of him with long brown hair and big brown eyes. She had subtle curves in all the right places, though he guessed that she'd probably been lankier with more of an athletic build as a teen. He wondered if she'd always had such an engaging smile.

"So, you're from Colorado originally, but now you live in Minnesota," he said.

Oh, shit! She'd never told him that.

"Yes."

Thank fuck. She didn't seem to notice his gaffe—she might think he'd learned her origins from Qing. *Tread more carefully, mate.*

"Still have family in Colorado?"

"My parents," she nodded.

"Any brothers or sisters?"

"Nope. I'm an only child."

"And what do your parents do?" He hadn't investigated her parents.

"They're both retired high school teachers."

"Oh?" That was interesting. "Did they work at the same school you attended?"

"Yes." She grimaced. He snickered.

"What did they teach?"

"Mom taught French, and Dad was bio and earth sciences."

So, her father was a science teacher. He imagined how the scene might have played out when she'd failed her eleventh-grade chemistry final. Maybe chemistry wasn't classified as an earth science, so perhaps her father hadn't been her teacher for that class. But still, a failed science class couldn't have gone over well with a science-teacher parent. He couldn't ask about it directly, of course, because it was too far-fetched that Qing would've told him *that* bit of information, but he could prod:

"Did you do well in those subjects?"

"Uh, no." She pursed her lips into a frown, crossed her arms over her chest, and looked away.

Okay, so she didn't want to talk about it. Maybe her mother's classes?

"Do you speak French?"

"I *took* French, but overall, it was a good report card if I got a 'B' in at least *something*. I didn't get decent grades until college. In high school, the ski team was my forte. It was interesting, having both of my parents around all the time." She rolled her eyes. "At least they didn't volunteer to chaperone prom." She chuckled to herself. He wondered what that meant.

"You don't get along with them?"

He kept his tone neutral, careful not to sound as though he was judging her one way or the other, which he wasn't. He was just making an observation. She seemed to take it that way, too, because she shrugged and leaned her elbows back against the side of the raft.

"No, my parents are fine. I visit back home every couple of years, text, e-mail, you know. But my mother has a very preconceived idea of how things should be, and I don't always fit her mold. Then she freaks out. She likes to be in control. I get along better with Dad. He lets me be me."

She'd tensed up while she was speaking, and her words seemed rushed. An edge of heat seeped through her tone. Ah. Parent issues. He understood that, to an extent.

But when she stopped talking, she straightened her shoulders, took a deep breath, and her whole body relaxed. She closed her eyes. Her brows knit and rose as though she were releasing pain. Then a serene smile played the corners of her mouth. She opened her eyes, and her smile deepened. She seemed at peace. He wondered what profound change, what deep, life-affirming understanding, had just happened for her in that fleeting moment.

Well, the best way to find out was to ask. Or maybe push a few key buttons?

"Did you leave Colorado to get away from your mother?" he asked.

"No, not entirely. I got a job in Minneapolis."

"What do you do?"

She hesitated as if reluctant to divulge her position. "I'm a production assistant at an ad agency."

"What does a production assistant do?"

"I help stage photo shoots."

"And how'd you get into that?"

She sighed. "By accident. Seven years ago, I applied for a copywriter position and got offered the job of receptionist by someone who *promised* I could work my way up. I accepted, and now I'm not much more than a glorified gofer on the opposite side of the building from the copywriters."

"What's a gofer?"

"You know, go-fer this, go-fer that. It's like a secretary who runs around a lot. But—seven years later—I am a much wiser individual." Then she brightened and grinned. "*And* I'm the reigning darts champ at McGlynn's Pub."

He cocked a skeptical eyebrow and barely suppressed a smile. It was difficult to imagine this perky, pretty little girl beating out a room of potbellied, beer-guzzling bar regulars at their own game. Maybe pubs in Minneapolis were different from those in other parts of the world?

Naw, probably not. It was funny. *She* was funny. And interesting. Durango could feel real, not-acting-for-the-job delight well up inside him. For the first time in a long time, he realized he was smiling of his own accord.

"You're a darts champ?"

"Two years running. Minnesota winters are *freaking* cold, and there's not a lot to do if you don't like ice fishing."

"You don't like ice fishing?"

"Not a fan. So, how about you?"

"Wouldn't know. Not a lot of ice fishing opportunities in Australia."

And there it was. Reality had tugged him back to earth. He'd automatically turned her question into a joke to avoid having to answer. But it was coming. She was asking about *him*, about his personal life.

Why was he so reluctant to lie to her? He did it all the time. However, he realized, those were people who didn't deserve the truth. All *she* was doing was being a nice person. Maybe he could avoid anything too deep and thus avoid having to lie to her.

"I meant 'what do you do in your spare time?'" she explained.

"I hit the bar with Qing and the boys, or some of my other mates, a few times a week. Nothing as ambitious as darts, mind you. And there's Facebook." He winked. She rolled her eyes. "Work keeps me fairly busy."

She nodded her head in concession to the work-thing, and he wondered what she would think if she knew what he really did for a living. Not that she could ever know. But what *if*?

"What do you miss most about Australia?"

Ah, an easy one.

"The people," he shrugged. "It's home." Even though he hadn't been there in over a year, he felt a twinge of sentiment. Faces popped into his head. Places. Smells. He did miss it.

"Yeah, I know what you mean," she said.

A distant look passed her features. Homesickness—he recognized it. He wondered where "home" meant for her. Minnesota? Or Colorado? But then she cocked her head to the side and looked at him.

"Hey, speaking of Australia, can I ask you something?"

"Sure." He braced himself.

"What's a *billabong*?" She almost whispered the word.

His eyebrows rose. That was not a question he'd been expecting. Plus, the way she'd said it, in a hushed voice, was almost comical. He stopped himself from bursting out laughing, but he had to know:

"What do you think it is?"

She bit her lip as though she were embarrassed. He couldn't wait to hear her answer.

"I think it has something to do with drugs," she confessed.

His eyebrows shot higher.

"Because, you know, it sounds like it comes from 'bill,' like a dollar bill, which gets rolled up for snorting coke, and 'bong,' which is for pot. Is that right?"

"Crikey." It was all he could do to keep his lips in a straight line. If she kept up with questions like this, maybe it wouldn't be so bad after all.

"Okay, clearly not," she mumbled. He hadn't done a good job hiding his mirth. She frowned and shrugged. She was embarrassed, he could see, but she was also completely adorable. He couldn't help but grin.

"No, but interesting etymological interpretation," he said, adjusting the rudder around a bend and trying to discourage her from feeling stupid. "A billabong is a stagnant, dead-end channel off of a river."

"Oh." She sat back, seeming to consider this. After a minute, she piped up again. "So, it's a good thing we caught you when we did the other night, huh? Or, rather, you caught us." She giggled, then knit her brows. "Were you getting ready to head out?"

She'd completely changed the topic. He wondered how her train of thought could have gone from billabongs to the unorthodox way in which they'd met two nights ago. But this was more the type of question he'd been expecting.

"Nope. I was done for the night."

"How come you never told Qing your real name before?"

"He never asked." Not that he'd have told Qing the truth. In fact, it was an incredible moment of weakness that he'd cracked at all. And it wasn't Qing he'd been telling, even though Qing had been in the room. It was her.

She was quiet for a moment, as though hesitating on an issue. He steeled himself.

"How did you learn to do… what you did… to the men in our hotel rooms?"

In other words, *'How did you learn to kill people?'*

Yeah, this is what he'd really been waiting for.

He could've given a simple answer: *I was in the military.* But he didn't want to revisit the time or the circumstances under which he'd left that profession.

For some reason, being around Kelly made him more acutely aware of the Incident from back then. Similarly, he couldn't tell her that the art of assassination was a useful skill, which he'd honed to perfection in his current line of work since leaving the military. He wondered what she'd think of him if she knew any of these things.

He didn't want to find out.

Doesn't matter. You're not going to tell her.

He didn't want her to look at him in any way other than the way she'd looked at him early this morning after he'd rescued her. He avoided meeting her gaze and kept his eyes trained upstream. He heard the bitter edge in his tone as he answered.

"Around."

26

He didn't add to his answer, and I sensed I'd crossed some sort of personal line with my questions. But before I could ponder for too long, the boat scraped bottom, and we had to get out to haul it across the rocks. I gritted my teeth and sank in the freezing river up to my ankles.

We passed a few small towns at first, then left civilization behind. At times we came across other boaters on the river, mostly fishermen, but as the sun rose higher in the sky, the fishermen went home, and we had the river to ourselves. Green mountains rose up around us.

I was surprised at how easy it had been to tell him about my relationship with my parents without getting defensive—and at how much insight I'd achieved. I'd suddenly realized that even though there was discord in my life, it didn't change who I was.

I'd closed my eyes, taken a breath, and literally felt an old load lift away. Maybe it was the river or the mountains, or maybe it was him, but I'd absolutely felt a release at these epiphanies. I was serene and at peace with my answers.

Maybe it was even *me*. Maybe coming to China *had* changed me.

Unfortunately, I began to second-guess my newfound serenity with Durango's extended silence. I grew more uncomfortable as the time passed, and he clearly wasn't going to elaborate. When he'd asked me about myself, maybe I'd overshared. *TMI?* And then, maybe my questions about him had been too prying. Perhaps I *had* crossed a line, and I ought to just keep quiet and let him guide me back to Qing and Li and then to safety.

Durango finally spoke his next words around one o'clock.

"We're good for a while now," he said. We climbed back in the raft after our fourth or fifth portage. He tossed a sandwich and a bottle of water toward me, onto the middle section crammed with our backpacks.

"Okay, thanks."

I settled back on my seat in the front, ignoring the food in favor of a chance to warm my pin-prickled feet. Flicking droplets away, I turned and stretched out sideways across the raft's v-shaped bow, resting my head against one inflated side, my feet against the other. I closed my eyes and turned my face up toward the sun, drinking in its warmth.

"Your toes are white," Durango said. He sounded concerned.

"I'm Caucasian," I deadpanned, keeping my eyes shut. I shifted my soles on the fabric of the inflated balloon, glad that its dark, tan color absorbed so much heat. The pinpricks intensified. I rode out the painful sensation.

"No, seriously," he persisted. "There's like… a line…?"

Oh, okay. We'll continue with the TMI. Smiling wryly, I brought a hand up to shield my eyes and turned my head, peeking at him with one eye. He was staring at my feet in bewilderment. I sighed. *Let the freak show begin.* I pulled myself to a seated position, with my knees under my chin, feet flat on the bench, making sure my toes were still in the sun.

"It's genetic. It's called Raynaud's," I explained. Durango raised his brows, curious. "I got it from my dad, who got it from his mother, et cetera. It just means that when I experience sudden coldness, the blood flow shuts down in my extremities."

"Your blood flow *shuts down*?"

"Yeah, see? It's stopped right here, this line you're looking at." I drew my finger across my toes.

"And then what?"

"Then I just gotta warm 'em up again. Happens more with my fingers, but in this case, the water's a bit brisk." I massaged my toes, aware that he was watching: a pink swirl broke through—the blood flow returning—and the white line began to dissipate.

"That's just bizarre," he said.

I smirked. *Yup.*

He looked away and maneuvered a bend in the river. "Does it hurt?"

I followed his gaze upriver. "It's not my favorite. But," I turned back, "it just means I need lots of sunshine in my life. Sunshine helps." I smiled and reached for the sandwich and bottle of water. "So, how about you?"

"Me?"

"Yeah. You must get lots of sunshine in your line of work?" That seemed like a good way to change the subject while also being a "safe" question to ask—one that wouldn't make him shut down again. If he was in the mood to talk, I wanted to keep it going. We were going to be stuck together for at least another day or two.

"Uh, yeah, sure."

"What made you decide to become a tour guide? Have you always been outdoorsy?" Questions about his job—that had to be non-offensive, right?

"Not always. When I was young, I used to sit around watching television, reading books. Read a *lot* of books. Got to be a bit of a tubster. So, my mum signed me up for footy in the same league as my older brother. I went kicking and screaming, but in the end, I turned out to be fairly good at it. By the time I was a teenager, my team had done really well, and I got the chance to travel a bit. Went to New Zealand, the UK, France, Italy, South Africa. Anyway, to answer your question, the travel opened my eyes to what else was out there."

"Does 'footy' mean football or soccer?"

"Where I'm from, it means rugby league."

"Oh." I wasn't sure what rugby was. "And you didn't want to keep playing?"

"Wasn't good enough to go pro or anything, but it helped me get in shape back then. What? You look confused."

"I have a stupid question," I confessed.

"No such thing."

"Okay, what's rugby? Is that the one with the stick with the net on the end, and you catch a ball in it? I think we have one of those teams in Colorado."

"I think you're thinking of lacrosse. That's an American sport."

"Really? Huh."

"Rugby is similar to your American football."

I thought for a moment and brightened up. "Mackay Cutters!" I exclaimed.

"Yeah," Durango answered slowly. "They're a semi-pro league team from Queensland. And it's pronounced 'Mah-*kye*.' How did you know about—?"

"Your shirt," I explained. "The one I was going to, er, *borrow* yesterday morning." I smiled and exhaled on a sigh, remembering the shirt's smell.

He chuckled. "Liked that shirt, did you?"

Crap, had I just made that sighing noise out loud?

"No, it's just that..." I could feel the flush creep up my cheeks and realized there was no explaining this one without dying of embarrassment. *Moving right along....*

"So, you have an older brother?"

"Yeah, one older brother, and after him came my two older sisters. I was the baby. And my sisters were merciless."

"How so?"

"Well, see, they wanted a baby sister, one they could dress up, and all. But when they got me, they decided it didn't matter. Dressed me up anyway."

"They dressed you like a girl?" I giggled.

"Let's just say that by the time I was five, there were more pictures of me in frocks than suits. Dad finally put an end to it. Said he was afraid I'd get a complex or something."

"And did you?" I asked in mock seriousness. Durango made a face at me and seemed to relax a bit. The tension I'd felt from him earlier was gone. He didn't seem to mind answering these questions about his past. So, I continued.

"You said you read a lot when you were younger. What sorts of books did you read?"

"Anything I could get my hands on, really. Especially the exciting ones. Adventure stories, mysteries, spy novels. Anything with a good plot and a map."

"A map?"

"Yeah, I've always loved maps. Makes everything more interesting when you understand it from a geographic standpoint. Might have become a cartographer if I hadn't wound up—"

He stopped speaking abruptly, gave me a sharp glance, and looked away upriver. He seemed flummoxed, and I didn't understand. Alarmed, I turned, scouting for the cause of Durango's concern, but unable to find anything, I pivoted back to him, waiting for him to explain. He offered no explanation. I wondered if I'd missed something else.

"If you hadn't wound up…?" I prompted.

He still didn't answer. I stared at him and tried to figure out the puzzle of this strange, gorgeous man with whom I was effectively trapped in the wilderness. I reviewed the conversation in my head. We'd been talking about his childhood, his love for books, maps… and suddenly, out of nowhere, it was over. It was almost as if…! *Wait.* Had he cut himself off on purpose? *"Might have become a cartographer if I hadn't wound up—"* Hmm…. Wound up here, maybe? I wondered how long he'd been in China. And then the next logical question burned through my lips before I considered whether or not I ought to ask it out loud.

"Why did you leave Australia?"

I leaned forward, bare feet on the cold boat bottom, all of my attention on him. Suddenly I needed to know more about Qing's friend, with whom I was now alone in the middle of sub-Himalayan nowhere. He ignored me as though I hadn't spoken, and I would have thought that I'd said it too softly, that he hadn't heard me, but for the fact that a knot pulsed at the back of his jaw. All of his earlier tension was back.

And then I felt bad.

I'd pushed too far again—my curiosity dancing along the edge of the boundary between casual acquaintance and actual friendship—and now he was angry. I could sense it coming off of him in waves. I didn't understand why, but I could guess that I was its source since no one else was around. *Duh!* And maybe I didn't need to know more about him, other than the fact that he was Qing's friend, and he was doing us this *huge* favor by getting Li and me to safety, for no reason other than his own altruism. My heart sank as I realized I'd caused him discomfort.

"Sorry," I mumbled. "I didn't mean to…" He remained silent, so I spun forward to face the bow, confused, contrite, and disheartened.

27

The scenery flew by—glimpses of lush valleys and cloud-shrouded mountaintops between the twists and turns we took on the river. Bird chirps occasionally lilted over the drone of the boat's motor.

At one point, I saw a strange sight: a large, red raccoon, sleeping on its belly, on a tree branch. Its legs dangled down on both sides, like a child with no cares in the world. I smiled at the thought of the weird comparison of the red raccoon to a human child. Then I thought of Li, a now-motherless, human child whose life was in danger thanks to me, and my smile faded. This place was beautiful, mystical, but it wasn't Colorado, and right now, that's all I wanted: to get out of this mess and begin rebuilding my life. I slipped my hand in my cargo pants pocket and fished out the bent nickel. Home.

An hour later, we needed to portage again. I put the nickel away and was out before Durango needed to say anything. We hauled the raft in silence over the shoals. I heaved, walking backward, not even trying to meet his gaze.

Suddenly the riverbed disappeared beneath my feet.

"Whoa!" I grabbed onto the side of the raft before I went under.

"You okay?" He halted and held the raft steady.

"Drop-off." No need to portage through *that*. I heaved myself up and flopped into the boat. Small torrents of cold mountain water ran from my pants and the bottom half of my shirt.

"Thanks for the warning."

I heard the mirth in his voice and turned to see him smirking. I scowled.

"Anytime."

It irritated me that he now found humor in my misfortune after his stoic silence of the past few hours. *Glad to keep you entertained.*

I wished I didn't care what he thought about me. Or whether he even thought about me at all.

He pushed the raft forward a few steps, located the underwater precipice, and managed to shove off and board the raft in a single, fluid motion. Figured. I paid him no more attention but retrieved the nickel and began flipping it again.

Minutes passed. The tranquil scenery eased by. I focused on the landscape, blocking out everything else. The bent nickel went over my middle finger, back down between my index finger and thumb....

Ironically, even though the focus/blocking technique was something I'd learned in Master Lo Wen's yoga class, I began to relax. *What Durango thinks of you doesn't matter.* He *doesn't matter. He's just a soul, passing through your life. He doesn't matter. None of this matters.* Over the finger, under, between...

Durango stiffened and looked upriver.

I continued flipping my nickel but followed his gaze. I saw nothing. Then my ears picked up on the anomaly. Human voices broke the cadence of nature. Rounding another bend in the river, we came upon two boats cordoned by a third. I stopped flipping my coin and sat up straighter. I looked back at Durango and raised an eyebrow. *What's going on?*

"It's a border patrol blockade," he said in a low voice, answering my unspoken question. "Highly unusual for them to come out this far."

That didn't sound good.

"What do we do?"

"Nothing. Just follow along."

Okay?

As we approached, I saw one guard standing on the southern riverbank and two in a small motorboat. Large guns hung on straps over their shoulders, and right now, those guns were pointed at people in the other two boats, who were handing over small booklets. The guards seemed to be checking passports and IDs. My chest constricted as I realized I possessed neither.

The guards let the first boat through, a man who looked like a fisherman, but they detained the two men in the second boat. They also looked like fishermen to me. The water-bound guards hauled a large box out of their vessel on the northern shore. One of the guards began to yell at the men. He pointed his gun and forced them face-down on the ground. I watched, transfixed and terrified.

"Arms smugglers," Durango said under his breath.

"*What?!*" I breathed. "What kind of river *is* this?"

Durango chuckled softly in a way that made me feel I was the only one out of my element. However, I didn't have time to argue because while the guards in the boat were handcuffing the arms smugglers, the guard on the bank was waving us toward him. Durango steered the boat over and idled the motor.

"Passports," the guard demanded in English.

To my surprise, Durango gave the guard a somber nod and pulled two passports out of his backpack. He handed them to the guard. The guard studied them for a moment, then gave them back to Durango. He waved us through.

I resisted the urge to give either Durango or the guard a *WTF* look. I was just relieved we'd gotten through. My heart pumped a million miles an hour. I couldn't believe they hadn't heard it thumping all the way in Beijing.

We pulled past the makeshift checkpoint. I twirled the nickel in my fingers. *Calm down. Breathe.* I looked up at my tour guide in gratitude for his mysterious passport-materializing abilities. I was about to mouth the words *thank you*—waiting until I could ask him where he'd gotten the passports—when suddenly the guard jogged up the bank next to our raft.

"Stop!"

Durango idled the motor.

The guard stared at me.

"What is in your hand?" his cold, cruel voice asked.

My stomach curdled, and I instantly knew. *The coffee shop.* Insignificant though the coin was, I'd played it through my fingers when I'd been there. Despite my best efforts to hide my face, and Qing's and Li's, they must have caught the image of the nickel on the security cameras.

Of course they had.

It was the talisman of my identification.

And even though we'd separated ourselves from Qing and Li, I still had the most damning piece of evidence with me.

The box.

Everything was about to be lost. I would go to prison, or worse, and Durango would go too, for helping me. Maybe Qing and Li had made it safely across the border, but I knew it wouldn't take much torture from my jailers for me to give us all up. I was such an idiot!

I did the only thing I could think to do. I dropped the bent coin, my last tangible memory of home, in the river.

28

"Oh, no!" I exclaimed, pretending I'd fumbled as it sank in the middle of the stream. A glance in Durango's eyes, and I knew he understood exactly what had just happened, that I'd dropped the nickel on purpose.

"I will get it!" the guard offered, to my horror.

With the eagerness of a leopard about to pounce, he unstrapped his holster and took off his shoes. Still wrangling their arms dealers on the opposite bank, the other guards were now alert to their colleague's interest. Just then, Durango spoke up.

"That's okay, I'll get it." He cut the motor and, with his shoes already off, hit the water right before the guard.

The inflatable raft started to drift immediately. I grabbed a paddle and stabbed it down toward the shallower shore to anchor it. Seconds ticked by. The guards on the opposite bank, the arms smugglers, and I were all transfixed on the river's current and the unbroken line of ripples that patterned the center of the waterway. Finally, the surface bubbled. The guard came up first.

"*Wǒ xiǎng qǐlái le!* I have it!" he exclaimed. The water undulated almost to his chin. But he held a flattened bottle cap. He looked at his prize and grimaced. Disgusted with himself, he cast it aside and was about to go back down when Durango's head and chest emerged.

"I got 'er!"

Something was off with his voice, but I was too distracted by the metal flashing in his hands to put my finger on it. What did he think he was doing? I'd dropped the nickel on purpose!

He waded over to the side of the boat.

"Hon, you have to be more careful," he scolded me. "We'll get it sized properly when we get back home."

It hit me then, what was wrong with his voice: he sounded as though he'd been born in Texas; his American accent was flawless.

He grabbed my left hand. I looked down as he slid a delicate silver ring with a single, small diamond over the smooth skin of my fourth finger.

I gasped inaudibly, and my heart leapt. Tears sprang to my eyes.

I mean, what girl doesn't dream of having a gorgeous man put a diamond ring on her finger, right?

But even as I thought the glib words, I knew that wasn't it. As insane and impossible as it was, I realized I'd developed feelings for Durango. I felt connected to him beyond the fact that he'd already saved my life once. And somehow, miraculously, he'd just done it again—saved us both.

"I'm so sorry," I gushed, returning to our present, dire straits and continuing his made-up story, though my cheeks flushed with warmth. "I can't believe you found it!"

He hoisted himself back up into the raft, drenched head to toe. I clamped a hand over my mouth as a small lake immediately began to run off of him.

"Yeah, it's funny when it's not you, isn't it?" he muttered in his own accent under his breath. I giggled harder.

"Anythin' for my puddin' pop," he drawled loudly, so the guards could hear.

Puddin' pop? I rolled my eyes at him. He was going a bit over the top. But, okay, if that's how he wanted to play it.

"Aw, who's my favorite sugar lump?" I cooed, batting my lashes.

The guards eyed us suspiciously. The ones on the northern bank looked for a cue from their wet companion in the middle of the river. He fumed for a second but then bought the story and waded back to shore, signaling for Durango and me to move along.

"Be more careful with your ring," he warned me.

Durango re-started the motor. I glanced at the guard, nodded, and then riveted my eyes back to my hand. The diamond glinted in the sun.

"Yessir. Thanks, y'all!" Durango waved as we sped away.

“Puddin’ pop? Really?” I scoffed as soon as we were out of earshot.

“It’s better than being a sugar lump.”

Water continued to stream off his clothes. He idled the motor and quickly stripped off his blue oxford and tank top, wringing them out and laying them across the backpacks to dry.

I tried not to gawk at his exceptional physique, but the thought crept into my head that Durango’s body was like a map, going from delicious deltoids to perfect pectorals to sartorial splendor to…! I laughed at myself.

Unfortunately, he noticed.

“What’s funny?”

“Nothing.”

Crap. Now he would probably be offended and think I was laughing at him. It was bad enough that I’d been sighing over the remembered aroma of his rugby shirt earlier. Now I was mooning over his drool-worthy bod, right in front of him. *You are* such *a moron.*

“I’m an idiot, that’s all,” I clarified. And before he could ask why I was an idiot, I spewed a new question that was now more important than the passport one. “So, cowboy, where did you learn to do an American accent?”

“Movies.” He avoided my gaze and shrugged his delicious deltoids.

“No,” I disagreed.

“No?” This time he looked me straight in the eye and knit his brow.

“No.”

“What makes you think—?”

“You mentioned books and sports in your past, but nothing about movies.”

“You don’t have to be an absolute theater buff to go to the movies at some point.”

“True. But that was a pretty good accent. It would fool *me* if I didn’t know better. I think you’d have had to sit through a lot of movies to be able to replicate that on the spot. And you live here, in China. Any American movies you’d have access to in theaters would be dubbed into Mandarin, right?”

“In Yunnan, yes, for the most part, you’re correct,” he agreed. He wore a half-smile as though he was humoring me, waiting to reveal the flaw in my logic. “But what about Internet streaming?”

"YouTube is blocked in China!" This, I knew from trying to watch it on my phone during downtime at the monastery.

"...not when you bypass it with a VPN, and what about DVDs?"

"Ha!" I pointed in triumph. "You don't have a television!"

"That you saw," he corrected.

"And your laptop didn't have a DVD drive!"

"Plus, I haven't always lived here."

"But...?"

I sat back, my train of thought temporarily halted by his roadblocks. I hadn't seen his entire house, especially not that other bedroom. And I knew from earlier in the day that he didn't want to discuss why he'd left Australia, so I avoided the "other places he'd lived" category, too. Chewing on my lip for a moment, but convinced the pieces of the Durango puzzle were starting to fit, I tried a different tact.

"Okay, fine," I conceded, "what movie did you learn it from?"

"*True Grit* with John Wayne," he nodded, focusing on steering the boat.

I narrowed my eyes, studying him. He was letting me partway in, then slamming the door on my foot, and I couldn't understand why.

But it didn't matter anyway.

Soon this would all be over, Li and I would be safe, and once I was home, I'd find a way to pay Durango back.

But I'd probably never see him again. The thought left a hollow sadness in my chest. I turned toward the raft's bow with a long, slow exhalation.

29

Alright, what is it?" he asked the back of Kelly's head. "You didn't like that answer, either?"

"Nope."

"Why not?"

He was genuinely curious. He'd thought it was a good answer, one that would have kept her happy. It surprised him that her brown eyes were cold and her jaw tight when she turned around to face him.

"Look, you have secrets you want to keep. That's fine. It's none of my business."

Her tone was aloof. She was clearly upset. She swiveled sideways and drew her knees up to her chin, hugging them, and looked upstream.

"No, seriously," he persisted, "why don't you believe I learned that accent from the movies?"

"Because you did a Texas accent, but you said you learned it from John Wayne," she responded without looking at him. "John Wayne was from Iowa and then California, not Texas. He had a distinctive way of speaking—his inflections possessed a drawl—but it wasn't Texan."

Durango had given himself a U.S. passport to match hers, and he had used the Texas accent, which he'd perfected through professional training. But his nonchalant explanation had fallen short. He'd honestly thought John Wayne was from Texas.

"You know a lot about John Wayne."

"I did a report on him in seventh grade. I also know what Texans sound like."

"You've met a lot of Texans, then, living in Colorado and Minnesota?"

"Yes, I've known several native Texans. I had friends who moved from there. Texas almost touches Colorado."

She hugged her knees tighter, then stopped and looked at her hands.

"Oh. Here."

She pulled off the ring and leaned across the boat. He opened his palm; she dropped it in. A million questions were in her scowling eyes, but she didn't ask any. She probably didn't want to deal with his sudden withdrawals anymore.

Which, he realized, happened when he tried to tell her the truth.

He couldn't explain that it wasn't because he didn't want to tell her about himself. The problem was that he *did* want to. Too much. It had been a long time since he'd let anybody in, even this far.

But the whole truth wasn't permissible. Not under these circumstances, not with his life. And not with what he still needed to get from her: the information she had and access to the box.

Unfortunately, her perception of him would be that he was pulling away and closing himself off. This would, in turn, he knew, cause her to close off from him. She didn't play games with people like he did. She was a victim in all of this, and he was making it worse for her. He couldn't let her shut down. He tried to lighten the atmosphere.

"Short engagement," he quipped.

Still scowling, she raised an eyebrow.

"You didn't find that in the river," she said.

He smiled. She was testing the waters by making a statement of the obvious, not asking a question. Maybe he could try being fully honest with her, just once.

"You're right. I had it on me." When she didn't push further, he added, "It was my mum's." He held it up in the sun, watching the rays dance off its facets.

"*Was*? Oh! I'm sorry."

"Thanks. It was about ten years ago. She gave it to me when she was in hospice. I was the only one of my sibs not yet married. Think she thought it would bring me luck. She died the next day."

He shoved it deep into the pocket of his soaked pants. He wondered what his mother would have thought about what he'd become. She wouldn't have approved of the way he was treating Kelly. He didn't approve of it, himself. It was just...

"Look, you don't have to tell me anything—" she started to say, but he interrupted.

"I'm sorry I get so abrupt with you," he blurted out. "It's just that I'm a very private person, and I don't usually tell people anything about myself."

"What about Qing?"

"Yeah, that's all banter online, and you go out with your mates to the bar. It's all just fun stuff. Nothing personal. You can just be who you are without having to talk about where you've been."

"And you don't like to talk about where you've been?"

"It's not that I don't like to. It's just that I don't. Ever. Because… well, I can't really go into it. But there's something about you that just… I don't know. Maybe it's because you sort of remind me of my mum a bit."

Kelly raised a skeptical eyebrow. "Er, thanks?"

He mentally facepalmed. *You're a nong. What girl wants to be told she reminds a guy of his mum?* "Naw, I mean that in a good way. You're very dogged, determined like she was. You get an idea in your head, and you don't let it go. I admire that. You're also very intuitive."

"Your mom was intuitive?"

"Yeah, she could read people like a book."

"I'm not that good at reading people," she said quickly. She thought for a minute, then cocked her head quizzically to the side. "So besides Texan, how many languages do you speak?"

He smiled as relief sank through him. Just like that, she'd accepted his apology and steered the conversation to a less-invasive topic. He loved her optimism.

"I think it's ten, right now."

"*Ten?* Right now?" She grinned and sat forward. "How did you learn ten languages? What are they?"

"In high school, I learned French and Mandarin. Then at UQ, I studied Indonesian. Later, along the way, I learned Malay, Thai, Burmese, Assamese, Hindi, Khmer, Vietnamese," he ticked languages off on his fingers, "and currently I'm learning Japanese."

"Wow," she laughed. "I don't even know what countries some of those languages are from. You remember how to speak the languages you took in high school?"

"Uh-huh."

"Wow. So what's UQ? University of Queensland?"

"Exactly."

"And you majored in Indonesian?"

"I dual-majored in international relations and Indonesian, and I got a diploma in geographical science."

"Geographical…? Maps!"

"Yes." He laughed at her enthusiasm.

"So why all the languages and the international relations? What did you want to go into?"

"Well, I've always been good with languages, and I thought I was going to go work for my dad. He was a banana farmer. My older brother was already working with him, trying to expand the business. But two months after graduation, Dad passed unexpectedly, and I lost interest in farming."

"I'm sorry."

"No worries. It all worked out." *In a fashion.* He smiled and shrugged, but found he couldn't look her in the eye anymore, so he turned his head and scanned upriver. To his relief—perhaps because she'd sensed his mood shift—Kelly switched gears again.

"How did you get your name?"

"From my parents." He glanced back in time to see her roll her eyes at his smart-aleck answer. He grinned.

"Yeah, I figured that part out. They named you after a city in Colorado?"

"No, they named me after a Basque town in Spain, after which the Colorado city is also named, as well as cities in Texas and Iowa and a state in Mexico."

"Huh. I didn't know that. Are you part-Spanish?"

"No. They were just visiting there about nine months before I was born."

She was quiet for a second, then—"Oh!" She giggled, a sound he realized he quite liked. "When's your birthday?"

"I'll be thirty-nine next December."

"You were a winter baby."

"Not Down Under," he corrected her. "I was born in the summer."

"Oh, right," she mused. "Cool."

She reflected for a minute, and that's when he heard more voices coming from somewhere around a bend in the distance. He cut the motor and listened. Voices demanding IDs, in Mandarin. Another border patrol. It would be too dangerous to continue following the river.

"Let's go."

30

Oh, crap!

I'd studied Durango as he'd cut the motor, and then I'd heard the voices, too. My eyes went wide. What if I'd been speaking too loudly? It was probably why he hadn't wanted to converse much in the first place. *You are such a dummy, Morrison!*

He pulled out a paddle and started for shore. I picked up the other one and tried to dip and pull as quietly as I could.

"Do you think they'll be up there, also?" I whispered. I jutted my chin at the ridge above the riverbank and looked up at him. He scanned the shore.

"Not the way we're going to go," he answered quietly. "Besides, there are only a few hours of daylight left. Everyone will be headed up soon. If we stay put for the night, we'll be fine. But we need to get a move on."

We reached the shore, jumped out, and hauled the raft onto a small ledge beneath the steep embankment.

"You're just going to leave it here?" I asked softly as we quickly put our shoes and socks back on. He strapped on his backpack and shrugged. I felt awful thinking of all the expense I was costing him.

Well, me, I reminded myself. *It's costing* me, *and this is a necessary expense.* I was going to pay him back for all of this, however long it took.

A foothold, a giant step, and he was up the embankment. He turned and held out his hand.

"Thanks," I said, trying not to be aware of the warmth of his palm as I took his hand and lifted my foot to get a toehold. He pulled me up as though me-plus-my-backpack weighed nothing and released me in one swift movement. I was pretty sure my pulse beat right through my palm.

Fangirling so hard right now!

I was relieved to note he seemed oblivious to my teenage regression moment.

The terrain sloped steeply upward, thick with trees and undergrowth. I was glad I'd already spent a month at altitude because I was having enough trouble keeping pace; Durango's broad steps nearly doubled mine. I'd kept in shape with a treadmill the past several years and had run three miles a day at the monastery, but I hadn't hiked like this in a long time.

We walked southwest, up the forested slope, and away from the river for almost two hours. The shadows deepened around us under the late afternoon sun. At one point, I saw movement in a tree nearby. It was a creature similar to the one I'd seen sleeping in the trees earlier.

"Is that a fox or a raccoon?" I asked in a hushed tone, halting to watch the red animal with the white-masked face and ringed tail as it munched bamboo leaves.

Durango paused a few steps ahead of me and turned.

"Neither. That's a red panda," he answered. "They're unique to this part of the world."

Given our remote location, probably not many people got a chance to see red pandas in the wild. And, I realized, I'd never have seen it myself if I hadn't been in this bizarre situation. I smiled at the irony.

We continued upward. The atmosphere became arider on the ascent. The temperature began to feel cooler with the sun descending in front of us against the mountain's other slope. But the views were still amazing. Before we reached the top, I turned, caught a glimpse of the layout behind us, and stopped in my tracks. Green, Berber-carpeted mountains spread out forever until they changed to white peaks of the snow-capped Himalayas, where they met the dusky sky. I spread my arms to open my lungs and took in a deep breath of fresh, mountain air.

"You look like you've just won the Olympics," Durango chuckled.

Besides having my arms spread wide, I realized I was probably also grinning like an idiot, but I didn't care.

"How high are we?" I asked.

"Probably about thirty-six hundred meters."

I did the math: right around eleven thousand, eight hundred feet. My grin deepened. Breckenridge, Keystone, Silverthorne.

"What?"

"I've skied this high," I sighed happily. "And I've hiked higher. Not in a long time, but it feels awesome. Just look at this view!"

"Wait until we get to the top. You'll like that view even better."

We continued up to the ridge until the trees ended. The ground dropped away in a steep slope in front of us. We were perched on what looked like the rim of an enormous, grass-and-forested bowl sprinkled with late-blooming colors. At the bottom of the bowl lay a round, clear lake, perfectly reflecting the sky above.

"It's beautiful," I breathed. "Like a fairytale!"

"Yeah," he agreed. "Tingming Lake. They say the gods treasure it so much that if you speak too loudly, you'll anger them, and they'll create violent storms."

I was reminded of the myth from the walls of Zhuang Dian, where the angry gods sent the water dragon to stop the fire dragon. But I didn't want to have this magical lake associated with my now-negative feelings of the monastery. I shifted the subject.

"You bring a lot of your tour groups here?"

"Sometimes," he shrugged.

He turned away, starting down the slope ahead of me, and I had the distinct impression he was upset with me again. He held out a hand to assist me, but I waved it away, put off by his mood swing.

"I'm fine," I said, taking a step down.

My recent yoga training had equipped me with solid core muscles and excellent balance. Tracking sideways, I found footing easily enough in clumps of the long grass that grew out of the hillside. Halfway down, I was proud of myself for keeping up with him when I froze mid-step.

Something long and dark slithered past where I had been about to place my right foot.

I shrieked, lost my balance, and set my foot too far forward. Then, in a rush to adjust, I caught my left foot on my right ankle. At that point, my backpack shifted, throwing me further off-balance, and I was falling, about to tumble down the remaining hundred yards of the sharp slope.

A sudden, firm clamp on my upper arm stopped my fall. My heart thumped as I stared straight down the long drop from my pivoted position. Twisting my head, I looked at him in amazement.

"All right?" His blue eyes were full of concern. He still grasped my arm tightly.

"There was a snake," I explained, but it sounded lame since he was so calm. I righted myself.

"Yeah, they come out to hunt at night. Mostly mice, though. Not too interested in people." A twinkle glimmered behind his concern, though his face remained serious.

I rolled my eyes in embarrassment and gave him a sheepish smile. I felt dumb for having refused his help earlier.

"Sorry," I apologized.

"Nah, don't be. You didn't know." He offered his arm again to help me the rest of the way. This time I took it. "Besides," he added, "you're a girl."

"Hey, wait a minute!" I started to protest, but I could already feel the silent chuckles shaking his body.

"Quiet!" he admonished me in a whisper, though he was still laughing. "You'll make the gods angry."

"Oh, go blow it out your boomerang," I mumbled.

"What was that?"

"Nothing."

31

The phone call from the police had come mid-afternoon—bodies found at a motel in far northwestern Yunnan. *Why would you inform me of this?* Bodies linked to the monastery. *Really? How is this possible? One of our guests is missing. You do not mean to say that she is...?* The bodies of two dead monks.

It was as though a hand had reached out from the grave and gripped his chest, cold and clammy. He wondered if the spirits of his ancestors had lost a new battle against their ancient adversaries, whose spirits would also forever haunt the castle's halls. Yat-sen Xun hung up the phone and summoned Ding Li-Liang.

"Tulku," Ding Li-Liang nodded.

"We do not have it." The words came out hoarse from Yat-sen Xun's throat.

"The box?" Ding Li-Liang's eyes grew wide. "How is this—?"

"My men were killed."

Ding Li-Liang said nothing. He looked at the floor, his brows still raised in surprise, though a thoughtful look passed his visage, as if, for a second, he was hopeful. Anger rose through Yat-sen Xun's dread.

Then Ding Li-Liang's mousy face paled in alarm. He raced to the computer. He pulled up a screen and located a signal. "It has been almost forty-eight hours since Kelly Morrison left the grounds with the box," he said.

"I am aware of this!" Yat-sen Xun snapped. "It is imperative that we find her soon! Where is she?"

"She is still in China." Ding Li-Liang pointed at the screen. "She is traveling where there are no roads. Would you like me to inform the police of her loc—?"

"No! I will take care of this myself!"

Yat-sen Xun summoned his two best men and sent them out. He instructed Ding Li-Liang to give them hourly updates on the movements of the box.

"Tulku," Ding Li-Liang said after the men had departed, "the box will be fine for up to a week."

"Yes," Yat-sen Xun agreed. He looked straight in Ding Li-Liang's dark eyes, giving voice to both of their unspoken fear: "Unless it is opened."

32

We set up camp on a shelf a dozen yards from the lake. With the sun already well below the rim of the crater, darkness descended rapidly. I shivered, searching for branches while Durango pitched the tent.

"What are you doing?" he asked.

"Building a fire."

"I'm not sure that's a good idea," he frowned. "Even this far down in the basin, it could still send the smoke up fairly high."

"Oh," I said in dismay. My damp pants were clammy against my legs, and my fingers were beginning to go numb. "Okay."

"Aw, don't give me that look like you just lost your best friend. We didn't bring any food that needs cooking." He raised his brows in realization. "You're not cold, are you?"

"A little," I understated. He glanced around and then rolled his eyes.

"Alright, fine. Give it a go."

He tossed me a lighter, and I lit my miniature pyre while he finished with the tent. However, no sooner had I gotten the first flame to catch than a brilliant flash lit the sky, followed by a roaring boom. A pea-sized hailstone bounced off the ground. Then another. Then a zillion.

Water dragon? Really?

I started grabbing gear and tossing it inside the tent. Durango secured the rainfly. Seconds later, we were inside, but we were both completely soaked. Lightning illuminated the tent walls against another deafening roar and the relentless pounding of hail against the tent fabric. My teeth chattered. In the flashes, I could see Durango's silhouette rummaging through one of the backpacks. Suddenly a bright light blinded me.

"Sorry." The light dimmed. He hooked a battery-powered lantern into a loop at the tent's apex. "There, that's better." He tossed me a power bar and a bottle of water.

From the outside, the tent had looked small, but inside, the six-by-eight space seemed roomy. I tried to eat, but I was too cold to finish. The harsh riddle of hail changed to a muted pelt of driving rain. Lightning and thunder continued. I was shivering even worse by now, so I removed my socks and shoes, tucking near the tent's front door, then stripped off my pants and oxford shirt. Ignoring Durango's amused smirk, I reached for a sleeping bag.

"Is this one mine?"

"Pick whichever one you want. Going to bed already?"

"Warming up." I undid the cord, unrolled the bag, climbed inside, and pulled it up to my neck, not caring that I probably looked like some giant, dopey, sitting snake.

"You're that cold?"

I rolled my eyes and reluctantly slunk an arm out of the bag, holding my hand out. His palm blazed as it enveloped my fingers.

"Qing was right. You *are* like a human meat locker."

I yanked my hand away and shoved it back into the bag. "Yes, yes, I'm a veritable enigma."

"You ought to try some ginseng."

"What's that?"

"Chinese herb."

"Sure, I'll go foraging as soon as this storm lets up."

"You and all the other nocturnal critters."

Another boom vibrated the metal tent poles. I jumped. "Nocturnal critters?"

"Yeah, in addition to the panda and the snake you met earlier, this neck of the woods is full of monkeys, gibbons, leopards—"

"Leopards?"

"The monkeys are just as dangerous. You ever heard of death by monkeys?"

"You're making that up."

"Nope. In the meantime," he reached for a flap on his backpack, produced a silver flask, and unscrewed the cap, "try some of this."

"What is it?" I asked, sitting up straighter. I took a small swig before waiting for his answer and made a bitter face as the liquor burned down my throat.

"Whiskey."

I took another larger gulp, handed the flask back, and returned my arm inside the sleeping bag. Durango took a draft and set the container down between us. He pulled a large, folded piece of paper out of another pocket on his backpack, unfolded it, and I smiled to myself.

"What?" he asked, noticing my grin.

"It's a map."

"Yeah?"

"I was just thinking about how much you said you like maps, that's all. And right now, I'm really glad you do."

33

Warmth flooded Durango's cheeks. She was looking at him that way again. Like she had at the motel when she'd thanked him for stopping the monk from killing her. It was like she put him on a pedestal—this time simply because he knew the terrain. He didn't deserve a pedestal. But it didn't make him less glad that he was able to help her.

"Right, then." He cleared his thoughts. "Look, we're here." He pointed at the map and showed her where they were in relation to the border.

"That's pretty close!"

"Yeah, but we're not out of the woods yet. We need to go up and over this ridge here, then down into Burma, via this valley, here. Qing and Li should meet us somewhere along here."

She took another sip of whiskey, studying the map. "Will they still have the car? I don't see a road."

"It's not on this map, but it's there."

"You sound pretty sure."

"Yup." He nodded but clammed up again.

Kelly didn't say anything, and he knew she was waiting for him to explain how he could be so certain of this terrain, even once they left the country. He wanted to tell her. In fact, right now, he wanted to tell her a lot more than how he knew about roads in Burma. Instead, he took another gulp of whiskey.

"And then we just cross Burma and waltz into India?" She was oversimplifying things to get him to open up. She was probably going to get miffed with him again.

"Not quite, but that's the general idea," was all he said.

She exhaled—more of a huff than a sigh—and took another draft. A few minutes later, she unzipped herself out of the sleeping bag and crawled over to her backpack. She didn't seem to be shivering anymore. And she didn't seem to care that all she was wearing was underwear and the tank top. Not that Durango minded the view.

"Now what are you doing?"

"I'm looking for the hairbrush." She spoke a bit loudly.

"I didn't think to bring one along." He raked a hand through his own short, damp hair.

"That's okay. I snagged one back at Qing's place." She knelt upright, swayed ever-so-slightly, then dug into her backpack and pulled out a smaller satchel. She found the hairbrush and combed out her wet tangles. He studied her shrewdly until she was finished. Then he leaned over, grasped her chin between his thumb and index finger, and looked her in the eyes.

"Morrison, are you drunk?"

She thought for a moment. She shook her head. "Nope. I'm only shlightly 'nebriated." She held her fingers up to show a small amount.

"You're slurring your words." He released her chin and sat back on his heels.

"Am I?"

"Yeah. How much did you have?" He shook the flask. "Not that much. Hmm. Not much of a drinker, eh?"

"It was a dry monastery. Haven't had any since…?" She counted on her fingers, gave up, and shrugged, grinning. "Oh well. Guess I'm a cheap date."

Fuck, he loved her smile. And he hated that he knew he was going to have to take advantage of her.

34

I giggled at myself, feeling the whiskey buzz. Durango rolled his eyes and chuckled too. Reaching in the satchel to return the hairbrush, my hand touched a smooth, sharp cube edge. A light bulb went off in my head.

"What's wrong?" Durango asked.

"I wonder…?" I mused, drawing out the box. "Maybe in my 'altered state of conshish… conshith-sis-ness'?"

I cocked my head to the side and began examining the edges of the block through my dreamlike haze, running my finger down the corners. Durango crawled over and shifted himself, so he was kneeling next to me, intent on what I was doing. Though my attention was on the box, I was keenly aware of his nearness. With my inhibitions lowered, I didn't try to ignore him. Instead, I embraced the thrill, relaxing into the comfort of his presence while continuing to work on the puzzle.

Wait a second…

I stopped, spun the box in my fingers, and frowned. The dragons were facing the wrong way.

"You're supposed to look at the baby," I scolded them. On impulse, I tried twisting one. It moved.

"Why do you think they're supposed to look at the baby?"

"So they match the emperor's door," I explained, remembering the scene on the grand, double doors at the monastery. I rotated the second dragon and appraised the cube through my anesthetized vision. The dragons still weren't bowing. "Come on," I encouraged them.

I gently stroked the neck of one. To my surprise, and maybe it was the alcohol, the dragon's neck seemed to uncurl and lengthen a bit. I stroked it again, and it lengthened some more. A third stroke, and I found that I could guide the dragon's neck downward. I did the same with the other one until both of their heads bowed down toward the baby's feet. "There, that's better. Good dragons."

I tried to twist and stroke the other images. The swan and starburst also rotated, but nothing happened when I stroked them. The baby and the square didn't rotate, and the baby was still scowling, so I really didn't want to stroke him. He'd probably bite my finger off. *Creepy baby.* In the end, I settled for making the swan upright to match the baby and the dragons, but I couldn't decide which way to turn the starburst. I checked for some sort of fissure or gapped joint at various rotations to tell me I was on the right track. The box said nothing. All of its edges were smooth and perfect. Finally, dejected, I exhaled.

"Mind if I have a look?" he asked.

My fingers instinctively gripped the box tighter, and I pulled it toward my chest. Durango was behind me, so close that he could easily take it from me. Why was he so interested in it? Why had the monk who almost killed me in the hotel in Pianmazhen also wanted it? What was up with this box?

"It's okay," Durango said gently, as though reading my thoughts. He laid his hand on my hip, emphasizing the fact that he was near but harmless. My body instantly relaxed at his touch. I let go of a breath I hadn't realized I'd been holding.

"I was just curious, is all," he added. Then he squeezed my hip. The touch at the hip had felt intimate; the squeeze inserted a hint of possessiveness, which a small, primal part of my brain responded to in the affirmative. It sent me over the edge.

You're being ridiculous. If he wanted it, he could've taken it from you at any time. Besides, you studied this thing last night and tonight, and it doesn't open. Also, you probably look like Gollum right now, clutching your "precious."

I relaxed fully and released my paranoia.

"Knock yourself out," I said, flipping my wrist limply over, handing him the box. "It's just a decoration."

He took it and held it up to eye-level for a closer look. I smirked and shook my head. No longer caring about the dumb box, I allowed the full effects of the whisky and my exhaustion to kick in. Sagging against the nearest support—Durango—I closed my eyes and drank in his scent.

"Mmmm, you smell good," I murmured. "Even when you're wet." He still had on all of his damp clothing. Another clap of thunder pounded overhead, hurtling rain against the tent with renewed vigor. A chill ran through my body.

"You still cold?"

"Usually am. But you're warm. Even when you're wet."

"Yeah, I'm always warm. Okay, hang on." I felt him push me upright, so I forced open my heavy lids to see him pull his blue oxford over his head and watched it sail into the corner. He let me lean on his ribcage again. "Is that better?" The muscles of his torso rippled through his tank top, and his scent was even stronger now. He put his free arm around my shoulder, and the cold went away. I closed my eyes against the stir of desire that rose in my chest.

"Mmm," I mumbled, breathing him in. "Woods and sunshine."

"What was that?"

"You're perfect," I breathed as I drifted off against his side.

****

In my dream, I heard a dull scrape and a click. "Aha!" I heard Durango whisper. Then I heard him swear. "Fuck me, they do have it! Aw, fuck, why did they have to have it?"

A snap, a click, and a scrape, then another click, and the space darkened. Rain pattered against the tent top. I felt his arm encircle my shoulder again. I shifted against him, now thoroughly comfortable, and his arm tightened around me. After a minute, I heard his muffled voice in my hair.

"What am I going to do with you, Miss Morrison?"

Do with me? I wondered what he meant by that, but my mouth was too tired to ask the question, and I drifted into a deeper sleep.

35

He sat with his arm around her, mulling his thoughts. He had two tasks now: finish the "tour guide" scenario of getting Kelly and Li to Guwahati, get the sample to his employer. He could probably do both, but if push came to shove, one was going to have to take precedence over the other. It wasn't a pleasant thought.

In the meantime…

It had been interesting to learn that she liked how he smelled because *her* scent was driving him wild. The only thing that stopped him from rousing her with his lips right now and letting his hands wander everywhere they wanted to go on her soft skin until she begged for more was the fact that she was drunk. It had been comically easy to get her to hand over the box, but that had been business. He wouldn't take advantage of her the other way.

Besides, he reminded himself grimly, he still needed to build her trust. He needed to know what she saw and heard in that room.

Instead, he picked her up, set her gently down into her sleeping bag, zipped her in, and kissed her forehead.

36

When I woke, it was just barely light enough to see inside the tent. I was zipped snugly into my sleeping bag, and I was roasting. Last night was a haze. Had I really been *drunk* off of what couldn't have amounted to more than two shots of liquor? I considered my light dinner and the length of time since I'd last had a drink. Still, what a lightweight. *Ugh!*

Disgusted with myself, I sat up. The acrid pungency of my own stink reeked in my nostrils. It had been two days since my last decent shower unless I counted yesterday's unintended forays into the river and the hailstorm. I would kill for some deodorant right about now.

Durango wasn't in the tent, but his backpack was stuffed, ready to go near the door. Unzipping myself out of the bag, I stretched and found my clothes. They were still slightly wet but considerably drier than they'd been last night. Before I put them on, I peeked my head outside the tent flap.

A muggy blanket of grey shrouded the crater basin. I could see about ten feet in front of me. I listened. The world, suspended in its moment between night and day, possessed a mystical stillness. I was seized by a sudden desire to be a part of it.

"Durango?" I whispered.

Thick fog dampened my voice and absorbed the sound into itself. I waited for a response, but it was as though I was alone with the lake. The thought electrified me.

Five minutes, that was all I needed.

Leaving my clothes in the tent, I stole outside. The sun hadn't yet broken over the rim of the crater, and the world around me slept. I tried to be quiet, to leave nature's silence as untouched as possible. It felt like the times in high school when I'd snuck out of my parents' house to go to parties and then had to sneak back in before they woke up. Only in this case, instead of my parents, it was monks and police I needed to watch out for. But compared with those high school parties, the draw of this hidden lake was even more magnetic in this otherworldly moment.

The wet grass felt soft and cool on my bare feet. I padded the short distance through the fog down to the water's edge. Wading down in my tank top and underwear, I located footing on the rocky bed below. I could see my feet beneath the crystal-clear water and my reflection on top of it, but the rest of the lake was veiled in fog.

Once I was up to my hips, I bobbed straight under once and came back up. Gasping quietly at the initial shock, I stripped off my tank, bra, and panties, gave them a quick scrub, wrung them out, and returned to shore, setting them on a broad, flat rock. Then I retreated back in up to my thighs and silently dove.

Cool liquid streamed through my hair. It enveloped and caressed my naked body as I undulated below the surface. Cleansing. Invigorating. Coming up for air, I broke through gently so as not to shatter the spell of nature.

I breast-stroked forward, not able to see where I was going, just feeling my way through the lake until I was in the center of the cloud, somewhere in the middle of the basin. The fog was denser out here, swirling in communion with the lake.

Peaceful.

Invisible.

Timeless.

I drifted on my back for a while, transfixed, breathing, existing in harmony with nature.

The grey veil overhead turned pink, then pale yellow. A sunbeam broke through, glittering the water next to me. I smiled, intoxicated with the languid activity of watching the diamonded reflection in the opening dawn.

Rebirth.

New life.

The chance to start over with a clean slate.

Day.

Day! Shit!

Reality crashed through, yanking me out of my reverie. I remembered the harrowing trek through the sub-Himalayan wilderness, the need to get myself and Li to safety, and the imperative task of getting my information into the right hands. Ming and the translator. Qing. Durango. *Durango!* I needed to return to camp so we could get moving.

Twisting to my belly, I took long, round scoops with my arms and legs, breast-stroking back in the direction I'd come. More sunlight danced around me; the fog was lifting faster than I could swim. I'd gone off-course but could see the shore now and was able to reset.

Finally, I could see the tent. Still no sign of Durango, though. *Whew!* I mustn't have been in the water that long.

I found footing and exhaled, easily returning to calm. A smile settled on my lips. I was glad I'd gone into the lake. I felt closer to it. Small stones dimpled the soles of my feet as I waded up the rocky incline. I paused to whisk droplets off my skin and squeeze water from my hair.

Suddenly I sensed a change in the stillness. Had I heard something? I froze, wary. Listening. Searching.

37

Thick, wet, gray fog had surrounded him when he'd slipped out of the tent early that morning. He'd buttoned his shirt on the hill, tracing back up the way they'd come down. As he walked, he assessed his damages.

He'd let himself get carried away with the charade they'd put on for the border patrol. That much was obvious. He replayed the moment in his mind. He'd grabbed her left hand, and she'd watched as he'd slid the ring over the smooth skin of her fourth finger. She'd gasped, which was good—played the scene nicely for the patrol.

But he hadn't been prepared for his own reaction.

It was as though someone had cracked a whip in his brain and sent a shock through his whole body. For a second, he'd had the sensation again of rushing toward the blind corner. He could almost glimpse the other side. But he'd no longer felt reckless about it. It was something wonderful and, at the same time, terrible. He shook his head at the memory. She was part of a job to him, and he knew better.

It bothered him that she kept trying to protect everyone yet had no qualms about throwing *herself* in harm's way. He was concerned about what she might try to do if she knew the box contained one of the most combustible elements in the world.

He still couldn't believe the monks actually had a Cadmium-201 manufacturing facility. Last night's confirmation had vindicated an entire year's worth of frustrating lurking, searching, researching, and head-banging deadends. Now he had the sample to bring back to his employer. From that point, either he or someone else would continue on to find the main lab. He wondered where there was enough space for a facility of that sort on their grounds, maybe hidden in some giant mountain cave on their property that his network hadn't been able to check.

Maybe Kelly knows where it is…?

The thought excited him until he realized the implications. If she knew anything beyond the two murders—anything at all about the existence of the facility—she'd be hunted forever until she was dead. He forced away a feeling of disturbing urgency and the concurrent thought that he had to protect her.

She's not your responsibility. Not in that way.

He neared the rim. The fog lessened, breaking fully before the end of the tree line. He took out his cell phone and walked around, trying to pick up a signal to report his news. No service.

He headed over the crest, down the eastern slope, and back into another thicket of trees. Still no service. After a few minutes, he reached the spot where Kelly had paused yesterday when she'd turned to gaze at the scenery. He looked out. White mist rolled in the valleys between the mountain ranges. Distant lines of peaks appeared as jagged black ridges against the early golden sky. He smiled.

She'd probably love this view even more with the sunrise.

After a minute, he realized he wasn't going to get cell reception and put the phone back in his pocket. As he did so, his middle finger touched the smooth band of his mother's ring and the flattened surface of Kelly's oddly-shaped coin. He'd found it immediately in the river but had forgotten to give it back to her. He took it out. It was small. The sort of thing that ought to be on a chain so it wouldn't get lost.

Or fall in a river.

He chuckled. If he hurried back, he could both return it to her and wake her in time to see the sunrise. He turned to go, and that's when he saw them on the right edge of his peripheral vision: two silent shadows moving up the hill. They were clad in the same, black garments as the two men that had come into the hotel rooms the night before last.

They were coming for her.

Or, they were coming for the box.

Icy calm settled over him.

They weren't going to get either.

His heart rate slowed; he measured his breaths. The nerves at the edges of his muscles waited like racehorses at the starting gate for his command. Everything else was gone.

This felt familiar.

This was who he was.

The monks approached from his right, tracking through the trees at the edge of the southern ridge that met the rim of the basin. With the new-morning light, and from their angle, they hadn't seen him. He remained still.

As soon as they passed him, he circled their flank to approach from the rear. Twigs and rocks littered the ground. Taking steady, stealthy steps, he used the softer grass clumps to mute his advance. It would have been easier if he'd brought his rifle and silencer. But those were back in the car, unbeknownst to Qing.

Fortunately, Durango's specialty was close-quarters combat.

They neared the rim of the basin. He was two meters behind.

With his right hand, he pulled out his Columbia River folding knife.

With his left hand, he picked up a rock.

He tossed the rock in a high arc and used the sound it made, skittering on the ground in front of the advancing monks, to mask the click-open of his blade. In the split second they turned their attentions to follow the rock, he flicked the knife into the head of the monk on his right. In the next second, he had his arms crossed around the head and shoulders of the other monk.

A quiet, violent wrench, and it was over.

He dragged the bodies into the underbrush. A quick rifle through their clothes revealed that one of them carried a cell phone. He checked the texts. The most recent incoming message was from a few hours earlier, but it was a set of coordinates. He suspected that if he checked his map, the coordinates would coincide with the location of Tingming Lake. *Damn.*

He tugged his knife out of the monk's head, wiped its blade on the grass, and put it back in his pocket. Then he started back over the crest.

If they had coordinates, then the woman from the restaurant hadn't been the reason the monks had found them at the hotel. The box must contain some sort of tracking device. He hadn't seen one when he'd opened it last night, but it was possible. He'd have to examine it again before Kelly woke up.

Picking up his pace, he trotted quietly down the hill. The fog had almost dissipated. Sunbeams danced on the lake. Something moved in the water near the shore. Durango paused and caught his breath.

Fuck. Me. Sideways.

She doesn't make any of this easier, does she?

38

Birds chirped, signaling the segue into day. A gentle breeze stirred the treetops. The fog lifted. What I'd sensed—the other presence—must have just been the mountain waking up. I gathered my clothes and slipped back up the hill into the tent.

Opting for maximal clothes-drying time, I laid out my bra, tank top, and panties. Then I slipped my arms into the blue oxford, like a robe—in case Durango came back before my clothes were dry. I wondered where he was.

I rolled up my sleeping bag. Then I knelt down to stuff it in the backpack and fished around for the brush to comb my hair. As soon as I pulled it out, memories of last night came back: giggling… the puzzle box… sleepy… *Or drunk. Crap!* Had I said aloud that I liked the way he smelled? No, that couldn't have been real. And… something about the puzzle box…. Had I let Durango examine it, or was that just a dream? I berated myself for being so careless as to endanger him.

But, wait! Did he open it?

I pulled it out, wondering, and studied the sides, trying to remember: was it click-scrape or scrape-click?

"G'day, Kells!" His voice boomed in the doorway behind me. I jumped, launching the box in the air as I whirled and instinctively grabbed the front of my oxford closed. The box landed softly on top of the backpack. A day's worth of stubble darkened the jaw around his grin, but his smile faded.

"What are you…?" His eyes darted suspiciously from the box to me. Then he noted my bra and underwear across the tent. "Sorry," he said gruffly, pulling his head out of the door. "Time to get a move on."

I shoved the box back where it belonged, zipped the brush through my hair, and pulled on my clothes, damp or not. I stowed the sleeping bags and emerged wordlessly, dragging both of our backpacks out.

"Get everything?" he asked. I nodded. He began pulling the spikes, so I went to the opposite side of the tent to help.

"Figure anything out with your box?" he asked.

"No," I admitted. "But I had a dream that *you* did." I met him around at the front and handed him the two stakes I'd pulled. "That *was* a dream, right?"

"Guess it'd have to be, huh?"

He took the stakes without looking at me and continued taking down the tent. Did that mean yes, it was a dream? Or was he deliberately avoiding giving me an answer? Was it *not* a dream? While pondering, I disbursed the evidence of my failed campfire, making the site look like no one had ever been there.

39

He had to work quickly. While Kelly was scattering the branches, he dug into her pack, pulled out the box, and opened it. Sunlight shone on the glass vial nestled in soft, black foam. *Damn!* It probably wasn't a good idea to be opening this thing again, especially in the sun, but he had no other option. He pulled the foam away from the edges until he found what he was looking for: a transmitter chip.

Several feet away, her back to him, Kelly put her hands on her hips and cocked her head as though satisfied with the effects of her campfire destruction. Ripping out the chip, he crushed it with a rock and closed the box. He shoved it back into her pack just before she spun around.

40

"Well, that's good," I said.

"What's good?"

"That I didn't stupidly compromise you by letting you get involved any deeper than you already are." I laid it on a bit thick and watched his body language closely.

He continued packing away the tent but shook his head, chuckling to himself. *Gah!* What did *that* mean? He shouldered his backpack, and I followed suit.

"Remember," he said, "we have to be quiet out here. Don't want to make the gods angry again."

Irked by his attempt to halt my line of questioning, I kept it to myself, shuddering at the thought of another hailstorm. We skirted the lake's southern shore and then headed southwest, away from it, up to the highest rim of the basin: back up to twelve thousand feet.

I stopped to drink in the show: the nubby, ribbed green sweaters on the lush, striated mountains, accented with sparkling-stream pendants which glinted in the morning light, like moving, silver water dragons. Beneath me, a few puffy, French-poodle clouds floated leisurely by. An automatic smile curled on my lips, relaxing my entire body.

"Yeah, I like it up here, too," he said quietly, gazing out next to me.

I sighed. It was impossible to stay miffed with anyone in front of this view. Durango put an arm around my shoulders, turned me northward, and pointed.

"We're going to trek across here, to that ridge, there. A few kilometers. Once we cross over into that valley, we'll technically be across the border."

"First of all, aren't we highly visible up here, and second: *technically*?"

"Political border disputes. Sometimes the Chinese patrol goes above and beyond the call of duty. But once we meet up with Qing and Li, we should be safe. From the Chinese police, anyway. And yes, we are more visible up here, but it's the fastest route, which means we won't be up here long."

His gaze fell on my damp hair.

"Go for a swim this morning?"

He started off along the crest.

"Oh!" I automatically fluffed my hair, which was drying quickly in the arid sunshine. "I, uh, the water just…" I fumbled. How could I explain myself? *I was stinky, and the water looked pretty? Um, embarrassing!*

"I indulged an early-morning whim," I blurted to his back as I hiked after him.

"No need to get defensive. I was just asking."

"Okay. Fine. By the way, speaking of this morning, you were gone when I woke up. Where'd you go? Some sort of walkabout?"

Not breaking his stride, he turned his head and gave me an amused smirk. "Yeah, exactly. Walkabout."

"Well, then where…?"

"I went up to the ridge to see if we could get cell service."

"I thought you said we weren't supposed to—?"

"I said you and Qing weren't supposed to try to communicate. In theory, no one's looking for me."

"Did you have any luck?"

"No. There's no service out here. Don't know why I bothered making an attempt."

"Who were you going to call?"

"No one on your radar."

"Oh." *Point taken: butt out.* "Fine."

"Meaning?"

"Nothing, just *fine*."

"Yeah," Durango muttered, "that's the second time this morning you've said that word. But when a woman says 'fine,' it means nothing is."

"That's *so* cliché."

Caveman.

We walked in silence for the next hour until we came to the ridge, crossed it, and started down, picking our way through undergrowth on the least drastic of the slopes leading to the valley. I sniffed the air.

"What is it?" Durango asked in concern. He paused and sniffed too.

"Hmm. It doesn't smell like a different country yet." I cocked my head innocently and bit back a smirk before continuing downhill. Without looking, I knew he was rolling his eyes at me.

"What am I going to do with you, Miss Morrison?" he muttered.

The smirk faded from my lips. My insides froze.

He'd said those exact words last night.

It wasn't a dream!

41

Durango was behind me. I kept my eyes straight ahead on the path and kept walking, but my mind raced. If it wasn't a dream, it meant Durango really had opened the box. I strained to remember what he'd said last night—something to the effect that he was upset at whatever he'd found. But why had he lied to me?

Just keep moving. Act natural before he gets suspicious.

Too late.

"Okay, now what? *Now* does it smell like a different country?"

"Um, no," I squeaked, marching forward, "just thought I saw another snake?" I swallowed hard.

We followed a small trickle that gushed out of the mountainside. The slope became steeper. He caught up to me as I shifted to a slower gait.

"No." His voice was serious. "Something's wrong. What just happened?"

Crap. He knew something was up.

As he had yesterday when we were descending the basin, he offered his arm to me, but I shook my head. He took a few steps ahead, pivoted his body toward me, and continued his descent sideways. I refused to make eye contact with him, focused on the trail, and kept walking.

Why had he lied about opening the box?

There was more to this man than he'd let on.

On the one hand, if he'd wanted the box, he could have taken it and left me out in the wilderness. Also, if Durango had wanted to, he could've killed me at any time. He was obviously capable of it. I remembered the dead monk at the motel and shuddered.

But he'd opened the box, and he knew what was in it. That meant something. I didn't know whether to be intrigued or terrified, but I was definitely upset.

"Kelly," he persisted. "There was no snake. What's wrong?"

"Nothing. Just concentrating on the mountain." Watching where I placed my feet, I was able to move faster.

"No, something's wrong."

He moved to block my path, forcing me to stop. On reflex, I snapped my gaze to his.

"Wow! You're extremely conflicted," he observed.

"Oh, you're an expert on me?"

"You're pretty easy to read."

"Did you inherit that skill from your mother, or was she made up, too?" I couldn't help the sarcasm that laced my tone.

His eyes grew wide. "What are you—"

"Never mind," I said, regaining some of my composure.

What did it matter? In the end, he hadn't killed me, and he hadn't taken the box from me. Let him make up whatever stories he wanted. Today we would get to Qing and Li, and I wouldn't have to be alone with him again, ever.

Ever!

And to think I'd allowed myself to develop *feelings* for him, listening to him talk about his life, thinking he might be some kind of Mr. Nice Guy hero. *Stupid girl!*

I broke eye contact and took a step forward, trying to brush past him. Instantly his hands locked around my upper arms. My pulse accelerated.

Take a breath, Morrison. He's just another bump in the road. Get over it.

A breeze wafted from behind him. I tightened my jaw muscles against his scent.

"We have to 'get a move-on,' as you like to put it," I said.

"I don't think so. Talk." His voice was less than gentle, conveying a sense of urgency.

"Let go of me," I said through gritted teeth. He didn't move. "Fine," I sulked into the distance. "You lied to me, and I don't like being lied to. Is that enough? Can we go now?"

"Why do you think I lied to you? About what?"

"About the box. I asked if you'd really opened it or if it was just a dream, and you told me it was a dream."

"That was hours ago. You've been upset this whole time?"

"No." I met his azure gaze square on. "Not until about five minutes ago, when I realized you hadn't told me the truth."

He raised a brow.

"When we came over the ridge, and I made the crack about it not smelling like a different country, you said, 'What am I going to do with you, Miss Morrison?' That's the same thing you said last night in my so-called dream. Exact same words. It *wasn't* a dream, and you *did* open the box. Why did you lie about it?" My cheeks flushed hot with anger.

"You think calling you 'Miss Morrison'—which, by the way, *is your name*—means I lied to you?"

It *wasn't* a dream. Why did I have to prove that I knew the truth? How dare he treat me like I was stupid! I knew I was right about this. The anger buzzing inside me shifted to calm realization.

"Okay," I agreed suddenly, knowing I now held the upper hand, "if this really is all in my head, then scrape and click won't work."

"Wha—?"

I wriggled my shoulders. The heavy backpack slid down. Its straps thudded on his hands, and he released my arms. In a flash, I'd unzipped it, whisked out the box, and stepped back from him.

"What are you doing?" he asked in alarm.

"Scrape and click," I explained. "That's also what I heard *in my dream*, right before I *dreamt* that you opened this. Which would mean..." My gaze slid to the box. *You'd have to slide something!*

I began pushing up, down, sideways on the various raised figures. The baby moved. Durango swore under his breath, but I took several more steps back from him and kept going. I thumbed the warrior infant carving upward with a scrape until the level of his feet was above the dragons' heads. *Of course!* A small, brown button sat underneath. I moved my thumb to push it.

"Kelly, don't!"

I paused and looked at him. "Why not?"

"Because it contains a highly unstable isotope that needs to be kept cold, either through refrigeration or for short periods in an insulated container, like this box. It's called Cadmium 201, sometimes referred to as—"

"Cad *two*!" I exclaimed. That's what Nathaniel Richardson had said in the monastery's conference room. It made sense now.

"Yes." He seemed surprised that I knew.

Before I realized what happened, he'd grabbed the box from me and slid the baby back into place.

"You heard that word there?" he asked.

I nodded—no point in keeping *that* a secret anymore.

"Do you know what it is?"

I shook my head.

"Cad-2 was manufactured for a short time in laboratories through an intricate and expensive process. It was used to produce some of the most advanced and powerful smart bombs in the world. Somehow Yat-sen Xun got a hold of some…? What? Your eyes just lit up."

"They have a mine," I gushed, puzzling together what the translator had repeated.

"A mine? That's impossible. Cad-2 doesn't exist in nature."

"Yes!" I nodded in excitement, finally understanding more of what I'd heard. "It *does* exist in nature! They have a whole plume of it!"

"A plume? A large one? Where?"

"And they're selling it to the highest bidders!"

42

His pulse raced. There was no way a mine could be possible, and yet here she was insisting that was what she'd heard.

However, the more he thought about it—incredible as it sounded—the more it made sense. Much of the Earth was unexplored. New minerals were still being discovered. Most of the "finds" for the past century had been lab-created elements, but who was to say there weren't untapped pockets hidden in the ground?

And what place on the planet made more sense for this sort of thing than China?

China contained some of the richest deposits of mineral resources in the world. A mine, where production wasn't required, rather than a lab, could be anywhere on the Zhuang Dian grounds. No refrigeration necessary. And it would never occur to anyone to look for a Cadmium-201 mine!

He had to know more.

"Bidders? Plural? How many buyers did you see? Did you recognize any faces?"

But Kelly paled and backed away from him.

"Is that why you haven't killed me yet?" she whispered. "You need to know who I saw? Are you working for some sort of competitive buyer?"

He jerked his head back in surprise. He had no intention of killing her anymore. But she was fairly close to the mark about his employer. She might have revealed more than she'd intended, but he'd done the same. He chuckled.

"Hardly." He knelt down to zip the box back into her pack.

"Then how do you know all of this?" she breathed. "And why am I still alive?"

She looked ready to bolt. Her eyes were huge with fear. For the first time, she seemed afraid of *him.*

The idea of her being frightened of him was bothersome, but he ignored it, having bigger issues to focus on. He needed to calm her down. He stood and held out her backpack.

That's right: get the task back on track.

The reminder slammed him like a mallee bull. Kelly was part of the job. Nothing more. Resentment twisted in his chest until the pang broke free and dropped off a cliff.

Keep to your job. It's all you have, and it's all you're ever going to have.

"You're alive because you've been damned lucky. As to how I know about the Cad-2? Discovery Channel. I'm just a tour guide, and in my downtime, I watch too much television." He wiggled the pack by its handle. "Now come on. Let's get a move-on." He flashed his best grin, the one that always worked.

Kelly's eyes narrowed, and her jaw hardened. But she'd stopped backing away from him.

"Too much television."

"Yes."

"In your house that has no television."

"That you saw."

She exhaled in what sounded like disgust. "You just keep shoveling it, don't you?" Stomping over, she yanked the backpack off his fingertips, slung it over her shoulders, brushed past him, and stormed off down the mountain.

Fine, if she wouldn't succumb to his charms, he could pick a fight with her. They could go that route, too. In fact, that route felt better. Teach her to think she could get all cozied up with him and fall asleep on his chest. He let the frigid calm descend, only it settled wrong, like ice laced with a thousand milligrams of caffeine shooting through his bloodstream. He ignored it and kept on grinning.

"What do you mean, 'shoveling'?" he called after her.

43

Shoveling shit. That's all this man was doing. He was full of it. Well, I was from Colorado, and I knew how to handle a shovel.

"This is not my first snowfall!" I yelled back at him.

"It's not snowing."

He caught up to me and seemed amused by my fury. My rapid pace wasn't helping me calm down, either.

The trickling stream widened into a rushing brook, following the valley's slope. We'd have to descend single-file. I pushed on ahead.

"And I'm confused," he continued, speaking to my back, "did the shoveling thing have to do with shoveling snow? Because if I'm already shoveling, then what are you worried about the snow for?"

I curled my right fingers into a tight fist. *No.* I took a deep breath and uncurled them. My emotions had run the gamut these past few days, but I did not need to lose control. *Just keep moving.*

He'd noticed.

"It's okay. You can hit me if you want. I'd probably want to hit me right about now."

Well, if it was okay with him…

My fingernails bit into the flesh of my palm.

No.

I made my feet move faster and picked up my pace to a jog. The heavy backpack jounced hard. Its straps strained at my shoulders. I used my anger to fuel the extra exertion.

"Whoa, you're going kind of fast now. For a girl."

It was obvious he was trying to push my buttons, but what was the point? Wasn't I already miserable enough?

"Of course, if we keep this up, I might work up a sweat." His voice was even, as though this were easy for him; he wasn't even out of breath. And then he added, "I might smell *really* good to you then."

That did it. I crunched my fingers, pivoted, and swung in one lightning blaze of rage. My fist fire-balled a diagonal line up to make contact with the side of his nose, just above his cocky grin.

Out of nowhere, his palm appeared. Still grinning, he'd caught my fist with one hand. I hadn't even seen him move.

"Good on ya!" he taunted, a wild glint in his eyes. "Get it all out!"

Get it all out? This was still some sort of game to him! I'd been honest and forthcoming, trying to protect him from deadly knowledge, and here he was *lying* to me, *wanting* that knowledge, and using what he knew about me—and my pathetic attraction to him—against me!? I finally understood what it meant to "see red."

44

With her rigid stance—muscles tensed, shoulders back, fingers clenched—and her chest heaving hard on her exhalations, Durango felt the fury emanating from her. He'd poured salt in all the right wounds, extracting every ounce of venom, bringing it to the surface at a rapid boil. He couldn't have her, and he wanted to make her hate him. All of Kelly's passion was directed at him, channeled into violence. In a cruel way, it made him feel better. Just one more dash of vinegar, something he noticed she'd reacted to another time:

"Come on, give it another go. You can do better. *I promise*."

Her eyes went wide with surprise and hurt. Then they narrowed, her jaw hardened, and her nostrils flared. She yanked her fist out of his grip and pulled back for a second hit.

Unfortunately, when she yanked her arm back, she shifted on the uneven downslope. Her backpack's weight also shifted. She gasped and toppled backward. He lunged for her but missed. She fell, backpack first, into the mountain stream.

For a brief second, he assumed she would just get wet and then stand up. After all, the stream wasn't that deep. But suddenly, she shot off with the current, arms and legs flailing in the air, like a turtle on its back. He caught a fleeting glimpse of her face, which must have mimicked his: jaw dropped, eyes popped wide.

Unbelievable! Yesterday afternoon on the way to Tingming Lake, and now again this morning! I didn't think I filled her pack with that much weight!

She was going fast. There was only one way to keep up with her now.

I can't even finish a decent fight with this woman!

45

Rushing water jetted me downstream over the riverbed's slick rocks. Just before I disappeared around a bend, I saw Durango roll his gaze skyward, flip his backpack around to his front, and jump in the water, belly-first, on top of it. He was coming to rescue me—if I didn't die first.

Rocketing down the steep mountain in the most nightmarish tubing experience of my life, I zigzagged blindly around turns, watching trees rush past in a blur. I instinctively pulled my knees to my chest and laced my fingers over my head in a hand-helmet to try to protect myself. I was going so fast I was afraid to try to flip over to my front for fear I'd hit a protruding rock or be forced under by the wet backpack as the river deepened. I craned my neck up but couldn't see Durango anymore. *What if he's been hurt?*

An entire summer's worth of algae-covered stones thwapped against the backpack in drum-roll succession. I slid faster and faster down the slope. I tried again to look for Durango, but my head was weighted into place by my speed. The trees grew larger at the lower altitude, and my ears popped with the rate of my descent. Mountaintops soared above me now. Random, shabby huts dotted the landscape.

Tributaries joined the stream, adding to the rushing flow. I couldn't hear the swish of rocks against my backpack anymore; the river was too deep, and the water was rushing so fast that it literally made a roaring sound. But the backpack continued to float, carrying me along at this insane pace. Would Durango's backpack support him, too? Finally, by engaging all of my stomach muscles, I was able to lift my neck and catch a brief glimpse of him several yards behind. He was still there, but he was waving his arms and yelling something at me. What was he—

Then, the world fell away.

My stomach dropped, and I plummeted backward off a waterfall. I screamed, grabbed my knees with my arms, squeezed my eyes shut, and tucked my head, waiting for jagged mountain rocks. But on impact, I went under, plunging down, down, with the force of my fall. Cold, soundless water enveloped me. Then the backpack hit bottom, and I began to rise again. I surfaced, still curled in my fetal crash posture, opened my eyes, and gasped air.

The last hill I'd just descended floated in front of me. It had felt like a hundred feet when I'd gone over but now looked as though it was really only twenty. I was still drifting but realized I'd reached a lazy section of river that meandered through verdant lower valleys.

Just then, Durango appeared at the edge of the waterfall. He let out a whoop, went over, then under at the bottom, and bobbed to the surface just as I'd done, except that he seemed to have enjoyed it. Grinning wildly, he pulled a few broad strokes over towards me.

"Excellent idea, Kells!" he called out. "The way I had us going would have taken about six hours through all that undergrowth!"

I'd drifted a dozen yards downstream from the falls. When Durango made it to me, he stood up, dripping, flipped his pack from his belly to his back, and raked his fingers through his wet, brown hair.

I exhaled in relief at the realization that he was okay. Seeing that the water was only up to the top of his thighs, I flipped over and tried to stand. Unfortunately, my earlier theory had been correct: the backpack weighed me down, and I struggled to find footing on the slippery rocks, even against this lighter current. Fighting to surface, desperately needing to breathe, I began to drift downriver again.

Suddenly, something tugged against my backpack, stopping me. Water rushed past my ears. The pack pulled upward; I was lifted in its straps. Durango set me upright. I coughed and spluttered, spitting out river water.

"We have to do something about you and this oversized pack," he commented. "You keep tipping over."

"You *said* I could hit you," I grunted, pushing plastered hair out of my eyes. "But thanks for saving me. Again." I stomped my foot underwater. "How am I supposed to stay mad at you when you keep rescuing me?"

"I wouldn't be a very good tour guide if I let my clients die, would I?"

He grinned, let go of my pack, took my hand, and led me to shore. To my dismay, my hand tingled with electricity at his touch. But I wasn't about to let go and drown. I would just have to accept that my body was going to betray me every chance it got.

Currents swirled around us as we waded over. A mechanical, whirring sound ground through the air, the same sound as the noise we'd heard when we'd left Qing and Li and embarked on the raft yesterday. Another dam was nearby.

He released my hand and hoisted himself up to the first ledge with relative ease. I clung to a sprawling tree root, managing to flop my upper body onto the bank before dragging my knees underneath me. Finally, I stood up, covered in mud.

"Well, I meant what I said in my note," I said as I wiped my hands on my wet-but-not-muddy butt.

"Come on." He took my hand again and helped me scale the mountain slope. "There's a road up here. What note?"

"You know, back at your place? The morning I tried to steal your car with Li?"

He didn't respond.

"You have no idea what note I'm talking about, do you?"

"Sorry."

We reached a poorly-maintained dirt road, about twenty feet above the river.

"Wait a minute. If you never saw my note, how did you know I'd left? And how did you know where we were headed? You got there before us."

"Your room was empty, and you weren't in the house. I made a lucky guess."

I shook my head with a soft groan. "Just… don't talk. No more shoveling."

Shoveling… the load of crap he'd fed me about how he knew about Cad-2 from the Discovery Channel, the substance in the box… *the box…!*

"Durango! The box!" I shrugged off my battered backpack and began digging through its contents. "All those rocks in the river! The box is probably damaged!" I couldn't find it. "Where is it? Did you put it in yours? And why is all of this stuff dry? It should be soaked after that whitewater freak show."

He crouched down, also sorting through his contents. "These are high quality, heavy-duty trail packs," he noted loftily, reaching over to remove several water bottles and a heavy coil of rope from mine and cram them into his. How had I managed to float with all of that in there? "And the box is still in yours. It was pretty sturdy, but because of what's inside, I stuck it in the middle of your sleeping bag for extra cushioning. My cell phone, however, was not as fortunate. I put it in one of the outer pockets so I could hear if it rang." He held up a phone with a rugged-looking case but a completely shattered screen.

Frantic, I shoved my arm down into the center of the sleeping bag's poufy spiral. My fingers touched the familiar, smooth, lacquered cube, and I drew it out. It was perfect, untouched, just as it was the first time I'd seen it when Li had pulled it out at Durango's house eons ago. I replaced it.

"Everything good?" he asked.

"Yeah, you were right. The box is fine. Sorry about your phone."

"Good! And no worries on the phone. We'll just have to find another way to let Qing know where we are."

I looked up at soaring mountaintops all around us. The sky was gray.

"Where *are* we?"

Durango got out his map. "Hmm. Does the air smell different yet?" he asked with a tone of mischief.

"No?" I sniffed the humid, botanical air. "Smells the same as China."

"Well, maybe that's because we're back in China."

"What? How did that happen?"

"Don't worry," he chuckled. "We're right close to the border."

"But the patrol?"

Out of nowhere, the sky opened up as though someone had turned on a fire hose. I began to shiver.

"The patrol is the least of our worries right now," he frowned, putting an arm around my shoulders and rubbing my arm. "Come on, let's get you out of this."

"No, I'm fine. Let's get to Qing and Li first," I insisted, though I didn't shrug off his warmth. Not yet.

"Alright, you're the boss. But here," he ushered me to the side of the road closest to the mountain, "let's not risk you falling down again."

We sloshed off.

46

After a few minutes, Durango let go and pulled ahead of me. I concentrated on the meter of his steps until I noticed that the stride of his right leg was faster than his left.

"Are you okay?"

"Yeah." He paused and turned. "Why do you ask?"

"It looks like you're limping."

"Aw, that. I twisted my foot about a year ago, and it never healed properly. Acts up now and again, but nothing big." He continued forward.

I recalled having seen his slight limp in the parking lot back in Lijiang. When I thought back, I realized that was the only time we'd been on stable ground. Since then, we'd pretty much been in a car, a boat, or hiking up and down mountains.

"So, you meant what you said in your note," Durango said, changing the subject, reminding me of my earlier comment. "What did the note say?"

"Well, I apologized to Qing for leaving without saying goodbye to him, and I apologized to you for 'everything else,' which, of course, you would eventually have discovered meant I'd taken your car, your shirt, and your baseball cap. And your atlas. And I promised to pay you back for everything, no matter how long it took me."

"Everything?"

"Everything."

"You were going to buy me a new car?"

"If I had to, yes."

"Wow. How much do you make at that secretary job in Minnesota?"

I smirked to myself—the job I'd already quit, and the state I'd already left, in my mind. "Production assistant, not secretary. And no matter how long it took me."

"Very professional of you."

"Thank you."

He seemed amused. "And a new Mackay Cutters shirt? That version isn't available anymore, you know."

"You might've had to settle for a Broncos jersey."

"Eh, the Broncos are fine, but I'm more of a Cowboys fan."

"Dallas? Really?"

"North Queensland. Townsville's closer to Mackay. Wait a minute, are you talking about American football? I thought we were talking about rugby league."

"Oh. I thought we were talking about sports apparel. I meant the Denver Broncos."

"Denver's in Colorado. I thought you said you lived in Minne—?"

"But the shirt doesn't matter because we're not doing it that way now," I interrupted. My personal plans were irrelevant to him. This was business. "So, tell me, how much do you usually charge for a three or four-day trip like this?"

"Dunno. Never done one quite like it before. Usually, I do day trips and such."

"Okay, how much for a day trip?" I pushed.

"Maybe five hundred."

"In American dollars?"

"Sure."

I added it up in my mind. "Okay, do you think about seven grand will cover it?"

"Seven grand? For what?"

"Well, I'm figuring four days at five hundred apiece, plus hotel, plus food, plus the boat you had to leave behind on the river, plus wear and tear on your gear, plus your return trip back… mmm, maybe ten grand?"

Durango didn't seem to be paying attention. "Seven's fine," he grunted. He picked up his pace and walked ahead again. I squinted at his form through the rain. Had I said something wrong? Again?

The road wound around curves and turns. We'd left the river and were following the road between hills, deeper into the mountains. Durango disappeared around corners again and again. I worked up to a jog, trying to keep him in sight. The pack was lighter now that he'd removed the rope and water bottles, but it still sagged heavily on my back every time I planted my sopping feet. I was lagging behind and having to push harder to catch up.

Wonder if this is what Marine training is like?

Despite the wetness, after fifteen minutes, my throat burned from gulping cold air, and a dull ache stabbed my left ribs. Stopping to catch my breath, I stooped forward, leaning my palms on my thighs. When I looked up, Durango was nowhere. Had I missed a turnoff?

Huffing too hard to call for him, I shielded my eyes and peered through the liquid gray lines that hazed the view.

Far ahead, a human form crossed the road from left to right. Was he that far ahead of me? I had a lot of ground to cover to catch up, though I didn't understand why he was headed to the side of the road. I jogged a few hesitant steps. He appeared to have gone around a corner, to my right, behind a hill. I walked with purpose. There was an inlet on the far side of the hill or whatever they called these strange, smaller roads here. I was still probably more than a quarter of a mile away, but I could see that on the inlet, nearly hidden by the hill, was a white house.

I noticed a van parked behind a tree on the left side of the road. Another form crossed the road from the van to the house, then another. Their movements were fast. Furtive. I slowed down. They were all too small to be Durango. More forms crossed, and I stared. I couldn't be seeing this correctly. I gaped in confusion while my feet continued to carry me, albeit at a slower pace, toward the scene. Disbelief began to give way to a sense of dread.

At the end of the line, a larger person crossed, appearing to be in a hurry. He—or she—stopped in the middle of the road, parallel to my position. I halted. We stared at each other through the rain, but I couldn't see the person clearly. Qing's words flooded back to me: *Myanmar's a cesspool… political unrest… drugs… human trafficking… child prostitution…!*

Then I knew. These were children. And not just a few. I wasn't witnessing a family or some sort of school group. Horror rooted me to the spot.

A hand touched my elbow. I jumped and whirled.

"It's just me," Durango said quietly.

"Where were you?" I demanded, unable to control the frustration in my voice and still in disbelief about what I'd just seen. "I thought I saw you, but…"

"Sorry, I saw you stop to catch your breath, and I thought you'd seen me take the side road back there."

Still in shock, I pointed down the road toward the white house and asked, "Is that…?" I turned my head to look. The other person was gone. "Was that…?"

"Yeah," he confirmed.

"But—!"

"Don't, Kelly. It's part of the ugly underbelly of this country. There's nothing we can do for them."

"They're children!" My lower lip quivered, and my eyes burned, filling with water that wasn't rain. He took my chin between his thumb and index finger.

"So's Li," he replied. "You have to think of him right now."

A large, hot tear rolled down my cheek. He was right. I had a responsibility to Li, and I couldn't leave him stranded to wind up in the same situation as these kids. Or worse. I bit my lip, conceding with reluctance but not acceptance. I turned my chin out of his grasp and studied a gray, tumultuous puddle that shuddered with the downpour.

"Come on," Durango urged gently. He slung his arm around my shoulder and started walking. "I've got something that might cheer you up."

I shivered, fingers and toes prickling, and glanced back down the road. The person who'd been watching me was definitely gone. Into that white house on that street, behind the hill.

I allowed myself to be led back a hundred yards to a bend where another, barely discernable inlet road jutted from the main branch. We walked silently for another mile or so until we came to a row of houses built against the sides of the mountain valley. These houses were very different from the house I'd just seen on the road. It had looked modern compared to these. In addition to being on stilts, these homes had walls made of wooden strips interwoven on a diagonal, giving them the appearance of parquet boxes on toothpicks. The windows were all shuttered against the storm. Rainwater rushed down the mountains, forming small ponds around the base of the stilts. I hung back in the road as Durango approached the third house, climbed the stairs, and knocked.

A beautiful woman in her late thirties answered the door. Her jet-black hair was pulled back into a ponytail, and—to my surprise—she wore a pale pink hoodie zipped up to her neck and black pants. I guess I'd been expecting more ethnic clothing, but her pink hoodie made me feel a certain kinship with her. Seeing Durango, the woman cracked a broad grin, which broke her face into a million friendly wrinkles.

"Min ga la ba!" She opened her arms and held out her hands. Durango grasped her hands and kissed her on the cheek.

"*Min ga la ba*, Sandy. How are you?"

The woman looked past him into the rain, noticing me. Suspicion clouded her features. She raised a perplexed eyebrow to Durango but followed his cue. "Come in," she responded in English and beckoned us both indoors.

The dimly lit room smelled of fish. A fire crackled from an open, square pit in the middle of the wooden floor. This appeared to be the dwelling's only source of heat. Two lanterns were the only other sources of light since the shutters were closed. Rain thumped rhythmically against the corrugated metal roof. As my eyes adjusted, I heard someone draw a sharp intake of breath. Suddenly something grasped tightly around my waist.

"Cow-li!" a small voice exclaimed jubilantly.

"Li?" I gasped. "Is that you?" I peeled the child off my legs to look at his face, and then I couldn't see anymore because of the tears that flooded my eyes. I hugged him tightly, not caring that I was soaked and he was warm and dry.

He was here, and he was safe.

47

Kelly? Oz?" Qing rushed over, grinning. "What are you doing here? I thought we weren't supposed to leave until tonight to pick you up in Pawakhu?"

"Mate!" Durango grabbed Qing's hand and punched him in the shoulder. "Glad you made it okay. Yeah, we would've gone that way, but your friend, here, had other ideas about how to get around."

I let go of Li and hugged Qing hard. Durango took off his shoes, leaving them by the front door. I dried my tears and followed suit. Sandy handed us both towels.

Qing looked even more confused. "Cow? What happened?"

I laughed and shook my head. "Let's just say that your friend, here, is the world's most aquatic tour guide. This was the wettest trek I've ever taken in my life." I messed up Li's hair and hugged Qing again. "It's so good to see you both! Did you have any trouble crossing?"

"Nope, we were fine," Qing answered. "We came right across, just two bros on a road trip. We've been hanging out with Oz's friend, Sandy, and her family since midday yesterday. Why didn't you call me to come to get you? How far did you have to walk?"

Qing was full of questions, and the four of us sat on bamboo mats around the open fire on the floor. Durango and I took turns answering, and Qing and Durango both translated for Li. I talked about the beauty of the river and about how I'd seen two red pandas. Durango mentioned that we'd left the river shortly after a round of border patrols.

He omitted the part about how we'd made it past—the fake IDs, the wedding ring. I didn't bring it up either.

He talked about the hailstorm on Tingming Lake and agreed with Qing about my "human meat locker" condition. I said that to cure it, I'd apparently have to risk death by monkeys.

Neither of us revealed our argument from earlier that day. I said that I'd clumsily tripped into the rushing stream on our way into Burma, and Durango had seemed to think of it as an amusement park ride. Retelling it now, I laughed; Durango grinned.

He said we got caught in the monsoon downpour after the river ride but neglected to mention the child-trafficking house, just a few miles away. I was quiet for that part and kept stealing glances at Li, who'd gotten bored after the first ten minutes and was now playing a board game across the room with Sandy's children.

Among the other things I hadn't brought up was anything Durango had told me about his past. I knew it had been difficult for him to share the little he had, and I felt privileged that he'd told me.

Neither of us said one word about the box, and I was glad Durango shared my desire to protect Qing from anything he didn't need to know.

Sandy brought us more towels and bowls of fish and rice soup that she called *mohinga* while we talked. I noticed that her pink hoodie was threadbare, with a hole in one elbow, and the zipper pull had been replaced with a safety pin.

After an hour, eight-year-old Naing, Sandy's oldest son and the middle of her three children, ran over to the window. He opened it to blue skies. The storm was over, and it was late afternoon.

"Well, the rain's stopped. Ready for the next leg of our journey?" Qing asked. He stood up. Sandy ran at him immediately from across the room, yelling, waving her arms in the air.

"No, no, no! What do you think you're doing? Two nights, that was the deal. Two nights!"

She waved her fists at Qing, who ducked, laughing. Sandy gestured at Durango and me.

"Let them rest. Besides, their clothes are still wet."

"Um, we've kind of got a timetable. So maybe when their clothes are dry?"

"It's dangerous to go out at night around here," Khin, Sandy's husband, said darkly. "Shadows grow long much earlier in the mountains."

"You accept my hospitality, Yang Qing!" Sandy shook her finger at him.

"Okay, okay!" Qing conceded. "Where'd you meet this dynamo anyway, Oz?" he muttered as he sat back down.

"Yeah," I chimed in, "and what does she mean about a two-night deal?"

Durango leaned back on his elbows and stretched his legs out in front of the blaze. "That night at my place, when we were figuring out which route to take, I e-mailed Sandy and asked if we could crash here for two nights, just in case Pianma was too difficult. Which it proved to be back at the restaurant."

"But back at your place, I hadn't told you which way I wanted to go yet," I protested. "We might not have gone this direction at all."

"I was being prepared," Durango shrugged. "Besides, I knew you'd come around to my way of thinking." He gave a cocky smirk.

I rolled my eyes and let my gaze wander to Durango's feet.

"You e-mailed someone with no electricity?" Qing asked. "That was smart. I suppose she has a wireless router in the garden shed out back, huh?"

"No, Einstein, but she does take the bus into town to check her e-mail. She and her husband are part of the resistance against Myanmar's current government. That's how I met her. In fact, I was the one who introduced them to each other."

Only marginally listening to their conversation, I scooted over, positioning myself cross-legged in front of Durango's feet.

"May I?" I asked, placing my hands on his socks.

"May you what?" he asked suspiciously.

"I want to see your feet."

He pulled his legs back and shot a baffled glance at Qing, who shrugged.

"Yuck. Why?" Durango asked.

"Just… trust me," I answered.

I gave him a mischievous grin. Durango warily stretched his legs back out. I stripped off one of his socks.

"Eew, doesn't that reek?" Qing asked, ready to pinch his nose from the other side of the floor-hearth.

"The fire eats up most of the smell," I explained. I pulled off the other sock. "Works with onions, too."

"Huh. Where'd you hear that?"

"Discovery Channel." I caught Durango's gaze for a fleeting, pointed moment before turning back to Qing. "When you chop onions, if you do it next to an open flame, your mascara won't run."

"I'll remember that the next time I wear mascara," Qing said, rolling his eyes.

"Said the boy, who I knew when he was in college."

"Hey, that was guyliner!" He looked desperately at Durango. "It was my clubbing phase."

I ignored Qing and directed my attention back to Durango.

"You were telling us how you knew Sandy?"

I visually compared both of his feet: the nails were trimmed, the skin around his heels was rough, and the right foot was slightly larger than the left—typical. But there was no noticeable sign of injury, which meant my hunch about his limp could be correct.

"Okay, but let me back up a bit," Durango started. "Burma is currently controlled by a junta government. Their military, the *Tatmadaw*, rigs elections and oppresses its people. In the mid-nineteen hundreds, Burma was one of the wealthiest economies in Southeast Asia. When the junta made their coup, it all went cactus. Now it's got one of the highest levels of poverty, worst literacy rates, and one of the least developed infrastructures. Even the little Internet access the people have is highly restricted by the government."

Listening to him talk, I began feeling my thumbs along the arch of his soles, then around to the top of his feet. Having shifted to a clinical mindset, I discovered I was able to caress his skin without attaching emotional significance to it—a relief since I was convinced I could help him. Eventually, I found what I was looking for: a large knot beneath the inside of his right ankle bone.

Using both hands, I lifted his foot into my lap and pushed my thumb hard into the knot. Durango's eyes bulged. He sat bolt upright and jerked his leg away.

"Mother… *of pearl!*" he cried angrily, couching his speech with a darted glance at the children present.

"Sorry," I apologized, reaching for his foot again, "this is going to hurt at first."

"What are you doing?" he demanded. He anchored his heel on the floor.

"You have a knot in your foot muscle, and it's aggravating the nerve endings. That's what's causing your limp."

"You have a medical degree I don't know about?"

"No, but when I was on my high school ski team—"

"Here we go." Qing threw his hands up.

"I had an injury that required physical therapy follow-ups, and I became interested in acupressure techniques. Look." I ran my thumb upward along the bottom of his right sole, then his left. "Feel the difference? That staccato on the right?"

"Yeah?"

"That's a little plantar fasciitis you've developed as a result of favoring the left foot. Your tendons need to be stretched."

"And she used to call *me* a nerd," Qing said smugly.

"You *are* a nerd," I said. "But there's nothing wrong with being interested in human anatomy."

"Can't argue with that," Durango reasoned. A twinkle glimmered in his eyes.

Warmth crept into my cheeks. That wasn't exactly how I'd meant it.

"She know what she's doing?" he asked Qing.

"She does give really good back massages," Qing admitted.

Durango cocked an interested eyebrow, and his lip twisted into an impish smirk. My cheeks grew hotter. Despite two-days' worth of scruff on his face, he still made me feel like I'd wandered into the football team's locker room while the quarterback was changing.

But I wasn't going to let myself be intimidated.

Clinical mindset, I reminded myself.

"Let's see if you can survive the foot massage first," I said quietly.

I reached for his foot, and this time he allowed me to lift it into my lap. I pushed the pad of my thumb back into the knot and held it there.

Durango drew a sharp intake of breath. I kept my smile private. The fire crackled, a log shifted in the momentary silence.

"So, Sandy's part of the resistance?" I prompted.

"Yeah," Durango continued. "There's an underground network of resistance fighters. Sandy is one of them. They are continually pushing to educate the people so that they can unify and eventually overthrow the government. There are other, more outspoken, non-underground leaders, but the *Tatmadaw* keeps imprisoning them."

I felt the knot give way under my thumb. Easing my fingers over, I continued following the line of the muscle, applying more stationary pressure to each spot as I went.

"And what does the Burmese resistance movement have to do with you?" I asked.

"I was stationed here briefly when I was in the military. Sandy speaks English, she taught me a little Burmese, and we've been friends ever since."

I tried to picture Durango in camouflage. "You've really been to a lot of places, haven't you?" I finished working out the knot and began pushing his foot into a flex to stretch the muscles.

"The military? Really?" Qing asked in disbelief.

I knit my brows at him. "You don't think he was in the military?" Had he lied to me again? But I didn't think so. Something about it seemed to fit—another piece of the Durango puzzle.

"Oh, I have no problem thinking Oz answered the call of duty. I mean, look at him. He's ripped. I could see him in uniform. But *here*? You were stationed *here*?"

"What's wrong with that?" I asked. "Military guys get shipped all over the place."

"No," Qing shook his head. "*Your* military guys get shipped all over the place. Not Australians."

"Sure they do," I protested. "Their guys work with our guys all the time." I switched to a light massage on Durango's other foot.

"In wartime, maybe. But when's the last time you heard of U.S. troops in Myanmar?"

I racked my brain. "You know, our guys are so many places. And the truth is, I haven't really paid much attention to politics or… army stuff," I added sheepishly.

"That's not a bad thing," Durango commented softly, "to be able to live your life how you want, without worrying about what everyone else is up to."

It was the first time he'd spoken since Qing began his line of questions. Qing and I stared at him. But he was gazing into the fire, lost in another world of thought. He relaxed back, then, lacing his fingers behind his head, and his lids drooped.

"If you don't believe me, why not just ask Sandy?" he mumbled with his eyes closed.

"I did. Yesterday," Qing said, apparently oblivious to Durango's exhaustion.

"And?" I asked.

"She said the same thing as he just did." Qing jerked his head at Durango. "That she knew him from back when he was—a serviceman, she called it—and he helped her with 'something.' She didn't say what, but she kind of alluded to it having something to do with political activities."

Qing's questions about Durango's past gave me an uneasy feeling. On the one hand, Durango had more than proven himself to me, Li, and Qing these past few days, and Qing was the one who'd brought us to him in the first place. On the other hand, there was still a lot I didn't know about this man. I needed to find out more about what was on my best friend's mind.

"Qing," I said in a hushed voice, "it's still sunny out. Why don't we go for a walk, just you and me?"

I traced my fingers lightly up Durango's left foot one last time, then stood up and walked to the door. Durango didn't move. Li jumped up, ran over to me, and grabbed my hand.

"Hey, Li," I whispered, "do you want to play outside, get some fresh air? Come on, Q, I need a translator. Please?"

Qing got to his feet. "Um, okay, but I thought…" He looked back at Durango, whose breathing was even. "Okay."

48

He wasn't really asleep, but the foot massage had relaxed him enough that he began to think about things he hadn't wanted to take the time to think about, and now he needed to sort them through.

He'd known the fact that he was in the military would come out if they went to Sandy's house. He was okay with that. The mission he'd been on during the time he'd met Sandy and Khin wasn't a bad memory. It seemed as though Qing had figured out that he'd been Special Forces. He was okay with that, too.

It was just the end part of his military career that he didn't want to have to think about.

The more time he spent around Kelly, the more the Incident came back to him. It was what had led to his leaving the army, it was what had made him choose his current career, and it was, ultimately, what had led to the knowledge that he would always be alone.

But why did her presence bring it back? Maybe it was because there was something about her that reminded him of his own lost innocence. He used to be optimistic once, too. Sometimes he missed that. Maybe it was because, except for about a minute right after she'd almost opened the box that morning, she'd never been afraid of him. Even when she knew he'd just killed someone. It was as though she could see the good in him, and he wanted to believe it was there. When she looked at him like he was her hero, he wanted to be who she thought he was.

Or maybe it was just her. Maybe he wanted to not be alone anymore. Maybe he wanted *her*.

But, again, back to reality.

Maybe it was better that she thought he was a tour guide, someone who would pass out of her life in a few days. She was so *real* and full of hope and wonder. But as attracted as he was to her body, smile, and vision of the world, he had no right to her. If he tempted karma and tried to keep her despite everything… well, she would probably just get hurt. Or worse, she'd become jaded—Like him.

49

I led Li out the door and down the wooden stairs. Sandy's boys, Naing and two-year-old Than followed. Qing brought up the rear.

When we reached the ground, I released Li's hand. He darted off with Naing and Than, and they immediately found the largest, muddiest puddle. I walked briskly for several yards until I hoped I was out of earshot from the house's open windows. Mountain shadows surrounded us, though the sky was still light. Qing caught up.

"How's he doing?" I asked, nodding my head toward Li. Qing frowned thoughtfully.

"He was upset when he woke up in the motel yesterday, and then again this morning. But he adjusts," Qing answered. "He's an amazing kid."

I glanced at Qing. A wistful smile crossed my friend's face as he watched Li laugh and run around. His expression made me curious, but I had to get to the real reason I'd wanted to get outdoors.

"So, what's the deal?" I asked casually, trying to keep my tone non-judgmental. "Why were you questioning whether or not Durango served in Burma? I mean, I know he's not super forthcoming, but you trusted him enough to bring us to his house. So what gives?" My voice rose as I spoke, and I realized I was afraid Qing was about to tell me something I didn't want to hear about the man who'd saved my life.

Qing listened, his head cocked to the side, his expression becoming more and more baffled. I could almost see the wheels turning as he processed what I'd inferred.

"Wait a minute," he finally said. "You think I was questioning his integrity? No way! I took us to him because I *knew* he was one of the good guys. I can tell these things, you know. No, Cow, I was questioning him because I think he was being overly *modest*."

"Huh?" I felt myself trade facial expressions with Qing.

"Look," he explained, "I'm sure Oz was in the military. But like I was saying back there, the Australian military rarely gets shipped out anywhere. Except for the commando units. And those guys are really highly specialized with their training and stuff. For him to say he was 'in the army' gives you, an American, an idea of some generic teenager just out of basic training camp—"

"Hey!" I interrupted. "First of all, that's not necessarily what I think. And second, we're quite proud of *all* our men and women and gender-fluid individuals in uniform, regardless of their age."

"Okay," Qing laughed, "but you get what I mean, right? Oz was… how can I explain it to you? He must have been like special ops, like the best of your army guys or your Marines. Aren't they the toughest ones?"

"You watch too many movies. But I get what you're trying to say now. He was an ultimate GI Joe." I mulled the image in my mind. It fit. "But if you believed he was in the military, and you accepted that he could've been stationed here, why did you even start questioning him about it in the first place?"

Qing gaped at me in disbelief. "It's cool! Duh!"

I stared at him for a second. *That* was what all of that had been about? Then: "Oh my gosh, you are *such* a nerd!" I laughed until tears came. Still giggling, I elbowed him in the ribs. Qing, also laughing, elbowed me right back.

Li ran around, playing happily with Sandy's children as the sky deepened into dusk. I wished I could freeze the world and let him stay here, but he wouldn't be safe. We weren't far enough away from the men hunting us. And the box.

I wondered what I would do with him once we'd made it to safety and delivered our information—and the box—into the right hands.

I thought about it for the first time. I felt responsible for Li, and I was definitely fond of him, but I had no desire to adopt a child. Not at this point in my life, with my uncertain future. Then a new idea began to form in the back of my mind.

"Hey, what's the deal with you two, anyway?" Qing asked.

"I don't know," I sighed, "but he's such an innocent little cutie, isn't he?"

"No, not him. *Him.*" Qing jerked his head back toward the parquet-walled house.

"Oh!" My cheeks became warm. He meant Durango. "I don't... I mean, uh, he's a nice person, but there's nothing... Why?"

"It's just something about the way you two seem around each other."

"What do you mean?"

"And the way you got so worried when you thought I was questioning his integrity."

"He saved my life a few times. I'm grateful, that's all."

"And the way he lets his guard down with you."

Suddenly, I was very interested. "What do you mean?"

"Oz always has this wall up. He's great, he's your buddy, and you know he'll close the bar with you every time, but he never lets you all the way in. You seem to be 'in' with him. I hadn't seen that before."

A ball of warmth grew inside me. Despite all the times he'd shut me out, was it possible? Did the connection I perceived with him exist in more than just my head?

"Maybe you've just never seen him with a female before," I said casually. Inside, I was fending off happy butterflies. For a whole two seconds.

"Oh no, Oz has plenty of women," Qing snickered. "Gorgeous ones. They're around him all the time, like flies. Flies with big boobs and—"

"Okay!" I pushed Qing's cupped hands down from in front of his chest. *Happy butterflies gone.* "I get the picture." An awful memory I'd worked five years trying to forget flooded back. It was that Other Thing, the humiliating reminder of the underlying motivation for the reason I'd moved to Minneapolis. It had all been a lie...

****

I'd been at the ad agency for a year and a half—a year and a half of flirtations and no-we-work-together-we-shouldn'ts. A touch of the hand at the water cooler. Innuendos as he'd leaned over my desk when no one else was around. The way he'd begun to lust at me from across the room. Little private affirmations, validations, thoughts leftover from my interview were coming to fruition. I was promoted from receptionist to personal assistant. *His* personal assistant.

And then the office holiday party.

He cornered me in a secluded spot, in the cold, on the outdoor patio, and I, naïve sycophant that I was, overwhelmed by the attention and the promises, knew that I must be in love. I gave in to his cajoles with very little resistance, right there, on the chair behind the plant, on the deserted country club patio. December air never felt so warm and cozy. He made me promise to keep "our little secret" before he left for a business trip the next day—office politics. I understood.

I didn't see him for a few weeks. When he returned, I was promoted again, this time to executive assistant.

But it was for the account execs on the other side of the building: office politics, the appearance of impropriety. I understood. At the end of the month, he'd hired a new personal assistant. Of course. He needed a personal assistant. He had to hire *someone*.

And a month later had been *that* day.

"Good morning, Megan." The frigid end-of-February air had rushed at my skirt as the door swung shut behind me. My arms were full of Starbucks trays and bags for a client meeting in a half-hour. Megan, the receptionist, shivered.

"Morning, Kelly. Brrr! I'm going to have to get a new space heater up here if this weather keeps up, I tell ya!"

"Totally! Hey, what's with all the balloons? Are we having a party?"

"No! Didn't ya hear? No, of course not. You just got in. Mr. Loomis proposed to Valerie!"

"What? *Percy* Loomis?" My smile froze, and I felt the blood drain from my face. My feet rooted themselves to the floor.

"You didn't think I meant his brother, did ya? Oh, my gosh! You didn't even know Mr. Loomis and Valerie were dating, did ya?"

"Valerie Bjorklund. The new personal assistant?" *With long blonde hair and big balloon boobs.* "She's only been here a month!" My mind reeled. There had to be something I was missing. He couldn't have been seeing Valerie. Certainly not enough to be *engaged*. And yet, the balloons…

As I escaped Megan and compelled my feet through the building to my desk, there were more balloons.

And streamers that said "Congrats!"

Passing Valerie's desk, I saw a monstrous bouquet of tulips, lilies, and gerbera daisies. In February!

I reached my own desk, dingy, gray, and barren, and it slowly penetrated my thick skull that the reason I'd had to keep my relationship with Percy a secret was that there was no relationship. Not with me. Any romance that I'd thought existed between us had only been in my head. His relationship was with Valerie. The others in the office seemed to have already known about it. If they didn't before, they did now.

No, the reality was that I'd been nothing more than a one-night stand. A crummy hump in the corner at a party. And now that he'd "racked his pool balls," so to speak, he was done with me. What he'd really meant when he told me it was "our little secret" was that he wanted it kept quiet because it didn't matter to him. *I* didn't matter to him. I wasn't good enough for him.

I'd gone home sick, taking the rest of the week off to alternate between sobbing into my pillow and staring listlessly at the ceiling. At one point, I even emailed Craig, my high school boyfriend, and on-again/off-again whatever-we-were. No response. Typical.

Finally, out of desperation, I'd accepted my Goth bartender-roommate Kim's invitation to a rave, thus commencing my own, brief Goth phase. Over the next few years, I'd tried multitudinous styles and countless dating methods, but the end result had left me void and unhappy. What I really wanted was to be able to be myself and for that to be good enough. For *someone.*

****

Now, however, listening to Qing talk about the beautiful women who flocked around Durango, I had a harsh reality check. *What had I been thinking?* Of *course*, winsome, capable, god-bod Durango could have any woman he wanted. Asian models. Aussie movie stars. Swedish secretaries. Whatever Qing thought he saw in Durango's reaction to me must have been imagined.

The sad thing, though, was that I'd momentarily allowed myself to be drawn into the idea that someone as handsome, heroic, nice, and *interesting* as him could actually be attracted to me.

My life, for the most part, was failed and mundane. I'd fooled myself into thinking we were getting to know each other as real people. Our long conversations, which I'd thought were honest and revealing, were undoubtedly the result of his impeccable manners—combined with the fact that he'd been stuck with me in the middle of the wilderness.

I was paying him to get me to India.

He'd been being polite. And counteracting boredom.

Also, for some reason, he was interested in the box.

Stupid girl! Stupid box!

"I *hate* men!" I yelled and stomped my foot.

"Whoa, Cow. Where did that come from? Are you okay?"

I sighed. Qing was one of the few guys I'd always been able to be myself around. He'd been there for me, no matter what phase I was going through. Goth, bohemian, *blonde*. Even this current "find myself" phase, which now involved mortal danger for *him*.

"I'm sorry," I said contritely. "Not you. I was somewhere else for a second." I linked my arm around his elbow, sighed, and leaned my head against his shoulder. "You're one of the good ones. Nori's a very lucky girl."

"Thanks, Cow." He relaxed and rested his head on mine with all the conviction and comfort of our close friendship. "But I'm the lucky one."

He sounded happy, and I smiled, content for my friend.

"Hey," I said eventually, "tell me again about how this Chinese-Japanese wedding is going to work."

Qing launched into an eager explanation of how they'd combined the cultural traditions for the ceremony, and I asked lots of questions. We watched the kids play until dusk deepened to dark. In the back of my mind, the idea I'd had earlier solidified. Yes. It was best for Li and best for everyone.

A woman's voice called behind us. I glanced back to the house. Sandy stood at the door. She swept her arm in an arc, motioning that it was time to come in. I nudged Qing.

"We should get going. *Come on, kids,*" I called out. Li and his new friends ignored me and kept on playing. "I thought Sandy's kids spoke English. How do you say it in Chinese?"

"No, I don't think her kids do. Just Sandy and Khin. But it's not the language. It's the motivation," Qing said.

"What?"

"Kids! Dinnertime!" Qing hollered in English. The kids stopped and looked at him. He rubbed his belly. Immediately they all started screaming and ran for the house.

"How'd you do that?" I asked.

"It's a gift," Qing replied with an air of superiority.

Under light emanating only from lanterns, Sandy had prepared a massive, multi-dish meal of mangos, rice, some sort of vegetables, something that smelled like chicken, and more soup. The kids took their places at the bamboo mats around the long, low table. I sat with Qing and Li. Durango wasn't there yet.

"This is a lot of food," I whispered to Qing.

"They did this last night, too," he whispered back. "Sandy said this is traditional Burmese custom."

Still stuffed from my late lunch of fish soup, I picked at a mango slice with my fork and watched as the family began to eat the food on their plates with their fingers.

"Where's Durango?" I asked Sandy.

"He said he was full and tired, and he went to bed," Sandy answered.

"Tired" didn't strike me as an adjective I'd have chosen for our energetic tour guide. *However…*

Recognition descended on my soul like a heavy blanket. It was a sign. With Durango out of the way, it would make it easier to follow through with my idea. Somehow, I thought he would've tried to stop me. But now, he would never know. Concurrent with the heaviness, though, came that now-familiar, wrong thrill—the one I'd had atop the monastery turret and a few times since. Was I sure I didn't have a death wish? My idea was dangerous.

I shook my head. Dangerous didn't matter. I *had* to do this. Especially now that the path had been cleared.

When the meal was over, I helped Sandy clear the table and do the dishes. Then I excused myself, saying I, too, was tired. Sandy showed me to a small, square room with a lit fire in the middle, just like the main room. Our backpacks were stowed in a far corner, and four mats lay around the square pit. Li was already asleep on one. I suppressed a gasp of surprise, seeing Durango was on another.

"This is usually the kids' room," Qing said quietly from behind me, "but the whole family is using the other bedroom while they have guests."

I raised my eyebrows in amazement, humbled that this family with so few possessions had shown us so much generosity.

"Wow," was all I whispered.

But Qing understood.

"I know, right?"

I took off my blue oxford and lay down, waiting. After an hour, the whole house became quiet. It took forever for Qing's breathing to become even. Then I waited some more to be sure he was in the deeper stages of sleep.

The last embers in the fire pit crackled and shifted until their glow went out.

"Qing?" I whispered.

He didn't answer. I knew I was the only one left awake.

Silently I rose, felt around for Qing's messenger bag, and stole out of the room. I paused in the hallway, listening. The rest of the house was dark and still. The fire in the main room had been extinguished for the night.

In a swath of moonlight that beamed through the open shutters, I found what I needed from Qing's bag—a pen and a piece of paper.

> *Qing –*
>
> *My journey with you might be ending here, tonight. I'm still going to try to make it to your wedding, but there's something else I have to do, so I'm leaving Li and the box in your hands. Please tell Durango that no matter what happens to me, he will still receive our agreed-upon fee for transporting Li and the box to safety. (He knows more about the box than I do, anyway.)*

Please give my pink hoodie to Sandy, with my fondest regards. Also, give my best to Nori. Love you!

– Cow

P.S. If you don't hear from me soon, please send this other note to my parents.

I quickly wrote a second note to my parents, telling them I loved them and instructing them to take all the remaining money from my savings and forward it to Qing, who would send it on to Durango. I folded the note to my parents inside the one to Qing and set them on top of his messenger bag near the front door. I didn't know if I would make it out of this alive. Picking up my shoes by the door, I snuck out into the blackness.

50

Screams—human shrieks that became inhuman howls—filled his ears, even above the roar of the flames. Smoke scorched his lungs as he tried to run towards it. No! No! No!

His eyes flew open. He was panting, gulping breaths of what he quickly registered as clean, non-smoke-filled air. Remnants of the nightmare faded.

He steadied his breathing. It had been a long time since he'd had the dream, and he wondered why it had chosen tonight to come back. The room was pitch black, but as he adjusted, he realized something was off. He lay motionless, listening.

He could hear the steady breathing of more than one person close by.

Kelly, Qing, and Li. Right?

He listened harder. Through the bedroom window, he could hear the swish of trees and cricket chirps at the back of the house.

Harder.

From the direction of the front of the house, he could hear the muted crunch of steps on the damp road. Fading. *One-two, one-two.* Human steps. Based on the interval of the footfalls, someone was running. A thought startled him:

Did I hear a door shut? Is that why I woke?

Reaching his hand into his pocket, he took out his penlight. Kelly's pack was in the corner, undisturbed. He'd already checked to make sure the box was still in it before he went to bed. If someone had moved it, he'd have known.

He shined the beam around the room. Qing was asleep. Li was asleep. Kelly's blue shirt was folded, but her mat was empty. He frowned.

Getting up, he padded into the main room. There was enough light from the moon that he could instantly see the room was empty. A dark bundle sat near the front door. There was something white on top of it. He aimed his light and walked over: Qing's bag. A note addressed to Qing lay folded on top. Durango's pulse sped up. He picked up the note, unfolded it, and read it. Twice. Then he quickly read the other note folded inside, which Kelly had addressed to her parents.

No!

He knew exactly where she'd gone.

An emotion he'd long ago purged from his permissible emotional catalog seeped back into his system. It stuttered through his nerves like fingernails on a chalkboard. His breathing became shallow. His heart drummed faster.

Panic.

What the fuck *does she think she's doing?*

Doesn't matter. You have the sample, and you have a good chunk of information. She's not your concern anymore.

She's going to get herself killed.

One less distraction to have on your mind.

She's insane! Nothing about this girl makes sense! She's not brave. She's crazy!

Probably. Stop worrying about her.

She's going to get herself killed! I can't let that happen!

You can. Let her go.

No! I can't! Screw karma! I can't let her die! What the bloody fuck does she think she's doing, and what the bloody fuck does she think she's doing to me*? I haven't saved her life, time and again for nothing!*

Panic switched to anger, which helped him regain control. He pushed everything else away. Even during his inner dialogue, he'd pulled on his shoes.

He opened the door and shut it quietly behind him. Then he sprinted around the side of the house to where Qing had parked the SUV, behind a row of tall bushes. He couldn't drive it because the engine would make too much noise where he was headed. But he needed something from the trunk. Over and over, the words seethed in his head:

What the fuck *does she think she's doing? Who the* hell *does she think she is? Screw karma!*

51

I sat on the stairs and laced up my sneakers, the old ones left behind by Qing's sister. Warmth and humidity enveloped me, a damp blanket on my bare shoulders and arms. Then I got up and walked forward quietly, with resolve. Once away from Sandy's house, I picked up my pace to a jog.

My feet fell in soft crunches on the sodden dirt-and-gravel road. Though my muscles were sore from all of my travels, an urgent sense of purpose propelled me forward. My eyes had adjusted to the dark quickly, and my ears picked up cricket chirps, the distant screech of monkeys, the wind stirring the treetops overhead, a distant, babbling mountain stream, and the sound of my own breath as I fell into stride. In this remote region, it was simple to feel part of nature without the hum of electricity.

I retraced my route from earlier in the day, though now, even in the dark, it was easier, lighter, and faster without the backpack and wet clothes. Reaching the intersection, I veered right.

The sound of the babbling mountain stream grew louder. After a bend in the road, I could see it: the white house behind one of the foothills. It glowed blue in the moonlight. The house seemed isolated in its small, inlet valley with its left side facing the road; my approach was from the rear. The van was no longer parked across the road. Hopefully, the children were still there.

I slowed to a walk, easing forward against the side of the hill, until the back of the house was diagonal in front of me, to the right. Water splashed loudly down the side of another foothill across the road. It wasn't a mountain stream, but rather a waterfall I hadn't heard earlier because of the rain. Fortunately, it served to muffle my approach. Probably, it also muffled the sounds of children, I thought. A high, chain link fence that I hadn't seen earlier, due to the rain and the distance I'd been at, surrounded the house. The fence was anchored into the slope of the hill on the house's back side. At least two cars sat parked across from the front entrance. I needed to see inside somehow.

I started forward, but there was movement near the front. I froze. A man strode around the corner of the wraparound porch. He kept his elbow bent at an odd angle. As he turned, a machine gun glinted under his arm in the moonlight. I shrank against the near-vertical hill, flattening myself behind a low-growing shrub until he'd passed back out of view. My heart raced. But I couldn't stop.

I'd have to try the back of the house.

Up was the only way to go.

I'd only been rock climbing once before, but I remembered the basic principles. Grasping a clump of grass, I raised my right leg and found a toehold. I pulled up and found a footing for my left foot. A nearby tree root made for another handle. This hill wasn't as severe as the ninety-degree rock wall I'd learned on.

You can do this.

I climbed to various trees and shrubs, managing to stay out of sight from the guard on the porch by taking my time, advancing when he paced out of view. Scaling until I was thirty or forty feet up, I shimmied left, around the face of the slope, and entirely out of the moonlight. Combined with the waterfall's noisy splashing, I was now virtually undetectable.

In the shadows, I flipped over to my back and slid forward to sit up in a crouch. I let my heart rate calm down for a minute and studied the scene. I was positioned over the inside of the fence. Peering down, I tried to see into the house. The shades were drawn, but there was a light on. As I watched, a small shadow crossed in front of the shade, then another. My heart thumped against my ribcage again. They were in there! I dropped my hands to my sides and angled my feet, ready to begin my descent into the yard.

Suddenly a black-gloved hand clamped around my mouth from behind, and a massive arm came around my torso, pinning my arms to my sides. Fear surged through my veins, and I twisted, trying to scream. I flailed my legs, but I was picked up and hauled back around to the moonlit side of the mountain. The next second, I was pulled in a vice grip into someone's lap, sliding at breakneck speed down the slope. *How did the monks find me here? What about Li?* My screams were lost against the firm glove and the loud mountain stream. As soon as our feet hit the road, the arms released me. I whirled and gasped.

Durango!

He wore dark clothing, gloves, a vest, a backpack, and some sort of utility belt that held what looked like binoculars and maybe a knife.

"What the *heck*?" I panted.

"Might ask you the same question." His voice sounded tight. His blue eyes blazed with fury, and his mouth held a grim line.

I'd never seen him angry before. He was quite imposing. This was not Durango, the handsome, affable tour guide. This man was fully alert, highly motivated, calculating, and extremely intelligent. *The tiger.*

I'd only seen a glimmer of this side of him once—the moment after he'd pulled Li and me off the roof of his apartment. And right now, he stood fully erect, towering over me. I shrank back instinctively.

He strode forward, grabbed my wrist, and pulled me down the road further away from the white house and into the shadows of the forest.

"What are you doing?" I whispered.

"I'm taking you back to Sandy's," he said under his breath.

"No!" I wrenched my arm out of his grasp, my frustration mounting. "I have to do this!"

"I thought we already went over this!"

"No," I breathed firmly, taking a step back toward the moonlight. "I'm out now. You can go on without me, get Li to safety. I need to do *this*." I took another step backward, my blood beginning to simmer.

"No, you don't."

"I'm sorry, I don't remember needing your permission," I said coldly.

I scowled at him, and he glowered back. I looked away, taking a deep breath, trying to calm down.

"Look, it's okay," I whispered, irritated. "You'll still get paid, and you know more about the box than I do, anyway."

"Yeah, I saw your note."

"Okay. Good. Go back to Sandy's, and please take care of Li. Thank you." If he'd read the note—which wasn't even addressed to him—why did I need to explain myself?

I'd lost my patience. Turning my back on him, I re-jogged to the base of the hill behind the house, reached for the nearest tree root, and began re-scaling the mountain. I'd just secured the first toehold and was hoisting myself to the next when I felt a powerful arm around my waist. Durango pulled me away from the slope, flung me over his shoulder, and began jogging back down the road.

"You're not doing this!" he grunted fiercely.

In a rage of disbelief, I tried to kick, but he held my legs tightly together. I tried to pound his back with my fists, but I was bouncing so violently with the impact of his strides that it was all I could do to brace myself against his back and stabilize my head.

When he'd turned the corner and gone several paces down the hidden lane toward Sandy's, he set me down. As soon as my feet touched gravel, my fingernails bit into my palms, and I punched as hard as I could, straight into his gut. He made no attempt to stop me.

My fist connected with what felt like a wall of steel. A blinding crunch shot through my knuckles, and I staggered back, holding my hand. What sort of gear was he wearing? Tears of pain and rage stung my eyes.

"Are you done?" he asked, his voice flat, harsh. "Let's go."

"What *cave* did you crawl out of?" I yelled, taking another step back from him. "I said *no*! My path ends here! There are *children* in that house, and I have to try to save them!"

"We've already had this discussion!" he yelled back. "You have another job to get on with!"

"*We* had this discussion? No! *You* gave me *your* opinion. And now that I've had time to think about it, I disagree. *This* is more important for me right now. Maybe this is the reason I wound up right here, right now. You can take better care of Li than I can, you can speak his language, and you know more about that damn box than any of us. *You* do that job; *I'm* going to do *this* one." I stamped my foot and glared at him.

He pinned me with an intense, blue-ice stare.

"You have *no idea* what you're doing, and you're going to wind up *dead*!" he roared. "Did you *see* the MP5 on that guy at the front door? Hmmm? And *then* those children will be no better off than they were *before* your blind attempt! This sort of shit is happening *all over the world*. Yeah, sweetheart," he added coldly, seeing my shock. "You want to save children? Donate to an organization where there are people who know what they're doing." He took a breath and seemed to downshift his emotions. His voice became lower and calmer, albeit no less brusque and demanding.

"But right now, you're a material witness to two murders and probably also to a major, illegal, international arms deal, depending on what all you saw in that room. *You* have to testify."

Instead of calming down along with him, my headspace went from red… to crimson.

"*You* don't get to order me around! You're not in the military anymore! And even if you were, I'm neither your subordinate nor your fellow countryman! I'm an *American citizen*. You wouldn't have any jurisdiction over me, *no matter what*." I squared my shoulders, lifted my chin, and leveled a look at him. "Just go back, finish tour-guiding them to India, and then you can go back home to your super-model harem. I'm not going *anywhere* with you!" I stormed around him, back toward the intersection, back toward the white house with the innocent children. I pumped my arms to go faster and ignored the throb in my right palm.

"Americans!" I heard him mutter. "Fine. Have it your way."

Before I knew it, he'd grabbed me, tossed me back up over his shoulder, and resumed jogging toward Sandy's house, the opposite direction of where I wanted to go. And there was nothing I could do to stop him.

Fury, with no outlet, became a long, slow, boiling fume. The one point he'd made that *did* penetrate was that I had no idea what I was doing and would only get myself killed. Which would help no one. There was, I finally realized, nothing I could do. I couldn't save them.

By the time he set me back down in front of the steps at Sandy's house, I was overwhelmed by feelings of anger, frustration, and powerlessness. My eyes filled as I hung my head and climbed the dark stairs ahead of him. However, conscious of the sleeping family inside, I opened the front door silently. Then, not having the desire to go back to my room, and not wanting to wake the rest of the household, I sat down on a mat next to the extinguished fire pit, hugged my knees to my chest, and stared at the white, moonlit ashes until they blurred with the shadows. Tears spilled down my cheeks. I buried my face in my knees and stifled my sniffles as much as I could.

Durango moved around somewhere in the darkness, but I didn't care anymore. After a few minutes, I was vaguely aware that he was kneeling next to me. Gently, he took my right hand. I winced at the pain and automatically jerked my hand away. Looking up from my knees, I glared at him. His eyes, however, were soft, full of concern, no longer angry.

"I'm sorry," he began softly, "I couldn't let you—"

"They're children!" I whispered before my eyes flooded again. A fresh wave of sobs escaped my throat.

"I know," he murmured.

Edging closer, he pulled me into a hug, and suddenly I was leaning on him, clutching the fabric of his shirt, sobbing silently onto his chest. He was no longer wearing the hard vest he'd had on before. It was just the soft, black knit shirt and his Durango scent. He held me for a long time, letting me cry until I was spent.

"Here," he said as I finally straightened up. He took my right wrist this time. "Let me have a look at that."

He examined my hand in the moonlight, feeling delicately for different areas of sensation. His touch was warm, tender, and with my emotions so raw, I couldn't help the electricity that pulsated through my fingertips.

"Think you bruised the bone," he said finally. He produced a roll of athletic tape and bound my hand.

"You have a medical degree I don't know about?" I ventured.

"No, but once when I was on the ski team…"

I managed a wan smile, but the gravity of everything that had just transpired weighed on me. The smile faded as I cast my eyes downward.

"Hey." His fingers gently lifted my chin until I made eye contact with him. He raised his brow slightly as if to assess how much damage had been done between us. In response, my eyes filled again, and I blinked away two large tears. He cupped my cheeks in his hands and caressed the drops away with his thumbs.

"Can I ask you something?" I whispered.

"Anything."

At that moment, the way he said it, I almost believed I could have asked for literally anything, and he'd have given it to me. But my question was trickier than that.

"Am I… your prisoner?"

I wasn't certain, but it seemed that his eyes hardened in the pallor of the moon. His shoulders sagged a little, and he dropped his hands from my face.

"Once I get you to safety, in India, you'll be free to do what you want."

I thought about that for a moment. "Can I ask something else?"

"Okay?"

"Why were you wearing all of that… stuff?" I gestured at his torso with my bandaged hand.

Durango looked away and glared at the ground, seeming to wrestle with himself. Suddenly he leaned forward, caught my head in his hands, and pressed his stubbled cheek next to my ear. "Because I didn't know what I was going to have to walk into to get you out," he murmured.

I caught my breath, and something inside me leaped.

He released me abruptly, stood, and by the time I'd gotten my bearings, he'd disappeared out the front door into the night.

52

I couldn't sleep. I destroyed the notes I'd written to Qing and my parents since they were now pointless. There was no reason to worry Qing if he accidentally found them. My stomach churned for those poor children, but Durango was right: there was nothing I could do.

It occurred to me to try to drive into town, find an Internet café, and then Google, and alert one of the types of children's organizations Durango had mentioned. But, in addition to not knowing the way, especially in the dark, I would probably stick out like a sore thumb in this region of the world. I couldn't risk dealing with Burmese police. Also, I was pretty sure Durango had only left to go stand guard outside, so I probably shouldn't even attempt to open the door.

I lay down on the mat, but too many conflicting emotions whirled in my head: frustration, powerlessness, sadness, and most disturbing: hope. Something in Durango's voice, coupled with what Qing had said earlier that evening about Durango letting his guard down with me, played in my mind. Had he only stopped me from undertaking my suicide mission because I was a "material witness," as he'd put it, and he had some overdeveloped sense of duty remaining from his time in the military? Or had Qing been right, and I correctly detected something more in his tone and touch?

I stood up and crossed to a side window. Kneeling in front of the sill with my chin on my good hand, I absorbed the warm, night air. The moon had crossed the sky and was now behind the mountains, leaving everything in almost complete darkness. From this vantage point, I could make out shadows of the two slopes on my left, between which the road disappeared. To my right, I could see the hulking ridge of mountains at the back of Sandy's house, silhouetted against constellations unobstructed by artificial light. Invisible treetops all around me swished an eerie lullaby with the currents, punctuated by occasional, far-off animal howls and screeches. My eyes drifted to the stars, a brilliant, though unfamiliar astral map. I could not find Polaris from this setting, and my mind went to maps, then wandered a tangent back to Durango, who loved maps.

The pieces of the Durango puzzle didn't fit anymore: Durango the bookworm and would-be cartographer. The athlete. The commando. The tour guide. Something didn't quite fit, but I couldn't figure out what. I'd seen all those different sides to him. Individually, they made sense. But together, somehow, they didn't complete the puzzle of *who* he was. I was missing a piece.

Birds began to chirp in the darkness, heralding imminent dawn. The sky lightened to grey. A click sounded behind me, and I turned to see the front door open. Durango entered. A dark line streaked across his cheek. I sat up, concerned.

"Are you bleeding?" I whispered.

"No," he answered curtly. He disappeared silently into the bedroom, returned with his backpack, and left again out the front door.

The first shaft of light gilded the uppermost leaves. The household began to stir. Sandy emerged and went to the kitchen to prepare breakfast. Her husband and children filed out of the hallway leading to the bedrooms, followed by Li a few seconds later.

"Cow-li!" he exclaimed, running to give me a hug. My heart filled with affection for my young friend, and I embraced him back tightly. If this was the job I was tasked to do, it wasn't without benefits.

"Good morning, Li," I smiled.

"Good morning," he answered back, to my surprise.

"Wow! You're picking up English quickly," I smiled at him.

"Yeah, he's one smart cookie," Qing said, entering the room. "Hey, Cow, what time did you get up?"

"A while ago," I said, evading a direct answer. I stood and quickly shoved my hands in my pockets to hide the bandage before he could notice. "I watched the sunrise."

"Nooo!" Sandy wailed from the kitchen.

Qing and I both spun around in time to see Sandy's toddler pull a full basket of eggs off the counter. The basket tipped upside down and thunked to the floor. Sandy lifted the basket with a grimace to reveal a white, brown, and yellow-pulpy mess underneath. Khin scooped Than up before the tot could try to help his mother clean up. Egg goo dripped from Than's bare feet. Khin carried him out the front door, scolding him, to clean him off by the stream.

"That was all of their eggs, wasn't it?" I asked Qing.

"I think so. Hey, why don't I run Sandy to the market with the SUV?"

"That's a very nice idea. Sandy?" I piped up, "I'll get that."

"Yeah, come on, I'll drive you into town," Qing added.

Sandy's eyes lit up. "Really? Oh, that would be wonderful! We won't be very long." She grabbed her market bag, and Qing escorted her out the door. I began scooping yolk and shells off the floor into a bowl I'd found, staining my bandage yellow.

"That doesn't look very appetizing," a familiar voice boomed above me.

"Sandy's baby decided to feed the floor and—"

I stopped short as I looked up at Durango Trunk, the jovial, tour-guide version. He wore his khaki pants and blue oxford again, and his relaxed face betrayed no hint of ambitious intelligence. I raised an eyebrow, trying to reconcile this man with the one from last night. Then I noticed he was clean-shaven, and his hair was damp.

"Did you *shower*?" I asked.

"Naw, I just did what you did with the lake yesterday. Only I used a waterfall." He gave a lopsided grin.

Yesterday? Was it really that recently that I'd plunged into the lake? That brief, carefree moment when I'd gone skinny-dipping seemed eons ago. I wondered if Durango had felt the same, freeing sensation in the waterfall.

Momentarily distracted by the thought of him naked, I shook myself out of it and winced when I put too much pressure on my right palm. I slopped the remainder of the shells into the bowl and began to look around.

"What else do you need, Kells?" I loved the familiarity he used with my name. He bent down and picked up the egg-mess bowl.

"Something to clean the rest of the floor."

"Hey, Nyunt?" He turned around and said something in Burmese to Sandy's ten-year-old. The girl ran to a basket in the corner and brought back an old rag. Then she brought over a half-full glass of water. She dumped a puddle on top of the mess, then grabbed a pitcher and ran outside. I mopped the floor with my left hand. Durango followed Nyunt outside, dumped the eggs, came back in, and began carting our backpacks to the front door. Qing and Sandy returned, carrying eggs, fruit, and a chicken.

"Wow, for a small town, they sure have a lot of police," Qing whistled.

"This is unusual," Sandy said. "People in the marketplace were talking about it. I forgot that you couldn't understand them. Early this morning, three Thai men were found tied up in the middle of a road nearby. Two were dead, and the third had been knocked unconscious and didn't know what happened. It was right in front of a house full of fifteen Tibetan children. The guy who was still alive admitted he and the dead men had been involved in trafficking for a prostitution ring."

"Really?" I asked in wonder. Sandy couldn't have been talking about *that* same house, could she? "What happened to the children?" I reached out to help Sandy with her groceries. Qing noticed the bandage.

"Hey, Cow, what happened to your hand?"

Sandy froze and stared at my hand. "The children are being turned over to people who will either return them to their families or will help place them in a decent orphanage. You two didn't go on any vigilante errands last night, did you, Kelly Morrison and Durango Trunk?" Her eyes narrowed. She glanced from me to Durango.

My vigilante errand was Trunk-cated, I thought. But before I could answer, Durango spoke.

"I would never want to place your family at risk, Sandy," he said.

I digested his words and then heard their subtext: *I* had put Sandy's family at risk when I'd gone on my unnecessary side-mission. Guilt sank in my belly. I hadn't considered the potential ramifications to our innocent hosts and their kids.

"Besides," he continued nonchalantly, "I was asleep, remember?"

Bits of reality flew at me like shards of glass: he was asleep until he'd woken up and retrieved me. Then he'd left out the door again. When he came back in, it looked as though he had blood on his face. But by the light of day, his face looked fine. *After* his shower. It was Durango. I'd assumed he was standing guard outside, keeping me from trying to leave again, but he hadn't been. He'd gone back alone. He'd done the thing I'd so desperately wanted to do. He'd saved those children. Fortunately, it hadn't been *his* blood on his face.

"Cow?" Qing was waiting for an answer. He glanced again at my hand.

"I smacked my hand into a wall last night," I said weakly. "Will you excuse me? I forgot something in the bedroom."

I hurried down the little hall, turned the corner, and closed the door behind me. Sinking against the wall, I clapped a hand to my mouth, engulfed in an ocean of feelings ranging from relief for the children to horror that I'd endangered Sandy's family. The emotions released themselves, sending a fresh round of tears streaming down my cheeks.

And then there were the Durango emotions: I was grateful to him. I admired and was astounded by his actions. And I was humbled that he'd risked his own life for something important to me. But in that moment, I also knew that beyond all his physical charm, and despite all the walls he kept throwing up and all of his "shoveling," I'd fallen in love with him. Not the teenage passion that had faded into a comfortable, once-every-blue-moon thing with my high school boyfriend, Craig, and not the pathetic infatuation I'd had for my boss, Percy. This was light-years from those. I loved him in a way that made me not care that I could never be good enough for him. I didn't even care if he never felt the same way about me because I couldn't help what I *knew*. Durango Trunk was an unbelievably brave and *good* human being and the best man I had ever known. And I loved him down to my core.

"Cow?" Qing knocked at the door.

I forced myself to suck in a deep, stuttered breath, then grabbed my blue oxford off the bedroom floor and dried my eyes with it.

"Yeah?"

He poked his head in. "Oz thinks we should hit the road, just in case the police start going door-to-door."

"Okay." I kept my back to Qing, slid my arms into the oxford, and swiftly folded the blankets neatly on each of the four mats we'd used—or not used—last night. "I'm ready."

"He also said you might need some more of this," Qing said.

I turned. Qing was holding the athletic tape. I opened my palm for it, but he pulled his hand back.

"What's wrong?" he demanded.

"Nothing."

"Your eyes are red, and you're acting funny." Qing frowned and drew himself up to his full height. "Did he do something?"

"It's not what you think."

"He did do something! I'm gonna kill him. I told him not to mess with you. What a douche bag!"

"You told him… what? Qing, he's actually pretty great." I picked the eggy bandage off my palm. My hand throbbed without the tape constricting it. "If anyone's the douche bag, it's me."

Qing helped me re-tape. "Cow, I know you lied about your hand. What happened? Just tell me," he begged.

I shook my head. "I can't tell you." I gave him a meaningful look. Understanding crossed his features, followed by a disapproving frown. He knew what Durango had done last night, too. He ripped off the end of the tape for me.

"Thanks. Suffice it to say that I could only ever dream of deserving someone as accomplished and cool and incredible and… *good* as him one day."

"Humph," Qing snorted. "He's got you snowed."

"I think it's the other way around," I said softly. Qing was the one who didn't see Durango clearly.

I pocketed the rest of the tape roll. We exited the room and crossed the empty house. The family had come outside to see us off. Durango hugged Sandy and shook Khin's hand. Li was already buckled into the front seat. Qing said his goodbyes and took his place behind the wheel. I opened the back-passenger door when I remembered something.

"Hang on!" I called. Running around to the back of the SUV, I found my backpack and dug through it until I found my zip-up sweat jacket. "Here," I said to Sandy, "from one pink hoodie girl to another."

Sandy smiled broadly and blinked back tears. She hugged the gift to her chest. "Thank you," she breathed.

"No, thank *you*." I squeezed her hand.

I climbed in the back seat next to Durango but couldn't bring myself to look at him. Qing started down the road. The car's engine purred as it lilted us side to side on the gravel. Now that my emotional palate was expended, the sleep that had eluded me last night weighed heavily on my lids.

"Sorry you're still stuck back here with me," Durango commented, "but it's probably safer this way until we get past the extra security in town." After a minute, he added, "That was a very nice gesture you made to Sandy back there."

I blinked and had to think to reopen my eyes.

"Least I got something right," I mumbled.

"What do you mean?" he asked.

I heard the question but couldn't answer. My head fell forward on my chest, and I was aware of the car moving, light filtering between the trees, through the window, the car jostling us on the road, but I was *so tired*. And then there was a pillow. I sank against it, slipping off in comfortable oblivion.

53

Somehow Kelly Morrison had managed to eliminate two pairs of his best servants. First at the motel in far western Yunnan, then in the mountains near the border with Myanmar. Their corpses had been found by hikers. Due to the location of the last coordinates from the transmitter, it appeared she'd been traveling west, but the transmitter's signal was now gone. It also appeared that she was traveling by foot, at least at the moment. It was unclear what her final destination would be, but he would make sure she never reached it.

He summoned twenty-five of his remaining fifty-four men and sent out five teams of five. Three teams would go by foot, beginning at Tingming Lake, the last known place the tracking device had sent out a signal. One team would travel north, one south, and the other west. The other two teams would journey by vehicle, scouring the major highways to see what they could uncover.

Yat-sen Xun fumed. She was very clever, this Kelly Morrison. But she had not been divinely chosen to succeed the greatest emperor in all of history. *He* had. Knowledge of the fire dragon had been entrusted to him for a reason. This American girl, and whoever she worked for, would not compromise the Mongol lineage. The sample and any information she had could not fall into the wrong hands.

54

Kells." Durango's voice murmured near the top of my head.

I opened my eyes and remembered where I was. The car had stopped.

"Sorry," Durango said, "just thought you might need something to eat."

I pushed myself up off the pillow, which turned out to have been Durango's bicep. "Sorry, was I…? Sorry," I blurted, my voice still thick with sleep.

"Quit apologizing," he laughed.

"Where are we?" I rubbed my eyes, blinked, and noticed Qing and Li weren't in the car.

"Myitkyina," he answered. "It's a big city close to the highway, but we took side roads to get here to avoid border patrol. This is a bazaar. There are heaps of other tourists here, so we'll blend in."

"Where's Qing and Li?"

"Li had to use the restroom. They're over there."

I could see the two of them walking away. They turned a corner and headed into the bazaar. Restrooms sounded good right about now.

We got out and stretched. The day was warm and bright, and I shielded my eyes with my hand to look around. We were in the middle of a line of cars in a large parking lot, which surrounded a series of low tents and kiosks. Throngs of people moved about the bazaar.

We delved into the colorful crowd and threaded our way between exotic booths. The pungent scent of human sweat tingled my nostrils. Music that sounded almost Chinese to me, with an oboe, drums, and gong, drifted overhead. Signs written in letters that all looked like circles hung above the various stalls.

"What time is it?" I asked. He checked his watch.

"Two."

"It's already two o'clock in the afternoon?"

"Yeah. You were tired."

"You must be tired, too."

"I slept yesterday, remember?"

He pointed to a row that looked like a chain of porta-potties. *Ugh.* Public restrooms in an underdeveloped country. Guess I had no choice. We headed over.

"By the way, my foot feels right as rain today, after your massage. Thanks for that," he said.

"Really? No soreness?"

"No. Did you think I'd be sore?"

"Yeah, for at least a day. Hmmm. Maybe it was well-stretched from all your acts of valor last night."

I stopped walking just across from the port-o-potties and touched him lightly on the arm. He stopped, too.

"Thank *you* for that."

"For what?" he cocked his head to the side, smiled politely, and knit his brows as if he had no idea what I was talking about.

I shook my head. "Aaaand… we're back to the shoveling." I started walking again. "You're going to turn into a snowman with all this shoveling, cowboy. Why do I even care?" I threw my hands up and walked into one of the women's restrooms.

It stank enough to make me nauseous, so I held my breath and did my business quickly. By a stroke of luck, someone had left anti-bacterial gel in the stall. I finished and almost jumped out to gulp "fresh" bazaar air.

Durango was nowhere in sight. Clothing stalls, produce stands, and jewelry booths lay in a dazzling array before me. I could feel my inner shopper clawing to be unleashed. Without money, however, that wasn't going to happen.

Something else caught my eye in the center of the square, though: a stand of computer stations. Keeping a lookout for Durango, Qing, or Li, I threaded my way through the crowd until I was in front of a row of terminals. Sure enough, it was the bazaar's version of an Internet café, with standing room only. I waited for an open terminal. A blond teenager in front of a monitor turned. Despite the line of people, he motioned for me to come forward.

"*Vill du använda detta?*" he asked.

I looked at him blankly. Was he speaking Norwegian? Finnish? Had all my time in Minnesota made me look Scandinavian?

"*Voulez-vous utiliser?*" he tried again, shifting to the more internationally-known language of *Français*, and pointing at the monitor.

"*Oui. Merci,*" I responded, nodding.

I stepped toward his computer. I couldn't believe my high school French had actually come in handy—in Burma, of all places. Mom would be proud. Or at least relieved.

He nodded back, departed, and I sidled up to the keyboard. The keys were damp and sticky from whatever the (Swedish?) teenager had been eating or handling, but twenty-nine minutes remained on the pre-paid meter. That was more than enough time. After everything else I'd been through, I could deal with sticky keys.

I Googled "Durango Trunk." The computer produced zero exact matches. Next, I tried "Trunk" and got way too many hits. *Duh!* But "Mackay Queensland Trunk" spat back a LinkedIn page for a Reginald Trunk. Curious, I pulled it up.

Assuming the photo of the man on the page had been taken recently, he looked as though he was in his late forties, and his hair was blond, where Durango's was brown. His cheeks were rounder than Durango's. But his smile was the same, and his blue eyes were strikingly similar. Reginald was the CEO of a produce company. His public profile didn't have any photos other than one of him, and his "contacts" list didn't have anyone close to the name Durango. But it was a start.

Durango's brother's name was Reginald. Maybe. Probably.

I glanced around. Still no sign of Durango, Qing, or Li. Or ninja assassin monks. The overhead music changed to a new song. I turned back to the screen. Deleting the history, I tried a new Google search: "Atomic elements." This led me to many pages with standard tables of periodic elements, but none had what I was looking for. Then I typed in "Cadmium 201" and found the following in a Wikipedia entry:

> "Cadmium 201, a derivative of Cadmium, is an unstable isotope that has only been manufactured in a few specialized laboratories worldwide. Because the process is difficult, costly, and time-consumptive, the production of Cadmium 201 was halted and is currently not being pursued.(Citation needed) Its primary application had been in weapons manufacturing, both chemical and explosive, though because of the difficulties, those weapons were never able to reach a level of mass production.
>
> Most explosives need extreme heat, shock, or friction to detonate. Cadmium 201 is an anomaly in this field because it requires such a low amount of heat, though the heat must be applied for an extended period.[1] This made it a wild card in the weapons of mass destruction category. (Additional sources needed)
>
> Cadmium 201, also sometimes called Cad-2, becomes extremely volatile at temperatures above 20°C (68°F), when it begins to degrade its half-life to a highly explosive state. Though not tested, it has been theorized that a single milligram of Cad-2, left to degrade over four days' time, could produce a hole 8-9 km in diameter and 300 m in depth, approximately the size of Crater Lake in Oregon, U.S.A.[2]"

My throat went dry.

Four days.

It had been three days since the box was removed from the refrigerator at the monastery. But even if the insulation in the box was enough to keep it cool, it had still been a day and a half since Durango had opened it. The box was an accident waiting to happen. A very big, hideously fatal accident.

My heart raced, and my breaths became shallow. I deleted the computer's history again, then nonchalantly backed away from the monitor and ducked back into the crowd. My feet couldn't carry me fast enough through the swarm of afternoon shoppers. The sun baked down on us all as though we were lamb shanks in a tandoori oven.

If it's this hot out here, what's it like inside the car with the Cad-2?!

My limbs seemed too heavy now for the speed I needed. I paced my steps back the way I'd come, only to find I'd gone the wrong way. Sweat beaded on my forehead and upper lip; it streamed in rivulets off my neck and down my chest. The sea of people began to swim.

No, Morrison, think! It's a square. If you keep walking in one direction, you'll come to the perimeter. Just go straight!

I forced myself forward, dragging my feet, keeping my eyes on the center of the lane, away from the congregations in front of the stalls. The lane grew longer and narrower. I passed a bunch of balloons that seemed to sway out as though they were going to clobber me. The tents over the stalls leaned. I staggered from the heat and the leaden weight of my own head. Pausing, I braced my hands on my knees, gasping.

How is no one else feeling this?

"Are you okay, miss?" a man's voice asked. He had an accent like Sandy and Khin.

"It's so hot!" I panted, fanning my face. "But I'll be fine. I just need to find my friends."

"Come, let's get you out of the heat." He put his arm around my back and half-lifted me down the row and toward a small canopy.

"Thank you, but I need to find my friends," I repeated, stumbling forward with the man's momentum.

"Your friends will be fine," he insisted. I hadn't even seen this man's face. Who was he?

I was too disoriented to resist when he gave me a slight shove, and I fell to my hands and knees through the canopy's shaded entry. The ground was a coarse, grasscloth rug. To my left was a bed.

"Oops, I guess you have had a little too much to drink," he giggled. He closed the flap behind us. The tent became dark, lit only by cracks of light from where its hem met the pavement.

"No, I didn't drink anything. I need to find my friends," I pleaded. I turned my head toward him and tried to get up. He grabbed my arms, pulled me up, and threw me onto the bed. My limbs weighed a ton as I tried to back-crawl to the edge of the bed, but the floor seemed so far away!

The man advanced. His face was extremely broad, with a black beard and mustache. He drew his lips back in an impossibly wide grin, showing crooked teeth. Shoving me onto my back, he grabbed my pants by the waist. He tugged impatiently, reaching for my belly to undo the drawstring.

"No," I protested weakly. This wasn't really happening. Not to me.

I closed my eyes. This *was* happening, and I had to try to stop it.

"*No!*" I said with as much strength as I could muster.

Opening my eyes, I slumped my leg out as hard as I could, panting with the effort of moving my overweight limbs. My foot made a solid connection with the man's gut.

"*Uuff!*" he cried. "You will pay for that, American bitch!"

He bent forward and slapped my face hard. Then he flicked aside my unbuttoned oxford and ripped my tank top down the center, exposing my bra. I tried to push him away, but my arms were impossible to lift and only cuffed him feebly. He snickered as he reached inside my bra, fondling my breasts with his awful, greedy hands. The room was spinning. My eyelids drooped. My pants were being tugged down.

Fight, Kelly! Fight!

Using every ounce of energy I had left, I took a deep breath and screamed as loud as I could: "*I… said… no!*"

The man tugged hard. The pants gave way past my hips, and he pushed them down to my ankles. *Noooo!* I tried to fight, but my body was useless. Tears leaked from my eyes. *Stop! No!* He grabbed my knees, opened my legs, and pulled me towards the edge of the bed. He let go of me for a second to quickly fumble with his pants. *No! Please no!*

Light flashed through the tent flap, and suddenly the dark canopy was magically filled with Durango's enormous, growling stature. His eyes were like lightning. He was the commando-Durango puzzle piece. And he was *very* angry. The man shrank in the corner, but before he could say anything, he became an unmoving heap on the ground.

And then I was in Durango's arms, cradled against his massive chest, being carried through sunlight. The bazaar disappeared behind us. We floated into the back seat of the SUV, and I heard Qing's voice.

"What happened?"

"Drive. Just drive," Durango answered. The engine purred in response.

"You're my Durango, no matter which piece of the puzzle you are," I whispered into his neck.

Blackness.

55

They got out of the car, stretched, and began to make their way through the bazaar toward the bathrooms. He tried to thank her for the foot massage from yesterday afternoon, but she turned it around on him, bringing up what had happened later that night.

"Thank *you* for that," she said.

She was doing it again, looking at him that way with her beautiful, soft, cocoa eyes. She knew what he'd done. On an objective plane, he'd killed two people. (Nearly three.) But the way she saw it, he'd gotten rid of bad guys and had saved children, which made him one of the good guys.

It erased any doubts he'd had about whether or not he should have done it. The respect and gratitude in her gorgeous smile lifted a bubble of pride inside him. He could live forever in her version of the world.

Of course, because the world was what it was, he couldn't admit any of these things out loud.

"For what?" he asked.

"Aaaand… we're back to the shoveling. You're going to turn into a snowman with all this shoveling, cowboy." Her disgust, as she stalked off toward the women's restrooms, was adorable. He headed into the bazaar to execute a new, quick mission.

It was a simple thing he wanted: to get a hole punched in the top of her oddly shaped coin, which he still had, and a chain to go with it. It turned out to be more difficult than he anticipated. One jeweler sent him to another, who sent him to another. No one seemed to have the right tool for the job. After five stalls, he gave up.

But then he couldn't find Kelly.

A woman who wasn't her emerged from the restroom. Kelly wasn't anywhere nearby. He figured she must have gone back to the car, but when he got to the parking lot, Qing and Li were waiting without her. He told himself he must have just missed her somewhere. She must have found something interesting to look at. Ducking back into the rows, he circled the bazaar in the opposite direction from how they'd originally entered, searching, scouring between the aisles, trying to ignore his growing sense that something was very wrong. He listened, straining to hear her voice through the shoppers and overhead music.

And then he heard it—weak, frustrated, terrified, yet still defiant:

"*I said no!*"

For the second time in twenty-four hours, panic augmented his heartbeat. He zeroed in on the closed canopy, two stalls up and to his right. Charging through the flap, he immediately assessed and confirmed what he'd heard. Only it was worse.

She lay slumped on a makeshift bed, her tank top ripped open, her breasts exposed above her bra, and her eyes glazed. She looked almost lifeless, except for the horror in her eyes and the tears streaming from them. Her pants were around her ankles, stopped by her shoes. A squat, hairy man stood at the foot of the bed, leering at her. He held his exposed dick in one hand, and the other hand reached for her shell-pink panties. Upon Durango's interruption, the man turned toward the doorway, scowled, and curled his lip in a snarl, like an animal being challenged over possession of its prey. Durango's lip curled in return.

The ice never made it into his veins.

Rage exploded in his mind, consuming everything. He strode forward and shoved his left palm under the man's neck. Lifting him off the ground by his jaw, he arced his arm down and slammed the man into the floor headfirst. While the man lay dazed, Durango sprang to a corner, seized a metal tent stake out of the asphalt, and drove it into the man's face.

"You'll never hurt another woman!"

The man screamed the horrible, inhuman squeal of animal reflexes protesting a death of exquisite pain. He clawed at his face. His body jerked and convulsed. Blood spurted up in the air and pooled on the floor beneath his head. The side of the tent sagged. Durango raised his foot and stomped on the man's neck, crushing his airway with his heel. Unable to breathe, the man stopped screaming. His arms fell to his sides. His body continued to twitch.

Seconds had passed. Durango whirled to Kelly. Her gaze was still unfocused. He swiftly pulled up her pants, lifted her bra back into place, and wrapped her oxford closed around her torso. Then he scooped her into his arms and rushed through the bazaar.

"You'll be okay now, sweetheart."

He hoped he was right.

They reached the car. Qing and Li were waiting outside. Qing's jaw dropped. "What happened?" he demanded. Li's eyes were wide with fear.

"Not out here." Durango shook his head. If they waited, they'd be detained and questioned.

Qing frowned but understood. He opened the back door, and Durango slid in, holding Kelly. Li jumped in the front. Qing stood at the open back door, waiting for an answer.

"Drive. Just drive," Durango growled at him.

Qing huffed in warning, jogged around to the driver's seat, and started the car. He pulled out of the parking lot and onto the highway.

Kelly whispered something that made his heart catch, though he wasn't sure he'd heard it correctly. It sounded like she'd called him "my Durango," and said something about puzzle pieces. He was about to ask her to repeat it. But then her head rolled back, and her entire body went limp.

"Kells? *Kelly?*"

She didn't respond. His heart hammered against his ribs, a combination of desperation and fury. *What did that monster do to you?*

He pressed two fingers against her carotid artery and turned his cheek to her nose.

"Oz! *What's wrong?*" Qing demanded.

Her skin pulsed against his fingers. Her breath warmed his cheek. He exhaled.

"She's unconscious," Durango answered.

"Why is she unconscious?" Qing pushed.

Durango pressed his lips together and met Qing's eyes in the rearview mirror. He was forced to admit it: "I don't know."

"What?!?"

Qing spun his head around from the driver's seat and bulged his eyes in anger. He quickly twisted back toward the front but re-met Durango's gaze with the same look in the rearview mirror.

"*Why* don't you know? *You* were supposed to be watching her! Didn't you understand that part? She saw a murder and was being chased by assassins across China! And she doesn't speak any other language! *You* were the one who convinced her to take this route through Myanmar! You promised me you'd be on your best behavior! But this morning, right after Sandy told us about those dead Thai men, Kelly lied about how she hurt her hand. And *then* she ran out of the room. I caught her crying. She wouldn't tell me why, but I knew it had something to do with you. I thought maybe you two had some sort of special bond going on, and I was going to stay out of it. But no more! If she doesn't wake up *exactly* the way she was before we went into that bazaar…!" Qing trailed off with one last fuming glare in the mirror. Durango bowed his head.

"You're right. This was entirely my fault. I should never have left her." His fingers remained on Kelly's neck. Her pulse was steady. He looked down at her, sleeping in his arms. He wished…

No. You don't get to have those thoughts, mate.

Strands of her dark brown hair had fallen across her pale face. He caressed them out of the way.

"Cow-li?"

Durango looked up. Li had twisted around and was kneeling, leaning on the console between the front seats. His lower lip quivered. The poor kid had just lost his mother. He didn't want to lose Kelly.

I don't want to lose her either, Li.

"She'll be okay," Durango told him in Mandarin. "She's just sleeping right now."

"Why?" Li asked. "What happened to her?"

Durango glanced at Qing. "I'm not sure," he replied to Li. "I left her alone when she went to the bathroom, but I took too long to come back to check on her. I think someone gave her something bad to eat or drink, and it made her fall asleep."

"Why do you think someone gave her something bad to eat or drink?" Qing asked sharply, in Mandarin, to include Li. "She didn't have any money. She couldn't have bought anything. And I didn't see any vendors with free samples. Besides, she's not stupid. She wouldn't take food from some random stranger."

Qing's brow furrowed in concern. He turned his head to glance back at Kelly. Just then, Durango shifted, and Kelly's oxford fell open, revealing her ripped tank top and exposing her bra. Qing's jaw dropped in horror. Durango quickly grabbed her shirt and pulled it closed.

"She wasn't alone when I found her," Durango growled in English.

"Put your seatbelt on, Li!" Qing said in Mandarin. He pushed the ten-year-old back into his seat, facing front. "What?" he cried in English. He rubbernecked between Kelly and the road. "Did she get…? Was she…?"

"Heard her call for help. Got there in the nick of time. Stopped the bastard."

The scene flashed through Durango's mind: the lecherous glare in the other man's eyes that had warned him to back off, and his own, instant surge of possessiveness in reply, even though he didn't get to think that way about her.

"Stopped him?" Qing demanded. "Does that explain the blood on your pants? What kind of a country have you brought us into, Oz?" Qing fumed a minute and checked back again. "How's she doing?"

She was so limp in his arms, but when he looked at her face, all he could see was the way her brown eyes turned golden in the sun and how her entire being lit up when she smiled. He loved her smile.

"She's still breathing. She's going to be okay. She *has* to be."

"She *has* to…? Oh, no, Oz. We had this conversation. She is not another one of your random good times."

"No," he whispered. "She's not."

"No," Qing shook his head. "This isn't happening. This is *not* happening. You know, I was going to introduce you two to each other at my wedding, but I've changed my mind. Nope, you don't get to meet her."

Qing's wedding. Durango hadn't even planned to be in town for it. He was going to cancel and go home. He *wouldn't* have met Kelly, except for the crazy collision of coincidences that had led her to land on his roof with a sample of Cadmium 201 on the very night that his last hope was dashed, and he was waiting to leave. They came from different countries. Different *worlds*. All things considered, they should never have met.

"Dude!" Qing went on. "Did you think it was *either* of our idea of a good time to go to *your* house—via *rooftop*, in the *rain*—the night she met you? No! It was an accident! An accident that was the result of desperation. I *never* would have come if I'd known *this* was going to happen to her! I'd have found someone *else* with a car!"

And yet…

Out of all the people Qing knew, he'd brought her to Durango. She'd come to *him.*

Durango gazed back down at Kelly in wonder. Was it possible?

He'd pulled her off his roof under a cloud of suspicion that night, but ever since that first time he'd looked into her eyes, his mind had been fighting against what his body and heart had been trying to tell him all along.

It was impossible not to have feelings for this beautiful, brave girl who saw the world through a prism of hope. And maybe "have feelings" for her was putting it lightly. But what if it didn't end there? What if the way she looked at him meant what he thought it did? What if *she* had feelings for *him*? Or at least *liked* him as much as he perceived? What if, somehow, she was *supposed* to be with him? She'd nearly been killed half a dozen times since he'd met her, but maybe he'd been *meant* to be there to *save* her.

What if he'd been forgiven for his past?

And maybe, if he could keep her safe… maybe he could keep her?

He hadn't done a very good job keeping her safe this time, though, had he? He'd gotten lucky that she'd been able to yell, and he'd been near enough to hear her. He'd have to do a much better job of it if… *Fuck*. Job.

The job.

What was he thinking? He had to finish the job first. As much as he'd love to whisk her away from everything, it would make them both wanted targets of his employer. No, he had to finish first, and he couldn't compromise on that. He had to turn the sample over. He had to get the rest of the information out of Kelly. And he absolutely, positively couldn't tell her anything more about himself until it was done.

56

I woke and barely registered that I was in a car before the wave of nausea hit out of nowhere. Someone held a bag underneath my doubled-over form, and I figured out I was in the SUV and that it was moving. Just then, the wave forcibly expelled itself from my system.

The engine slowed, and I felt the car move to the side of the road and stop. We were on a bridge.

I jumped out, ran to the guard rail, and leaned over. My initial round of sickness was followed by another, then another. Finally, I took a deep breath, gripping the railing for support.

It was dark out. Where *were* we? What time was it? Was I carsick? Durango handed me a bottle of water. I took in a mouthful, swished it around, and spat out the acrid vomit aftertaste.

"Sorry about that," I said. I wiped my face on my sleeve and noticed my shirt was buttoned over my tank top. *That's weird.* "When did I button my…?"

Suddenly I remembered the man on top of me, smacking me, tearing my tank top, snickering, groping me, pulling down my pants. I clutched my shirt over my breasts, and a startled cry escaped my throat. In horror and feeling completely exposed, I looked up at Durango. Then I began to shake all over. In one step, he closed the gap between us, enveloping me in his arms.

Another memory surfaced: Durango rescuing me into the sunshine. His scent. Safety.

"He… you…" I tried.

"Shh, don't try to talk yet," he murmured. I clutched his shirt.

"What happened?" I demanded, ignoring his instructions, though my voice still shook. He sighed and tightened his arms around me.

"Come on. We have to keep moving. We can talk in the car."

He ushered me back into the SUV. Qing started the engine again.

"Hi, Cow-li." Li twisted around from the front seat, his little brows knit with worry.

"Hi, Li," I tried to give him a reassuring grin and reached out to touch his cheek. Li shivered. "Yeah, my hands are cold. But that's normal for me." The corners of his mouth finally twisted up, and when he returned to facing-front, I allowed the smile to fall from my own face.

"Where are we?" I asked.

"We're on the Ledo Road. Still in Myanmar, though," Qing answered, frowning at me in the rearview mirror. He massaged the back of his neck for a second, then returned his eyes to the highway.

"What time is it?"

"Seven-thirty."

"And"—my tone had shot up an octave—"where did four and a half hours of my life go?"

"We're not sure," Durango said quietly. "Did you eat or drink anything?"

"No."

"Told you!" Qing reproached Durango. "She's not stupid. She wouldn't have done anything that dumb. This wasn't her fault." The way he said it, he'd already decided whose fault it was.

"Why don't you tell us everything you remember?" Durango suggested, ignoring Qing's attitude. He put his hand on my knee. "Start from when you last saw me."

My gaze drifted down, and my focus hazed over into reverie. "Well, I used the bathroom, and when I came out, you weren't there. I remember lots of stalls, lots of colors, and then I saw the computers. I went over to the Internet station in the middle of the bazaar. There was a blond boy, a teenager. He said something in Swedish or Norwegian or something, and I didn't understand him. But then he switched to French, and he asked if I wanted the terminal. I said yes, and there was time left on it, so I used it."

I looked up and focused on Durango's face as I remembered what I'd Googled. My gut instinct told me to skip that part. I took a sip from the water bottle and shifted back to remembering.

"I left to try to find the car. It was *so hot*, and I was sweating, but nobody else seemed to be. And my body felt heavy. Did I have heat stroke, maybe? And then this man came along and acted like he was going to help me, but I said no, I have to find my friends. But he just kind of steered me over to his tent, and…" My throat went dry. I didn't want to remember that part. I took another sip of water, swallowed hard, and then met Durango's gaze. "You saved me. Again."

"No, *you* saved you," he answered.

I knit my brows in question. Durango sighed.

"I think you were targeted for a transdermal sedative."

"A what?"

"Like a date rape drug, but instead of mixing it into food or drink, it's absorbed into the skin."

I thought about that. "There was a bottle of anti-bac gel in the bathroom?"

"That could've been it, though it's less likely since anyone could have used the bathroom. The blokes running a scheme like that wouldn't want to draw too much attention to themselves by having random people blacking out in public. They're better off if they can select and control their targets. I think it's more likely the computer keyboard you used was laced with it, and the teenager was a scout looking for an easy mark, like a single female. Did you touch anything else?"

"I don't think so. But now that you mention it, the keyboard was sticky. How did you find me?"

"Like I said, you saved yourself. You were able to yell loudly enough that I heard. I wouldn't have found you otherwise."

"You shouldn't have left her in the *first* place," Qing said, his temper rising.

"You're right," Durango agreed solemnly, "this was entirely my fault."

"You know, it's bad enough…!" Qing left his sentence unfinished and pounded the steering wheel.

"I know, I know," Durango nodded, somehow able to follow Qing's mysterious train of thought. He stared out the window, his hands like white-knuckled sledgehammers in his lap.

"By the way, Cow," Qing said, still sounding peeved, "when you used the computers, you didn't check your e-mail, did you?"

"What?" I asked, startled. "No."

I didn't want to go into this. I didn't want to admit to Durango that I'd looked him up and had found his brother. Somehow, I thought it might make him upset. And I couldn't talk about Cad-2 in front of Qing, though I needed to figure out a way to handle the box very soon. It had been two full days now since the box had been opened and—I counted—four days almost to the hour since it had been removed from refrigeration.

Qing's mood, however, was pissed, and that made him dogged.

"Okay," he sounded slightly relieved, "then what did you do on the computer?"

"I forgot."

"You forgot? Bullcrap. You're the world's worst liar. Answer!"

"Nothing important." I squirmed in my seat.

Durango turned his head, suddenly fully interested in me. His eyes narrowed. Intelligent, ambitious, *calculating*. He was daunting when he was like this.

"Qing's right. You're a terrible liar. What did you do on that computer? You might as well come clean."

"I Googled some… stuff," I mumbled.

"Like what?" Durango asked.

After a long pause, I answered. "You."

"Me?" he laughed, as though he knew his cyber footprint was invisible—at least to someone of my average tech-abilities. "Did you find anything?"

"Not exactly. But sort of."

His smile faded by a fraction. "What does 'sort of' mean?"

"Well, I couldn't find anything about you, but I think I found your brother, Reginald, right? Runs a fruit company? He looks a lot like you, even if he's not your brother."

"You have a brother, Oz?"

I looked up at the back of Qing's head and paused. How was it that I knew Durango had a brother and Qing hadn't? I mean, I knew he wasn't an open book, but he must have told his *friends* about his family, right? Unless my initial instincts were right, and I'd just done something wrong.

Slowly I turned back to study Durango's face. He showed no emotion at first, his face blank and unreadable. Finally, a slight hardness crept into his eyes, and a small knot formed at the back of his jaw. He was angry and upset. Knowing that I was the cause of it made my ribs sag with hollow sadness.

"Yeah, I have a brother," Durango spoke to Qing as though they were having a normal conversation. "Reg. Back home in Australia. Didn't I ever mention him?" His smile looked forced.

"I don't think so," Qing replied.

"Huh. Well, go on. What else did you do on the computer, Miss Morrison?"

The use of my surname reminded me of the other times he'd said it, when I'd thought maybe I was dreaming during the storm on Tingming Lake and the next day when we were hiking down the mountain. There had been affection in his tone then. But now, he seemed to use it as a way to remove himself from me, to be more distant, cold. At that point, I knew I couldn't tell them what else I'd found, even though, upon reflection, Qing probably deserved to know about the ticking time bomb in the back of our car.

"Nothing," I muttered, looking away out the window into the darkness.

"Kelly?" he warned.

Refusing to answer, I pressed my forehead against the cool glass, letting the fog of my breath on the window distract me from the hollow ache of knowing he didn't want me to really know him. The car slowed down and pulled over to the side of the road. It rolled to a stop. Ghastly florescent light filtered through the windows.

"What are you doing, mate?" Durango asked.

Qing got out and leaned back in. "The car needs fuel. She needs food," he pointed at me. "When's the last time you ate?"

"Yesterday," I mumbled.

"Okay, she *really* needs food, he needs to use the restroom—*again*," he pointed at Li, "and you two need to talk. Qing out." He stuck a pump in the side of the car, helped Li down, and the two of them walked inside the store, beneath another sign with circle-lettering. Yup, we were definitely still in Burma.

"All right, they're gone. Now, what else did you look up?"

"Why do you do that?" I asked bitterly.

"Do what?"

"Let me in, shut me out. Let me in, shut me out. Whenever I think I'm connecting with you, you turn around and act like it's a bad thing. I can't get a straight answer out of you, so I Googled you to learn more. Sorry. If this really is a game to you, and all you've been doing is buttering me up to get information, then happy birthday. Here it is:

"Nathaniel Richardson." The words came tumbling out. "That's the man I saw in the room with Yat-sen Xun. They were negotiating for Richardson to get the Cad-2 for whatever their original price was, 'plus three hundred.' At first, I thought that meant an additional three hundred million dollars, but then I thought maybe they wanted three hundred of whatever it is that Richardson's company produces. Richardson was worried about Pathos as a competitor, but Richardson said he had a manufacturing plant, and Pathos didn't. But then Richardson wanted proof, and that's probably where the box would have come in. Richardson got mad and said the words 'Cad-2', and that's when Yat-sen Xun had the translator killed. And then Ming made a sound to stop Li from digging in the fridge, Yat-sen Xun heard her, and Li and I have been running ever since." I took a deep breath. "And now I really need to go."

I pulled the door handle, but he grabbed my wrist and held me in the car. I whirled to face him. A strange light shone in his eyes.

"Why did you just tell me all of that?"

"Because it's what you wanted."

My secret was out; I knew there was no more reason for him to force himself to be around me. Emptiness expanded in my chest, gripping my ribcage, threatening to crush in upon itself.

"And what do *you* want?" he asked, still holding my arm.

I sighed. "I want to stop playing games. I can't live like that. I want to be and feel *for real*." I looked him straight in the eyes, gave a wry half-smile, and pulled away from him, out the door.

I returned the finished nozzle to the pump, walked around to the SUV's hatch, opened it, and dug around for the box and Li's smaller backpack. Durango came out and stood, watching me.

"Now what are you doing?" he asked.

One last thing for me to reveal. Not that it mattered anymore. He already had the big info.

"It turns out Cad-2 isn't just used for making weapons. It *is* a weapon, all by itself. This box is a ticking time bomb. That's the other thing I found out on the Internet today." I put the box in the smaller pack and zipped up the light load. "You can take Li and all of the information to safety now, but I have to get this thing out of here before it makes a five-mile crater."

"You think you're just going to go? Waltz away from here?"

"I have no choice. We had a four-day window, and it's almost up. If I don't go, Qing and Li and you and everyone else around us will be, I don't know, incinerated or whatever. This is something I can do that's *real*." I slammed the hatch closed.

"You know, four days is only a theory. They don't really know."

"You knew about that?"

"I've seen the Wikipedia entry before. I'm assuming that's what you read. Besides, the box is pretty well insulated."

"But you opened it!"

"That was two days ago. If the theory is correct, then we still have two more days left. That's plenty of time for our purposes. But I don't think they're right about it. I've heard convincing arguments that it can take longer. Plus, you know the other thing doesn't work like that."

"What other thing?"

"The part where I let you leave."

Hope surged inside me for a second, then: "Oh." I remembered his overdeveloped sense of military protocol and something he'd said about me having to testify to what I'd seen and heard. My heart sank back down. "Secondhand testimony is only hearsay, is that it? Sorry, it's going to have to do."

"No, not that." He stepped closer, towering over me, and my heart fluttered in my chest again.

"Stop," I begged. He was too close, and my pulse quickened.

"Stop what?"

"Don't do that." I looked away from him, down at the ground.

"Do what?" He lifted my chin until I made eye contact with him. His blue gaze was full of amused concern.

"Please don't make me think that you care," I whispered, my eyes filling. The empty void became palpable pain, burning a hole in my sternum. "It's not necessary."

I stepped back, right into the SUV. He placed his hands against the car on either side of my body, trapping me between his arms.

"But it is necessary," he whispered, lowering his body in until his massive chest was inches from my breast. His blue eyes shone with an intensity that electrified my pulse. "Because I *do* care."

He touched his lips to mine gently, as though asking a question. My lips parted on a small, inhale-gasp, and I kissed him back. And then he crushed me in a maddening embrace. Desire exploded in my mind. A ball of hope expanded in my chest. The backpack slid from my fingers to the ground. Tears rolled from my eyes, dissolving into joyous delirium. Our lips throbbed hungrily together, and he wrapped his arms around me, lifting me against his body. I threw my arms around his neck and wound my fingers into his hair, pulling him in even closer, our tongues caressing.

Suddenly he pulled his mouth away, set me back on the ground, and leaned his forehead against mine. "I'm sorry," he panted. "This is not… I'm not…."

He was doing it again, letting me in, then shutting me out. *Enough.* I cupped his cheeks in my hands until he looked at me.

"You're sorry?" I asked gently. "Do you want to take it back?"

"No!" Intensity returned to his eyes, a glint of light. "There's been no going back for me since the moment you fell into my arms: a muddy, wet girl with the heart of a lion! I have never felt like this before about anyone. Ever."

He brought his mouth to mine again. I responded with enthusiasm.

A pointed cough caught our attention, and we pulled apart. Qing stood a few feet away, a bag of food in one hand and his other hand over Li's eyes.

"I *knew* you two just needed to talk," he crowed, beaming. "And to think: I was going to wait to introduce you to each other at my wedding!"

I blushed, grinning back. A black sedan pulled into the gas station behind the SUV.

"Come on, we're taking up the only pump space." Qing removed his hand from Li's eyes and headed for the car.

Durango's body stiffened, his arms tightening around me. I looked up at him. He'd shifted into commando-mode. Puzzled, I followed his cold gaze to the sedan. Three doors began to swing open.

"Go!" he ordered.

57

Before I realized what was happening, Durango had hurled Li and me into the back seat, told Qing to take the front passenger seat, and sprinted around to the driver's side. A ping on the rear window shook the car. Then he was in the driver's seat, tossing Li's backpack over to Qing, locking the doors, and igniting the engine.

"They're shooting at us!" Qing yelled.

"Car's bulletproof," Durango grunted as he threw it into gear.

I twisted to look as two more pings hit us. A Chinese gunman in a suit and dark sunglasses aimed at us from behind the sedan's open passenger door. Somehow, despite his business attire, I knew he was a monk from Zhuang Dian. And despite Durango's bulletproof reassurance, I shrank down, instinctively capping my hand on top of Li's head.

Two more monks, also in suits—minus the sunglasses—ran up next to the SUV and tugged at its back-passenger doors. One of them held something that looked like a Dremel tool in his hand. *What the—?* They stared with black, soulless eyes. Li squirmed as close to me as he could.

Durango peeled out of the parking lot. The men leaped onto our moving vehicle like spidery acrobats. There was a thump and a scrape on the roof of the car, and suddenly one of them appeared upside down in the rear window. He held a small, whirring saw against the seam where the window met the car's frame and began cutting into the rubber. *No!* If they couldn't shoot through the window, they were going to take it off!

Durango swerved the car back and forth, but the man only swayed with the motion, undeterred.

The saw was already halfway across the top of the window. Durango put the car on cruise control and unrolled his window.

"Take the wheel," he told Qing.

He let go, and Qing reached over. Durango started to hoist himself out toward the roof when a bullet whizzed past, pinging the window frame just below Durango's back. Swearing, he threw himself back into the car. I turned and peeked over the seat to see the black sedan veering back into the lane behind us. The sunglass-wearing gunman hung out the passenger window, lowering his aim toward the tires.

"Fine, if that's how they want to play it," Durango said through his teeth.

He gunned the engine and reached under his seat, pulling out a semi-automatic pistol. Something zinged under the car. Steering with his knees for a second, Durango loaded a magazine in the grip and unlocked the safety.

Qing raised his eyebrows at the gun and gaped at me. I stared back, as stunned as he was.

"Hang on!" Durango called, shifting gears and spinning the steering wheel in one rapid movement.

Li and I were thrown sideways as the SUV whipped around in a one hundred eighty-degree turn. A monk went flying off the car's roof and down the mountainside, but saw-guy managed to hang on.

With barely a pause in the motion of the vehicle, Durango shifted into reverse and reaccelerated. A vicious grin curled his lips as he simultaneously navigated backward at a reckless speed and leveled the pistol out the window at the gunman. Facing the black sedan, I saw the gunman aim once more, just before his sunglasses split cleanly in two and a hole appeared in the middle of his head. His upper body slumped, and his gun bounced away off the side of the road. Too late, I thought to shield Li's eyes.

"*Shì a!*" the boy cheered with his fist in the air.

The sedan slowed while the driver reached over to pull the gunman's body back in the window. He began to speed back up. Durango spun the SUV back around.

Saw-guy was across the top of the rear window. He started down the side.

"*Now* take the wheel," Durango ordered Qing again. He re-set the cruise.

Qing leaned over and then arched his legs over the console to take the driver's seat. Durango pulled himself all the way out the window. I pressed my head against the side window and craned my neck upward, desperate to know what was happening, but I couldn't see the roof. Suddenly, Durango rolled down onto the hood of the car. He hung on to the side of the windshield, his fingers curled around the open driver's side window, and his body splayed diagonally across the hood as a warrior monk jumped next to him. The monk straddled Durango and grabbed his head. Saw-guy continued his assault on the rear window.

"No!" I screamed.

"Where did that one come from?" Qing yelled. "I thought there were only two of them up there!" He swerved the car side to side. The monk lost his footing but managed to hang on to Durango's neck. Durango's legs and torso were tossed so that his body slid over, parallel with the left side of the hood.

"Cow-li?" Li tugged on my shirt sleeve. Sick with terror, unable to pry my eyes away from Durango's face, I put my arm around Li and hugged him tightly.

Qing kept swerving the car. The monk hung on. Between the weight of the monk and the force of the swerves, Durango almost flew off the hood. He shot Qing a look of incredulity.

"Sorry!" Qing yelled, steadying the SUV.

The monk regained his balance and re-straddled Durango. Durango released the side of the windshield and slid down to grip the lip of the hood over the wipers. The monk clamped Durango's head. With one hand, Durango ripped off a wiper and swung his arm around, stabbing backward, deep into the ninja's side. As the monk instinctively grabbed his bleeding torso, Durango reached back and threw him off the car.

"Cow-li!" Li tugged my shirt urgently.

A loud crack and a whoosh of air rushed into the car. I whirled. Saw-guy flipped through the open window into the back of the SUV.

I screamed and pushed Li toward the front of the car, shoving him over the console. Li scrambled to the front passenger seat. Saw-guy lunged forward. I whipped backward, flattening my spine against the seat bed, and kicked up with both legs. My feet connected with his face, sending him reeling. But only for a second.

A red stream trickled from his nose as he reappeared over the seat. An angry sneer curled his lip. I twisted around, backed up against the console, and kicked at him again. This time he caught my foot.

"Kelly!" Qing yelled, helplessly twisting his attention between me and the road.

Saw-guy yanked me forward and jumped over the seat, crouching on top of me. I socked toward his face with my bandaged right fist. He caught that, too, squeezing my hand. Fireworks burst before my eyes as pain detonated from my palm, down my arm, and I cried out.

A massive arm snaked around his neck. He released my hand. Panting, the pain in my hand subsiding, I scrambled up to see Durango drag saw-guy back over the seat. He tossed saw-guy out the window onto the road, where he was run over by the black sedan right behind us.

The sedan kept coming. Once he'd flattened his associate, the driver accelerated, almost touching the SUV's rear bumper. Qing sped up more. Suddenly, the driver rolled down his window and pulled himself out to sit on the ledge, shouldering a rifle. He lowered the muzzle, aiming for the tires.

Durango was already ducked down in the rear, tossing backpacks and other gear aside. There was a loud thwack. The SUV lurched violently to the left, its rear tire impaired.

"You got run-flats on this thing?" Qing hollered.

"Too right!" Durango called back. "Keep going!"

He opened a suitcase. My jaw dropped to see large, black gun parts, which he began rapidly assembling. The SUV jerked left with another pop. Its rear sagged down, grating loudly as we went over bumps in the road. Durango took the jolts in stride, bouncing his knees like a horse jockey, and finished assembling the rifle.

"Swerve to the right!" he yelled. I watched him insert a red-tipped bullet into the chamber.

"I can't get over any farther!" Qing shouted. Large oak trees towered over the road, flanked by blooming rhododendron shrubs.

"Just get over and hold us there!"

Qing careened to the right. A salvo of rhododendron branches peppered the side windows. The SUV screeched as its undercarriage jogged over rocks and gravel. It sounded like the vehicle was going to come apart. The sedan driver hugged his body over the front of his windshield and aimed for our front tire. A bright red line flared from Durango's rifle, hitting the sedan's gas tank.

"Okay!" Durango roared.

He whirled his back to the orange fireball that burst from the sedan. Throwing his hand over the seat, he pushed my head down. The heat blast radiated into the open rear window. Qing powered back onto the road and shoved Li's face away from the blast as we gained distance from the explosion.

Durango moved his hand off my head. I peeked up over the edge, coming face-to-face with his dancing blue eyes.

"You okay?" he asked, shrugging out of his blue oxford. Its backside was browned and smelled like smoke. He tossed it aside.

"*Me*? Are *you* okay?"

"Yeah, we're fine up here," Qing piped in sarcastically.

"That was a bit of fun, wasn't it?" Durango joked, climbing over and plopping down next to me. To my relief, he didn't seem to have sustained any burns himself. He reached up and slapped Qing on the shoulder.

"Nice driving, mate!"

"Mad skills!" Li agreed. He hi-fived Qing and Durango.

I shook my head in disbelief.

"What?" Durango asked.

"You are *such* an adrenaline junkie!"

"When I have to be." He shrugged.

"Really? You don't need a daily dose of ninja assassins to be happy?"

He grinned wickedly and grabbed me around the waist. "This, from the girl who surfed backward down a rushing river and then scaled a mountain to take on—" He cut himself off with a quick glance at Qing. Qing didn't know I'd tried to rescue the children. But Qing was studying the instrument panel, not paying attention to us. Durango leaned in and said low in my ear, "If I'm an adrenaline junkie, then you're a proper kamikaze pilot!"

I giggled, reflecting on myself in this light.

The SUV listed sadly to port. The sedan driver had gotten off his last shot. He'd taken out our front driver's side tire, leaving us running essentially on one good tire and three oversized rims. Though the tires were designed for this kind of punishment, the vehicle bounced precariously low to the uneven ground.

"Hey, guys?" Qing said. "We're leaking oil."

No sooner had he said this than the engine began knocking. A few seconds later, we coasted to a stop. A hush settled in the air. Hills shrouded in trees rose before us. Behind us, a long shiny trail glowed iridescent in the moonlight.

58

Well, the good news is we're not far from India," Durango said. "The bad news is we have to walk."

We exited the SUV and began loading up with our backpacks. By the light of the car, Durango studied one of his maps.

"We're here," he explained, showing us a spot on the map where the road twisted close to the Indian border, then south, back into Burma, before curving northwest again for the crossover. "The easiest way for you two to go," he pointed at Qing and Li, "would be the road. You could cross easily, no questions asked. Unfortunately, Kelly and I can't. We have to go from here to here." He pointed diagonally from the first twist, southwest across the terrain, until his finger touched the road again, some distance inside the border.

"That's about two kilometers, right?" Qing asked. "That's not bad."

"It's 2K on paper. But this region is all hilly jungles, full of wild animals and thieves. It will take us a while, especially in the dark."

"You gonna bring your guns?"

"No. That's the last thing I want to have on us if we do run into thieves. Or worse, border patrol. But it's fine. I can leave them here. They're untraceable. So, what do you want to do, Qing-o? Split up? You two take the road? Or stick together and risk the perils of the jungle?"

He was leaving the decision to Qing, but I knew what I wanted. The road sounded so much safer, and I liked the idea of at least having Qing and Li farther away from the ticking bomb. While Qing was thinking, I moved the box from Li's backpack back to my own. *This stays with me, no matter what.*

Qing chewed his lip, frowning. "Let's stick together," he decided.

His eyes darted from Durango to me to Li to the back of the SUV and back to me. I knew that look. Something else was on Qing's mind.

"All right. Let's get a move on," Durango said.

We started off on a long, diagonal downslope into the black jungle. With the moon as our only source of light, we picked our way between massive oaks and around thick rhododendron underbrush. The jungle was alive with sound. I recognized monkey shrieks and gibbon howls from the night at Sandy's house. But when a guttural snarl rent the darkness, I gasped and froze.

"It's a leopard, Cow," Qing said calmly from in front of me. He led Li down the hill.

"He'll go after the monkeys and squirrels before us," Durango called from behind.

A few seconds later, something large landed with a soft plop, shaking the branches in the treetops just over my head. I ducked and jumped away from the tree.

"Flying fox," Qing called back.

"Or giant flying squirrel," Durango pointed out. Li stood erect, calmly navigating next to Qing.

I berated myself. *Quit being a baby, Morrison! If the ten-year-old isn't scared, you can suck it up, too.*

Straightening up, I forced myself to take deep breaths, concentrating on placing my feet and ignoring the ecological din. A few drops of rain began to fall, *pelt-pelt* on the overhead canopy of leaves, but the moon shone between the clouds. The others kept going, and I followed suit, determined not to be the cause of a delay.

Right foot, left foot, you can do this!

The sky opened up. It was still monsoon season. But I had gotten into The Zone.

Right foot, left foot, step over the roots, step around the bush…

The rain came even harder. We kept going. *Left, right. Left, right.* I didn't notice until too late that Qing had stopped. Right in front of a steep hill. Pressing onward, blinking water out of my eyes, I walked hard into Li.

My feet flew out in front of me. Li landed in my lap, Qing was dragged down with Li, and all three of us went sliding feet-first, screaming, down the muddy decline. I heard a muttered "Oh, fuck," and knew Durango had come after us. Li and Qing lost their handhold. I hugged my arms around Li.

Down, down we swooshed and veered with the curvature of the landscape, zinging under branches, a sloshing rush roaring in my ears. I was certain we were going to smack into a tree. One hundred feet… two hundred feet… three hundred feet…! We came to an abrupt splash and tumbled over sideways in tall grass and mud at the bottom of the ravine. Water churned around our waists and legs as the storm's runoff continued down the valley.

"Li! Are you okay?" I cried.

The boy began to giggle and stood up as Qing slipped down with a yell, landing behind us. He was followed by Durango, who somehow managed to skid his feet neatly in-between me and Qing, almost as though he'd figured out how to steer on the mudslide.

"Everyone good?" Durango called. Then he jumped up and helped me to my feet. "All right, Kells! Way to show that mountain who's boss!"

He whooped, grabbed me around the waist, and kissed me. I couldn't help but smile. I began to laugh.

"What's funny?" he asked.

"How do you manage to turn every death-defying moment into something fun?"

"There must be something wrong with me!" His grin was full of mischief, and he kissed me again in the rain. "Come on, let's get a move on!"

He released me and went to hoist Li up to the line of tree roots to begin the diagonal ascent on the other side of the valley. Still giggling, I glanced at Qing. I expected him to roll his eyes or say something sarcastic. Instead, he hung behind, his face serious.

The smile drained from my lips. I lingered back with him.

"What's wrong?"

"Kelly, I'm sorry, but..." He trailed off.

And he wasn't using my nickname.

"What? Spit it out!"

Durango and Li were gaining distance. Frustrated that my friend couldn't be happy for me, I began to hike after them. If Qing had something to say, he'd have to do it on the way.

"Look," he said as he caught up to me, "I don't want to alarm you, but I've been thinking. You know Oz's firearms? The Heckler & Koch USP and the F88S Austeyr rifle?" He kept his voice low, and I almost couldn't hear him with the rain.

"Uh, sure. Yeah?" I hadn't known what brands they were, but apparently, Qing was familiar with guns. I grabbed a tree root, stepped on a shrub, and pulled myself up, favoring my uninjured left hand.

"How did he get them?" He hauled himself up faster, so we were climbing side-by-side.

"I don't know. Probably when he was in the military?" I dropped my voice to Qing's low level.

"But he's not in the military anymore."

"And…?"

"And there's no way he'd have been able to get those past customs when he came into China."

"How do you know so much about guns and world militaries and stuff?"

"I'm a guy, and I game online." His tone suggested I'd missed an obvious connection.

"Okay, so he bought new guns?" I didn't see what was so difficult about all of this.

"Not legally, he didn't," Qing observed. "Foreigners are very heavily restricted on stuff like that in China. *Plus*, he said they're untraceable."

"So how do you think—?"

"I'm wondering what kind of people he knows."

I didn't like the implication Qing was making. "Well, I thought he knew *you*."

"He *does*. I mean, I *do* know him." Qing softened his tone, backpedaling. "And he seems like a great, standup guy—"

"And you have good instincts with people."

"Yes, usually I do. And he did just save all our lives. On the other hand, what kind of stuff is he involved in that he needs to drive a *bulletproof car*? Look, maybe I'm just being overprotective, not wanting you to get hurt. But, Cow," he touched my wrist, and I paused to look at him, "I'm beginning to wonder if he's really a tour guide."

"Don't be silly! He was in the military, and now he's a tour guide." I shrugged and started climbing again. "What else could it be?"

I'd seen him outdoors; he loved it; it was part of him. It made sense. Then again, why hadn't I been able to find anything about him on the Internet when I'd Googled him? Shouldn't he have had a website for his business or something? And then there was everything he knew about the box. He'd opened it, knew what it contained, and he'd questioned me about what I'd heard and seen in the room long before I'd actually told him. It was more than curiosity on his part.

"You two doing okay?" Durango's voice boomed down.

I exchanged pointed glances with Qing.

"We're coming!" I yelled, still looking at my friend. A knot grew in my stomach.

"What do I do now?" I whispered. "I'm already… he's already… I have feelings for him."

"Ask him about it," Qing said. "See if he can answer. You need to know what you're getting into before you get in any deeper."

"Before I get in any deeper?" I hissed. "Wait a minute! You were the one who said, 'you two need to talk,' back at the gas station! I thought you were all for this! Or are you the only one who is allowed to have a happy relationship?"

"That's not what I mean, Cow, and you know it! Oz is a great guy, and I've never seen him around *anyone* the way he is around you. I know I said that before, but, *man*! You didn't see the way he was when you were passed out, and we weren't sure what had happened to you. He kept making sure you were breathing, checking your pulse. And the way he looked at you! I think it literally might have killed him if you hadn't made it. That guy is in love with you."

I felt my heart leap. "You think so?" I asked softly, unable to hide my grin.

"Totally. But you need to know more about him before you go any further. Did you tell him how you feel about him?"

"Sort of."

I thought I'd made it pretty clear to Durango that I was into him. But I wasn't ready to say "those three words." I'd only ever said those words to a man once before. It wasn't even my boss, Percy Loomis, with whom I'd thought I'd been in love for a millisecond. It had been Craig all the way back in high school. And then, ever since he broke up with me the summer after senior year, I'd learned my lesson. It wasn't something I would let myself say easily again, even though it was precisely what I felt now.

"You're confusing me, Q," I said. "We were in trouble, so you brought us to him—this tour guide buddy of yours, whose real name you didn't even know—and one minute you think he's this cool commando who you totally trust, but the next minute he must be hanging out with shady company because he's got some guns? Which are okay for him to use to save our lives, just as long as I don't get too emotionally attached to him? Have I got it right?"

"When you say it that way, you make it sound like I'm crazy, or I invented all of this up."

I sighed. "Maybe you're just very stressed out with everything that's going on in your life. You're getting married in a week and a half, and here I've come and dragged you into a life-threatening trek across Asia. If you're crazy, I blame myself."

"Cow, this wasn't your fault. And you saved that little guy's life. That was a really good thing. He's a great kid; I've grown really attached to him. But I didn't make this up, either. I'm telling you, I sensed something was off with Oz the second he carried you back into the car this afternoon after the bazaar, and by the time we were in that high-speed death chase, I *knew* I wasn't looking at the same guy I thought I had brought us to."

I couldn't argue with that because I had already seen multiple sides of him—the Durango Puzzle.

The rain stopped abruptly, a faucet being shut off. Durango and Li had halted in the trees several yards upslope from Qing and me, waiting.

"One last thought," Qing said under his breath before we reached Durango. "Is it enough to know who someone is without knowing what they are?"

Qing pulled ahead of me for the last few feet. Lost in ponderance over his words, I didn't notice until I reached the others that we weren't alone.

59

"There's really no need for those, mate," Durango was saying.

He held Li behind him with one hand. I came up from behind a clump of large rhododendron bushes and saw a group of young males, three of whom held guns on Durango and Qing. In the post-rainstorm moonlight that filtered through the jungle, they looked barely older than teenagers.

The youths snapped their attention toward the bushes at my approach. One of them trained his gun nervously on me. My mouth went dry. I stopped and threw my palms up to show I was unarmed. The teen motioned for me to line up with Durango and Qing. I stepped forward, and Durango put his arm around my waist, pulling me so I was next to him.

"This isn't going to help your cause, mate," Durango said. His voice was calm. "We're just naturalists here to observe the local ecosystems. Put the guns down. Please."

"What do you know about our cause?" one of the youths sneered in Indian-accented English. He looked as though he was the oldest of the three, possibly nineteen or twenty.

"You're separatists, right? From Nagaland? A bit far north, though, aren't you?"

Durango moved his hand from my waist to my shoulder, giving me a reassuring squeeze.

"There are no boundaries to the lengths we will go to to see our sovereign rights restored," one of the younger teens answered. His voice quavered with uncertainty.

"My apologies," Durango replied politely. "I thought we'd come into Arunachal Pradesh." How could he be so composed in the face of these edgy, armed boys?

"This territory *should* be part of Nagaland!" the oldest one snarled. "As should parts of Assam and Manipur, where our people also dwell!"

While the youth was talking, Durango's fingers slid from my shoulders and rested on my backpack. It was as though he was afraid that one of these kids was going to pull the trigger—either accidentally or on purpose—and he was getting ready to push me out of the way. I remained motionless, with my right hip pressed against his side.

"But the Naga have fought and will continue to fight against those who oppress us," the youth continued. "An unjust government will not remain in power forever. We will have self-governance, and until then, we will refuse to recognize false borders! Under those rules, you are trespassing on our land unless you pay taxes."

"Look," Qing blurted out, "all we have is some food and stuff. We don't have any money."

"Then we will relieve you of your *food* and whatever *stuff* is in your bags," the oldest teen said.

"Oh, come on!" Qing protested. "Do you have any idea what—" He stopped short as one of the younger ones thrust his muzzle at his chest.

"No!" I gasped.

"Okay, okay, take it easy," Durango said. "You can have our bags." He moved Li out of the way and unstrapped his own pack, throwing it on the ground between the teens and us.

"What!?" Qing bugged his eyes at Durango. "You're going to let them get away with this? We have no money, and now they're going to take our food *and* our sleeping gear? What are we going to do?"

"Well, they're the ones with the guns," Durango pointed out.

I stared in disbelief, trying to catch Durango's eye. I couldn't give these kids the box! Had he forgotten about it? Or was he trying to make a Naga-thief crater?

Then he looked at me and ever-so-slightly… winked.

Trust me.

Surprised and doubtful, I removed my pack.

Qing unshouldered his, grumbling under his breath. I could barely make out what he was saying.

"Oh, sure, *they're* the ones with the guns. But does anyone listen to me when I say, 'let's take the guns?' No! That would be too obvious. Because then *we* would have been the ones with the guns! I should have stayed back at the..."

"Better our things than our lives, right, mate?" Durango slapped Qing on the back, drowning out anything else he was going to say.

"Hey, listen," Durango extended his hand to the second-oldest teen, "thanks for not shooting us."

The startled teen took Durango's hand without thinking and shook it. Durango clapped him on the shoulder. Then he shook the oldest one's hand, then the youngest, cuffing them on the shoulders, too, like good friends.

"There is a town, Taipi Duidam, about ten kilometers down the road, that way," the oldest teen said, pointing northwest. "Someone there will probably take pity on you."

The youths picked up our packs and marched off into the darkness. As they disappeared, I grabbed Durango's wrist.

"Why did you let me give that to them?" I panicked in a whisper.

"I didn't." He held up his hand. Moonlight glinted off the box's lacquered surface.

"How... how did you?" I took it from him in wonder.

"When they were talking."

"Oh, good," Qing said sourly. "We're stuck in the middle of Indo-Burmese nowhere, but we have the world's most wanted paperweight. Excellent."

"We're not exactly stuck anymore, either," Durango said. He held up his other hand: a cell phone. "Nicked this off the little guy. Come on. Let's get a taxi and blow this black stump." He started up the hill, checking for service.

I crammed the box into one of my lower cargo pockets. It was bulky, but it fit. I smiled and looked at Qing. He shook his head in a dubious exhale.

"Well, at least he's on our side," Qing muttered. He took Li's hand, and we started off.

60

Five minutes later, we heard Durango talking up ahead of us. He'd reached an area with service. And the road. There were no cars at this late hour. We headed west. After twenty minutes, a pair of yellow headlights grew larger and larger. I noticed the vehicle was being driven on the left side of the road. It slowed down. The driver rolled down his front passenger window and leaned over.

"Guwahati?"

"That's us!" Durango announced. We crossed the road. Durango pulled a wad of bills out of his pocket and handed it to the driver. "Half now?"

The driver nodded. "That is fine."

Qing opened the rear passenger door and climbed into the back seat, followed by Li. Muddy, exhausted, and relieved, I paused and turned to Durango.

"You're amazing," I sighed. "Thank you."

"It's almost over," he said gently, reaching to stroke a lock of hair behind my ear.

It's almost over! Really?

I climbed in next to Li. Durango shut my door and got in the front passenger seat. The driver made a U-turn and headed back the way he'd come.

It's almost over! Could it be true? Were Li and I finally about to be delivered to safety, our information placed in the correct hands, and the box destroyed? And Qing could get back on track with his wedding to Nori? And Durango…?

A lump rose in my throat as I considered the other implications of "it's almost over."

Despite the noisy, rattling motor, Qing and Li nodded off almost at once. Even Durango, directly in front of me, leaned back in his seat. Soon his breathing became even. But I, having either slept or been unconscious most of the day, watched out the left-side window as the nighttime landscape passed by.

We descended through the fertile land of the Brahmaputra River valley. Farmhouses flecked myriad pastures that appeared as silver and black squares under the moonlight. The sky was clear, now that the clouds had rained themselves out, but I noted that the starscape was broken by an earthly glow from the cities we passed, all of which seemed to have electricity. It was a stark contrast to Burma, just miles behind us. What a difference a border made!

After a while, the driver noticed I was awake. "We don't have many Australians out here," he commented over his shoulder. "Do you and your husband come here often?"

"Oh, we're not married," I answered in a hushed voice, glad for the darkness because I knew I was blushing. "And he's Australian. I'm not."

"Ah, you're American. And your other friend? And the little boy? They are Chinese?"

Crap! I was giving out too much information to a stranger—time for a few inventions.

"No," I replied, leaning forward to communicate more easily over the engine's rattle. "We're all three American."

Qing was more American than half the people in Minneapolis. He could pull it off any day. And Li? Well, if he woke up, hopefully, he'd stay quiet like he usually did.

"Oh," said the driver, sounding puzzled, "so this one is your husband?" He jerked his head toward Qing.

"No!" I laughed. "He's my friend. And this is his little brother." I indicated Li. "I'm not married." *Time to make a friend.* "I'm Suzie."

"Well hello, Suzie-who-is-not-married. I am Amalesh." He held his hand over his shoulder. I shook it.

"How about you, Amalesh? Are you married?" I'd already noticed the ring on his left hand.

Amalesh's face lit up, and for the next hour, he told me all about his wife, their five children, his wife's mother, grandmother, and the family's pet goat. I asked polite questions. I enjoyed his enthusiasm, which kept me from brooding. But after he'd exhausted his narrative, he came back to his original topic.

"So, you and he," he jerked his head toward Durango, "you are dating?"

"Um, not exactly."

"But you are in love, no?" Amalesh knit his brow at me in the rearview mirror.

Durango's profile looked almost regal in sleep. Even wet, dirty, and disheveled, all I could see was the adorable way his hair curled unruly when it was damp, the stern line his brow took when he was trying to protect me, the way his jaw knotted when he was upset, the deeper crease on the right side of his lips where his easy smile turned up a little bit more…

The hollow in his neck where I'd lain my head and inhaled his woodsy-sunshine scent.

The place on his cheeks where I'd placed my hands the first time we'd kissed.

I closed my eyes.

"Yes," I whispered. It was true for me, even if not for him.

The lump in my throat returned, threatening to constrict my airway. It was the first time I'd admitted it out loud, even though no one other than me, and possibly the cab driver, could have heard. Suddenly I felt even more vulnerable than when the monk had had his hands around my neck. I sat back, gritted my teeth, and stared at the landscape in silence again. *This is almost over.* With every mile that flew past, I could feel him slipping away, this man who I knew so well. And didn't really know at all.

He'd wanted the information I'd given him. Why? When this was done, when we'd reached our destination, where would he go? What would he do with the information? Why wouldn't he tell me more? And when we arrived where we were going, would I just get on a plane and go home and never see him again?

He said he'd never felt like this about anyone, but what did that mean? We came from such separate worlds, across oceans of difference. Though he'd hidden much of his identity from me, I knew he'd had experiences and had done things that dwarfed any of my achievements. How could he possibly remain interested in me, with my ordinary life?

We'd only known each other for a few days. True, they were a very full few days, but I knew that while I would never meet anyone close to his caliber—anyone who could possibly make me feel so *alive*—the same could not be said in reverse. He was a superhero; I was only a mortal.

The weight of anticipated loss sagged like a lead balloon in my breast. I shivered as a thousand pins pricked my fingers and toes. This was worse than the emptiness.

61

The sky was blue and bright with morning sun when we pulled up in front of a hotel hours later. We were in India: we'd made it. We were safe. The weight of living on the edge of life and death and having been hunted for the past four days began to lift. At the same time, the poignancy of *'it's almost over'* took its place. I knew in my head that he was right, it was almost over, but I didn't want it to be.

The car stopped. Qing stirred.

"What time is it?"

"It is seven-thirty in the morning," Amalesh replied.

Qing checked his watch. "Was there a time-zone change?"

"You Americans and your time zones! No, all of India is in one time zone. Very convenient for business. Although," he reflected, "I suppose it is not so convenient if you like to always rise with the sun, and you live all the way over in Mumbai, and it is winter."

"Well, China's in one time zone, too," Qing protested.

"Yes, there are a few countries like that," I threw in quickly. "But now, old buddy, we have to get you, your bubba, and me back home to the States."

I kicked Qing's foot. He sighed in an overly dramatic fashion. He understood, but he wasn't happy about lying.

"Yes, and I'm going to make sure that bubba and I sit far away from you on the plane. You *stink*." He woke Li and hustled the boy out of the car before Li could betray his true heritage.

Durango rolled his eyes. "They fight like this all the time," he said to Amalesh. "You'd swear they were actual siblings." He paid Amalesh and got out.

I pulled the handle to leave the cab. Before I exited, Amalesh turned to me.

"Miss Suzie, may I say that I have enjoyed making your acquaintance?"

"Thanks, Amalesh. Likewise." My smile was sincere.

"And I hope you can work out whatever differences are keeping you and him apart." The taxi driver indicated Durango.

I tried to smile again but wound up tensing my jaw instead. I swallowed hard, bit my lip, and got out.

I walked past a courtyard with lush foliage and into a seven-story marble- and glass-fronted building, following the others. A large, white marble Buddha sat atop a gigantic, black marble ball that spewed water in crystal-clear plumes in the foyer. Durango was already at the front desk checking us in.

"All right," he said, coming away from the desk, "I've got two suites ready, and room service should be up there with food by the time you get off the elevator." He handed a key card envelope to me and another one to Qing.

"You're not coming?" I asked.

"I've got some calls to make," he said. He hesitated, as though he was about to say something else, then changed his mind and just said, "I'll see you later." I couldn't read his tone and suddenly wondered if he meant we would actually see him later or if that had been a friendly signoff. *Goodbye?* My breath caught in my throat. He handed us each a wad of Indian currency. "Here, if you need anything."

I looked at the money in my hand in disbelief. It was already the beginning of the end, wasn't it? *It's almost over.* When I looked up, Durango was already out the hotel's front door. My inhale went shallow, creating a hollow feeling in my chest of surprise and hurt. He hadn't even said goodbye.

Qing waited by the elevator with Li. He studied me with a look that bordered on sympathy as I walked over, but he didn't say anything. I was grateful for the silence because I wasn't sure what had just happened, so I wasn't sure how I felt emotionally. Physically, though, I was suddenly very tired.

We went up to the seventh floor to find corner suites across the hall from each other. Qing's key led to a room with two luxurious-looking queen-sized beds. My room had a single, well-appointed king-sized one. Room service arrived just as we were letting ourselves into our respective suites, which was good timing because I'd decided on the short elevator ride that I needed sleep before I tried to process my emotions. I was probably being ridiculous because I was over-tired. I tipped the servers and then turned to Qing.

"My clock is all screwed up. I didn't sleep on the ride over. Think I'm going to shower and go to bed. How about you?"

"Showers, yes. Definitely. And I'm going to check in with Nori. Make sure the wedding's still on." He grimaced. "But did you see the pool downstairs? He did!" He pointed at Li. "We're going to have to pick up a couple of swim trunks from the hotel shop and try that thing out. It has a waterslide." Qing grinned, said something in Mandarin, and Li grinned back with a thumbs-up.

"Hey, that's awesome. Have fun!" Emotions were overwhelming me faster than I could deal with them. *Yes, definitely sleep.*

"Hey, come here, you." Qing leaned in and bear-hugged me. "We made it! It's over." I hugged him back fiercely, not wanting to give in to the trigger of his 'it's over' statement because of the obvious relief in my friend's voice. I didn't want to break down in front of anyone right now, let alone Qing, and ruin his good mood. I released my friend and kissed Li on top of his head. Then I pushed the cart into my room, locked the door, wolfed down some scrambled eggs and cantaloupe, and headed for the bathroom.

I stripped, leaving my muddy clothes on the floor, and picked the dirt-caked athletic tape off my bruised right hand. Though exhausted, a twenty-minute pulsating shower helped. I shaved my legs and blow-dried my hair for the first time in days. That alone was like therapy for my spirits and left me feeling a little better. Maybe my sadness really *was* the result of just being exhausted. Then I re-taped my hand and pulled the lacquered box from my cargo pants, shoving it under one of the bed pillows. Too tired to worry about anything else, I donned one of the plush bathrobes, drew the sun-blocking curtains shut, and crawled under the smooth, cream-colored satin sheets. I fell asleep almost instantly.

When I awoke, it was already three o'clock in the afternoon. I found that I was feeling much better. I smiled and rang Qing's room.

"Hey, how's it going?"

"Fine. We went swimming earlier. Then we ate lunch, and Li found this weird, Indian kids' show that he thinks is hilarious. Now we're getting ready to go back down to the pool. Wanna come?"

I laughed. "No, thank you! I've seen enough water the past few days to last me until next summer. Have you heard from Durango?"

"No. Why, have you?"

At Qing's answer, my good mood dissipated, and my heart felt heavy again, as though I hadn't just slept. "No. I was just wondering, that's all." My voice sounded weak. I ignored my shift in feelings, shook my head to clear it, and changed the subject. *Enough about me.* "Did you get ahold of Nori?"

"Um, yeah?" He seemed hesitant.

"Oh no, was it that bad?"

"Let's just say she's pretty mad at you."

"At me?"

"Well, I told her it was all your fault."

"You did not!"

"Yeah, I sort of did, just for now. I couldn't tell her the truth, really, could I? Not till I see her in person."

"Yeah, good point," I agreed. "And you're probably right about the rest of it, too. None of this would have happened if I hadn't butted in."

"Cow—!"

"Okay, okay. Have fun at the pool. Bye."

"Bye."

I hung up and stared at the phone.

Durango was gone.

My eyes threatened to fill. I didn't understand why the loss of this man who I'd only known for a few days was hitting me so hard. I also felt stupid for not having seen the extreme temporariness of our *thing*, whatever it was. How could I have let myself get so close to him in that short amount of time? I remembered something he'd said, back at Sandy's house: *Once I get you to safety, in India, you'll be free to do what you want.* Reflecting on that now, I realized he'd meant "free to do what I wanted" without him. He'd already known he was going to be out of the picture once we got here.

The lead balloon threatened to crush my heart. I pushed back against it.

Stay alive! He is not your only lifeline!

But I'd let myself fall in love with him. *How? Why?* And that kiss!

No! I would not let my blindness for some sweet-talking superhero-hunk ruin my life. But why had he kissed me like that, and said those *things*, if he'd known it was all for nothing?

My cheeks burned. Anger rose to replace my sadness, and the need to *do something* took over. I couldn't sit around and mope. In fact, now that we were safe and far away from people who wanted to kill us, I suddenly *really* wanted to go shopping. Retail therapy. But to do that, I'd need to have clothes to wear to actually leave the hotel. The thought of putting back on the ones I'd left in the bathroom made my skin feel unsanitary.

My eyes fell on the wad of bills on the desk. Maybe that was why Durango had left it, so we could get clothes.

But suddenly, that money felt like some sort of parting gift. I realized I was loath to touch what now felt like a pile of kiss-off cash. How could I have let myself even think this thing with him could go anywhere? *He* clearly hadn't. He hadn't even said goodbye!

A rebellious epiphany struck me: I was my own woman. Why did I have to rely on his money?

I was losing it. I needed to get out of here. In a blind, "do something" frenzy, I called my credit card company and explained that my card had either been stolen or I'd misplaced it. After confirming that it was really me, the company not only agreed to send a new card to the hotel by tomorrow but had cash wired to the front desk within the hour. Next, I called the hotel's boutique. After a brief discussion with a sales clerk, I asked them to send up a simple shorts-romper and sandals. When they arrived, I got dressed. Then I went to the front desk, collected my wired cash, and left for an afternoon of shopping.

62

One of the teams of his servants had called him from the road. They had found Kelly Morrison in Myanmar and were in pursuit. She was with a Chinese boy and man, neither of whom they'd gotten a good look at, and a big Caucasian man who was dressed like her—another American, most likely. Yat-sen Xun had smiled and waited for his team to call back with confirmation of their success. He worried she might have already delivered the box to her people, but his servants knew that they were to take precautions in the event that the box was still in her possession.

Nothing, however, prepared him for the next call he received seven hours later. It was from the Tatmadaw, the military police of Myanmar, inquiring about the bodies of five similarly-clothed men, found in various locations along the Ledo Road, and the charred remains of a vehicle registered to the Zhuang Dian Monastery.

For a second, Yat-sen Xun's heart stopped beating. She had defeated him again! How was this possible? *Who was Kelly Morrison?*

Numbly, he feigned ignorance and answered the Tatmadaw's questions. Then he hung up the phone, cleared his head, and focused on the option of last resort. He had avoided telling the government of the People's Republic about the substance. There was, however, someone he could contact who was well-connected to governments around the globe. This person would be able to locate Kelly Morrison. And this time Yat-sen Xun, himself, would make sure that she did not evade him.

"Do not worry, Ming," Yat-sen Xun said aloud. "When I bring my box home, I will also bring your son. And I will send him and Miss Kelly Morrison to you. Then you may tell her in person how she should not have involved him in this!"

63

He contacted his employer for the first time in four days and gave them an update on everything that had transpired.

He couldn't believe what she'd told him. The pieces that she knew were staggering. By rights, she should be dead by now. If anyone else learned that she knew these things, there would be more than just assassin monks and Chinese police after her.

Not to mention his own employer.

He'd have to negotiate carefully when he gave them the info. He wondered, though, why she'd told him all of it when she had, back at the petrol station, voluntarily. It was almost as though she'd *known* everything he needed to hear. As though, maybe, she was trying to help him end the job that much faster? His heart had begun to thump out of rhythm.

"And you have the sample now?" his employer asked.

"It's in a secure location."

"Excellent. So. Nathaniel Richardson and Alexander Pathos are both competing for this. Interesting. We'll have to keep an eye on them. Now, the team you've requested, I'm assuming you want…?"

"Yes."

"Fine. And this girl, Kelly Morrison, she's the one we did the background check on for you?"

"Yes."

"She's American, right?"

"Yeah?"

“That could be a problem. We might need her.”

“What for? I’ve just told you everything she knows. She’s been through enough!”

“Whoa! Getting a little testy there, Trunk. Is something else going on with you?”

“No, sir,” he responded, composing himself immediately. He’d been afraid of this, of them wanting her for more than just the info she had, which he’d just delivered. It frustrated him, but he needed to keep his cool so he would be allowed to finish the job. Otherwise, he wouldn’t be able to protect her from whoever else they sent.

“Fine. There’s a preliminary team in Dhaka that will be with you by the end of the day. The ones you requested will follow. You have a lot of work to do in the meantime. And, may I remind you that you are, as they say, still on the clock.”

“Yes, sir.”

64

It was well after eight and dark outside by the time I returned, my hands full of bags from the local stores. I knocked on Qing's door first. He answered, stifling a yawn. Maybe he needed a pick-me-up.

Which was exactly why I was here.

But first, I couldn't help asking, even though I was pretty sure what the answer would be:

"Hey, Q! I bought you some clothes!" I handed him two bags. "This one's for you, this one's for Li. Um, you haven't heard from Durango, have you? I picked a few things up for him, too." I tried to ignore the knots in my stomach as I asked.

"Wow, thanks, Cow. No, I haven't heard from him."

I'd figured as much. I'd prepared myself for the "getting over the bump in the road and moving on with life" stage that had happened the last few times I'd actually tried opening my heart to someone.

"Huh," I said as nonchalantly as I could. At least I hadn't said I loved him.

But I did still feel the need to do a getting-over-him/let-my-hair-down night out. It was either that or sit in my room eating ice cream and watching sad movies, but I was fresh out of ice cream. I looked at my best friend.

"Wanna hit the town?"

"You look nice, but—"

"Thanks! I'm not even dressed up yet. I found the cutest little outfit! Wait till you see it!"

"Your clock is really screwed up, Cow. Li's already asleep."

"So just you and me then?"

"Who's going to watch Li?"

Watch Li? "Oh. Right." I don't know how that part hadn't occurred to me. I deflated a little.

"By the way, thanks again," he said, looking in the bags. "Wow! You really did some damage out there. Looks like there's more than one outfit in here."

"Thought you'd like a selection."

"That was really thoughtful. Maybe we can all hook up tomorrow? I'm kind of tired tonight, too. That kid wore me out."

Qing smiled. But it was with a look of contentment I hadn't ever seen on my friend's face. I took a step back and studied him.

"Not that I don't appreciate that you thought of us," he added hastily.

We. Us. Qing had taken to Li in a way I couldn't have imagined. It was suddenly easy to picture a future where Qing, Nori, and Li were all together. I was happy for them, if that turned out to be the road they took. But Qing's new family vibe also somehow made me feel even more alone. I shook off the feeling.

Whatever.

"Okay. See you tomorrow. Good night." I breezily hugged him, gave him a kiss on the cheek, and returned to my room.

Sitting on the edge of the bed for a minute, I stared at the phone. No messages.

It's almost over.

It *was* over. He wasn't coming back. The lead balloon began to sink in my heart again.

I could order ice cream from room service?

No! I refused to let the lead balloon win. *Screw relationships!*

Jumping up, I undressed and put on new, light blue lace panties and a strapless, adhesive pushup bra. Then I donned a deep blue, low-backed, thigh-high halter dress that hugged my curves in all the right places and had looked killer on me in the store. This was followed by taupe strappy heels that totally showed off my legs. I finished with makeup—some bronzer, mascara, eyeliner, and lipstick. *Ha! I knew I could rock a nude lip!* Fluffing my hair, I grabbed my new purse. I opened it and shoved in my remaining cash, the tube of lipstick, my key card, and the box. The purse was just barely big enough. Then I left the room and descended the elevator to the first floor.

I made a pit stop at the hotel kitchen.

"Excuse me." I smiled at one of the sous chefs. "Could you please help me out? I have some medication that needs to be refrigerated."

The sous chef looked irritated, but he relented when I gave my best "pleeease?" look. He gave me a paper bag, told me to put my room number on it, and went to check on an order.

I did as instructed, put the box in the bag, and folded the top down. When the sous chef returned, he motioned with his arm. I followed him. We walked through a large, brightly lit kitchen with two separate commercial ranges. Ginger, cinnamon, mint, and cardamom scents wafted through the air. The sous chef led me to the left and around a dividing wall.

"We keep our surplus storage out here," he explained. "This way, you won't have to worry about one of the other chefs accidentally moving your medicine."

Three large freezer doors lined the back wall. He opened the middle one and walked in. I peeked inside. Huge blocks of butter, giant bags of potatoes, and different meats lined the shelves on the back and right. But on the left, the entire wall was taken up by boxes upon boxes of fireworks. I raised my brows at the fireworks and looked at the chef.

"Gandhi's birthday is coming up. It is a national holiday," he explained.

"Oh."

He held out his hand. I gave him the bag, and he set it on the top shelf, next to some butter. Then he shut the freezer.

I smiled brightly. "Thank you so much for all of your help."

"You are most welcome, Mademoiselle," he smiled back, bowing slightly.

He led me back out. I exited the kitchen, turned the corner, and walked down the long corridor toward the hotel's nightclub. It was nearly ten. I could hear music thumping, even from a distance. Ready to relieve my tension, I hurried between the bouncers. The inside was thronged with rhythmically pulsating bodies. Apparently, it was a popular hangout. The song was unfamiliar, but the beat worked for my purposes. So did the bar.

"Mojito, please!"

I pulsed my hips with the beat and slid onto a vacant seat as the bartender delivered my drink. Sliding several hundred Rupees across the counter, I quickly downed the mint and lime-infused drink, then signaled for another. A few moments later, as I took the first sip of the second cocktail, the effects of the first began to hit me. A group of Indian women wearing name badges on lanyards approached the bar, giggling.

"Ooh! That looks good!" one of the women said, pointing at my drink.

"Hey! I'll buy y'all a round!" I gushed. I signaled four more mojitos, then pointed to the women's name badges. "What are you here for?"

"Medical conference," another one answered. "How about you?"

"Just passing through on my way back home," I answered, smirking bitterly to myself.

"What happened to your hand?" another woman asked, pointed at my athletic tape bandage. The bartender delivered the other women's mojitos.

"Accidentally hit a brick wall a few nights ago." I started to grimace, then shook my head. No, I wouldn't go there with my thoughts. The women sipped their drinks and offered enthusiastic thank-yous. I pasted on a smile. "But tonight, I'm gettin' my girl on!" I held up my drink.

"Wooo!" the other women cheered, raising their glasses.

The song changed to one I knew. Drinks in hands, my new friends and I hit the floor.

The woofers were turned up to maximum capacity. Every punch of the bass vibrated through my bones. My feet and calves worked with the song, bouncing me right into the midst of the thrumming mass. I was assimilated into the mindless sea.

My second drink half-gone, I allowed the room to take on a blur. Bodies pressed up against me; I didn't care. I didn't want to feel anything but reckless relief. A few men copped a feel; I ignored them.

I let the spin in my brain lead my movements, numbing everything beyond immediate sensory overload. The crowd hemmed me in, tighter and tighter; I held my cocktail all the way in the air, above the pulsating mass that pushed up against me.

Don't think, just go with it. Forget everything else.

I closed my eyes, bent on oblivion.

"What are you doing?" a familiar voice said low in my ear.

My eyes popped open, and I whirled around. *Durango!* For a second, my heart skipped a beat. Then I remembered: he was leaving my life. I pushed the pain away.

"I'm gettin' my girl on! Wooo!" I hollered above the thumping din and took another sip. Nearby, the female doctors echoed me—"*Wooo!*"—and held up their drinks, too. I tried to think happy thoughts, like shopping.

"Hey," I said over-brightly, "I bought you some new clothes! Except…" I gave him the once-over for the first time, "you already have new clothes." He wore charcoal dress slacks and a crisp, white button-down with the collar open. Durango was already hot, in general, but right now, he looked corporate-hot, which was a whole new thing for me…

No. Do not *get any more emotionally invested, no matter how delicious he looks. He's just another guy passing through. Just treat him like any other guy. Okay, like any other really smoking-hot guy.*

"Wow! You look great!" I smiled coyly.

"Thanks. So do you." His voice was flat, his emotionless response like a slap. How perfunctory of him. My smile faded.

"How many of these have you had?" He pointed at my drink.

In a day—maybe less?—I would never see him again. He didn't get to be picky about my life anymore. His job was done. He had tour-guided me to India. I downed the rest of my drink before the balloon could sink any further. He wasn't going to ruin my party. I gave him my brightest grin.

"Only two! Come on! Let's get another round!"

I grabbed his hand and bounced my way through the crowd. Electricity flew through my fingertips, but I was beyond caring; it hurt too much, and I didn't want to hurt. Not tonight. Just a little break.

I let go of him, set my empty down on the bar, and waved for more. He caught my hand. His expression was hard to read, though his jaw was set.

"No thanks. I'm good. I think you're good, too."

Humph. What did it matter to *him*?

"Not yet I'm not."

I removed my hand from his grasp and turned to lean my back and elbows against the bar. I pretended to study the crowd while being acutely aware of Durango standing right there, waiting for me to turn and look at him. The swarm continued to pulse, my hips automatically gyrated with the music. Turning my head, I caught the bartender's eye and indicated another drink.

"Kelly, what's going on?"

"I told you, I'm gettin' my girl on!" I continued to casually survey everyone else in the club except Durango.

"Yeah, *wooo*, I got that. I mean with you. Did I do something?"

"Nnnope." *Yup. You're leaving me.* I turned my chin up stubbornly, watching the dancefloor.

"Okay, then what happened? What did I miss?"

"Nnnothin'. Every-thingsh fine." *Except that I'll never see you again.* I set my jaw, fighting my emotions. My next drink came. I turned to grab it, but he was faster. He slid it down the bar, out of my reach.

"Kelly." His tone was harder now. "Where is the box?"

"*What?*" I whirled on him.

"The box. I went to the room, and I couldn't find it. Where is it?"

The box. *That damn box!* That's what he wanted to talk about? Shock blazed into white rage. My whole body went stiff. Hot tears burned the edges of my eyes.

"Why do you want to know?" I asked through my teeth.

"Because I need it."

"Why?"

He paused. "I can't tell you that," he finally answered.

"Fine. The box is safe," I said calmly. Too calmly.

I wouldn't let the tears leak out. My nostrils flared with my exhalations, and I continued to stare at him, attempting to bore a hole into his soul.

But he could play that game, too. Leveling my gaze with his own icy-hard stare, he asked again.

"Good. Where… is… it?" He annunciated each syllable as though I was stupid.

"Safe," I replied, matching his tone, seeing him through an aquarium-haze.

Furious, bewildered devastation crashed my buzz. I had lost my desire to dance. I wanted to be away from here, away from *him.* I needed to be alone.

"Excuse me, miss, is this man bothering you?" A handsome, broad-shouldered British man put his hand on the bar, inserting himself between Durango and me.

"We're fine, thanks, mate," Durango snapped, his blue eyes not leaving my watered stare.

"I wasn't talking to you, *Aussie*," the Brit sneered over his shoulder. "I was speaking to the lady."

With a smile, he turned back to me. Durango's hands curled into fists.

I kept my eyes on Durango. Part of me wanted so badly to answer, "Yes!" and leave the bar with this man, to have him escort me back to my room, just so I'd know I could get there alone, without Durango.

But this was Durango. *Durango.* I knew deep down that no matter how angry I was with him, or he with me, that he would never, ever hurt me, no matter what. I knew this the same way I knew that on some level, Durango was in as much pain as I was.

And that's when the tears decided to come.

"No. Thank you," I squeaked. I met the Brit's amber gaze with sincere gratitude for his attempt at chivalry and touched him lightly on the hand. I fled the nightclub as the rivulets began to stream.

Out the door, down the hall, around the corner. My heart thumped against the chase that wasn't. He didn't follow me. The elevator came. I took it to the seventh floor. I removed my heels and ran barefoot back down the hall to my room. Then I shut the door, threw myself on the bed, and sobbed into my arms in the dark.

65

What the bloody hell was wrong with her? He stood at the bar, marinating in a strange mixture of anger and worry that only she seemed to be able to provoke in him, and he couldn't follow her to find out what was going on until he'd gotten rid of this asshole.

The Brit watched her go, then turned, puffing his chest out. He swaggered toward Durango and narrowed his eyes. A lanyard, like the ones on the women Kelly had been dancing with, dangled around his neck. *Clive Thornfield, pharmaceutical rep.* Figured. Cocky fucker. Clive seemed in a mood to pick a fight. Not that he wouldn't have loved to knock the man's block off. He was one of several who'd been ogling Kelly in that jaw-dropping dress she had on. But it would only draw attention, which would slow him down. It took him nearly thirty seconds to distract Clive by pretending to ignore him. Then the nong's attention went to one of the women Kelly had been dancing with, and Durango slipped out the door.

He still had to retrieve the box. It was what he tried to focus on as he boarded the elevator.

Unfortunately, the other thing he was trying *not* to think about was exactly where his mind wanted to go.

He'd been both relieved and disturbed to find her in the club. She hadn't been in the room upstairs, and Qing had had no idea where she'd gone after she'd come back from shopping—shopping? Today? Did she not understand that she was still being tracked by assassins?—so he'd worriedly started scouring the hotel. And there he'd found her, dancing in the middle of a throng of people, as though her life was no longer in danger. He was as mollified as he was miffed. But she was clearly already upset with him, and he had no idea why. And when he'd asked her, and she hadn't wanted to tell him, something inside him had gone all cold and controlling—all caveman, she'd probably say. Then, like an idiot, he'd demanded to know about the box rather than waiting for her to calm down. He'd also made her cry, and that unsettled him even more.

He reminded himself that she'd been through extraordinary circumstances over the past five days. Maybe it was all just too much for her.

Or maybe she'd decided she didn't feel the same way about him as he did about her.

He couldn't blame her. In addition to that small mountain of everything he hadn't been able to tell her about himself, which was a constant barrier between them, it might also be that she just wasn't that into him. He didn't want to think about that.

But he had to know.

The elevator stopped. He hoped she'd gone back to the room. His nerves jittered as he walked down the hall.

He held the key card above the slot in the door and hesitated.

He'd raced toward the blind corner, and now he was afraid to find out what was on the other side. This was it. Maybe he didn't have to know. Maybe he didn't want to know. Maybe he should just leave and not complicate things any further.

But the box.

Fuck.

He still had to do his job, which, unfortunately, still involved her. He swiped the key card, opened the door, and shut it quietly behind him. In the dim light cast from the bathroom's nightlight, he could see her, face down on the bed, sobbing.

It was too much. Forget the box. He had to try to comfort her. She might push him away, but at least he had to try.

Lifting her into his arms, he pulled her to his shoulder. She didn't resist. Instead, she clutched his shirt, her body shuddering with each breath. He stroked her back. Her skin was like silk, and there was so much of its smoothness beneath his fingers right now. Wafts of her scent taunted him the short distance that it took to get him into full arousal. It didn't matter. He would ignore his body's urges and hold her like this forever if she would let him.

But then she pulled away. She sat ramrod straight, and her eyes blazed. She looked furious.

His confusion and frustration returned. But something primal also rose inside him to counter her fury. Heat surged in his veins.

Electricity crackled in the space between them.

An angry growl escaped her throat. She began pounding his chest with her fists. He caught her wrists, stopping her. Her cheeks were flushed. She was breathing hard, and rage sparked in her eyes. Hope rose in him.

He kissed her forehead, her cheek. Her scent incited a riot in all of his functions, and she didn't stop him, didn't pull away. His breathing rose in unison to match the rapid rise and fall of her breasts. He grazed his teeth along her earlobe, tugging it, and brushed his lips down the side of her neck.

He pulled back. The electricity between them had only intensified.

Apparently, she felt it, too.

The blaze of fury, the pang of potential loss, were consumed in a rush of passion. Her mouth found his, desperate, eager. She wrenched her wrists out of his grasp and began rapidly undoing the buttons on his shirt. Pushing aside the fabric, she caressed his skin, laying her hand on the place where his heart hammered under his chest. His erection went rock-hard. He threw off his shirt.

He kissed her mouth, her neck, her throat, relishing the taste of her skin. He slid his hand from her waist, up the side of her dress, and caressed his thumb roughly over her breast. This elicited a low moan from her, which nearly sent him over the edge.

His fingers found her dress's clasp behind her neck, and she knelt up so he could undo it and peel it down, revealing a barely-there bra that cupped her gorgeous breasts. He kissed the upper mound of her left breast, diving his tongue down to the edge of the bra. She inhaled sharply and grabbed his shoulders. He yanked her dress down farther, past her perfect, unmarred stomach, past her hips and lacy blue bikini panties, kissing her skin as he went. Her hands moved to his head, pulling him closer. The scent of her arousal hit him, and he swelled painfully against his trousers. He kissed her through the panties, and she tightened her fingers in his hair. Bloody hell, at this rate, he might just take her *through* the clothes. But he was going to do this right.

He pulled away and rose up. He positioned his right hand on her back. Scooping under her right buttock with his left hand, he lowered her down onto the bed, tossing the dress aside. He glanced at the bra, assessed it—the sticky, self-adhesive kind—and deftly rolled it down and away. She gave a gasp of pleasure and gently raked her nails up his arms and down his back, trying to pull him closer. His hands curved around the length of her hips. He hooked her panties and slid them off her legs. She was gorgeous. A goddess. He was completely smitten.

She wrapped her calf up and around the fabric of his trousers, curling her leg around his thigh. Her fingers went for his belt. He helped her out, kissing her neck, kissing down between her breasts as he kicked off his trousers and underwear. She used her feet to help him get rid of them, and then she groaned and arched her back as he deliberately sucked and swirled his tongue around her right nipple before making his way back up to her neck. He kissed her lips and positioned himself, ready to drive his swollen cock straight into her clit. Shit, she was already wet. He was dying inside. This was it. It was *her*. Yes!

No, mate, you need to make sure.

He paused. He knew the voice in his head was right. He needed to make sure. With every ounce of willpower, he forced himself to wait one more second.

"Kells," he asked huskily, "are you sure this is what you want?"

66

His warm, bare chest grazed my erect nipples, and the sensation detonated even more small shockwaves of pleasure in my brain. Every inch of my body screamed for his skin to touch mine in every way imaginable. I heard myself moan, and I was just about to breathe out a *"yes!"* when an alternate, possible meaning in his words occurred to me. My eyes flew open.

"Wait," I whispered.

He froze his face an inch from mine, his breath warm on my cheeks. Oh, man, this was *exactly* what I wanted—but not like this.

"What I want is… so much more…" I trailed off softly.

"Then tell me what you do want," he whispered back. He kissed me again, and then his lips moved down, behind my jaw and just below my ear, and fire raced through my body. *Holy shit!* I'd never been kissed there before and had no idea it was even a hotspot. I almost lost my mind.

But this was Durango.

"*Mmmm*—wait, *no*," I forced out. "Stop."

He lifted his head, pushed up with his arms, and I slunk my legs out from underneath him, hating myself for stopping but knowing I couldn't do this to him. I rolled to the side of the bed and jumped to the floor, disgusted with myself. I couldn't find my bra, but I found my dress and panties in the dark and threw them on.

"What I want"—I exhaled hard, my nerve endings still flush and racing—"is for you to get what *you* want without having to resort to *this* to get it."

"Kells, what are you—?"

"Oh my gosh, I'm so sorry. This isn't right. You should never have had to… *ugh*. I'm so sorry!" I began feeling around on the floor.

"What are you doing?" He clicked on the side-table lamp.

"I'm looking for my purse. Here it is."

"No, *why* are you looking for your purse? What just happened?"

I hung my head, exhaling wearily, and raked my hand into my hair, holding my forehead against my palm.

"I'm giving you the box. You should never have thought you had to stoop to something like this. *Ugh!* I can't believe what I almost let you do to yourself. I'm so sorry. You didn't deserve that." Full of remorse, I looked up at him.

His blue eyes were full of confusion. He stood, pulled on his underwear, and crossed to within a few feet of me. I tried not to stare at his well-tented boxer briefs.

"Why are you getting the box right now?"

"Because you want it."

"No, I don't want it, actually—"

"But you said—!"

"That I needed it, yeah, but that doesn't mean I want it—wait." He frowned. "Did you think I was doing all of this just to get you to give me that thing? Are you… do you think you're *protecting* me? From *you*?"

"Well, from having to… you know…." I gestured toward the bed. "Because you should never, *ever* have to do that for anyone. Especially not me." I mumbled the last part and hung my head.

By the time I'd finished speaking, he'd already closed the gap between us, wrapped an arm around me, and was holding my chin up between his thumb and index finger.

"Aw, Kells. What part of how I feel about you do you not understand?"

My eyes stung, and I turned my head to the side.

"But you're leaving," I said softly.

"*That's* what that was all about in the club before? You're experiencing some sort of disconnect? Who said I was leaving?"

"Well, we're here, in Guwahati. That was the plan, right? Get Li and me here so I can get Li squared away, get the box in the right hands, and then I go back to the U.S., and you and Qing go back to China. Right?"

"Well, that *was* the plan. But that was before."

"Before what?"

"Before. I'm not sure when everything changed. But at some point between rafting up the Timing River and hauling you off the mountain above that house in Burma, I knew… well, I knew things were different. And by the time I'd lost you in the bazaar…" He shook his head, looked straight at me, and I knew he wasn't seeing anything about the way I looked. He was seeing *me*. "After I found you, I knew I wasn't going to let you walk away from me." He cupped my cheeks in his hands and kissed me gently.

Then he stopped.

"Unless that's not what you want?"

I took a deep breath. "I know exactly how I feel," I whispered, "and it terrifies me. I've never been so sure, and yet at the same time so unsure of anything as I am of you."

"I know you probably have a lot of questions about me, and I promise to answer everything as soon as I can. You just have to trust me on this."

"Durango," I said quietly, "I already do trust you. With my life. But trust goes two ways. The real question is do you trust *me*?"

He opened his mouth to answer and then closed it.

"I see your point: how it looks like I'm keeping things from you because I want to, and not because I absolutely, positively am not at liberty to share everything about me with you. Because I do want to, you know. I am desperate to tell you all about my life."

It was as though he was trying to convey his secrets to me telepathically through the piercing intensity in his eyes. He pulled me into a tight hug, sighing with his chin on my head.

"Can you hang on this crazy ride with me a little longer, Kells?" he whispered fiercely. "Please?"

The ache in his voice poured out through his entire being. I couldn't speak. Instead, I threw my arms around him, pressing my fingers into the warmth of his skin, pulling him in even closer. The lead balloon in my chest doubled in size as though I could carry his load with mine. But if a little extra time with him was all I had, I'd take it. Especially if it could somehow make him happy.

As terrified as I was of the swift, deep relationship we'd formed, I knew with perfect clarity that it was real. I might not know *what* he was, but I absolutely loved the *who*.

I sighed against his skin. Durango leaned down and nuzzled my neck.

"For the record, you look *extremely* sexy tonight," he murmured.

Desire stirred in my chest, pushing the lead balloon to the background.

"So before, that was all because you wanted to?"

"Are you crazy? It was all I could do not to rip your clothes off in that club." He trailed his lips lightly up the length of my neck, causing me to gasp in ecstasy and drop my purse. He paused to breathe in my ear, "Might have had to fight off some of your male fan club members, though."

"I have no idea what you're talking about." I kissed his chest up to his neck while my fingers trailed down his back to play with the waistband on his underwear.

"Of course, if this is how you shop, I'll get you more money." He found the clasp on my dress again. "Uh, Kells?"

"Mmm?" I traced my fingers around to the front of his underwear.

"Did you do *all* of this shopping today?" The far side of the room was still littered with bags, now illuminated by the bedside lamp.

"Mmm," I affirmed, leaving wet, languid kisses on his neck again. "Plus the stuff I got for Qing and Li." I tugged his waist, trying to lead him back to the bed, but his feet wouldn't move. I paused. "Did you want to see the stuff I got for you?" I asked politely. Shopping was the last thing on my mind right now.

"You got all of this stuff," he puzzled, ignoring my question, "and you still have all of that money left?" I followed his gaze to the wad of cash on the desk.

"I didn't use your money," I shrugged.

"Then what did you do?" His voice carried a strangely urgent tone.

"I used mine."

"What do you mean? How?"

"I called my credit card company and told them my card was lost," I shrugged. "They wired me cash, and they're getting me a new card tom—"

"You called your credit card company?" He grabbed my shoulders.

"Um… yeah…?"

"Okay, what time did you do that?" His fingers tightened.

"I don't know, like maybe three or four when I woke up. Why?"

"Because they're going to trace you, that's why!"

"But, no, it's okay," I tried to explain, "it's a *new* card."

"No," he shook his head, "it doesn't work that way! You're American! Your cards are tied to your social security numbers. They can still trace it!" He closed his eyes for a second, lost in thought, and when he opened them, he was my commando puzzle piece again. "We need to move you. Get your things together. I'm going to go get Qing and Li."

"Okay… uh, should I go get the box first?"

"You have to leave the room to get it? I thought it was in your purse! Where did you put it?"

"I told you it was safe. I had one of the chefs put it in the fridge down in the kitchen."

"You put the box containing Cadmium-201 in the hotel kitchen refrigerator!?"

"It's in a paper bag," I defended myself. "No one knows what it is."

"Why on *earth* would you do that!?"

"You know: to try to keep it cool. Or at the very least to not have it warm up any more than it already is until I can get it to the American embassy—"

"Whoa! Remember how I said I need it? Sorry, but it's going back to my government."

"What? Why would we give it to your government? I'm American. And so is Nathaniel Richardson."

"But I'm Australian."

"And? You're not in the military anymore. You don't have to answer to your government."

"*Ugh!*" he exploded. "Kells, we're going to have to argue about this later. Right now, we need—!"

"—to get a move on!" I finished with him, to his apparent surprise. A grin broke on my face; I couldn't help it. This was my Durango, in his element.

"I love you," I sighed.

I'd never said those words to him before, and I hadn't intended to now, but they just slipped out. And it was true.

Durango's jaw dropped, and he froze.

67

She was smiling at him. Her cocoa eyes shining, her entire face radiant. Innocent, genuine, stubborn, beautiful girl with the heart of a lion. The woman he loved more than anything. Who knew him better than anyone.

And she'd just said it.

The words had passed her lips with no provocation, no resistance, no backtracking.

She loved him.

He reached the blind corner, and a bomb went off. His heart swelled to bursting. She was his. He got to keep her. Durango Trunk would never be the same.

He crushed her in his arms.

"I'm the one who has never done anything to deserve anyone as wonderful as you!" he breathed. He drew his head back. "We *will* get out of this, and I *will* tell you everything!"

The warmth in her brown eyes deepened to an emotion that almost knocked him over. Then she reached up and placed her palms on his cheeks.

"You're my Durango, no matter which piece of the puzzle you are," she whispered back.

She'd said that to him once before when they were leaving the bazaar, but he wasn't sure he'd heard it right. And now, he still had no idea what it meant, but it just about sent him over the edge when she called him *hers*. It was all he could do not to take her in his arms and run away with her on the spot.

But she was in danger, and so were Qing and Li. Any running they were going to do would have to be as a foursome for the moment.

68

We kissed again before he tore himself away, and I watched the subtle shift as he went back to commando-mode. He threw on his pants. I hooked my strappy sandals with my fingers, grabbed my purse, and turned to leave the room so I could go to the kitchen. In a flash, he'd crossed the distance and put his hand on top of mine at the doorknob.

"I'll go. Just tell me where it is." He slipped his arms in his shirtsleeves.

"It's in the one fridge that's kind of farther back…?" I held my hands at angles, trying to create an air diagram. "Sorry. It's a big kitchen. I kind of need to show you."

"All right, come on," he agreed reluctantly.

We padded barefoot down the hall to the elevator. The first one arrived, and we stepped into the empty car. Durango punched the button for the first floor and began pulling on his socks and shoes. Before the doors shut, a ding sounded from the hall, signaling the arrival of the other elevator. Just as our doors were closing, I caught a glimpse of someone exiting the other elevator and starting down the hall in the direction of my room.

The long, black robe.

The long, gray, grizzled beard.

Fear convulsed through my system. I clapped a hand over my mouth and recoiled against the elevator wall. Even though he hadn't been facing me, I recognized his profile from the side, just as I'd recognized his reflection in the long, glossy tabletop at the monastery five days ago.

My elevator door closed.

"What is it?" Durango demanded. The elevator started to descend.

"That was Yat-sen Xun!" I whispered, pointing at the closed door. "He's here! He just missed us! Or, *we* just missed *him*!" Then I remembered: "Qing and Li!"

Commando-Durango punched the button for the sixth floor. The elevator stopped one floor down.

"I'll go," Durango said. "You stay right here." He disappeared around the corner to the stairwell.

69

D*id he mean "right here" on the sixth floor or "right-here" right here?*

While I was thinking it through, the doors closed, and the elevator began to descend since he'd already punched the first-floor button. Decision made. I prayed Durango had already made it to Qing and Li and that they were safe—all three of them.

On the second floor, three Indian men in suits got on. They wore medical conference lanyards like the women I'd met earlier. Two of them nodded politely and re-punched the already-lit first-floor button. The doors closed, and the elevator continued its descent. The third man turned toward me, grinning broadly.

"Hello! Are you going down, also?"

"Oh, er, yes." *Obviously.* I wondered whether they thought it was weird that I was carrying my shoes. I put them on.

"There's a wonderful club down there," the man continued. He winked. *Winked!*

I blinked in disbelief before recovering. "Thanks. Maybe I'll check it out later."

We reached the first floor. A well-dressed Caucasian man waited at the elevator doors. I needed to get back to Durango. (*"Stay right here!"*) But I was afraid of drawing too much attention by riding the elevator without pushing buttons, so I followed the three Indian men out into the lobby. The Caucasian man did a double-take and followed me.

Oh, great! Of all the times! I never got hit on in my life, and they pick tonight *to start? It's because I'm not wearing a bra, and somehow they can tell, isn't it? Perfect.*

Trailing the other three men down the hall, I ducked into the club after them. The Indians went to the bar.

I shimmied through the crowd and found a spot at a table across the floor from where I could watch the club's door. The Caucasian man entered, and, rather than heading for the bar, he scoured the crowd, spotted me, and made a beeline. At this point, there was nowhere I could go, so I sat, watching his tall, blond approach. He was attractive, maybe forty-ish, with serious, steel-gray eyes. The sooner I could get rid of him, the sooner I could get out of there and back to Durango.

But as the man got closer, his expression remained stoic. He didn't crack a smile. I began to question whether he was about to drop a pick-up line on me or if this was something else.

"Miss Morrison?" he said over the music.

I froze. It wasn't just that he knew my name, but the fact that his accent was so familiar. He was Australian. When I didn't answer, he continued.

"I work with a man whom I believe you've met. Or at least, I used to work with him." His tone was not entirely unpleasant. "He's gone by several aliases, most recently by the name Oswald Kelso."

Who?

The man paused for a fraction of a second, studied my expression, and then held up a photo on his phone. "His real name is Durango Trunk."

Durango has aliases? Then it registered: *Oz*. That was what Qing had called him, and I had assumed it was a nickname for Durango being from Australia. But maybe it had been short for Oswald. Oswald Kelso. "You worked with Durango?"

"Yes," he nodded. "My name is Colin MacAyers." He held out his hand.

Still stunned, I shook it.

"You're a tour guide?" I ventured weakly.

"Surely you know by now that Trunk is not a tour guide," he scoffed. He sat down across from me.

Not sure whether I should be talking to this man, I glanced around. No one was paying us any attention.

"I… I had a suspicion," I conceded.

"I'm an officer with the ASIS. The Australian Secret Intelligence Service. It's comparable to your CIA."

I processed this for a moment. “You’re a spy?”

MacAyers shrugged. “Intelligence agent. And so was Trunk.”

More processing. The pieces of the Durango puzzle began to shift around in my brain. But….

“Was?”

“He retired about twelve months ago, and we believe he’s been contracting his services out to a well-funded terrorist organization. He had possibly even begun this contract before leaving his post. We’re not sure what damages have been done back in Canberra.”

I didn’t know what or where *Can-bruh* was—maybe he’d said Canada? Which wouldn’t make sense—but…!

“Wait a minute. You think Durango is working for *terrorists*?” I shook my head. “No. There’s no way.”

“‘Think’ is too light of a word,” MacAyers frowned. “We have compelling evidence that he is. And at this point, we’re fairly certain they’re trying to get their hands on next-gen WMDs.”

The puzzle whirled around. This guy must be talking about a different Durango Trunk. Could there be more than one person in this world with that name?

From Australia?

The spy part actually made sense. Durango was so intelligent, capable. He knew things that regular people just wouldn’t have known. Like everything he knew about Cad-2.

But *terrorists*?

MacAyers kept talking, and as much as I didn’t want to hear what he had to say, I couldn’t turn away.

“There is a rare Cadmium derivative that has been discovered on the grounds of the Zhuang Dian Monastery. The monks have been attempting to broker a deal for its sale to help fund their order. If handled correctly, this element could be an incredible energy source. However, because one of its unique applications is catastrophic weaponry, they’ve been trying to keep news about their discovery secret. They are afraid of making a bad sale and having the Cad-2 fall into the wrong hands. If an unethical person were to get hold of, say, a sample of this stuff, they could use it to leverage pressure against the monks and force a sale.”

"How could having a sample of Cad-2—?" I began.

"For one thing, the person could threaten to tell the Chinese government about the discovery of the plume," MacAyers explained. "The Chinese government doesn't yet know. If they did, they would come in and take over. The monastery wouldn't see a *yuan*."

The box. Durango could have taken it from me at any time if that's what he'd wanted, but he'd let me carry it because that's what *I'd* wanted. MacAyers couldn't be right about this. Durango couldn't be involved with brokering a deal for terrorists. He was one of the good guys.

But doubt crept in, a sliver of a voice in the back of my mind: even though I'd carried it, he was getting it in the end, wasn't he? He'd said that it had to go to his government. Sure, at first, I'd resisted. But by now, I'd practically thrown it at him, hadn't I? What if this man with the steel-gray eyes was right?

Suddenly, MacAyers's whole stance changed. He sat straight up and leveled an accusatory glare at me.

"Miss Morrison, we know that you were a guest at Zhuang Dian's retreat program. You left early—fled the monastery's grounds as we understand it, leaving all your possessions behind—at the same time that the son of one of the monastery's workers went missing. You are wanted by the Chinese police for kidnapping that young boy and also for the theft of one of the monastery's priceless artifacts."

My heart raced. I couldn't breathe. All I could see was the stern face of Colin MacAyers. The rest of the club vanished against the gravity of the immediate trouble I was in.

I knew the Chinese police wanted me for kidnapping. Li was traveling with me, and I wasn't his parent or guardian. It wouldn't look good from a Chinese police perspective, but they didn't know the whole story. And apparently, in their desperation to get the Cad-2 sample back, the monks must have also said I'd stolen a "priceless artifact." I knew the police wouldn't have known the real story on that, either.

On the other hand, maybe *I* didn't know the whole story myself. Maybe the box *was* a priceless artifact, despite what was inside it. *Crap!* What if I really *was* traveling with not only a kid who wasn't mine but also a piece of stolen, historical art?

Somehow the legalities of my situation hadn't seemed so bad when I was surrounded by people who didn't speak my language. But MacAyers did. To be accused by a westerner—someone who spoke my own language and had a similar system of government—made everything so much more real. And so much worse.

And not only was he saying these things about me, but he was saying awful things about the man who'd saved my life, the man I'd fallen in love with…!

The Durango puzzle whirled in my head. But the danger I had been in before I'd even met Durango was hemming me into a corner. *India was supposed to be safe! I was supposed to be able to get from here to an American embassy where people would listen to me!*

MacAyers leaned in, his brow furrowed in sympathy. "Ms. Morrison, you have no criminal record. *We* do not believe you are some sort of art thief with underworld connections. Similarly, *we* do not believe you are involved in any child trafficking ploy."

We *do not believe.*

Meaning someone else *could* believe it. Someone could make a case for it. I remembered the seedier side of Burma. My stomach churned at the thought of being lumped in with people like that.

The club music thumped along. The energetic crowd was a surreal contrast to the conversation I was having—the nightmare of how I was being told the world could perceive my actions. All I'd meant to do was help Li!

MacAyers continued. His tone became compassionate. "My people are willing to think you somehow got it into your head that you were acting to protect this youngster. Am I correct?"

I nodded vigorously. "Yes!"

"Tell me what happened."

"I was just trying to help Li find his mother," I blurted out, desperate to have someone in a position of authority see my side of things. "But they *killed* someone! I saw it happen!"

MacAyers narrowed his eyes. "Describe exactly what you saw," he said.

"There was a translator at a long conference table at the monastery. At one point, Yat-sen Xun got angry, and he nodded at one of the other monks, and the monk came up behind the translator, and he twisted his neck, like this," I demonstrated in the air with my hands, "and then the translator was dead! And then he killed Li's mother, and now a bunch of ninja monks have been trying to kill me, and Li, too! All because we heard them talking about Cad-2!"

The words came out in a rush. I couldn't stop them. Tears began running down my cheeks, so great was my relief at finally being able to talk about what had happened. I took stuttered gulps of air to fend off having to ugly-cry in front of this stranger.

"Whoa! Slow down." MacAyers held his hand up. "You saw them kill the boy's mother?" He seemed stoically unimpressed by my emotional display, maybe even offended by it. The thought unnerved and embarrassed me. I tried to get my shit together.

"Well, no," I admitted, regaining some composure and wiping away the wetness with the backs of my fingers. "We were running out the door by then, Li and me."

"Miss Morrison, the boy's mother isn't dead."

Silence.

Dead air.

My world stopped. Despite the pumping beat around me, all I could hear was the rush of blood in my own ears.

"What?"

"She's alive," he repeated, "and so is the translator. True, they knocked him out temporarily, but it was because they suspected he had other motivations. You can't actually kill someone that way, you know. You can just temporarily immobilize them. I suspect those 'ninja monks' you're referring to were trying to do the same thing to you? Probably because they thought you'd kidnapped the child, and they were trying to save him. I mean, for pity's sake, if actual *ninjas* wanted you dead, you'd be dead by now. Right? Think back to what you saw. Does any of this make sense?"

I sat agape, the scene blurring through again in my mind: the limp translator, the look in Ming's eyes, the assassin at the hotel who ultimately *hadn't* killed me, the ones who had jumped on the car but *hadn't* killed either me or Li. Was it possible?

"I… but I was so *sure*. The translator just slumped over, and…" I trailed off. Had I really misunderstood *everything*?

MacAyers continued: "They're being very careful about this discovery, as I said. In the meantime, the mother wants her little boy back, the monastery wants its artifact back, and I want Trunk. Can you help me out? If you do this, no charges will be filed against you."

"Ming… is… alive!" I breathed.

MacAyers nodded.

I clapped my hand to my mouth, sick with horror in my gut, thinking of everything I'd needlessly put Li through. And Qing! I had usurped his life for a colossal *mistake*. All those times we could have all been caught or *killed*. We could have been run off the road on a Burmese highway or shot by the Nagaland teenagers. We could have been caught by any number of police. Or we could have been destitute in the middle of nowhere.

Except for Durango. He'd been the reason we'd survived.

"I can see you realize this was all an error, Miss Morrison. But now you have a chance to make it all right with no time spent in one of those dungeons the Chinese call a prison. Where are Trunk, the boy, and the box?"

Holy crap! But…

"You're wrong about Durango, Mister—er, Officer MacAyers. He's been protecting me. Saving my life *and* Li's. He's not working for any terrorists."

MacAyers chuckled grimly.

"Ah, he's gotten to you, hasn't he? I forgot about that effect he has on women. They think he's all dashing and dreamy, and they get all doe-eyed around him. It's nice to know my friend hasn't lost his touch after all this time." MacAyers's tone held an edge of bitterness. "Has he worked his charms on you, too? Made you think he's some sort of hero? Are you in love with him yet? He fancies himself quite the lothario. You should hear some of the stories he would tell at office parties. He's rooted more females than a champion stallion on a stud farm."

My jaw dropped. I gaped at Officer MacAyers. His words had the same effect as if he'd reached his arm down my throat and manually squeezed out the air. It was like coming in to work that day in February, a year and a half ago. I was speechless, with the same sick feeling growing in my gut, but with the new, aching emptiness reaching its tentacles back around my ribcage.

Everything Durango had said.

Everything I'd felt.

Had I been mistaken about all of that, too? According to MacAyers, Durango had done this before. It was Percy Loomis all over again, a man with a sick fetish for reeling women in, just to see if he could do it. Had he really been playing me all along? Had I learned *nothing*? Was I still the same, *imbecilic* female, falling into the same *pathetic* trap, making the *exact same mistakes I'd made before, all over again?*

MacAyers smirked and continued, "Well, you've only known him a few days. Can't be too much damage done, can there? You're probably anxious to get home to the States. Do you still have the artifact, or have you given it to Trunk already? No doubt he's been quite persuasive."

The room spun; my stomach twisted and coiled. Ming was alive. The translator was alive. I'd dragged Qing and Li across the country for four days for nothing. And Durango, my *Durango*, was an ex-spy now working for terrorists.

A conniving lady-killer.

Qing's words rang in my ears: *He has women around him all the time.*

The puzzle pieces shifted wildly, spinning, shattering on the floor.

70

It was hard to breathe. I stood up but had to grip the table. The club had become too much for me: too many colors, too much noise, too many people. I couldn't think straight; I wanted to puke. MacAyers stood with me.

"Miss Morrison, do you still have the box?"

The box. *That damn box!*

"I need air," I begged.

"Fine, we can walk together," MacAyers snapped.

"No, please, I just want to think alone right now. Please."

"Miss Morrison, I can't let you do that. I need an answer. *Now.*"

Looking wildly around for any sort of relief, I locked eyes with the broad-shouldered Brit from earlier in the evening. He trotted over at once.

"Everything okay, miss?"

A rush of appreciation surged through me toward this gallant young man.

"No, it's not," I answered. "This man won't leave me alone."

"All right, you heard the lady. Time to blow, bub."

The Brit puffed his chest and inserted himself between MacAyers and me. He clasped MacAyers's arm. MacAyers threw him off.

"Oi!" MacAyers protested. His eyes darted to the lanyard around the Brit's neck. "Excuse me—*Clive*—but this is Australian government business."

"Seriously, mum, what is it with you and these sheep shaggers tonight?"

"Sheep shaggers means kiwis, *pommy*," MacAyers growled.

"Fine. Wallaby welders, koala copulaters, the lot of you take what you can get *down under*, right?" Clive smirked, clearly trying to pick a fight.

"Wait a minute! There was another Aussie tonight?" MacAyers snapped to me. "Trunk was *here* tonight, wasn't he? Is he still here? In the building?"

I stepped closer to Clive. I couldn't talk about Durango anymore. I couldn't talk about any of it. Not now.

"Leave the lady *alone*."

"Butt out, mate! Like I said, this is *government* business."

"Well, excuse me, *mate*," Clive sneered back, "but the way I see it, she's an American, and this is India, so you've got no jurisdiction in these parts. It's all right, Luv. I'll take it from here." The Brit folded his arms across his chest.

"Thank you!" I looked up at him gratefully and took quick steps away from the table. When MacAyers tried to follow, Clive blocked him. By the time I'd reached the club's exit, I could still see my new friend standing his ground.

Rushing around the corner, I made sure I wasn't being followed and then made a beeline for the hotel kitchen. Though they offered twenty-four-hour service, there was only a skeleton crew of cooks staffed at this hour of the night, and they were all stationed on the right half of the facility with their radio blaring Bollywood-sounding music.

I crossed the kitchen's empty, dimmed, left side and made my way around a dividing wall to the now-darkened section where the auxiliary refrigerators sat, the ones least-used. Entering the middle cooler, I remembered the sous chef reaching his hand… there. My fingers found the light switch, and once on, I easily found the paper bag on the shelf between huge blocks of butter and packs of pre-sliced prosciutto. I pulled it off the shelf, letting the slight weight of the box inside the bag be enough to drag my arm back down.

But now what?

This was all for nothing. Everything that had seemed so dangerous and urgent had all been in my head. I still couldn't wrap my mind around the dichotomy between what I had perceived and what I now knew to be the case. I had separated little Li from his mother and had told him his mother was dead. Though it was a relief to think that Ming was alive, that poor child would be lucky if I hadn't done him irreparable psychological damage.

And Qing! I'd convinced Qing I was in danger, too, and—loyal friend that he was—he'd given up almost a week of his time *right before his wedding* to risk his life and help me. I may have singlehandedly ruined Qing's marriage, depending on how angry Nori was.

The one saving grace in this whole scenario was that Colin MacAyers had never brought up Qing's name, and neither had I. If Qing could miraculously be kept out of this, at least that would be something. This escapade had already tested his friendship to the limit; he might never forgive me once he found out the truth about what had really happened. In fact, I might never forgive myself.

And then there was Durango.

My knees suddenly weakened. I managed a step backward into the wall of firework boxes, sliding down just as my legs crumpled to the freezing floor beneath me, my hands limp on the ground. My eyes burned. How could I have been so wrong, yet again?

"I'm such an *idiot*!" I whispered.

Coming to China was supposed to have helped me find myself. Instead, I was still the same lost soul I'd been for the past several years.

The problem was I had *thought* I'd changed. I'd thought I'd figured out who I was. Flying on instinct—especially these past few days—I'd been so sure about everything, particularly him. He was the child who'd grown up loving books and maps, the teen athlete who enjoyed travel. By adulthood, he'd morphed into an army commando and later a tour guide. It had all made sense. Even the spy part made sense.

But then, he hadn't told me that. MacAyers had.

If Durango really was working for terrorists, then it meant he wasn't a tour guide, either. And if he was also only feigning interest in me for sport, then how much else of what he'd said had been designed to draw me in, make me another notch on his bedpost?

What Durango said.

What MacAyers said.

No.

No!

My breaths came in frosty puffs. Pins and needles stabbed at my fingers and toes as the emptiness snared my being, sucking it in tighter and tighter upon itself.

I didn't know anything anymore.

I closed my eyes.

Let it come.

I breathed in deeply, welcoming the arctic temperature that seared my lungs, embracing the emptiness, allowing its weight to crush me as I exhaled. My head sank against my chest. Blackness enveloped me, and I let go, refusing to fight any longer.

Exhale.

Hollow.

Nothing.

Empty…

…

…What about you?

…?

A tiny point of light appeared in the darkness. What *about* me? I had a crappy, nothing job. I'd never seen the world before. I didn't speak any other languages. And I was in a situation that was way over my head.

But I was still a person, and I still mattered.

Trust yourself.

That was it—and it was all I could do. I couldn't guess at reality based on what everyone else said it was. I had to stop listening to other people's words and trust myself. I was *not* an idiot. This was my life, and *I* was the one who got to decide what counted in it.

Him.

No matter what else was true, I loved him. Even if I was nothing more than a passing conquest to him, even if my body had willed me into believing a false seduction, I'd still looked into his eyes and had seen *him.* I knew that much was true. And I loved him.

The point blazed into a torch. I could see in the darkness now.

I opened my eyes. MacAyers was wrong. I *knew* what I'd seen at the monastery. The translator was dead, and Ming had known she was next. And the assassins *had* been trying to kill Li and me. I'd seen it in their eyes. Durango had saved us, no matter *what* he was—a tour guide or an ex-spy. Even if he was a textbook womanizer who was somehow mixed up with terrorists, it didn't matter.

Everything else about *who* he was stood tall in my mind, defying the accusations MacAyers had leveled.

Pain interfered, now that my thoughts had crystallized. I looked at my hands. The tops of all my fingers were as white as the athletic tape around my right palm, halfway down to the second joint on some of them. It hurt to flex. My toes were the same. Crunching the bag clumsily in my left fist, I stood.

Now, what to do about this box that everyone wants?

I took the box out of the bag and placed it on my palm. To my surprise, it was warm, despite having been in this freezer for a few hours. It seemed to be radiating its own heat.

Oh, no!

My heart began to race.

Suddenly I knew exactly what I had to do.

71

He entered the sixth-floor stairwell and rushed up toward the seventh floor. Anger rose inside him. He'd used the Oswald Kelso identity to register both rooms, and even though Kelly's name wasn't on the registry, the hotel staff knew which room the American woman was staying in. He only hoped they hadn't given up the location of the two Chinese "brothers." And that Kelly stayed put.

Above him, the door opened. Two black-clad men headed down. They stopped, startled, and made eye contact with him. Recognition registered between both parties. He read in their faces the same thing that went through his own head.

I'm going to have to kill you.

"Well, alright then," he said.

The men jumped one after the other over the railing. Durango grabbed the metal rail next to him and powered his feet into the stomach of the first one to land. The man went flying back into his partner, both monks falling on their backsides.

The top one jumped up and swung a roundhouse kick at Durango's head. Durango ducked, caught the man's foot, and flipped him, prone, onto the stairs, dragging him down a few steps. The man's face bumped off the concrete edges.

The other monk leaped into the air, twisted, flipped, and landed on Durango's shoulders, locking his legs around Durango's neck. His hands clamped Durango's head. Durango grabbed the monk's hands and launched himself backward in the air, pulling his knees into a cannonball. His shoulders and the entire weight of his body crushed the monk as they crashed on the lower landing. He jumped up, whirled, and powered his heel into the monk's neck, breaking it.

The monk on the stairs got back up. Blood dripped from his bent nose and the scrapes on his cheek and forehead.

I don't have time for this! I have to find Yat-sen Xun!

Durango whipped his knife from his pocket, engaged the switchblade, and flicked it underhand. It lodged in the other monk's belly. By the time the monk doubled over to grab the knife's handle, Durango was already next to him. He twisted the monk's neck.

"I'll take that," he said, pulling out the knife as the man fell away to join his partner.

Damn! Now I need a clean-up crew. Where the fuck is my team?

He re-pocketed the knife and raced to the seventh floor, emerging near the elevators. Their rooms were to the right.

An Indian man and woman, both with silver-streaked hair, walked toward the elevators from the left. Some distance behind them, two more black-clad monks also approached. The Indians wore lanyards like some people in the club, and they were engaged in an animated conversation in Assamese about cost-value versus quality of care in teaching hospitals.

Durango smiled at the Indian couple and nodded politely. Waiting. Listening.

"Yat-sen Xun will not be pleased," he heard one of the monks say in Mandarin.

"He wants to be the one to kill the American girl," his partner answered.

Durango's mind raced, but he kept his exterior nonchalant.

How many of these yobbos are in the building? And where is Yat-sen Xun?

Next to him, the Indian man pushed the "down" button.

"Oh, can we go to the rooftop?" the woman asked in Assamese. "I heard they have an outdoor patio."

"The patio's open," the man replied, "but they don't have service until after the rainy season. I need a drink."

"Me, also," the woman nodded.

The elevator doors opened, and the couple got on. Durango pushed the "up" button and continued waiting. The monks passed the elevators and continued around the corner, down the right hallway, toward Kelly and Qing's rooms.

"Yes, but *we* must find and eliminate her companions," the first monk muttered.

The doors shut on the Indian couple. Durango spun around and walked up behind the monks. Just as he was on top of them, they turned. A flash of understanding crossed the first monk's face. It was too late. Durango seized their heads in his hands and smashed their skulls together. They slumped in his grasp.

"Not if one of her companions eliminates you first," he muttered.

He dragged them to the stairwell, broke their necks, and tossed their bodies over the rail. They landed in a heap on top of their colleagues.

Durango sped back down the hall. He tested the door of Kelly's room. Locked, as they'd left it. Using his key card, he entered. The room was a disaster. The bed had been stripped. Drawers sat open. All of Kelly's shopping bags had been emptied, and the clothing strewn around the room. But no one else was inside.

He hurried across the hall. Using another key card, he entered Qing's room and flicked on a light. Two forms each lay motionless in their respective beds. Durango held his breath, focusing on the smaller bulge of blankets beneath the tuft of black hair in the left bed. The bulge rose and fell ever-so-slightly.

Li was alive.

Durango walked to the other bed. He shook Qing's foot.

"Hey, Qing-o!" he whispered. "Wake up, mate!"

Qing groaned in protest and rolled over. Durango exhaled in relief.

"Oz? What time is it?" Qing rubbed his eyes and reached for his glasses.

"Almost midnight. Listen, has anyone come by your room?"

Qing sat up, scowling in thought. He glanced over at Li, who was still asleep.

"Well, yeah, Cow was here three and a half hours ago. I think she was looking for you. Did you find her?"

"Yeah, thanks. Not her. I meant anyone else."

"No. Why? What's going on?"

Good. They don't know where Qing and Li are yet.

"Okay, listen: I need you to lock the door after I leave and don't answer for anyone. I don't care who it is."

"What's going on, Oz?"

"I'll call you when I know more. I won't use my name. I'll just say, 'It's Oz,' so you'll know it's me. Flip over the security bar on your door, too."

"Oz! What the—?"

"You'll be fine, mate." Durango winked and smiled. Qing rolled his eyes and threw his hands in the air.

Durango went back into the hall. His smile faded. He needed to find Yat-sen Xun.

On second thought, forget that. I need to find Kelly!

72

Carrying two fireworks—a huge rocket and a medium one—and the bag containing the box, I exited the walk-in refrigerator. I snuck into the dimly lit auxiliary kitchen, trying not to let my heels click too loudly on the tile, and snagged a wand lighter from near the stove. There was one more thing I needed—*aha!* A roll of twine sat on the counter by the rotisserie ovens.

Knowing I only had seconds to work, I put everything on the floor, took out the box, twisted the dragons, stroked their necks, and slid the baby figure upward. *Scrape.* It was difficult with my prickling fingers, but the small, wooden button stared up at me once it was up. I rubbed my hands briskly to try to restore blood flow and thumbed the button. *Click.* The box hinged open, revealing a narrow glass vial nested in foam. The vial contained a small crystal less than half the size of my pinky nail. However, unlike most crystals I'd seen, this one had rounded edges instead of jagged ones. And the entire rock glowed white. It was definitely producing its own heat.

Prying my fingernails into the insulation surrounding the Cad-2, I managed to free both halves of the foam from the top and bottom of the box. I carefully closed the foam back around the vial and set the whole insulation block aside. Then I yanked out a length of twine and tried to cut it with a serrated knife I found in a drawer. My numb fingers fumbled, and I dropped the knife. It clattered to the floor.

I froze, staring at the active right-hand side of the kitchen. A shadow moved near the division between the two rooms. I held my breath. The shadow passed. Laughter rolled from the staff. I exhaled and went back to work.

Retrieving the knife, this time, I managed to cut the twine. I bound the foam block to the medium rocket. My pin-prickled fingers burned with every movement, though the deteriorating Cad-2 inside the foam helped to warm them. My bruised right hand throbbed beneath its bandage. I tied a messy but secure knot.

Next, I cut off another length of rotisserie twine and tied the medium rocket to the large one, staggering them so that the bottom of the medium one was closer to the top of the large one. Finally, I closed the empty box.

One more thing to do.

I picked up the kitchen phone and dialed Qing and Li's room number. To my relief, Qing answered.

"You're okay?" I asked quietly, below the noise of the staff and their blaring radio in the next room.

"Yeah, we're fine. Why wouldn't we be? Would one of you please tell me what's going on?"

I closed my eyes, drinking in the comfort of knowing they were safe. Everything was going to be okay, at least for my best friend and sweet little Li.

"Qing, is Durango there?"

"No, he was here earlier. He told us to stay put."

"Okay, good. Keep doing that."

"Why? Where are you? What is that music?"

He sounded peeved. That was good; he didn't know anything, and Yat-sen Xun hadn't gotten to them. I hung up.

The fireworks were too big for me to hide under my dress. I found a white tablecloth and wrapped it around them. Then I grabbed the now-empty puzzle box and the lighter.

Go time.

I peeked out the door. The coast was clear. I dashed across the hallway, through the empty lounge area, and past the back side of the elevator-shaft wall until I came around to the two elevator doors. Punching the "up" button, I waited, hugging my odd tablecloth bundle, with the box and the lighter pressed up against my chest. My heart raced a hundred beats for each second that passed.

A commotion echoed down the hall behind me. I turned to look. Colin MacAyers sauntered from the club, ushered by a burly bouncer. Some distance behind him, another bouncer ushered out Clive. The Brit held his hand to his nose, a line of red streaming between his fingers. He exited onto the street without a backward glance.

I tried to sink into the shadows, but MacAyers spotted me before I could hide. He walked toward me at a crisp clip, a grim smile curling his lips. I whirled my head to the elevator door and pressed the button rapidly with my finger, as though it might make one of the doors open faster.

Suddenly a set of doors slid open. I stopped dead in my tracks, aware that some distance away MacAyers had done the same.

"Kelly!"

Durango walked out. Relief flooded his features.

But all I felt was horror.

I shook my head and backed away, my mind racing. He was the last person I wanted to see right now. There had to be a way to keep him safe from the Australian government *and* the impending disaster under the tablecloth in my arms. If MacAyers didn't take him in, I knew Durango would try to stop me from what I was about to attempt. I had to push him away.

"What's wrong, Kells? And what—?"

"Mr. Trunk," I interrupted, forcing my voice to be cold and clinical. "I believe you've met Officer MacAyers?" I nodded across the lobby. Durango did a double-take.

"Colin? What are you…?" For the first time since I'd known him, Durango looked completely at a loss.

"Why don't you go stand over by your colleague?" I suggested icily.

"Kelly, what's going on?"

"Now!"

I yelled so loudly that the front desk clerk leaned over the counter to see what was going on. One of the club bouncers had his attention on us, too. Durango held his hands up and backed away.

"Alright? Now, will you please tell me what this is all about?" His eyes darted between MacAyers, me, and the tablecloth bundle I held.

The elevator doors closed. *Crap!* One chance missed as the clock ticked its countdown.

Get rid of MacAyers and save Durango.

"Officer MacAyers here was telling me all about your *past*. And your *present*." I sneered with disgust. "He seems to remember you being quite the charmer, racking up bedpost notches for kicks and bragging about it later to the boys at the office."

MacAyers smirked.

"Kells," Durango shook his head, "Colin has an ax to grind because—"

"But that's not even *half* as interesting as the other things he said about you," I interrupted him again, re-pressing the button for the elevator. "Did you know he and your other former *mates* think that after you retired, you began working for terrorists? And they think you were interested in brokering a deal involving Cad-2! Fascinating, huh?"

Durango's mouth opened and closed. He cocked his head to the side and frowned.

"But the funny thing," I continued, directing my gaze at MacAyers, "is that no one ever suspected me. *Me!* Oh, stupid American girl! *She* can't be the one finding out who the competition is for the terrorist organization. She can't *possibly* have discovered the exact geographic coordinates of the plume to leverage negotiations with the monks. There's *no way* she could know a computer hacker to lay out compelling evidence against a well-positioned tour guide in China. And she *definitely* wouldn't want to bypass a few laws and adopt a kid of her own along the way." I shrugged with a cynical smile.

MacAyers jaw dropped in disbelief. I knew Durango was staring at me, too, but I couldn't bring myself to meet his gaze for fear I'd crack.

"So you see, Officer MacAyers, Mr. Trunk isn't the one you're after. It's me."

"Kelly, you don't have to do this," Durango spoke quietly.

I felt a catch in my throat. It was all I could do to muster up the anger necessary to glare at him.

The elevator dinged, and the doors re-opened.

"My path ends here," I said, with as much spite in my tone as I could muster. "You've served my purposes handsomely, handsome. You can go now. Time for you to 'get a move on.' Go back and do what you were hired to do."

I ripped my eyes away, but not before I saw the utter disbelief that crossed his features. I backed into the elevator.

"Here, Mr. MacAyers. You want this thing? Take it." I pulled the lacquered box out from where it was wedged between the tablecloth and my stomach and dropped it on the floor outside the elevator doors.

"It's just a dumb box," I added, kicking it across the lobby toward the two men. I stabbed the button for the top floor.

"Kelly, *no*!" Durango yelled. Both men dove after the box. The elevator doors closed.

I exhaled a small sigh of relief as the elevator began to shiver and ascend. Clapping my free hand to my mouth, I stifled a cry. I'd been as vicious as I could be, and I'd tried to believe the words as I was saying them so he couldn't tell I was lying. I needed Durango to think I hated him.

Beyond that, MacAyers had my word that I was guilty. Hopefully, my story would be enough to exonerate Durango from whatever the Australian government had on him. And also enough to push him far away from me. I wanted him to take Qing and Li and leave before Yat-sen Xun found them.

My eyes fell on the bundle in my arms. Whipping off the tablecloth, I looked at the double-decker firework I'd assembled. This *had* to work!

73

Both men launched themselves through the air, sliding across the floor. They landed on their bellies, outstretched fingers touching the box at the same time. Durango reached and managed to grab it with his other hand, too.

I know she hates the damn box, but I can't believe she just practically gave it to Colin! I'm going to kill him for whatever he's told her!

Instead of trying to wrestle the box away, MacAyers grabbed Durango. His arm shot around Durango's neck. He rolled onto his back, pulling Durango's upper body on top of him. Using the crook of his elbow, he yanked Durango's jaw up and reached his other hand around, trying to rip out Durango's throat.

Durango dropped the box, grabbed MacAyers's palm with one hand, and drove his elbow hard into MacAyers's gut. MacAyers loosened his grip for a second. It was enough for Durango to roll away and jump to his feet. MacAyers did the same. But not before he managed to kick the box to the side. They faced each other, locking their cool, even gazes.

A small crowd watched the two men face off—the night desk clerk, a hotel guest, the club bouncers, and two of the maids. They'd also heard Kelly's "confession."

"Always had a way with women, didn't you, Trunk?" MacAyers smiled.

"Get over it, Colin." Durango shrugged. Unlike Kelly, both men kept their voices low, so no one could overhear them. Force of habit.

"Me? Naw, I just thought she ought to know who she was getting into bed with." MacAyers smirked.

"You've told her quite a bit about me, haven't you? But terrorists? Really?"

"Didn't tell her anything that wasn't true, did I?"

"I suppose it's your right to look at it any way you want." Durango smiled.

MacAyers's gaze suddenly cut to the side, towards the box. Durango followed his line of sight. As soon as Durango looked away from him, MacAyers swung a left hook. Durango instinctively blocked it with his right hand, and MacAyers landed a right uppercut to Durango's jaw.

Durango's head whipped back and bells rang. He shook it off, locked his palms behind MacAyers's neck, pulled the man's head forward, and rammed his knee into MacAyers's sternum, knocking the wind out of him. Then he pivoted and threw MacAyers to the ground.

MacAyers landed on all fours, coughing, but rolled quickly away and jumped to his feet. Durango now stood between MacAyers and the box. Five men in casual business attire walked into the hotel. MacAyers took one look at them, turned, and bolted toward the back exit.

Durango gave a half-step in chase, but on second thought, whipped around and dashed back for the box. The five men approached Durango. One man held up an ID. Seeing that Durango was rushed, he spoke quickly.

"Officer Trunk?"

"Yes."

"I'm Corfield. This is Gilroy, Yulara, Howden, and Bunroo."

"From Dhaka?"

"Yes."

"Good." He pointed at Howden and Bunroo. "You two go after the blond man who just ran out the back way. His name is Colin MacAyers. He's formerly one of us."

"Got it." They smiled, nodded, and ran.

"You two." He pointed at Gilroy and Yulara. "Yat-sen Xun is presumed to be somewhere in the building. But I've got four bodies on the sixth-floor stairwell. Secure it, shoot it, and handle clean-up."

"Four. All you?" Gilroy asked.

"Yes."

"Fuck!" Gilroy grinned. Yulara chuckled in admiration, and they headed for the stairwell.

I've got to find Kelly.

"Is that the sample?" Corfield asked. He pointed at the box.

"Yeah," Durango answered. A thought struck him cold. "I think so."

He opened the box. It was empty. His heart plummeted to his stomach. *No!* She was doing it again: trying to save the world by risking her own life. *No!*

"Should you and I fan out and find Yat-sen Xun? Maybe he got hold of it."

"Forget Yat-sen Xun," Durango said in a strangled tone. "We have to find Kel-ly!"

74

I reached the roof-access level and ran down the corridor, hugging the bundled fireworks. The Cad-2 heated my neck, even through its foam insulation. The heat provided me with an urgency that overrode the fact that I'd just shredded my heart to pieces. I reached the door and made my way out to the rooftop. The outdoor bar was shuttered. Empty wrought iron tables lay scattered around the perimeter. Apparently, the patio lounge didn't see much use during monsoon season.

I dashed to a corner railing. On this side, the patio overlooked the Brahmaputra, a swollen, glittering swath in the moonlight. It looked wider across than the Mississippi, but it wasn't as big as the ocean. Or even a lake. Still, it would have to do; there was no other alternative.

I tried to prop my makeshift extended firework up against the smooth railing corner, but it kept sliding down. I was running out of time. MacAyers would eventually catch up with and arrest me. But if I didn't get this done first, the Cad-2 would crater us all.

Abandoning the fireworks for a moment, I ran over to grab one of the round, iron tables. The clock ticked as I scraped it across the concrete. Finally, I managed to butt it up against the railing corner, creating a small triangle. I balanced the rocket between the table and the railing, with its stick and wick going through the triangle, hanging below the tabletop. I bent to grab the wand lighter from the ground.

"Celebrating your victory early, aren't you, Miss Morrison?" a wizened voice crackled.

I stood and whirled. *Yat-sen Xun!*

"You!" I breathed. "You killed Ming! And the translator!"

"They should not have overheard my private business dealings. Nor should you have!"

He lunged at me, grabbing my upper arms, shaking me.

"Who are you, *really*, Miss Morrison? How did you uncover the heart of my plans to wrest control of China from the 'Peoples' Government'? *I* am the lineage of China's last *true* emperor! *I* will rule China, and the *world* will respect us once again! How did you manage to plant yourself in exactly the correct places? Was it Ding Li-Liang? *Who are you? Who do you work for?*"

By rights, I knew I ought to be terrified. The man I'd been running through hell to escape had caught me, and he was clearly a complete lunatic. But after everything I'd been through, and with a bomb about to kill us all, something shifted inside me. Instead of being fearful, I got mad.

"I'm nobody!" I shouted at him. His long fingernails bit painfully into my flesh, which pissed me off more. "I'm just an American tourist, and I wish I'd never come to your *stupid* monastery!"

Yat-sen Xun studied my face. His eyes widened in shock.

"You are telling the truth!" Then a sneer of disdain curled his lips. "And you are pathetic. A hapless fool."

He released my shoulders. His hands shot to my neck, and his thumbs gored into my soft palate, just like the ninja at the hotel. I clawed at his fingers with my left hand.

"Now, where is my box?"

"I've already turned it over to the authorities," I squeaked.

The wand lighter was still in my right hand. I ignored the pain that shot through my bandaged palm, flicked it on, and lifted it to Yat-sen Xun's robe. His clothes flared up. Howling in pain, he released his grip on me and fell to the ground, rolling.

Dropping to all fours, coughing, I crawled under the table. I re-lit the wand and touched it to the wick. The wick caught and began to sizzle.

A hand grabbed my ankle, and Yat-sen Xun yanked me out from under the table. Rough concrete scraped the skin on my bare arms. I dropped the lighter with a yelp. Twisting swiftly onto my back, I kicked out with my other foot, smacking

Yat-sen Xun's face with my sandal heel. It was enough of a hit that he dropped my leg. I scrambled to my feet and ran toward the door.

Yat-sen Xun dodged with lightning speed, catching my arm. His shirt was charred to his chest, and his beard had been badly singed; burnt hair and flesh reeked in my nostrils. But another layer of scent clouded the air: the faint, acrid odor of cooked foam. The Cad-2 was melting its insulation.

The wick sizzled to its end. The large rocket roared off with a loud whoosh.

I pivoted and raked the fingernails of my free hand down the scorched flesh on Yat-sen Xun's torso. He shrieked and lashed his foot out, making contact with my ribs. I heard a crack. Acute pain stabbed my thorax. I screamed and staggered sideways.

The first rocket reached its apex and exploded. Pops and crackles blistered overhead. A piercing whistle screeched over the first firework's snapping: the smaller rocket had ignited.

Clutching my side, panting, I hobbled for the door, but Yat-sen Xun blocked me again. He seemed to only have been temporarily hampered by his pain. I backed away as he advanced.

And then it happened.

In the millisecond between being hit by the shockwave and knocked off my feet, I understood: the Cad-2 had exploded. I flew backward through the air and then crashed. *Hard.*

Excruciating agony shot through my body as my already-compromised ribs hit the pavement, forcing air from my lungs. Burning pain scalded my skin as my bare back skidded across the cement patio. A paroxysmal clonk thundered in my head as I smacked against a patio wall. The entire building shook.

But I had done it. I had succeeded in getting the epicenter of the Cad-2's detonation as far away from people as possible. The hotel was still standing. That meant that Qing and Li, and Durango were going to be okay.

Durango…

The image of the soles of Yat-sen Xun's feet lay on the ground in the distance. The sound of car alarms squealed below. My eyes lost focus. And the last thing I remembered before darkness became oblivion was the scent of woods and sunshine.

PART 3
American Prisoner

75

It was a mile to the nearest hospital, and the streets of Guwahati looked like a bomb evacuation zone. Then again, that was exactly what it was—or what it had almost become, but for the limp, lifeless woman in Durango's arms. Police and ambulance sirens wailed from every direction. The power was out, windows were shattered, and a couple of buildings nearer to the epicenter had large cracks fracturing their sides. The worst was the people, panicked and desperate, pouring out onto the pavement. They were bewildered, yelling in the moonlight, some of them crying, searching for their loved ones. Finding them, they held them close despite the hot, sticky September night air. But they were alive, which was more than he was sure of for her right now. She didn't seem to be breathing.

Hold on, sweetheart! We're almost there!

The armpits of his white dress shirt were soaked. Sweat beaded on his brow and trickled behind his ears. He blinked it out of his eyes and concentrated on powering his legs forward, planting his feet, and pushing off in rapid motions through the darkness. It had taken him ten minutes to get this far since he'd found her on the hotel's deserted rooftop patio. He'd heard a series of pops, like fireworks, and had a horrifying, split-second view through the door-glass to see that she was in a face-off against Yat-sen Xun. Then the blast hit.

She went flying backward in one direction, Yat-sen Xun in another, and the door to the patio was forced shut, even as he tried to push it open. The glass shattered. Instinct forced his arms up to shield his face as shards barraged him. The entire building shook and hadn't finished settling before he was through the metal frame of the door.

Her body lay motionless, bathed in moonlight, with her head butted against the brick wall. Panic clutched his heart, dragging it back to cower against his spine. It was the third time in more than ten years he'd felt this level of fear, and all of those occasions had happened over the past three days. All of them had been because of her.

He sprinted toward her, flicking glass bits off his shirtsleeves as he ran. Her eyelids sank shut. He reached her side, crashed to his knees, and called her name, rubbing her shoulder, stroking her cheeks. She didn't come to. His eyes began to burn around the edges, but basic first aid from his military training kicked in. She had a weak pulse. Her chest rose and fell—just barely, but she was breathing. Quickly, carefully, he scooped her up. He had to get her to the hospital.

The city all around him was dark. The power was out. Corfield, on his heels, had followed him through the broken door and was dealing with Yat-sen Xun. The head monk was also still breathing, though his face was bloody and badly burned. Corfield already had a mobile pressed to his ear. They nodded at each other as he crossed the patio, carrying her. He hurried back through the door into the darkened hotel. The dim, auxiliary backup lighting had been his only illumination as he'd bypassed the useless elevators and sprinted eight floors of stairs down to the street.

He'd tried to run through the masses that had emerged. Upon seeing him carrying her, most of the crowds parted to let him through. It became more difficult, though, the nearer he got to the hospital.

A block away now, it was clear she was not the explosion's only casualty. Two men carried an older man who clutched his chest. Another apparent heart attack victim, an old woman, was lugged by a couple of teenage girls. Three very pregnant women had gone into labor. Their husbands argued over a lone wheelchair as the women huffed the last hundred meters on their own. Dozens of people had bloody bandages pressed to various body parts—probably they had been cut by glass or things that had fallen off shelves when the buildings shook. But the structures were all still standing, and the people were all still alive.

He wanted to shout at them: "Back away! *This girl* is the reason you weren't all vaporized tonight! She gets to go to the front of the queue!" But he couldn't do that. He wasn't allowed to speak of the events, about which only he and a select few others knew. Instead, he muscled his brawny, six-six frame through the crowd, ignoring the cries of protest as he reached the hospital doors.

Two security guards stood outside, attempting to staunch the incoming rush. They began to point, telling him in both Assamese and English that he needed to go to the back of the line, but a nearby physician took one look at her and stopped them. The doc raised an eyebrow in question.

"She was on a rooftop patio when it happened," he said in English. It took every ounce of his training to keep his voice steady. "She was thrown and hit her head on a wall." The doctor nodded and lifted Kelly's eyelids, shining a light in them. "I don't think she's breathing," he added softly.

The doctor brought them forward into the ER's well-lit main entrance and grabbed a gurney. He laid Kelly down gently. He could see that her lips were tinged blue under the bright lights powered by the hospital's backup generator. When he removed his left arm from behind her back, he was alarmed to see that his white shirtsleeve was covered with blood. *Her* blood.

The doctor began to examine her, but he stared at his sleeve. She must have landed on the concrete patio floor before hitting the surrounding brick wall head-first. She must have skidded, and her blue halter dress had provided no barrier between the skin on her back and the pavement. He quickly explained this to the doctor, privately shuddering to think of the pain it would have caused her. The doctor nodded. While listening, he applied a stethoscope to her chest, first on one side, then the other, then back again, frowning.

"What is her name?"

"Kelly."

"Why is her hand bandaged?" He indicated Kelly's right hand.

He couldn't exactly tell the doc the truth about how she hurt her hand, the same way he couldn't tell anyone the type of bomb that had gone off. It was classified. Instead, he gave the same explanation Kelly had given Qing:

"She smacked her hand into a wall in the dark."

The doctor frowned again, turned, and began wheeling Kelly down the hall toward a room. He followed.

The doctor barked into the air in Assamese. "I have a head trauma. Female, late twenties, unconscious—pupils unequal and non-reactive—probable concussion, lips cyanotic, bilateral abrasions along the scapular region." Another nurse joined them.

"Where's Chakraborty and Puntambekar?" the doctor demanded.

"They were at the medical convention at the hotel, along with everyone else," the nurse answered. "Hopefully, they are all on their way in right now."

He remembered the women Kelly had been dancing with in the nightclub just a few hours earlier. They'd been wearing conference lanyards, as had half the people in the club and another couple he'd come across on the seventh floor. He looked around and saw what appeared to be a skeleton staff. Any doctors trying to make their way in right now would have difficulty with the mob outside. The hospital was severely understaffed for a major catastrophe.

"We need a CT and an X-ray," the doctor said. He switched to English. "What is your name, sir?"

"Oswald Kelso." It was the same identity he'd used to reserve the two rooms at the hotel.

"You're going to have to wait out here, Mr. Kelso." The doctor punched a code on a large double-door marked: *Caution! X-ray equipment in use.* "We'll know more about her injuries in a few minutes." He and the nurse pulled the gurney through to the other side. The doors clicked shut behind them.

Durango stared at the doors for two full minutes, lost, before he sat on the edge of one of the brown upholstered chairs that lined the wall in sporadic clumps. He leaned forward with his forearms against his knees, ready to spring up the second anyone came from the room.

The clock ticked. And ticked. He sat back in the chair and leaned forward with his head in his hands. Other people began to fill the other chairs.

Tick. Tick.

There was a commotion behind the doors, and some kind of code was called on the loudspeakers, but no one came out.

Tick. Tick.

Forty-five minutes later, they reemerged, the doctor, the nurse, and Kelly. She was still unconscious on the gurney, only now she'd been fitted with a temporary oxygen mask, held in place by the nurse, and her face was ghostly white. Wires trailed from the skin above her dress's plunging-V in a garish sort of necklace.

They were attached to a heart monitor, which right now registered only forty beats per minute. Durango ran forward.

"What's wrong with her?"

"She needs surgery," the doctor said as he pulled Kelly down the hall toward a wide elevator.

"What for?"

"In addition to the concussion and the lacerations on her back, she's got a broken rib and a pneumothorax."

Durango spoke Assamese and ten other languages, but he didn't speak medical-ese. "What's a pneumothorax?" he demanded, keeping pace.

"Punctured lung." The doctor answered. Durango felt the blood drain from his face.

They reached the elevators. The nurse pressed the button going up.

"And, oh!" The doctor's tone became testy. He leveled an accusatory glare. "Somehow, that 'wall' she inadvertently 'smacked' managed to give her a fracture. She'll need a cast to stabilize her hand. If she makes it through surgery."

Whether the doc was ticked off that he knew he'd been lied to about her hand or was implying that perhaps Durango had hurt Kelly, Durango ignored the man's attitude. He was too worried by the news about her punctured lung. Stroking Kelly's pale cheek, he caressed a stray lock of dark hair off her forehead.

"You're going to be okay, sweetheart," he murmured, wishing he believed his own words. "I'll be right here with you."

"You can't come up to the OR," the doctor said curtly.

"We'll send someone down to the waiting room as soon as we know something," the nurse added with more compassion. She squeezed the bag on the oxygen mask.

Durango neither moved nor broke eye contact with Kelly's face. He wasn't going to leave her.

Another nurse appeared at his side.

"Sir, I need you to help me fill out the paperwork," she said. "What is the patient's name?"

"Kelly. Kelly Morrison," he answered. He continued to stroke her cheek, afraid to hold her hand now that he knew it was so damaged.

"Does she have any allergies or other medical conditions that we need to be aware of?"

"No." He thought for a second. "Wait. She has Raynaud's, if that matters?" He knew all of Kelly's medical history—and a lot more about her, too—even though she didn't know that he did.

"We'll keep her fingers and toes warm," the first nurse reassured him.

"Are you her husband?" the second nurse asked.

A lump caught in his throat. "No," he answered. "She's not married."

The elevator doors opened.

"Sir, you need to step away," the doctor bristled.

Durango leveled an icy stare back at the man. *Make me.* Fear registered in the doctor's eyes. Just then, the heart monitor let off a series of high-pitched beeps. Kelly's heart rate dropped to thirty-five beats per minute… thirty-two… thirty... Panic gripped him all over again. He backed away, keeping his eyes locked on her frail form. The doctor and nurse wheeled her into the elevator.

"We'll send someone down as soon as we know something," the nurse reiterated. The doors closed; everything that mattered to him was behind them.

"Sir," the second nurse persisted at his elbow, "if you are not related to her, does she have any immediate family members I can notify?"

The sudden realization jolted him to a new level of fear. He ripped his gaze from the elevator doors and stared at the nurse.

"Sir?" Her eyes widened in alarm.

"Her parents," he said. Her parents would need to know. *Hello, we've never met, but I'm madly in love with your daughter. Only, I may have just gotten her killed.*

"Do you have their names and number so I can call them?" the nurse asked.

"No." He shook his head. "I'll do it."

76

B*rrrrring!*

The shrill ringtone echoed off the cream-and-blue tiled backsplash and black laminate countertops. Two rooms away, the man folded his newspaper. He creaked out of his brown Lay-Z-Boy recliner.

"El, can you get that?" the woman's voice called down. "I promised I'd help out with French club up at the school, and I've been running *late* ever since my doctor's appointment." An aerosol hiss followed, along with overloud clicks that he knew were made by her slamming the wrong bracelets on top of her dresser while she searched her jewelry box for the correct one.

Brrrrring!

Already standing, he sighed and crossed the recently-buffed, honey oak floors from the living room through the dining room. His wife was closer to a phone upstairs in the bedroom, but she'd already been cross at him for taking too long to choose between eggplant or chicken parmesan at the grocery store after her appointment. She'd have made the decision in two seconds flat. Her supercilious tone and refusal to pick up the receiver was her way of saying that it was *his* fault she was running late. But then, after thirty-five years of marriage, he was used to this. It wasn't the grocery store or being late that was bothering her. It was the travel. Carol hated having to go too far from home. The farther she had to travel, the tenser she became, and the doctor's office had been an hour away—all the way over in Aurora. It made her snippy. She'd always been insistent on order and routine—she hated chaos—but the travel aversion had become more pronounced over the past decade or so. He wondered whether she was borderline agoraphobic.

Regardless, she needs to take it easy, he thought with concern, *or that expensive blood pressure medication we just bought will be for nothing.*

Bright, mid-afternoon sunshine splashed the kitchen and the small, neat backyard, which he could see through the house's back windows. He folded the *Denver Post* he was still holding, set it on the countertop, and glanced at the cordless phone's base. The caller ID displayed a number that didn't begin with a local area code but rather 061. He frowned. A foreign country.

A nagging thought tugged at his brain, but he dismissed it. *Probably a wrong number,* he reasoned, *or some sort of overseas scam.*

"El?" his wife called down. "Why aren't you answering?"

"It's just a telemarketer, Care."

The phone rang two more times then went to voicemail. Instead of staying on the line to leave a message, however, the caller hung up. Relief flooded his system. It must have just been a telemarketer. But no sooner had he turned away from the counter to go back to his chair than his cell phone rang. The nagging thought returned, and apprehension prickled his heart. He crossed the house to the front door and looked at the phone, still attached to its charger. His heart beat faster. The same three digits appeared at the front of the number.

This was more than a persistent telemarketer. Butterflies danced in his stomach. He unplugged the charger and picked up the phone.

"Hello?"

"Hello. Elliot Morrison?" The man had a deep voice and a foreign accent. British, maybe.

"Yes?"

"Sir, I'm calling about your daughter. Kelly. She's been in an accident."

Five minutes later, he stared at the cell phone in his hand as his wife descended the last stair. "I'm ready. Let's go." She whirled toward the front door. Fumes from the judicious use of hairspray that helmeted her coif arrived a second later. She stopped short. "El? What's wrong?"

"It's Kelly," Elliot said, feeling his face go cold as the blood drained from it. "She's in the hospital."

"The hospital? What happened? How bad is it?" she whispered.

Elliot gulped, afraid to tell her. But he'd made a decision. "It's bad. We have to go to her, honey."

"To China?" She issued the words in a breathy shriek.

"No, Carol," he responded firmly. "India. We're going to India."

77

For Colin MacAyers, the nice thing about the explosion was that it took everyone by surprise, including the blokes who were tailing him. He recovered more quickly and could use their distraction to hide and then double back behind them. He felt a twinge of remorse but let it go. It wasn't like he'd ever worked with either one—single gunshot wounds to each of their heads. Poor greenhorns never saw him coming, and in the ensuing panic on the streets, no one else noticed. Afterward, as he dragged their bodies behind the arched columns of one of Guwahati's myriad temples, he sorted out what the explosion had meant.

The sample had been destroyed.

Frustration and fear mounted in his chest. His failure to retrieve the box and the girl—and the subsequent Cad-2 sample annihilation—wouldn't bode well for his new relationship with Yat-sen Xun. Nor for his existing relationship with the Omanis. He had to make things right. He needed the money.

He moved away from the temple, blending into the crowds in the darkened streets. Maybe the destruction of the substance wasn't a bad thing. The wrong people didn't have it, and it couldn't be traced back to the monastery. His heart accelerated as he considered for a moment what it would have meant for him if it *had* actually been recovered…

And if Trunk had been the one to bring it in!

Heat surged to his face, having nothing to do with the subtropical climate. Oh, how he *wished* he could have just pulled out his sidearm then, back at the hotel! Put a nasty cap right in the middle of that face women found irresistible. That would bring balance back to the world, wouldn't it?

Unfortunately, there'd been too many witnesses. The Indians had their own military-level police force and competent Intelligence Bureau. Better to make it look like a fistfight. People would forget him faster. Plus, Trunk had far more hand-to-hand combat experience and would have easily disarmed him at that close range. *Bastard!*

No, he had to forget about it. He had to get back to the hotel, find Yat-sen Xun, and figure out how to solidify the deal between the monks and the terrorists. Then he would get paid.

The Omanis had gotten wind of the monastery's Cad-2 cache a few months earlier and had tried to approach Yat-sen Xun on their own. Yat-sen Xun had been more interested in dealing with weapons manufacturers, not buyers, at the time. MacAyers had done a few side jobs for the terrorists—intelligence background checks on men in their organization the leaders didn't trust. Two were just nongs with drug problems and bad debts; another had turned out to be a spy from a rival, Syrian-based terrorist group. Pleased, the Omanis had asked MacAyers to make contact with Yat-sen Xun, which he'd attempted without success a week ago. He was surprised, therefore, when Yat-sen Xun had called him out of the blue yesterday.

As soon as Yat-sen Xun had described what was going on, MacAyers had had a hunch Trunk was involved. He'd kept his opinion to himself, but deep down, he'd known he was right. Just as MacAyers had been retiring, Trunk left for a post in China near the monastery. Plus, he was one of the few men MacAyers knew of in the world who had the experience, the physical abilities, and the language skills to escape highly trained Shaolin monks across rough, sub-Himalayan terrain, through Burma, into India.

The girl, however, was an unknown quantity. Yat-sen Xun had been convinced she was some sort of specialized American operative, but MacAyers's cursory rundown had turned up nothing to that effect. Therefore, he'd played on his own assumptions when he'd met her face to face and quickly realized he was right: she was nobody. Just a tourist who'd been in the wrong place at the wrong time but who'd had the dumb luck to run into the right person to keep her alive. MacAyers's gut was usually spot-on.

And his new gut feeling was that either she or Trunk had blown up the Cad-2 sample on purpose.

It had to have been one of them—either the girl, Kelly Morrison, or Trunk—but his money was on the girl. He sneered at the thought of her. *Bitch!* She must have taken the stuff out of the box before she showed up in the hotel lobby. Why else would she have dumped it in front of him before she'd ducked into the elevator? And, of course, it would have been a rocket of some sort that she'd had under that sheet. He remembered hearing pops and turning around to see fireworks near the hotel just before the blast. Yeah, it'd been her alright.

Stupid bitch! His story had been perfect! She should have given him the box when he'd asked for it earlier, *with* the substance still in it. He *knew* she'd believed that he was an active-duty officer, and Trunk was not. When he'd cornered her at the hotel's attached nightclub earlier, he'd heavily insinuated that she could be arrested for kidnapping and theft, and he'd seen the sheer terror in her eyes as she'd weighed her options. Instead, she'd not only gotten away from him, but later she'd lied and had given *herself* up. She was trying to save that wombat, Trunk! Bastard must be a really good root. Trunk would only use her and toss her. The man cared about nothing except his job. MacAyers should know. He was all-too-familiar with Trunk's fallout.

He made his way back through side streets and neared the hotel. Some of the employees might remember him from having been in the fight with Trunk in the lobby. It had been twenty minutes since he'd run out the doors. MacAyers knit his brows and sidled next to the agitated guests who thronged the outdoor courtyard. They murmured quietly to themselves, their eyes round with fear—time to rabble-rouse.

"What *was* that?" he asked in a stricken voice.

"It felt like an earthquake," the man next to him responded.

"No!" another man said. "I heard members of the staff talking to each other as I was on my way out here. They said that it was a bomb!"

"The hotel was *bombed*?" a woman shrieked. Other members of the crowd chimed in.

"My brother just texted me! He felt it over on the North Bank!"

"Maybe someone tried to blow up the Guwahati Refinery!"

"This hotel seems to be in much worse shape than the other buildings around us."

"Was it the separatists or one of the liberation fronts?"

"Probably it was the Bodos."

Yeah, a rocket from the rooftop, MacAyers thought. *I wonder...?*

"Was anyone hurt?" he called out.

"A man carried a woman out of here. She was unconscious."

"Or maybe dead."

"What was she wearing?" MacAyers asked quickly.

"A blue dress. And she was Caucasian, like you! Do you know her?"

MacAyers clapped a hand to his mouth and gasped. "Excuse me," he muttered, turning. People clucked in horrified sympathy and parted to let him hurry back out to the street. Once away from the crowd, he headed for the nearest hospital. The thought of blasting a nine-mil into Trunk's face had become more and more appealing. The man had ruined MacAyers's life, and now he'd ruined MacAyers's business deal. Killing Durango Trunk sounded like a good idea right about now.

He thought about what it would feel like to watch the dark hole appear in the space right between the man's eyebrows. The hole would be black, for an instantaneous breath, before the blue-red appeared, changing to bright blood-red as it bubbled forth into the oxygenated atmosphere, warm liquid beginning to stream down his nose just as his body began to topple backward. Bits of skull bone and gray matter would already be on the sidewalk, above the place where his head would land.

He frowned. It was always the gray matter that got to him. He didn't have a problem with the killing, and certainly not with the damage to the front of Trunk's face. But to take out the brain, the center of someone he *knew* and had *worked* with... that was a problem. It upset the balance. That bothered him. Things had to be "equal," and the equality wasn't necessarily quantifiable or tangible but more about something he sensed. He could sense balance. Or, he could sense his version of it. It was how his mind had always worked, and destroying the brain of someone he'd worked with felt *un*balanced.

Well, he'd make an exception in this case and figure out another way to restore order to the world.

It took him quite some time to wade through the crowded streets to the hospital. A line of patients waiting for triage streamed out the door. When he finally made his way to the front, he explained to the guards that he was only there to see whether his friend had been admitted, and they let him past. He went to the desk.

"I think my friend, Kelly Morrison, was brought in here tonight?" he asked.

"Yes," the receptionist nodded, looking at her computer screen. "She's in X-ray right now. The waiting room is over there." The receptionist pointed to a set of double doors.

MacAyers went through and was halfway down the corridor before he stopped short. Trunk was there, practically in front of him, across from a large door with a *Caution* sign. MacAyers ducked into an open room and held his breath. He exhaled silently, but he was shaking. Trunk was a formidable opponent. In addition to his size and strength, the man was incredibly intelligent, with catlike reflexes, and he'd had years of elite training before joining the Service. MacAyers's sternum hurt and would probably ache for days from their fight earlier. He wondered why Trunk hadn't injured him more severely. Deference to the job? Guilt? Regardless, one false move now, and MacAyers would be the one who was dead.

After a minute, he peeked back out. Trunk sat on the edge of a chair, not two meters away, tapping his heel on the floor and alternating glances between the Caution-door and his watch. His shirtsleeves were bloodied. He seemed oblivious to MacAyers's presence.

MacAyers smirked and reached for his compact Beretta. Just then, the doors to the X-ray room opened. Kelly Morrison was wheeled out. Trunk jumped up. MacAyers froze, his fingers touching the pistol's textured backstrap.

The doctor and the nurse pushed the gurney down the hall, away from MacAyers. Trunk moved with them, staying next to Kelly. They stopped at the elevator on the far end. Another nurse, carrying a clipboard, passed the room MacAyers was in and walked briskly toward Trunk. MacAyers ventured a bold step forward, listening to Kelly's diagnosis. The doctor told Trunk that Kelly would have to have an operation for a punctured lung, and clipboard-nurse ran him through a list of questions. Then Kelly's heart monitor began to beep wildly. As MacAyers watched, he observed Trunk's devastated reaction.

At first, he was confused. It almost seemed as though Trunk was behaving like a man in love. Then it hit him: it had happened. Trunk actually *was* in love! He'd fallen for the American girl!

MacAyers's thoughts shifted and rearranged. The more he considered it, the more perfect he knew it was. It would solidify his standing with Yat-sen Xun, thus giving him a way to repair the bridge between the monks and the Omanis, and it would eliminate a key witness against himself, as well. Plus, there was the beauty of the personal satisfaction that MacAyers would get out of it: the balance. If MacAyers had to be companionless because of Trunk, then Trunk would get the same thing, and he would be the one to do it.

No, he wouldn't kill Durango Trunk. He would kill Kelly Morrison.

78

It was just after five. The sky outside the hospital windows shifted from dusky apricot to deep golden. Saffron-colored, the Indian people might say. He hadn't appreciated a sunrise for years until he'd seen the world through her eyes. It was like taking off night-vision goggles and finding out you were in the middle of a child's birthday party. Only now, this beauty that she would enjoy so much was spoiled by the fact that he didn't know if she'd live to see it again.

His stomach remained suspended in a half-clamp through the endless seconds of waiting. Important issues demanded attention in the back of his mind—including serious breaches to Australia's national security—but he couldn't make himself care about any of it. He didn't know how she was doing. He didn't even know if she was alive.

He'd contacted her parents, and in the broadest terms, explained to them what had happened. He'd maintained a calm voice over the phone, but the thought of meeting them in person added to his turmoil. They would arrive in two days from Denver.

He'd resisted calling his office again, but he'd needed help to get her parents' Indian visas expedited. In the process, he'd been forced to inform his director that the Cadmium 201 sample he was supposed to be bringing in had exploded.

Behind him, people in radiation protection gear filed through the corridors. Due to the immense strength of the shockwave, Indian officials were afraid the explosion over Guwahati might have been a nuclear bomb. They'd started testing everyone who came through the doors, especially those who'd been nearer to the center. They'd run their dosimeters over him, too.

Of course, no one had tested positive.

Casualties trickled in more slowly now, along with standard ER patients. From somewhere near the entrance, a young female doctor announced another new arrival.

"Head trauma, male, mid-sixties. He's conscious but disoriented, with severe burns to the upper torso. He was found on top of the same hotel as the female with the pneumothorax from earlier."

Durango whirled, already knowing. Sure enough, some distance away, Corfield stood answering an admitting nurse's questions about the new patient.

Anger boiled in his belly, and resentment tugged at the edge of his upper lip. He curled his hands into fists and strode toward the front of the waiting room, across from the registration desk. Kelly's life-and-death condition was Yat-sen Xun's fault. It was small comfort to see the old monk mumbling and thrashing feebly on his gurney. Charred bits of hair stuck out of shiny, red patches of skin around his mouth and chin. Plasma oozed from a long swath where his black robes appeared to have melted into his chest. Durango wondered if Yat-sen Xun had been burned trying to stop the firework.

A middle-aged female doctor joined the first one.

"This man was on the roof of the same hotel with the woman up in surgery?" she asked, taking Yat-sen Xun's vitals. "How many more were up there?"

"The man who brought him in said they were the only two on that rooftop."

"Are they related?"

"I don't think so. She's Caucasian, and he looks Asian. Maybe they're a couple?"

"There's quite an age difference. Although… who knows?" She jotted notes on a medical chart, and then they both began to push Yat-sen Xun's gurney toward the hall.

"I heard she's wanted by the Australian government."

"She's a criminal?"

"I don't know. That's just what I heard."

Their voices trailed off. It sickened Durango to hear the rumors already being spread. Kelly had saved their lives, and they'd never know it. She was a hero.

"Oi!"

Durango spun around. Two tall, younger men in suits walked toward him: Officers Ciprian Van Diemen and Blake Tavish of the Australian Secret Intelligence Service. His coworkers. They were part of the team he'd initially requested yesterday morning after he'd gotten Kelly, Qing, and Li safely squared away at the hotel. Some of the tension eased from his shoulders.

They could take care of the other details.

He could stay with Kelly.

"Chip. Blake." Durango nodded. "Are the others here, too?"

"Jim, Rob, Oscar, and Al," Blake said. "They're back at the hotel with Corfield's group."

"Do they have power at the hotel yet?"

"No," Chip answered. "That's why Corfield didn't try to bring in Loony-Xun earlier. He waited for medical transport." He glanced around at other people in the waiting room.

Durango took the cue and led them back by the window, where they could speak without being overheard.

"We've been briefed up to what you told the Director, but apparently, there've been some new developments in the last twenty-four hours. What happened?"

"Colin MacAyers happened."

"MacAyers…" Chip mused. "That bloke who resigned a year ago?"

"That's him," Durango nodded.

"Don't think I ever knew him," Blake said.

"I didn't know him well, but he struck me as a decent fellow," Chip shrugged. "Got a bit moody after his divorce, but I think the general consensus was that he needed a change of scenery. How'd he get involved in all this?"

"He *was* a decent fellow," Durango agreed, "and a good officer, at least for a time. But last night, he showed up at the hotel and told Kelly that I was working for terrorists who were after the substance."

"He did what?" Chip blinked.

"Why would he do that?" Blake asked.

"Two reasons: one, because he has personal issues with me. And two, because *he's* working for terrorists."

"Why do you think that?"

"Because of some things Kelly said. Also, because his presence in the hotel coincided with the appearance of Yat-sen Xun."

"Things *she* said…?" Chip asked. "Oh, you mean the statements she made in the hotel lobby?"

"Yeah," Durango said, "how'd you—?"

"Jim and Rob are still interviewing all the witnesses who heard every word. She dug herself in pretty deep."

Durango grimaced. "I was afraid of that."

"Are you sure this is the same woman we ran the background check on?" Blake asked.

Durango scowled at him.

"Fine," Blake shrugged. "But if she's clean, why would she make up that kind of story?"

"Because she believed what Colin told her, and she thought she was protecting me." He rolled his eyes at the ceiling. If he could have just told her who he really was, none of this would have happened.

"She doesn't know your identity?" Chip asked.

Durango sighed. "She knows my real name and bits and pieces about my past. Other than that, she thinks I'm a tour guide."

Chip and Blake were quiet for a minute. He didn't care what their silence meant or how transparent his feelings for her were. They shifted the topic.

"Something else you should know…" Chip said. "When we arrived earlier, the hotel staff was in the middle of trying to account for all its guests. By luck, we ID-ed and snagged your friend Yang Qing just before IB arrived on the scene."

"Shit!" Durango shook his head in self-reproach. "IB" was the Intelligence Bureau, India's internal intelligence agency. He'd forgotten all about Qing and Li. Though IB would have to be told what was going on, ASIS needed to control the flow of information on this. The fewer people who knew about Cad-2, the better. "Was Li still with him?"

"The little boy? Yeah, he was there. They were both polite, but neither would talk to us. Qing explained that he was under strict orders from you not to speak to anyone until you came back for him."

"Why didn't you just call me?"

"We tried."

Durango checked his phone. He had five messages. "Sorry. I've been preoccupied."

Blake's mobile rang. He walked a few steps away to answer it.

"Where is MacAyers now?" Chip asked Durango.

"He took off when Corfield's team showed up. Two of them went after him. Less than five minutes later, the explosion happened."

He relayed his version of events on the rooftop.

"My guess is Kelly thought the substance was going to explode on its own. I'm pretty sure she somehow secured it to a firework and tried to send it up as far away from the city as she could."

"That's consistent," Chip said, nodding. "Multiple witnesses reported seeing fireworks over the general area of the hotel just before the blast. From what a couple of them have indicated, the tail end of the pyrotechnic display was consumed by the explosion, which seems to have originated from the same location." He cocked his head to the side. "How's she doing?"

"They took her up to surgery over three hours ago. I haven't heard anything yet."

"How are *you* holding up?" Chip knit his brow.

"I'll be fine once I know she's going to be okay."

Blake returned, still holding his mobile. "That was Jim. The two members of the Bangladesh team who went after Colin MacAyers were found dead not far from the hotel. MacAyers is gone."

The half-clamp on Durango's stomach tightened. In addition to being a witness about Cad-2, Kelly could also testify against MacAyers. He might try to come after her.

As if on cue, a woman in surgical scrubs walked up to Durango. "Are you the man who brought in Kelly Morrison?"

"Yes." The clamp bore down on his stomach, seeming to cut off his airways.

"I'm Doctor Nadeem. The surgery went well. She is still asleep, but you may see her if you would like."

"Yes. Thank you."

79

"Trunk."

Durango blinked his eyes open and was immediately alert to the stocky man sitting next to him, whose closely cropped hair accentuated his sagging jowls. He knew why the man was there.

"Jim," Durango grunted back.

"Didn't they tell you that you could go back?" The nuance in Jim Powers's tone was half jibe, half reprimand, and it was straight to the point. Jim wasn't a fan of small talk. By "they," he meant the head office in Canberra, and Durango was well aware he'd been told to return. He was disobeying orders, and he'd known it would catch up with him. But he couldn't leave her.

He gazed forward, saying nothing. A clear, plastic curtain divided the hospital room, creating an antechamber on their side. Behind the curtain was a plastic tent meant to protect outsiders from possible radiation contamination. Inside the tent, underneath tubes, wires, bandages, and not at all contaminated, was Kelly. It was ridiculous because there had been no radiation, but it wasn't as though he could tell them that. The Indian doctors, left to trust their government's guesses on the type of explosive, were being overly cautious while they continued to run tests on her blood and tissues. Right now, he wasn't allowed to even touch her.

Not getting a response, Jim tried again.

"When's the last time you slept?"

"It's the twelfth?" he asked.

"Yeah. For twelve hours, now."

"I rested in the cab on the way to Guwahati on the ninth."

"How about in a bed?"

Durango shrugged. "Doesn't matter. Her parents are on their way in. Should be here soon."

"You're going to meet them looking like that? Nice first impression." He smirked. Then he leaned forward, his gaze on Kelly, and rested his forearms on his knees, all business. "What have you told them?"

"I said a bomb exploded over Guwahati, and she was seriously injured and needed surgery. They wanted to know why she'd left China. I said she'd become involved in an international incident and that I couldn't tell them any more until they got here."

Jim nodded. "That's good. I'll take over from there."

"What? No. I'll do it."

"No. You're too close. How long have you been staked out in her room?"

"Ever since you told Blake that Colin got away," Durango answered evenly.

"That was two days ago."

"Yup."

"We could post a—"

"No thanks."

"You can't sit here and play guard dog. You've been ordered to go home."

"Have you caught Colin yet?"

"No, but she's American. Let her own people watch her."

"Right now, *we* are her people. She's in danger from one of us, and she's our witness." Durango was one of the few people who couldn't be bullied by his older colleague's aggressive style.

"Witness? Sorry. Guess you haven't heard. Based on everyone we interviewed at the hotel, as well as all of the circumstantial evidence, she's been classified as a suspect."

"*Suspect?*" Durango turned and gave Jim an incredulous glare.

"Yes. *Suspect.*" Jim's tone was low but decisive. "The other eyewitnesses' stories all corroborated what she said about herself. Someone even recorded the tail end of her little speech, telling off you and Colin."

"There's video?" Though not unexpected in today's world, video footage was either a help or a new layer of complication. In this case, it was definitely the latter.

"Yeah, but fortunately, the young lady who shot it with her mobile decided to nix the audio and instead synced it with a Cardi B rap. It's trending on Tik Tok under the heading, 'I don't need no hot-ass boy-toyz.' With a z." He added the last two sentences as though he was a prudish aristocrat being forced to speak a crass foreign language—and as if he didn't have a thorough command of colorful language in his own tongue.

"I've already told you *and* the ADG why she said what she did," Durango shot back. "She's a *witness*." He didn't bother to keep heat out of his tone. He was relieved about the lack of audio, but it wasn't the first time he'd wanted to punch Jim Powers. The man was a dickhead.

"Regardless of whether she's a suspect or a witness, you need to step back and distance yourself. You know the drill. Go home. That's not from me, and it's not a request." Jim had seemed none too pleased about the Tik Tok, but he also seemed to favor the "suspect" decision that had been made.

The weight of the trouble Kelly was in had suddenly deepened. Between Yat-sen Xun, Nathaniel Richardson, and Colin MacAyers, she already had an impressive list of formidable individuals who posed a threat. But now, being classified as a suspect instead of a witness, she would have even less claim to official protection.

Here she is, unconscious, helpless, in a hospital bed, and none of it is her fault!

He clenched his fist in anger and pounded it on the chair arm; a quick, frustrated huff came through his nostrils. His disbelief that they could even think she was a suspect was now juxtaposed against the cold reality of the position she'd put herself in. It infuriated him that his own word hadn't carried more weight with his office. His mind raced through everything she'd said in that hotel lobby. A horrifying thought struck:

"Did anyone else record her? Specifically, talking about—"

"No," Jim answered, knowing Durango had meant whether anyone had recorded Kelly talking about Cad-2. "That part seems to be contained."

He sighed, grateful that at least one thing had gone right that night. *Still!* He looked back at her, isolated behind quarantine protocols, hooked up to a ventilator to breathe, and pounded the arm of the chair again.

"Hmph." Jim narrowed his eyes and studied Durango. After a pause, he asked, "How's she doing?" He nodded toward the plastic tent.

Durango sighed. "They repaired her lung and re-set her broken rib. Her concussion was minor, thanks to the fact that she skidded on her back before hitting the wall. But she hasn't regained consciousness yet. They don't know if she's…"

The faint *hiss-hush* of the respirator finished his sentence. Kelly's status was still critical.

Jim slapped his knee. "Well, the doctors know what they're doing, and *you* look like a set of swaggie balls." It was Jim's attempt at sympathy, with a not-so-subtle dose of *get over it and get a move on.*

Durango rubbed the well-past-stubble overgrowth on his jaw. Eight days ago, he'd been sitting in a rental house in China, waiting to be sent home to Australia at the end of what he'd thought was a futile, year-long mission. He'd been better rested, but he'd been dead on the inside. It was *Kelly* who'd given meaning to his work, to his life. He could handle physical fatigue if it meant protecting her. He frowned, though, thinking Jim might be right about his appearance. It had been three days since his last shave.

"I'll shave when her parents get here, but I'm not leaving her unprotected."

"You don't have a choice."

"Meaning?"

Jim gave him a funny look and snorted. "Even the ADG got a whiff of something from your phone call. He pulled me aside before I got on the plane. It's obvious to everyone. The iceman grew a heart. Did it thicken your skull, too?"

Durango clenched his jaw, forgetting momentarily that it wasn't personal. Jim was always an arse. However, the alarm had finally begun to ring in his brain. He realized now that Jim hadn't been sent as a nudge, but as the last straw. He may have pushed his disregard for his orders as far as they would let him. Even as he thought this, another plan began forming in his mind.

"Okay, Trunk, since this is unusual for you, I'll spell it out. First off, it's not your call if she's protected or not. You've been ordered to leave. Every hour you fail to return home, you're not only getting *yourself* in trouble, but you're also compromising the investigation. *And* if she wakes up and you're still here, you risk compromising *her*. It creates the appearance that you could be feeding her information. Second, investigation aside, you're too close, and you haven't thought of the next step."

"Meaning...?"

"Do you really want to be the one to tell the Morrisons their daughter can't go back to the U.S.?"

Durango snorted. "Better me than you. Or anyone else, for that matter. I've been with her this entire time, and I know the whole story—which I relayed to you all, yet somehow I seem to be the only one on her side. She's innocent. I'm not leaving her."

Powers's mobile buzzed. He answered it, then turned to Durango.

"That was my contact in customs at the Guwahati airport. The Morrisons just went through."

Durango checked his watch. "They're early. I'd already sent a car to pick them up, though. They'll be here in thirty."

"You can't be here."

"I'm going to stay until they're here, and I'll be the one to talk to them. It's only right, and you know it, Jim. And as far as her protection goes from here on out..."

Durango pulled out the new mobile he'd managed to procure and proceeded to make a phone call.

80

P*ain!* Vague images of spacemen examining me, probing me.

No! Stop! So tired… *What are you do—?!* Sleep….

Bright, round lights overhead, tubes and wires protruding out of my mouth, my arms, my chest, more spacemen—*What are they doing to me?*

Dizzy, sleep….

My mother and father's stricken faces behind a plastic sheet; my mother's hand pressed against it.

Mom? Dad? Where am I? No, mom, please don't cry. Sleep…

MacAyers's stern features frowning down at me from the other side of the plastic sheet. Him reaching for my monitors… *achiness*, sleep…

My father's face looming in a spacesuit, trying to smile, my mother's hand gloved in blue rubber stroking my cheek, *exhaustion*, sleep…

81

My back itched. I opened my eyes.

The room was different. The bright, overhead lights were rectangular, and they were farther away. I wasn't flat on my back either; I was semi-propped up. My dad sat next to me on my left, reading a magazine, but he wasn't in a spacesuit or behind plastic. *Are we in Colorado?*

I glanced down and saw something that looked like an electronic, plastic clothespin clipped on my left index finger, as well as a long, thin tube taped to the back of my hand. I followed it to an IV bag hanging from a stand.

For some reason, my right arm felt heavy, but my back itched like crazy. I automatically lifted my right arm to scratch and saw that my hand was in a cast that extended halfway up my forearm. That explained why it felt heavy. I tried to sit up to get a better angle to scratch. The small effort made the left side of my ribcage roar with piercing venom. I made a weird yelping sound and realized there was a plastic tube hanging from my mouth. I dropped my arm and sank back into the pillow.

"Hey, Kell-Bell, you're awake." My dad's hazel eyes crinkled gently behind his glasses. He put down the magazine and stood.

A dark-skinned nurse with jet-black hair came into the room.

"Is she ready?" She had a thick accent. *Are we still in India?*

"I think so." My dad responded to her, nodding. He put his hand on my shoulder and gave it a gentle squeeze.

"Okay, Miss Kelly, on the count of three, I want you to cough. Ready? One, two, three!"

I coughed, my ribs screamed, and the nurse pulled the tube out of my mouth. I panted, dizzy with the effort, sick to my stomach from the pain in my ribs. My head sank back into the cool pillow.

My dad turned away, and I understood why when the nurse pulled back the sheets and lifted my hospital gown. I wasn't wearing anything beneath it. A tube came out of my vagina and went off the bed somewhere between my legs. A thick wad of gauze was taped beneath my left ribs. With practiced movements, the nurse whisked off the bandage and changed the dressing.

"The wounds from your thoracotomy tube and VATS port are healing nicely," she commented. She replaced my gown and pulled the sheets back up. I wanted to ask questions, but she kept talking. "Okay, Father," she said to my dad. Dad turned back around. "She should try to drink something as soon as she feels able." My dad nodded, and the nurse swept from the room.

I watched her go, having no idea what she'd just said. *Thor-cotamie-2? Vatsport?*

An Indian woman in a police-type of uniform entered the room and closed the door behind her. She cleared her throat.

"Miss Kelly Morrison, I must inform you that you are restricted from discussing any of the events that transpired in your life from the time of your departure in the United States of America through now. This restriction will hold until you are otherwise informed by the Commonwealth of Australia. Do you understand what I have just told you?"

Wait, were we in Australia? Bewildered, I looked at my father.

"Dad?"

My voice was a cracked whisper. Not what I'd intended. I tried to clear my throat, but my ribs protested anew. Settling for a rasp, I tried again.

"What happened? Where are we?" The last thing I remembered was being blasted off my feet by the Cad-2 explosion.

Dad frowned and handed me a cup of ice water with a bendy straw. I craned my neck up and took a small sip, letting the cool liquid linger at the back of my parched throat for a second before swallowing. Setting the cup back down, he leaned forward and took my hand. Despite the tubes coming out of it, it didn't hurt; it was reassuring now the same way it had been when we'd walked along the train tracks so many years ago.

"We're in a hospital in India. There was a bomb. You had a punctured lung, a concussion, a couple of cracked ribs, some road rash on your shoulder blades, and a fractured bone in your right hand, though they said that one looked like an earlier injury because it was already bandaged. Do you remember any of this? What happened to your hand?"

I thought back to something that seemed like ages ago.

"I hit a wall," I whispered.

"You hit a wall?"

"It made me mad."

My father stared at me with a single, raised eyebrow. I looked away, then glanced back up to see his lips pursed in thought.

"At any rate," he continued, and I exhaled with gratitude that my father never pushed me for more than I wanted to share, "initially they were afraid you were exposed to some sort of radiation from the bomb, but all the tests came back negative. You needed surgery to repair your lung, but you're healing nicely. The doctors tell us you're lucky to be alive. Your mother and I got here as quickly as we could, once we'd heard. There's an Australian gentleman who explained that you became involved in some sort of international incident. They really haven't told us much, other than the medical stuff."

An Australian gentleman? My heart leapt for a second and then sank as I realized who my dad meant: MacAyers.

I tried to think back to the last thing I could remember. Suddenly:

"Qing!" I croaked out. "Is he okay? And Li?"

It hurt to talk with emotion. I breathed heavily with the effort.

"Miss Morrison!" the policewoman warned. I ignored her, imploring my father for answers with my eyes.

"Honey, I don't know who Li is, but Qing is fine. Worried sick about you, but fine. He had to go home to China. He's been texting me every day to check on your progress. He was ready to call off his wedding if you didn't make it, and he told me to tell you that he and Nori are adopting a little ten-year-old orphan boy."

Qing and Nori were adopting Li!

I closed my eyes, grateful for that wonderful piece of news. It would be so nice to see them both again.

"Dad," I breathed, "I have to get back to China for the wedding." I paused to pant. "I'm supposed to be in it." I forced the words to come out slowly, conserving my breath. "When can I leave?"

"Hon, you're not going to be able to make it out in the next three days to make it all the way back to China," my dad said gently.

"The wedding's in three days? How long have I been…?"

"The bomb was six days ago, and they say you have another few weeks in here until your lung and ribs are fully healed."

"Six days?" I huffed. *"Another few weeks?"*

"Kelly, don't strain yourself," my father warned.

He gave me more water and put his hand on my shoulder, guiding me back to the pillow. I found the bed controls and raised myself to a more upright position.

"Dad, I have to get home," I croaked.

But even as I said the word "home," the wrong image popped into my mind: Durango. Only, I'd deliberately pushed him away. Hopefully, he was safe, somewhere, by now.

"I… I have to quit my job," I added lamely.

I would probably have to go back to Minnesota to tie up loose ends and then move to Colorado and in with my parents until I figured out what I wanted to do with my life. Again.

"Kell-Bell, I need you to listen to me." My father's tone was serious, and his countenance was grim.

I was suddenly afraid to hear what he was about to say. He cast a sideways glance at the policewoman before continuing.

"You might not be able to come home. Not right away. Remember when I said 'international incident?' Well, it seems they need to question you about a few things down in Australia. They won't say what, but we've got a lawyer working on it…"

My gaze drifted out of focus as my dad continued talking. They'd hired a lawyer? I felt bad, wondering how much that had cost them. They were retired teachers, and my mom had health issues. They couldn't afford legal fees like this. Besides, what was I thinking, going home and moving back in with my parents? As if it would be that easy! I'd known this was coming, that I'd be questioned and arrested. I'd realized it just before I'd decided to blurt out that I was a criminal mastermind to MacAyers. It had been the only way I could think of to save Durango. He was innocent. He wasn't who they thought he was.

"...The Australians say they're going to take you as soon as you're fit to travel, and the worst part is that *our* government is actually backing them up on this! I mean, gosh darn it! I thought our countries were supposed to be friends!"

Maybe once I got to Australia, I'd be able to make them see my side of things, make them understand that Durango couldn't possibly be involved in any of this. He must have been set up.

"... But don't you worry. The attorney your mom and I retained has threatened to go public with this—and I mean to the press, the Internet, everything—if they don't let you come back home to the U.S...."

Then again, I'd been pretty blatant with my lie about working for terrorists. The night-duty desk clerk had probably even heard what I'd said. And, if I remembered correctly, I'd detonated something tantamount to a nuke over Guwahati. Suddenly I realized: not only was I in deep shit, but if any of this came out in public, my parents would be embarrassed and harassed beyond belief.

"... Don't get me wrong, it's not like they've been rude or anything, but—"

"Dad?" I croaked.

"Yes, Kell-Bell?"

"It's okay."

"What's okay?"

"I'll go to Australia," I sighed. "Save your money. Call off the lawyer."

"Honey, we don't care about the money. You're our daughter!"

"It's okay, dad." I met his gaze and held his hand as best as I was able with both of mine. "Just call him off. And *don't* let him go viral."

"Kelly, honey—?"

He stopped himself and pressed his lips together against whatever protest he'd been about to issue. He sat back. His hands were clenched, his brows were knit, but he'd heard my words. He was going to respect whatever decision I made.

Gratitude surged inside me for the fact that Dad had been the one in the room with me when I'd woken up and not Mom. I wondered if he'd planned it that way.

"Dad?"

"Yes?"

"I need you to do something for me."

"Anything, Princess."

82

Now that I could speak, I was very strictly re-instructed not to utter one word of the events that had taken place from the time of my arrival in China up through the day I landed in the hospital. That said, no one ever came in to question me, but a local police officer stayed with me at all times—probably to ensure my silence on the matter. Based on the few things the local officers would say to me ("That is up to Australia," "You will have to ask the Australians that question," and—my favorite— "Once you have been repaired, you will be shipped to Australia"), the best I could figure was that an agreement had been made to treat me as property of the Australian government. I wasn't sure how I felt about that.

I could not get any more information out of anyone, and I was afraid to specifically ask anyone else about Qing or Li, just in case they'd managed to steer clear of the whole mess. I definitely wasn't going to bring up Durango's name. The farther away I could keep him from all of this, the better.

When I felt stronger a few days later, I was transferred to another room in the hospital, where one of the nurses said I would remain until I could be discharged. It was the day of Qing and Nori's wedding.

My father assured me he would take care of "shutting things down" for me in Minneapolis. This meant getting out of my apartment lease with my roommate Kim, selling my things, and communicating my intent to quit my job to my boss. Then my parents left.

Four days went by. On September 22, I celebrated my thirtieth birthday alone. Well, alone except for my constant police guard. On the way back to my hospital room after my physical therapy session, the guard held the door open for me, and

I saw MacAyers standing at the opposite end of the hall. I wondered how much trouble I'd created for everyone—my parents, Qing, Nori, Li, Durango… the local police force, the U.S. government, the Australian government?

MacAyers glanced up, saw me, and gave me a look like I'd made him eat nails, and now he had to poop. Then he walked away. Guess that answered my question.

Yeah, probably a lot of trouble. Perfect.

I sagged my shoulders and walked into my room. At least I still got to see blue sky out of my window, for now. I wondered what they called the Supermax prison in Australia. Or maybe I'd be extradited to the U.S. and thrown in the ADX in Florence, Colorado, or whatever the female-equivalent was.

Six more weeks passed. By early November, I felt pretty well recovered. I could walk easily with no pain, I could get dressed alone, I could reach all of my body parts when I showered, and I could perform most of my other, everyday activities. My cast had been removed two weeks earlier, and I was doing hand exercises to regain strength. The abrasions on my back had healed, leaving only minor, pink scars, which the Indian doctor said would fade in time.

Not that it would matter what my back looked like under an orange jumpsuit.

My lung function was back to normal, though the doctor warned me that I was not to resume strenuous activities like running or lifting heavy objects for at least another month as she discharged me to the Australian authorities. This didn't bother me. I didn't plan on having the freedom to do much of anything once I was questioned and thrown in prison.

Somehow the things from my hotel room in Guwahati had made their way to the hospital with me. I donned one of the new outfits I'd bought in India—a cream-colored t-shirt, shirred around the collar, brown capris, and brown sandals—for the plane trip to Australia. This turned out to be a nine-hour flight on a sleek, comfortable jet. One of my two burly, Australian police escorts made a disdainful comment about me getting "special treatment." Though I agreed the jet seemed like a waste of taxpayer money, it didn't make the policeman's remark any easier to swallow. I clenched my jaw, steeling myself for the days ahead. Terrorists were probably viewed with the same hatred in Australia as they were in the U.S.

We lost five and a half hours to the time difference. It was close to midnight when we arrived in Canberra. The policemen brought me to what seemed like a very nice hotel (again, how much did they tax their citizens, that they could afford to treat criminals like this?) where they handed me off to a new, sturdily-built guard. (Did they really think I was that dangerous that they had to keep their biggest men on me?) Shaking my head at the irony, I checked into the hotel room and crashed hard, numb to any sensation but sleep.

I was awakened the next day, and the next day, and the next, and was brought via armored car through the city, and then through an underground tunnel, to a dank, windowless room. There, I was made to sit on a hard, armless chair at a cold, steel table and answer question after question after question for six hours, with a small break for lunch in the middle.

For the first few days, I had to answer to men in suits, then to men in uniforms. Over and over and over, I repeated my story, sticking to the fibs I'd told MacAyers in the hotel lobby.

I considered trying to tell the truth but couldn't figure out how to do it without naming Qing or Durango. Plus, my monologue had been corroborated not only by the night desk clerk but also by one of the club bouncers, two physicians' assistants from the medical convention, and a maid.

Note to self: next time you throw yourself under the bus, don't speak so loud!

They asked me for the name and contact information of the computer hacker I'd said I'd used. I said I didn't know him—or her; I'd only met them online through an anonymous Facebook page. When they pointed out that I didn't have a Facebook page, I merely answered, "That you know of," and then I wouldn't say any more on that topic. They didn't push too hard, though. There were other things they seemed more interested in.

When they began to press for information about the plume's exact coordinates, I would either claim to have forgotten, to have misplaced my notes, or that I wanted to see a lawyer. Of course, I didn't really know where the mine was, but I had to stick to my story to be believable. I wanted to get past the questions so I didn't have to keep up the pretenses anymore.

I was also vaguely worried about the "alternative methods" of persuasion I'd heard some countries used on terrorists. Was I actually considered a terrorist, or just a terrorist accomplice and a thief? Then again, did it matter? Hopefully, they could just get past this part and on with the sentencing, or whatever.

I avoided any discussion of Durango, and when asked about the Australian tour guide/ex-spy, I would simply say, "He has nothing to do with the information you're after." I shoved thoughts of him out of my head each time, and with practice, trained myself not to wince at the sound of his name. These days, the lead balloon was my best friend, numbing me inside.

After four days of law enforcement officers—plus a break in the middle of that for the weekend—a litany of scientists was brought into the room. I spoke with bio-physicists from the Australian Department of Health, geologists from a few Australian universities, and a few other doctors and researchers. They asked me all sorts of things about my experience with Cad-2, and these I answered truthfully.

Yes, I'd read the Wikipedia entry on the Internet.

Yes, it really did glow white, not yellow, and the crystal had rounded edges—at least at the point I'd seen it, when it had been warm.

Yes, it heated up despite having been placed back into a refrigerator.

No, it didn't appear from my test results that I'd sustained effects from any radiation.

And so on, the questions continued.

They ran more medical tests on me and took more blood and tissue samples, further validating the results from my Indian doctors.

Back at the hotel by four o'clock each afternoon, I made my way to the small workout room and walked on the treadmill for an hour, increasing my time by five minutes each day until I was up to ninety minutes. Then I began to increase my speed.

"Are you sure you should be doing that?" Peta, my afternoon-shift police escort, asked, watching me start a slow jog. Peta was young, cute, and petite, but the huge nighttime guards gave her plenty of respect. Clearly, she was just as over-qualified as the rest of my wardens.

"If I fall off, I guess we'll know," I said. I kept jogging, determined to vent my frustrations with a physical outlet.

After almost two weeks in Australia (plus two long, boring weekends in my luxury hotel room), a letter arrived, via Peta, from my father:

Kell-Bell—

I sent this to Qing, but he says he's unable to forward it to where you'd wanted it to go, so he sent it back. Sorry. Maybe you can do something with it down there.

Love, Dad.

In the envelope was a money order for just over twenty-one thousand dollars: the proceeds from the sale of all of my possessions, plus my father had closed my savings account and sold my stocks, as I'd requested.

So, Qing had lost track of Durango! I hoped that meant Durango was okay, just keeping a low profile. The tightness in my chest at the thought of him was accompanied by a strengthened resolve to keep his name out of the remainder of my questioning, however much longer that would be.

The weather was cool in Canberra—November being spring for this part of the world—and I only had the clothes I'd bought for September in India. I'd tried to ignore it in the dank, underground room when the chill rippled my skin into goosebumps, and my fingers took turns losing blood flow. Controlling my breathing between answering questions and sometimes sitting on my hands for warmth, I'd managed to keep the worst of it at bay. But now, staring at the check in my hand, the thought of a slight reprieve occurred.

"Peta, I need to go shopping," I said as we re-entered the hotel room after the latest science-geek fest—my eighth official day of questioning.

I began changing into the hospital scrubs I'd been using for my workouts. Peta knew my routine by now and was already dressed in sweats.

"Sorry, no-can-do," Peta shook her head, bouncing her wavy, dark bob against her brown cheeks.

"Please, Peta. I'm freezing. At least let me get a hoodie." I handed her the check.

"Oi!" Peta's eyes bugged out. "Not sure if 'hoodie' means something different in America, but just how exy do you think they are? That's big bickies!"

"Look, this is everything I own, and I don't have any cash. Most of this needs to be converted into Chinese currency, but—"

"Chinese currency? Why?" she asked suspiciously.

"Actually," I reconsidered, "I'm not even sure China's right anymore."

Where *was* Durango? Qing was going to have to take the money. He'd have a better chance of finding Durango than I would from a prison cell.

"I owe somebody a lot more than this, but it's a start," I explained. "For now, I just need a sweatshirt or a sweater or something to keep from freezing in that room. At least until…" *Until I go home? Yeah, right.* I gave a wry smirk.

"Until what?"

Until they give me something permanent to wear. An orange jumpsuit? Or maybe they used a different color over here. I chuckled darkly to myself, shaking my head.

Peta pushed the check back at me. "I'll see what I can do," she said.

The next morning, while the night guard was waiting for me to finish getting dressed so he could escort me into the van and clock out, Peta popped her head into my room. She'd brought me a navy zip-up sweatshirt.

"Thanks," I said gratefully, pulling it on over an embroidered white tank top, which I wore over a cute black skirt—the last clean things in my small wardrobe. "How much did it put you out?"

"It's mine. Consider it a loaner until you're done here," Peta said.

"Okay. Thanks, Peta. See you later."

It couldn't be much longer now. How many more questions could they have to ask me?

But today was different.

83

When we arrived at the underground parking garage, they escorted me to the same dank room. The men in suits from the ASIS were back. The one with sandy-cropped hair and a broad jaw that reminded me of a bulldog was Officer Jim Powers. Officer Gelen "Rob" Coorabie, the dark-skinned one with a straight, thin nose and cropped, curly brown hair, was the other. They both looked to be in their forties. Neither man seemed to possess the facial muscles necessary to smile.

They sat down across from me. Powers plopped a thin manila file on the table in front of himself.

"Miss Morrison," Coorabie began in a flat tone, "you've been cooperative with our scientists these past few days. Thank you."

He paused, staring at me with a blank, unreadable expression that didn't feel like 'thank you.' I tried to mimic a vacant response on my own face. When I didn't speak, Coorabie continued.

"We hope this means you've decided to be more forthcoming with us as well."

Powers slid the file across the table toward me. Unable to contain a rise in my curiosity, I cocked an eyebrow at Powers.

"Take a look," he ordered. He nodded at the folder, his expression as unreadable as his counterpart's.

My fingers clenched in trepidation as I began to worry about what I would see when I opened the file. *Please don't let it be anyone who died from the Cad-2 explosion!* Gulping hard, I flipped the front flap aside.

It was a set of satellite photos, which I quickly realized was of the monastery grounds. No bodies.

I exhaled a small sigh of relief. As I flipped through the images, Powers grabbed one of the ground's northeast region and pointed.

"This is the monks' prayer garden. It's off-limits to visitors, but it butts up to this mountain ridge. Is this where the mine entrance is?" he demanded.

Great. This again. I'd dodged countless questions already, and now, apparently, they wanted to try photos. I had no idea where the mine entrance was.

Over the past several weeks, I'd considered telling the truth. In fact, I'd considered telling the truth about all of it, not just about the mine's location. I tried to rationalize with myself that things could have a happy ending if I told the truth. But then I would remember what MacAyers had said about them having "compelling evidence" against Durango. And every time I thought it through, the scene kept playing out in my head with some version of the following:

ME: I lied. I don't know where the mine entrance is. Also, I didn't steal the Cad-2 on purpose, I don't know any terrorists or computer hackers, and I wasn't trying to kidnap a child. I was trying to save him from getting killed.

THEM: Oh? Then why did you lie?

ME: Because I didn't have time to argue because the Cad-2 was going to blow, and I thought it would protect Durango. You guys have him pegged all wrong. He's a good man.

THEM: Nope, we don't think so.

ME: Please, if you would just listen to me about all the times he saved—

THEM: It's irrelevant. We have evidence he's working for terrorists. And since you admit that you lied, we have no reason not to resume our pursuit of him. Also, now you're going down for obstruction of justice.

Either way, I knew I was screwed. But this way, with me sticking to my original story, Durango could be safe, or at least he could have a head start on going underground. Also, if we could get this over with as simply and quickly as possible, there was a chance that the case could stay under the radar, and my parents might be spared a grueling media circus—or worse. I was worried they might receive death threats because of my self-professed terroristic behavior.

So much for telling the truth. I had to stick to my original story.

I glanced at the area of the photo indicated by Powers's thick index finger, a small, elongated hump that rode up the mountain until it blended into the crest.

A memory tumbled in: the striated vista from the ridge over Tingming Lake, the exhilarated breath I'd taken, and the unadulterated joy at knowing he'd appreciated the moment every bit as much as I had. I started to smile, but then pain rent my heart as if I'd been freshly speared. Clenching my jaw, I ripped my vision from the image of the mountain, trying to banish the memory, and closed my eyes.

Breathe. Compose yourself. Get it back together, Morrison.

"Is that the entrance?" Powers insisted.

I looked up, able to meet his gaze with steady apathy.

"You seem pretty certain without my help. Why don't *you* tell *me*?"

"The monastery closed to visitors just after you left," Coorabie said. "No one has been allowed on the property, and our satellites haven't been able to make out any human activity outdoors. Without some sort of proof, we can't justify a reason to try to get onto the grounds."

"Why not just alert the Chinese government of your suspicions?" I asked. My voice sounded monotonous, dead.

"We don't want to do that just yet," Powers replied. "Why don't you take another gander." It was an order, not a request. He slid the photo back toward me.

Avoiding the mountain image, I pushed the other photos around, spreading them on the table. Powers and Coorabie sat back, their arms folded, glowering at me with hostile stoicism. They weren't nearly as intimidating as Durango could be, I thought, with a small degree of smugness.

After a few minutes of aimless picture-pushing, I decided to kill time by arranging the photos in order so that, eventually, I had a large aerial map. I had no idea what to do with it, though; I still didn't have a clue where the mine was located. Holding my chin in my fingers and frowning, I pretended to strike a pensive posture.

If I was going down, I was going to have fun doing it.

I let my eyes roam the sculptured gardens in which I'd been allowed to wander, the reflection ponds, the majestic range ringing the grounds, even some of the areas that were off-limits that I'd never seen. Eventually, I landed on the castle itself. The satellite shots weren't nearly as spectacular as the real thing. I glazed out of focus, remembering my time at the monastery.

When I'd arrived, I'd been a nervous, uncertain mess of a human being. Then there was learning to sit still in the meditation sessions, the sculpting classes that never materialized into a finished piece for me, and the yoga classes that left me sore but more flexible and better-toned. All these things had taught me about myself, but I hadn't been able to internalize any of it until the day I ran out the monastery door.

My favorite yoga class was the one I'd been at just before this whole ordeal had begun. The reason I'd signed up for the once-a-week, punishing, two-hour session was the same reason it had been my favorite: the view. The class was held outdoors on the highest turret ever made available to visitors, and in the five minutes of downtime after the class, I'd been allowed to walk to the wall, where I'd gazed out at the scenery.

From the mountains—layers of green and purple in the far panorama with white striations visible on the nearby Jade Dragon Snow Mountain range—to the grounds of the Zhuang Dian Monastery itself—lime and emerald dotted with cheerful accents in butter, magenta, azure, and vermillion. As I bent my neck down, my eye traveled the vivid field of vision in my memory from far to near, ending up at the ancient, gray stones of the castle itself.

I'd loved the view so much that I'd "borrowed" a key and would sneak out there late in the afternoons, before dinner. At that time of day, there was always a tiny line of workers leaving the monastery from somewhere around a corner far below. I could see them now, disheveled, dirty. I couldn't see their faces, but I'd empathized with the weariness in their slumped shoulders and drooping arms. Simultaneously, I envied them for the rich scenery they were allowed to travel through. None of the visitor paths crossed this section of the grounds, and the workers' trail hugged the castle so closely I hadn't ever been able to see it to find out where it intersected the main path.

Wondering this now, with a full satellite image in front of me, I regained focus and cocked my head to the side. I twisted my fingers in my lap. There was the main path… there was the yoga turret… where was the workers' path? It didn't seem to exist.

In fact, following visually, backward, along the route the workers had taken, I saw that the castle turned a corner away from the workers' route. Could that be correct? I had seen them come from right… there…!

I sat up, my heart rate accelerating. I was looking at three giant boulders embedded into a hill.

I was looking at the entrance to the mine.

No one would ever find it. The mine was under the castle.

"What is it?" Powers demanded. Both men leaned forward, interested.

"Do you remember something?" Coorabie hounded.

I swiftly averted my eyes from the photos, carefully considering my options. If I told them, they would say I'd been cooperative. It might lighten my inevitable sentence for working with terrorists. It might even get me off the hook altogether.

But if I told them where it was, and if, by some chance, Durango was in any way involved with this, it could make things worse for him. According to what they'd said, my word would be enough for them to be able to go onto the grounds to collect physical evidence. But what if they found something that implicated him?

No. Right or wrong, I loved Durango, and I wouldn't do that to him. I wouldn't do that to *myself.* I would hate myself for betraying him in any way. Whatever his involvement was, it had to have been for a good cause because he was a good man. A government vendetta against one of their own wouldn't be the reason one less hero walked the earth.

Not because of me.

"Miss Morrison!" Coorabie badgered.

"Sorry." I shook my head, allowing my mouth to curl into an innocent smile. "I just thought I saw the place I lost a contact lens."

"You don't wear contact lenses, Miss Morrison!"

Officer Powers was not amused. He slammed his fist on the table and stood up so quickly his chair fell backward. Circling the table, he advanced on me, grabbing my arms, yanking me roughly to my feet. My heart thumped. *Oh, crap!* Were they ready to pursue alternative methods of interrogation?!

"What did you see? Where is it?" he yelled, shaking me so that my ribs knocked around and my head ached.

I received the full furor of his glare, and I felt my eyes go round with shock. *Oh, crap. Shit just got real.* My body felt like he was still shaking it because my limbs quivered from fear. My feet automatically tried to step back from him, but his grip on my arms was tight.

Coorabie's cell phone rang. He answered, listened for a second, then looked at his partner and jerked his head toward the door. Powers gave me one more seethe of hateful disgust before he threw me down into my chair. Storming out of the room, he picked up my lunch tray and threw it against the opposite wall. Lettuce burst everywhere, the tray clattered to the floor, and discs of cucumber stuck to the cinder blocks.

Still shaking, I placed my arms on the table and lay my forehead down against the softness of the hoodie sleeves. *Don't cry, Morrison! It's a mind game. Suck it up! Focus!* I forced my breathing to even out with long, deep inhalations and measured exhales. By the time a guard entered the room some long minutes later, I was sitting upright, fully composed.

It was earlier in the day than I was used to being dismissed, but it had also been a more violent session than I'd experienced thus far. However, instead of taking me to the parking garage, the guard took me to an elevator. This was different. Were they done with me? Were they sending me to prison to await trial?

He took me up to the fourth floor, down a hall, and through a door that led to a large room with one wall made entirely out of windows. Sunlight! Another wall, to my left, seemed to be made out of mirrors. Given that it was a government building, I figured it was one-way glass. The room's only other door was in that wall. Two new men in suits faced me from across a conference table in the center of the room, with their backs to the sunshine. They were younger than Powers and Coorabie, probably closer to my age. One had sandy hair, green eyes, and very pale skin, as though he spent too much time in front of computers. The other had brown hair, hazel-brown eyes, and the cut of his suit suggested a tall, sinewy build. The guard directed me to a seat facing the men, then left the room through the one-way glass door.

"Hello, Miss Morrison," the pale, sandy-haired one said. "I'm Officer Oscar Tindal." His voice was courteous, and he gave me a friendly nod. I nodded back. "This is Officer Ciprian Van Diemen."

"Chip," the brown-haired officer amended.

I nodded politely. He grinned with a quick wink, and I blinked in surprise. Was he *flirting* with me?

"Tell us how you first met Colin MacAyers," Tindal said.

I narrowed my eyes, taken aback by the question. Why did they want to know about their colleague?

"He followed me from the hotel elevator into the nightclub in Guwahati," I answered truthfully.

"And then what happened?" Van Diemen asked.

"He introduced himself, and then he began to tell me things."

"About what?"

"Well, he said he knew I was wanted for kidnapping and for the theft of an artifact."

"Anything else?"

"I believed someone—two people, actually—had been killed; he informed me I was mistaken." I remembered my brief conversation with Yat-sen Xun before I'd lit him on fire. "But Officer MacAyers was wrong about that," I blurted out. "Whatever line of bull Yat-sen Xun—"

"What else did he discuss?" Tindal interrupted.

I hesitated. I had tried to keep Durango's name out of it, but this part would help clear his name, right?

"Miss Morrison?"

"He told me things about my tour guide. He said Mr. Trunk was an ex-spy whom he and his colleagues… I guess that would be you guys… believed had contracted services with a terrorist organization."

"Which terrorist organization?"

"He didn't say."

"Go on."

"Well, he said you-all had a theory that Mr. Trunk was the one who was trying to broker a deal for Cadmium 201, which the monks at Zhuang Dian had discovered on their property."

"Is that all?"

"Pretty much."

"Did Mr. MacAyers mention anything else about Mr. Trunk?" Van Diemen asked. "Perhaps something about his personal life?"

I blinked at the men. Did they really want to know?

"He may have used the word 'lothario' in conjunction with Mr. Trunk."

Van Diemen sniggered a little, and I felt blood rush to my cheeks.

"Look, I don't know what Mr. Trunk has to do with anything," I said. "He was just my tour guide, that's it. Can we please leave innocent people out of this?"

The men composed themselves, nodded at me, and got up, heading for the door. I swiveled my chair, watching them exit, wondering if I was supposed to go too. I heard the one-way mirror door open and my guard entering, but a horrifying thought occurred to me. The two men who'd just left: were they going to go after Durango?!

"*I'm* the one who was working with the terrorists!" I called out after them, just before the door shut.

"Kells, you've got to stop saying that," a voice said quietly behind me.

84

A ping of joy from some primal, irrational part of my heart caused me to feel a surge of hope before logic took over. I froze and swallowed hard. The voice was familiar, but I was in Australia. They all sounded like that, right?

"Kells," the voice insisted.

Time slowed. I felt like I was moving through water, like a fish in an aquarium, but I finally got my chair swiveled back around. He sat in the chair opposite me at the table, his back to the windows. Rays of sun danced on the shoulders of his crisp, white shirt and behind his now-short, neatly combed reddish-brown hair. His face was serious, but his blue eyes held the faint impression of a past twinkle.

"What are you doing here?" I breathed in wonder.

"I work here."

"No, you *used* to work here. But you were supposed to…" I trailed off.

"Run? Is that what you were going to say?"

I shrugged and raised my brows. *Yes.*

"When you gave me an out? Did you really believe I worked for terrorists?"

"No, I didn't believe that part. At least, I didn't want to," I admitted. My voice faltered and sank. "I didn't know what to believe."

I remembered my epiphany in the walk-in freezer but didn't want to go there right now. Not with him so close. I might lose my resolve. Plus, I'd said some pretty hurtful things; he probably hated me by now. I remembered the money order in my pocket.

"Here," I said, pushing the folded paper across the table at him.

"What's this?" He unfolded it.

"I know it doesn't begin to cover the cost of your car, but it's probably all I'm going to be able to get back to you for a while."

Durango looked up from the check, his countenance stern. He tapped the folded paper on the table.

"You still think I'm a real tour guide?"

"Aren't you? But…" I chewed my lip, frowning.

"But what?"

"Well, it fit, that's all."

"What do you mean, 'it fit?'"

"You were like a puzzle that I had to figure out. The ex-spy thing seemed to be the last piece, and it fit in, right between the army commando piece and the tour guide one."

"'*You're my Durango, no matter which piece of the puzzle you are.*'" He quoted my words, a distant look in his eyes. "That's what that meant."

"Yeah," I mumbled, trying to quash the stimulus that came with the memory of how close we'd been in that moment. "Only, I had trouble wrapping my mind around the whole deal-broker-for-terrorists thing. And you never corrected me when I was telling you what he'd said about you. You even agreed with some of it!"

My eyes stung as myriad emotions tried to break free inside me. *Deep breaths!*

"Agreed with it?" Durango frowned for a second until the light bulb went off. "Oh, that. Like I was trying to tell you that night, but you didn't give me a chance: Colin has an ax to grind with me. A few years ago, he went through a messy divorce, and during one of their blues, his wife let it drop that she and I had hooked up a week before their wedding."

"You slept with his wife?"

"It was one night, several years ago, and I didn't know who she was." He looked away, shifting uncomfortably in his seat. "And they weren't married yet," he added.

"Okay," I said, "so MacAyers is angry with you. But how does he go from that to terrorists?"

"I couldn't figure it out at first either. You see, I never quit the Service."

"You…?"

…*never quit the Service?* He really did work here? That would mean…!

I felt my eyebrows shoot skyward. Durango was still a spy.

"But..."

The momentary relief I'd felt clouded over into upset. My instincts about him had been correct, but, *All the guessing! All the doubt!* I bit my lip. My breaths came rapid and shallow, and my eyes stung again, this time with the pain of betrayal and confusion. My voice came out in a whisper:

"Why didn't you just tell me?"

"I wanted to. So badly," he said softly. His eyes were full of compassion, and a knot pulsed at the back of his jaw.

Our last conversation in my hotel room. Before the lobby. He'd said something about desperately wanting to tell me everything but not being at liberty to do so. His hands had been tied. A tear rolled down my cheek as I understood what had happened. Brushing it away with the back of my finger, I nodded.

"Go on."

"Shortly after his divorce, Colin did quit," Durango continued. "Now, fast-forward a year. By the time you met him, two months ago, I'd been away from home for just over a year, living in China. And I'd been out of communication with my office for a few days while you and I were on our little road trip. The morning we arrived at the hotel in Guwahati after I'd dropped you all off, I'd gone and called in for support. The team hadn't yet arrived, and my first thought when I saw Colin coming toward you at the elevator was that he'd re-enlisted, and they'd sent him.

"But as you talked, I began to figure out that everything he'd told you about me was really about him. *He'd* been contracting out his services, and at that point, he was working for Yat-sen Xun. Made sense, though: Colin found out about the Cad-2 rumor the same time the rest of us did, just before he put in his notice. We think he's used half a dozen leads from this office to cultivate his 'retirement activities.'"

"Wait a minute. *MacAyers* is working for terrorists? But I saw him at the hospital. I thought he was monitoring my arrest and checking up on my guards."

"He was at the hospital? Did he speak to you?"

"No. I just saw him there a few times."

Durango's jaw hardened. "I'm pretty sure he was there to kill you."

"Excuse me?"

"It's one of the reasons you've been under guard. When Yat-sen Xun's own men failed to terminate you, he sent Colin to finish the job. Colin knew I was embedded in China, and he guessed that I might be involved with your escape from the monastery. He's much smoother than I ever gave him credit for. He knew exactly what buttons to push to make you believe he was on the up-and-up. Though you did throw him for a bit of a loop when you fell on the sword yourself, instead of tossing me to the sharks." Durango smirked at the memory.

I remembered my devastation in the cooler and my rambling speech in the hotel lobby in front of the elevator doors.

"So all that time I was saying it was me—that I was the terrorist's broker—you both knew it wasn't true," I clarified slowly.

"Yeah," he agreed. "I think we both realized you believed him and that you thought you were covering for me. And then your little stunt with this thing."

He reached down to the chair seat next to him and set something on the table. It was the despicable, black, lacquered wooden box. I jumped up from the table.

"Whoa! Kells!" He held up his hands in surprise.

"I hate that thing!" I growled.

Scowling at it, I returned to my chair, ripping my eyes away from the baby that stared back at me. Durango pressed his lips together, looking like he was suppressing an urge to laugh at my superstition. He moved the box back to the chair.

"In retrospect," I continued, "I still would have said the same things. Although maybe not quite as loud. I wanted you to take Qing and Li and get as far away from the hotel as possible. And regardless of the truth, I needed for MacAyers to think that I believed him, so he'd be distracted by… *that* thing… while I did what I needed to do."

"You mean while you went off to save the world all by yourself." He frowned.

"I really did think MacAyers worked for the ASIS, and I thought he believed what he'd told me about you. So when I said what I said in such a public forum, I thought he'd have to arrest me. But the Cad-2 was already getting hot. I didn't have much time."

"It was a smart idea to use the fireworks," Durango admitted. "But I distinctly remember telling you to stay put."

"I *did* stay put, but the elevator started to move," I informed him. "And then there were these Indian guys and MacAyers, and I just wanted to get away from them all to get back to you, to know that you and Qing and Li were safe from Yat-sen Xun. But then MacAyers said all that stuff, and I didn't know what to believe."

"How did you finally figure it out?"

"I didn't," I conceded. "In the end, I just had to go with what I knew to be true for *me*."

"And what was that?"

Having no idea how he felt about me, months after I'd very deliberately tried to break his heart, I looked down at my hands in my lap.

"That I loved you for *who* you were, no matter *what* you were," I said softly to my thumbs.

Durango didn't say anything. I heard him stand. He came around the conference table. I looked up. He handed me back the money order and clasped my upper arm, pulling me to my feet. In his other hand, he held the box.

"Come on, we're going," he said curtly.

That was his response to me telling him I loved him? *Oh, man.* It was bad enough that I'd just laid it all out there, but now I'd also created what was probably going to be a super-awkward situation for both of us for however much longer I needed to stay in this country.

He opened the main conference room door. Once out, he slid his hand to my shoulder, guiding me forward.

Deflated, I shoved the check in my pocket and allowed him to lead me through aisles of office cubicles until we came to the main corridor. Maybe it was upsetting to him that I could possibly love someone whom I'd believed might be linked to terrorists.

Or perhaps he just didn't feel the same by the light of day, two months later.

Come to think of it, this was actually the second time I'd told him I loved him. I'd also said it at the hotel in Guwahati. He'd definitely responded better that time, but he hadn't said the same back to me back then, either. *Maybe he never felt that way*. After all, we *had* only known each other for a few days. Maybe I was just part of a job to him.

My heart sank, but I was surprised to find I wasn't embarrassed about my feelings. I was, however, determined to keep a lid on it and not make him any more uncomfortable in my presence, for however much longer that turned out to be. He stopped us in front of a desk before a door.

"This witness is now in my custody," he told the gray-suited clerk behind the desk.

"Yes, Officer Trunk," she acknowledged pleasantly.

He directed me out the door, over to the elevators, and onto the first one that opened, going down.

"You said 'witness,'" I commented after the doors closed. "Didn't you mean to say, 'suspect?'"

"Nope. You *were* classified as a suspect, but you are now a key witness to an international incident involving China, India, the U.S., and Australia. And since one of our former members is one of the main suspects, we get to keep you here, in protective custody. Your country has already agreed to it."

"But after everything I said? To all of your other colleagues, for *days*...?"

"Yeah." He made a face. "You're lucky I do work here, or you *really* would've been in some hot water. You're one of the most stubborn, obstinate... Here." He handed me the box. "Open it."

Relief had begun to flood me upon learning I wasn't a suspected terrorist. Confused but curious, I took the despicable cube from him, rotated the dragons into place, stroked their necks, and shoved the baby up with my thumbs. I pushed the button.

With a click, it hinged back, revealing new, black foam. In the center of the foam lay a flattened, bent nickel. *My* nickel. I gasped.

"How did you? Where did you? This is..." I looked up at him.

"I found it in the river the same day you dropped it," he confessed. "Don't know why I didn't return it to you sooner, but I got it into my head that it needed augmentation. Look."

He nodded toward the nickel. A small link had been punctured through its top, and as I picked up the familiar, ridged edges, a silver necklace followed.

"So you won't lose it again," he explained. "That's actually where I'd gone that day at the bazaar, to see if I could get something like this done, but I almost lost you. Very unprofessional of me. Here." He helped me put it on, and I bit back sudden tears. After all the hostility I'd encountered the past few weeks, his unexpected gift was so sweet and thoughtful.

"Thank you," I whispered, looking up at him.

Durango's lips pressed firmly together, but this time he wasn't suppressing a chuckle. A knot formed at the back of his jaw, and his brows knit in consternation as though he were wrestling with his thoughts. For a second, I thought he was going to kiss me but quickly realized I was wrong.

"You're welcome," he said stiffly. "Now, how about if we find you somewhere better to stay than a hotel? You're going to be here a while."

85

The elevator shuddered to a stop.

"The hotel is fine," I mumbled. I was still trying to find the correct emotional balance from my inability to read Durango's signals in this new setting. "I probably can't even afford to stay there, let alone anywhere else. I quit my job."

"I heard."

We exited the elevator into the same underground parking garage I'd been taken to for the past week. Only this time, we walked right past the row of tinted-window vans. He led me to a shiny, black SUV.

"By the way, who is Ralph?"

"Ralph?" I asked, startled. "Where did you hear that name?"

Durango opened the front passenger door on the left side, and I got in. He strode around to the driver's side on the right before answering.

"At the hospital in India, your father said to me, 'When you see my daughter again, please tell her that Ralph said to say that he loves her, misses her, and wants her to come home.' He said something like, 'Ralph would never want Kelly to be walled-in by him, but he was her first love, so when she's feeling better, she should know that he's sick.'"

"Oh no! He's sick?" My heart sank.

"Apparently." His eyes narrowed as he purred the engine to life, peeling out of the garage rather quickly.

"Why didn't Dad tell me?"

"Maybe he didn't want to worry you while you were recovering. So, who is he?"

"Wait a minute. You were at the hospital? You met my parents?"

"Yeah, Elliot and Carol. Nice people. Who's Ralph?" Durango pressed.

I puzzled my head to the side. Maybe I was numb from all the questioning I'd been through the past week, but Durango seemed overly curious about Ralph. I remembered my father mentioning a "nice Australian gentleman," but I'd assumed he was talking about MacAyers.

And what had Dad meant by 'Ralph would never want me to be walled-in by him?'

The light bulb went off: I'd told Dad I'd broken my hand by hitting a wall that made me mad. Dad had extrapolated from there, and for some reason, my father had chosen his wording to make Durango think Ralph was human.

"Ralph is my dog. My parents' dog, actually," I explained.

"I thought you said your parents' dog was named Sampson."

"His name *is* Sampson, but when he was a puppy, we used to call him Ralph because that's the sound he made when he barked. 'Ralph-ralph.'"

"Oh. I see."

Durango's eyes glinted with sudden understanding, and the corner of his mouth twisted into a smirk. He shook his head and suddenly seemed relieved.

"Sorry about your dog being sick, by the way," he muttered.

"So, you were at the hospital?" I asked again.

"For a little while," he replied. "Long enough to meet your parents and know that you were going to make it. But I wasn't allowed to actually see you. Not until you'd finished being deposed. Unfortunately, it took until today for them to realize you weren't going to give them a straight answer unless you knew I wouldn't be hurt by it." Durango shook his head and chuckled. "Heart of a lion."

"So, you're not mad at me? For all of those hateful things I said in the lobby? And for not trusting you more?"

"First of all, I was never mad at you for anything you said in the lobby. Like I said, I figured out what was going on pretty quickly. But the other, well, like you said back at the hotel, trust goes two ways. How can I expect you to have trusted me when I couldn't even tell you the truth myself?"

I thought about his words for a few moments. There was still a chasm between us on the trust issue, and I still needed to know more about that night.

"What happened when you left me in the elevator to chase Yat-sen Xun?" I asked.

"I never found him. Your room was open, and it was a mess. Clearly, he'd scoured it looking for the box. But he'd worked fast because he was gone by the time I got there, though I did get delayed by some of his associates. I checked on Qing and Li—woke them and told them to lock in until I got back. Searched around the other floors, met a couple more of your Shaolin monk friends in one of the other hallways, but never found the big dog."

I was sure Durango had done more than "meet a couple of Shaolin monks" in the hallway. We drove in silence for a few minutes, and my gaze drifted out the window.

"What do you think of Australia so far?" he ventured.

"You have hills!" I exclaimed, looking at the green mounds in the distance.

"Those are mountains," he chuckled. "Not exactly what you grew up with in the Rockies, but we're not all desert. You can even ski on those in the winter. Haven't you seen them before?"

I shook my head. "Until today, all I've seen is the inside of my hotel, the inside of a van, and the inside of a cross-exam room. The toilets swirl around the other way, though. That's kind of cool."

"You've been in Australia for almost two weeks, and all you've seen are the toilets? Why didn't you ask to go out?"

"Well, first, I was kind of tired from the time change. Then there was all the questioning. Plus, I thought I was under arrest. But even when I did ask, Peta wouldn't let me."

Durango grinned. "She was being over-careful. That's Peta. She's quite fond of you, you know."

"You know her?"

He pulled up in front of a small, modern house with an impossibly tiny yard and sculpted shrubbery in an uber-trendy-looking neighborhood. "Peta's my niece. My sister Brenna's oldest. Come on, see if you like this one."

"Peta's your niece? She never said anything!"

I followed Durango up the steps. He walked through the front door.

"Um, are you sure this is okay?" I followed him in. The house was empty.

"Yeah, I called ahead to the landlord."

We went through the tiny foyer to the small living room, a combo kitchen/dining area, two bedrooms, and one bath. Everything had super-straight, clean lines and looked brand new. I felt like I was in Millennial Clone-Land Hell.

"What do you think?" he asked.

"Sure," I shrugged. "I could stay here for a while." It wasn't my taste, but I didn't want to make waves.

Besides, it would just be until I testified, right?

"Naw, you don't like it." He shook his head. "Come on. I've got another place to show you."

We drove for another fifteen minutes to a gated-community suburb, ending up at a sprawling house with four large bedrooms, three and a half bathrooms, a swimming pool, a theater room, a kitchen with black granite countertops and gigantic professional cooking range, and a few other empty, cavernous rooms. "What do you think?" he asked.

I strained my ears, listening hard.

"What is it?" he whispered in alarm.

"Sssh! I'm waiting for the echo," I whispered back.

"Aww, crikey," he rolled his eyes, grinning. "Come on. Let's try the next one."

His grin still made me melt, but I did my best to not let it show. The rapport between us had settled into comfortable familiarity, and I was relieved it didn't feel awkward. I could do this: I could be friends with him.

This time we drove for ten more minutes, coming to a subdivision near the center of town. Durango parked in front of a mid-size, single-story house with a small, well-manicured front lawn. Suddenly, before we looked at another rental, I wanted more information.

"Tell me what happened after I told you to take a hike, gave the empty box to MacAyers, and jumped in the elevator."

"Well, I didn't know the box was empty," he confessed. "I was dumbfounded that you would give it to him, even though I figured he'd fed you a pretty convincing line. And by that time, I'd figured out what was really going on with him. So, of course, I couldn't let him have it. We wrestled for a bit, I got hold of it, and he got away."

"Which is why he was able to show up at the hospital," I realized, finally piecing together the danger I'd been in.

"Yeah, that's one of the reasons I'd called in a favor to the Indian government, to have the police watch you while you were there, and why you're now in protective custody. Colin can run, but he'd have to go troppo to try and come back here."

"Troppo?"

"Crazy. From too much tropical heat."

"Ah. But that's how you got the box." I wondered whether he'd sustained any injuries fighting his former colleague. Not that he'd ever admit it. "And then did you feel the blast?"

"*Everyone* felt it. No fatalities, but, as you've probably heard, it shook all the buildings in a one-kilometer radius, and it knocked out the power grid for a few hours. But I saw it, as well."

"You saw it?"

"Yeah." Durango took a deep breath and stared straight ahead at the dashboard. "I still couldn't believe you'd given Colin the box. Once I got it away from him, and he ran off, I opened it. Right then, I knew what you were up to. Didn't know you'd got ahold of fireworks, but it didn't make sense for you to go back up to the room, so I figured you were probably taking the elevator all the way to the top.

"By then, my support team had arrived. We made it to the rooftop door in time to see Yat-sen Xun cornering you, and that's when the shockwave hit. He got knocked one way, you went flying the other, and you just slammed into the ground like a rag doll. I couldn't run fast enough. With the power out, I got you down the stairs, and by the time we got to the hospital, I couldn't tell if you were breathing..." His voice trailed off.

I thought about it: the hospital was at least a mile from the hotel. That meant he'd probably carried me the entire way.

But something struck me.

"I remember," I breathed.

"You remember that?" he asked in disbelief.

"No, I remember *you*. The last sensation I had before completely going unconscious was the smell of woods and sunshine. That was you. Thank you for saving me. Again."

Durango's hands gripped the base of the steering wheel. The knot in his jaw bulged, and his eyebrows lowered as he continued to stare ahead in a long exhale. Was he angry?

"Come on, let's take a look," he said gruffly. We exited the car and went up.

86

Entering the house, I paused. It had clean lines and an airy, open floor plan. Three bedrooms, two baths, a slightly dated kitchen, and large windows. Something about this house felt homey. Then the backyard caught my eye.

I walked to the sliding door. Past the covered concrete patio was a small green expanse, oddly angled, with a gnarled tree in the corner. Something hung from the tree's branches. I gasped.

"Kells?" Instantly he was at my side with his arm around my shoulder, in full-on protective mode. I ignored the little leap my heart gave at his touch. He followed my gaze.

"It has a tire swing!" I explained, feeling the smile blossom on my face as I spoke. The sight of the swing tickled me, and childhood memories swept me over the top. I loved this place.

"Figures," he muttered. "She picks the one that has a tire swing." I felt his stance relax, but his arm stayed around my shoulder.

"Really?" I looked at him in disbelief. "I can stay here? The rent isn't too high?"

"Stop worrying about money. It's yours."

Pleased, I grinned up at him. He'd avoided eye contact with me for most of the day, but now his blue eyes blazed into mine.

"*I'm* yours," he breathed.

Whoa—what?

My jaw dropped, and my heart thrummed against my chest.

"I don't want to have to keep any part of me from you ever again. And I don't deserve you, but I am *not* losing you. I love you, Kelly Morrison."

He dipped his head, brought his lips to mine, and my heart exploded. I knew right then that I'd read all of his other signals correctly, and he'd just been holding himself back. This was the most real and true thing in the world. *Us.*

I threw my arms around his neck. He moved his hand to my waist and pulled our bodies flush. I couldn't stop the smile on my lips as we kissed. And *kissed.* He pulled himself away with effort and planted another kiss on my cheek before pressing his forehead to mine.

"I wanted to quit my job a hundred times out there on that road trip and just run away with you—*anywhere*. To hell with national security!"

I'd had no idea he'd felt that way back then, and the thought curled warmly around my heart. *But...*

"But that's not who you are," I murmured. "Plus, you would never have left Qing and Li high and dry."

"You're right," he sighed. "And you would never have gone along with that part either. But now, keeping this job is what's kept me close to you. I wouldn't have been able to monitor you or this whole case if I wasn't in this position."

"But now I'm in your *custody*?" I grinned.

"Twenty-four, seven," he responded, nuzzling into my neck, which felt *very* nice. Then he stopped with a sigh. "I know this is a lot to ask, being with someone who does what I do. And I don't plan to do it forever. But do you think you could hold out at least until this case is over?"

"Durango," I said softly, "I meant what I said. I love you for who you are, no matter what you are. You do this job for as long as you want to be here. But...?"

"But?"

"Are you going to leave for months at a time to go on missions?"

Relief swept his face. "No!" he said definitively, kissing me one more time. "Come on. We have a lot to talk about, but not here."

"Where are we going?"

"Back to my place."

87

Durango lived in a modern hi-rise southeast of the R. G. Casey Building, where the ASIS was headquartered, overlooking Lake Burley Griffin in Kingston. Taking the elevator to the eleventh floor, we walked down the hall. He opened the door, stepping aside to let me enter first into a large, very black-and-white room.

On the right, sable leather sofas and onyx-stained end tables faced an ebony fireplace, set three feet up into a narrow section of stark, white wall. Beyond the fireplace, the rest of the wall was taken up by a floor-to-ceiling window.

To my left, the white wall was lined with chunky, half-empty, espresso-colored cube shelves. In front of those sat a black, modern desk with a computer monitor, several stacks of papers, and a cardboard box full of file folders.

Facing me on the blank, far wall, eight high-backed black leather chairs surrounded an inky dining table. Underneath it, an alabaster area rug adorned the charcoal slate floor tiles. A doorway lay on the right of the back wall, through which I could see snowy cabinets, obsidian granite countertops, and sleek, black appliances from a kitchen lit by the continuing bank of windows. A broad opening to the left of the dining room led to an unadorned, milk-walled hallway. I shivered. Despite the luxe furnishings, the place felt sterile. Nothing about it meshed with the warmth of Durango's character. He, however, seemed impervious to the apartment's clinical austerity. Or maybe he just ignored it.

"How long have you lived here?" I asked.

"Uh, 'lived' is a strong word," he replied. I followed him into the kitchen. "I bought the place five years ago. But I've been gone so much I never really moved all the way in. It's kind of more like a crash pad."

It was a relief to know my instincts had been correct: he didn't call this place home, either. But I was curious about the fact that he said he'd bought it, not rented. Maybe spies got paid really, really well, but it seemed a bit over the top for a place that never got used.

Durango's cell phone rang. He checked the caller ID and groaned. "Sorry, he's been texting me all afternoon. I have to reply to him. I'll just be a few minutes. Make yourself at home."

I walked back out to the living room.

"Want a beer?" he called out.

"No thanks, I'm good."

I wandered over to the bookshelves. Several cubes were lined with bestselling titles, many of which centered on nautical themes. Four were entirely devoted to atlases. I smiled, remembering Durango's love of maps. There were also a dozen books about business practices, and on the bottom shelves were binders of quarterly reports for Beach Produce, the company his brother ran. Five boxes labeled "books" sat taped shut in front of the rest of the empty shelves.

A few framed family photos sat on some of the shelves. I recognized a younger Peta in one. She had three younger brothers, and all four of them had the same brown eyes, curly hair, and dark skin as the man in the photo. The red-headed woman smiling next to him had green eyes, but otherwise, her facial features were very familiar: that must be Durango's sister, Brenna. I found the woman who must be his other sister in a Christmas photo: she had blue eyes and brown hair, like Durango, and she smiled serenely, surrounded by her husband and six children, all of whom were wearing suits. I found his brother, Reginald, in a couple of photos, one with a pretty blonde woman and three blond-haired, blue-eyed girls. An old black and white photo showed a bride and groom, each of whom shared some of Durango and his siblings' features—probably their parents.

Set off to the side was another aged photo, this one in color, of two boys in swim shorts walking on the beach. I picked it up. They both had their backs to the camera, but the older boy, a skinny blond of about ten or twelve, held the hand of a youngster with unruly mahogany hair, whose belly pudged out farther than his shorts. The toddler grinned up at his brother in complete hero-worship. Warmth spread in my chest, having nothing to do with the cold, ascetic apartment.

"So, what do you think?" Durango asked.

"I love it!" I said, turning. Durango looked surprised.

"You do?"

"How could I not?" I smiled, but, confused by his tone, I held up the photo in my hand. "Isn't this you and your brother?"

"Oh," he chuckled. "You love the picture. Yeah, that's Reg and me when I was about two. Fat little tyke, wasn't I?"

"What did you mean, 'what do you think?'"

"I meant this place." He gestured around the room.

"Oh! It's very… clean. And expensive-looking."

"Yeah, I don't really like it much either. It kind of screams 'urban snob.' We can unload it as soon as we get the house the way you want it."

"We can unload—?"

"Spewin' *arseholes*!" Durango exploded as his phone rang with another incoming caller. He looked at it.

"I'm sorry," he sighed. "It's my boss."

I nodded in understanding as he stalked back to the kitchen. Setting the photo down, I peeked in the cardboard box on his desk. On top of a stack of files sat a fat envelope with my name on it. The envelope was open, so I picked it up. Inside were my driver's license, cell phone, China visa, and passport. *Hallelujah!* I tried the cell phone. It was dead, probably from lack of charge. But I pocketed it anyway, along with the other things with my name on them. It felt good to have a piece of "me" back. I wondered what had happened to my purse, credit cards, and all of my clothes from the monastery.

Durango was still on his call. I was just about to go try out the sofa when a large cardboard box on the floor caught my attention. It was wedged in the corner between the desk and the bookshelves. The top flap wasn't all the way shut, and something glinted underneath. I crouched, lifted the flap, and peeked. Half a dozen rugby trophies lined one side. Next to them sat a row of plaques, diplomas, and framed certificates. I knelt on the cold slate, moved the trophies around, and flipped through the certificates. They all bore the name "Durango Archibald Trunk," "Captain Durango Archibald Trunk," and "Officer Durango A. Trunk." A smaller box was tucked behind the plaques. I lifted it out and opened the lid.

Inside, a golden starburst medal on an orange ribbon and a pewter cross on a crimson ribbon sat, unheralded. I wondered if they were rugby medals or something else.

Snippets of Durango's end of the conversation floated into the room. My ears perked up.

"... no, she's *already* been through enough... She's answered that already... Yeah, but it was *obvious* she made it up... No, I didn't see today's. Was it different from last week's? Oh, for the love of...!"

I got off the floor. Still on the phone, Durango walked to the kitchen door and made eye contact with me. His lips were pressed into a thin line, and his entire body was rigid.

"Yes, sir. We'll be right there, sir." Durango shoved his phone in his pocket. He exhaled. The knot in his jaw pulsed. I raised my eyebrows in question.

"Sorry," he said, "we have to go back to the office."

"Okay?"

I closed the lid on the small box containing the medals, set it on his desk, and crossed the room to him. Durango gave me a quick kiss on my temple. Then we left.

88

"They think there's a discrepancy," he explained on the way over, though he seemed to be talking more to himself than to me. He drove at his slightly alarming light-speed rate. Then he shook his head. "I mean, kick my arse. You're the *worst* liar. A monkey could tell, so you'd think some of the world's best-trained professionals wouldn't need to go through this."

"Uh, thanks?"

"Look," he said, seeming not to have heard my joke, "just go in there and tell them the real truth—on the record—now that you know I won't get hurt by it, right?" He parked in the garage, then reached across and took my hand. "Then we can go home and… start moving forward."

"Forward," I grinned. After months of stagnating in the acceptance of an awful fate and being worried about Durango, and now to know that not only was I *not* going to terrorist prison, but Durango was back in my life in a *big* way—moving forward sounded *awesome.*

Late afternoon sun shone through the building's windows as we entered. We got on the elevator, the doors closed, and I thought of something.

"By the way, whatever *did* happen to Yat-sen Xun after the explosion?"

"He was injured but alive. He was brought to the hospital and treated for several days. We had a guard on him. Our intent was to take him into custody when he was released, but he escaped early—possibly aided by Colin—and we lost him. We were able to discover that he'd somehow made it back to the monastery, where he's now holed up in seclusion. We're close to getting a man on the inside, but that's a delicate operation, too, with Colin on the loose. And we haven't reached out to the Chinese government for help because we don't want them learning about the mine. For now, we're just watching the grounds via satellite, as best as we're able to. Yat-sen Xun is definitely there, but he hasn't had any visitors. He knows he's being watched."

The elevator doors opened. We walked down the hall through the cube maze and entered the conference room. Durango rested his arm around my shoulder, pulling me close.

Three of the four officers who'd questioned me, Jim Powers, Gelen Coorabie, and Chip Van Diemen, were already seated in the conference room. An unopened laptop sat on the table in front of Coorabie. All three men looked up as we entered. Powers flared his nostrils, making no attempt to hide his disgust.

"Oh, brilliant," Powers muttered with a glance at Durango's posture.

He crossed his arms on his chest and looked away. Coorabie shifted in his seat. Chip rolled his eyes at Powers. Durango ignored his colleagues.

"Where's Oscar?" Durango asked.

"Busy," Chip answered. "And I don't see why it takes more than one of us to depose a friendly Yank." He looked at his watch, scowled at Powers and Coorabie, and huffed.

"Well-said," Durango concurred.

He pulled out a chair for me on the door-side of the table and then walked around to sit next to the other officers. It was on the same side of the table as I'd sat earlier today, only now I knew I wasn't a terrorism suspect but a witness. I lowered myself into the seat.

"Unless it's because she's hot," Chip added under his breath, with a wink and a quick nod at me.

I bit back a smile as Durango's elbow slipped into Chip's ribs.

"Or because she actually knows something," Coorabie said dryly.

"We've been through this, Rob," Durango sighed. "I explained it all to you. And *you* agreed with me."

"That was before today," Coorabie said.

He opened the laptop, punched a few keys, and angled the monitor toward Durango and Chip. I heard the beginning of the session I'd had that morning in the dank cross-exam room in the basement.

Suddenly I knew exactly what this was about.

My stomach sank. Having forgotten my morning revelation while reuniting with Durango, I'd since re-thought the situation and just wanted it to go away. But *that* wasn't going to happen.

Trying to quash the panic rising in my chest, I looked on helplessly as Durango and Chip watched the video. Listening to the audio, I replayed the event in my mind.

Powers and Coorabie asking me to be more forthcoming, sliding the photos across the table. Powers, asking about the possible entrance to the mine being on the property's northwest corner. The memory of being with Durango at Tingming Lake—a memory that had been so unbearable, I'd had to push it away for fear of sobbing my heart into pieces—a memory now decadent with the texture of future possibilities.

I stole a glance at Durango as he watched the video. He sat stoically, his face as unreadable as his counterparts'.

Coorabie, prodding me for answers; me, obstinately answering their questions with questions of my own. And then the long minutes where I'd pushed the satellite photos around, mocking Powers and Coorabie with my body language.

The edge of Durango's lip smirked up for a second. He understood exactly what I'd been doing.

Silence, during my long daydream about my time at Zhuang Dian.

The photo-staring had gone on for quite a while. Coorabie leaned over to fast-forward the video.

"I don't see what this shows us," Durango exhaled in exasperation. "She made up the part where she said she knew the coordinates."

"Just wait," Powers snapped. "It's coming."

Coorabie clicked the video back to play speed. I reviewed the timeline. I knew exactly where he would have stopped it and what they wanted Durango to see.

The memory of my yoga classes, the majestic view, the workers below. My curiosity about the workers' path. Regaining focus on the image.

Durango sat up straighter, leaning in slightly to the monitor. He frowned. His eyes narrowed.

And then my light bulb.

Durango's eyebrows shot up, just as Powers and Coorabie had also been interested. Their voices began to press me for details on the video.

My silence as I weighed my options. Coorabie's insistence, my smart-aleck response about a contact lens.

"You see?" Coorabie demanded. He reached for the monitor, but Durango and Chip were still glued to the scene.

"Whoa, mate!" Chip blocked Coorabie's hand as the video continued.

I didn't want to relive this part, either, and I didn't want Durango to see my humiliation. But there was nothing I could do from across the broad table. I stared at the floor, embarrassed, my fingers finding the familiar edges of the bent nickel strung around my neck.

Powers slamming his fist on the table, getting up, grabbing me, shaking me like a pit bull with a toy. Coorabie's phone ringing, Powers throwing me down as he left, but not before he'd also thrown my lunch at the wall. Me, sitting traumatized, with my head down on the table.

A click and two quick shuffles sounded in my ears. I looked up. The laptop was shut, and Durango and Powers stood frozen, staring at each other, fists clenched. Durango easily had six inches and fifty pounds on Powers.

"Thought she was a witness, not a suspect," Chip said in a low voice from his seat, looking over at Coorabie.

"That changed once we realized she had tangible information," Coorabie said evenly.

"*She's* the one who positioned *herself* as a suspect!" Powers yelled at Durango and pointed at me. "She told us over and over that she was working for terrorists!"

"And *I* told you why she did that," Durango growled. "She *thought* she was protecting *me*, courtesy of *our* former colleague. On top of that, need I remind you that she saved millions of lives when she managed to send the center of a *five hundred kiloton* blast into the troposphere *while* fighting off a warlord! *She's* a hero!"

I'd never thought of myself in those terms—I'd been too busy feeling horrible about betraying Durango—and I was stunned now to hear him speak that way about me. Durango, who modestly downplayed his own countless, selfless, epic actions, including rescuing me repeatedly.

"Hero, my *arse*!" Powers screamed. "It's *her* word that the sample was getting hot and was going to blow. She saved her own neck by destroying the Cad-2. Maybe she was really destroying evidence that could incriminate her. She knows something, and you know it! Look at her! She's having a lend of us, you worst of all!"

"She already told me everything she knows, and I've already written it all up. *You've* seen the report! I know this girl; I've spent a great deal of time with her. And just because you and I have become jaded on the human condition doesn't mean everyone else has. In her world, right and wrong really do exist! She thinks *we're* some of the good guys—yeah, even you, Jim, believe it or not. Whatever was going through her head this morning, it wasn't what it looked like! So, lay off!"

My heart sank. Durango was defending me, but this time he was wrong. The expression they'd read on my face had been for exactly the reason Powers and Coorabie had thought. I ripped my fingers away from the nickel and forced my hands into my lap.

Breathe, Morrison. Think this through.

"Oh, I get it," Powers sneered. "She acts like she worships the ground you walk on, and it gives you some sort of superman complex, so you keep rushing to her aid, defending her. You get off on that? Nice."

"Least he doesn't use force with women to try and get what he wants," Chip muttered.

Powers's eyes bulged, and his face went red. He took a loaded stride toward Chip. Durango stepped toward Powers, and Chip stood.

"You want to go down that road?" Powers growled at Chip. "*I'm* doing my job." He slashed his gaze back to Durango.

My stomach roiled, knowing I was the cause of this volcanic moment. I also knew that whatever followed next, I probably wasn't going to make things any easier.

"Don't get off your bike, mate," Coorabie warned. Powers fumed a few breaths.

"Okay," Powers countered, looking at Durango, "let's say you're right. This girl is completely innocent. She doesn't know where the entrance is. Ask her. Right now! Ask her!"

Powers and Coorabie stared expectantly at Durango. Chip looked at Durango and shrugged. I swallowed hard as Durango gave one more glare at Powers, then rolled his eyes and turned to me.

"Kelly," he sighed as if he already knew what my answer would be, "do you know where the entrance to the Cad-2 mine is?"

My heart pounded, and my breathing became shallow again. I wanted to be anywhere other than here right now. But I'd made up my mind.

"No." I squeaked.

The expression on Durango's face changed in slow motion. The word I had spoken was the one he'd expected to hear. But I knew that *he* knew that I'd just told him the exact opposite of no because I was, apparently, a horrible liar. His brows lowered in concern, confusion, then lifted in shock. He blinked, and his jaw dropped.

My insides twisted in on themselves. My fingers interlaced so tightly they threatened to cut off their own blood supply.

"Kelly," he repeated slowly, "do you know where the mine entrance is?"

I couldn't look at him. Studying my thumbs in my lap, I mumbled, "It's just a guess. I don't really *know*… anything…"

"Well, tell us where you *think* it might be," Durango said, his voice still rife with disbelief.

Hating myself for what I was about to do, I mustered all of my courage, took a deep breath, and looked Durango straight in the eye.

"No."

All four officers stared at me, waiting for an explanation. My senses were suddenly very alert to the fact that I was the only female in a room full of huge, dangerous men. I was aware that Powers was seething, his hatred for me realizing its full potential. Out of the corner of my eye, I could tell that Coorabie, the only man still seated, glared at me from across the table. Chip took a step back, as though surprised. But it was the shock of betrayal in Durango's blue stare that made my eyes burn. I looked away, back to my hands in my lap.

"This morning, as I looked at the satellite images," I began quietly, "I figured something out—at least I think I did—and it's something I was in a fairly unique position to know. Yat-sen Xun would have figured *that* out as soon as he realized who it was that had taken his box from the monastery. But I didn't put it all together until today when I saw the photos. And maybe I'm wrong about it. But I don't think I am.

"This morning, the reason I didn't say anything was because of you," I explained, speaking to Durango but looking at my hands. "If I was right, and if by some remote, hideous chance there was anything there that might be tied back to you… Well, I couldn't take that risk."

A tear rolled down my cheek as I berated myself. How could I possibly have ever doubted him?

"I'm sorry," I whispered, then glanced up at him for a split second.

His face was an incomprehensible mask, staring back at me. The knife in my heart was probably equal to the one he thought I was stabbing in his back. Severing my gaze, I looked back down.

"But now," I continued, "I've started to think it through, and I can't let go of something MacAyers said to me. He said that one of the things someone could do to leverage negotiations of the Cad-2 with the monks would be to threaten to tell the Chinese government. He said the government didn't yet know about the plume's existence, and if they got wind of it, they would come in and take over the whole thing, and the monks wouldn't see a penny. Because for the monks, it's all about the money, MacAyers said.

"But it's also about secrecy. In fact, *you* guys haven't told the Chinese government about the mine either, for the exact same reason."

My resolve strengthened as I spoke. Firmer in my thoughts, I was able to look back up, meeting Durango's eyes. I directed my words at him, willing him to understand my intents, even if I communicated them in a less-than-perfect manner.

"So, here's how this plays out in my head: let's say I tell you what I think I know, and then you have to do something about it, right? Well, what then? The Australians go in and take it out, and then they have control of this stuff?

"Or maybe you tell some of the countries you're friends with, so the 'good guys' all share it. Or worse, maybe you guys go in, and you get caught by the Chinese government—who are the 'bad guys' to our countries—and then you're stuck in a Chinese prison, which I'm told is somewhere no one wants to be, and then China's mad at the rest of the world, and then *they* have this stuff, and… you get what I mean?

"It's a hideously unstable substance. *You* know that. People *will* die in some fashion if they pursue it.

"But right now, it's a secret! No one is even mining it right now because the one thing Yat-sen Xun is doing right is keeping this stuff a secret. And this is just too big of a secret for me to be the one to unlock the door."

I finished speaking, but I bit my lip and broke my gaze, still unable to read Durango's expression. Hearing a guffaw, I looked back up.

"You were right, mate!" Chip laughed, clapping Durango on the shoulder. "Heart of a lion. She still thinks she's got to save the world, doesn't she? Now, who does that remind me of? Hmmm."

"I don't think she's courageous at all," Coorabie said with a dour expression. "In fact, I think she's a complete coward, trying to avoid having to deal with the responsibility that's fallen to her. We *will* find the mine entrance without your help, Miss Morrison. It may take us months, using thousands of hours of manpower and millions—maybe even billions—of dollars. And that way, you can pretend you don't know and that you never had anything to do with this. Is that what you'd like?"

"Lay off her, Rob," Durango ordered.

"Yeah, don't worry about a thing," Powers chimed in, "because our entire government operation is just here to make *you* happy!"

"I said *no*," Durango reiterated. "Lay *off*."

"Aw, shut it!" Powers roared. "You aren't the only one who's been busting his dick on this for the past twenty-three months! You aren't the only one who was in the line of fire! Oh, but hey, your little girlfriend—who, by the way, has already cost this department hundreds of thousands of dollars—is uncomfortable! So by all means, let's just kiss her seppo butt and walk away!"

"There's no call for that!" Durango snarled. "This is an *accident* for her. She didn't sign up for this. If you want to take your anger out on someone, take it out on me. *I'm* the one who failed to find the target sitting right under my nose for a year!"

"Hey, mate," Chip interjected, "you weren't the only one out there. Me, Oscar, Jim, Rob— even Blake Tavish, Ollie Chang, and Al Prospers. We all took rotations at every hostel, farm, monastery, and tourist trap in a two hundred kilo radius of the Three Rivers area, including Zhuang Dian. We've *all* been working like dogs trying to nail this down. We all failed. But we had no way of knowing Colin was out there thwarting us."

"Yes," Coorabie purred, "our people were made, while this nobody-American stumbles around and manages to get all the information and proof we're after. But then, when she falls into our laps, she destroys the proof, and *we* are unable to extricate said information from her. Pity." He stood, picked up his laptop, directed a pointed gaze at Durango, and headed for the door.

"Spit it out, mate!" Durango spluttered.

"He's just saying what we're all thinking," Powers sneered. "Why don't you just fuck the story out of her?"

I heard a gasp come out of my mouth. I stared in horror at Powers and shrank into my chair. Coorabie snickered. Chip plopped his head in his hand, perhaps disagreeing with his colleagues' delivery method, though not with their idea. Durango's knuckles whitened, and his face got red.

"Or I could do it for you," Powers suggested.

Durango launched himself across the room, knocking Powers off his feet. Both men rolled on the floor, using each other as human punching bags.

I jumped up in alarm, backing away from the table. What had I done to Durango? What kind of position had I put him in by refusing to tell them where I thought the mine was? To have to defend my moral compass about the mine—a position he didn't even support—and then be at odds with his co-workers, all because of me! There had to be another way around this.

The monastery's ancient story of the dragons made a cameo, floating randomly through my whirling thoughts. Annoyed, I swatted it away.

And then a nugget of an idea occurred to me.

What if…?

That's ridiculous, dummy! Don't be stupid!

Still, the nugget grew.

This is right! It has to be! And it might actually work! I should tell Durango!

But, wait. With his job, there might be different rules he had to follow. *Ugh!* I couldn't involve him in this and have him facing any more political difficulties than he already was. But *who*, then?

Coorabie threw his laptop down and rushed around the table. Chip dashed across the room, and then he and Coorabie began trying to separate Durango and Powers.

Suddenly Durango's words rang in my ears: *He'd have to go troppo to try and come back here.*

That was it. It was *me*. I could neutralize the Cad-2 mine, and I was possibly the only one who could get away with it. I was the last person they'd expect to go back to China. But I had to act quickly.

Swallowing hard, I silently turned the knob, exited the room, and closed the door. *Please understand*, I begged.

89

Angrily brushing away a few stray tears, I made my way to the elevator, then the lobby. Hailing a cab, I was able to make it to a bank a few blocks away and cash the money order in my pocket for traveler's checks. The driver took me to Canberra International, where I purchased the next available flight on China Eastern Air to Kunming.

I made it to my first layover in Sydney. As I exited the plane, two airport security police blocked my path.

"Miss Kelly Morrison?" the female cop asked.

I gulped. "Yes?"

"This way, please," the male said.

Each officer took a firm grip on one of my elbows and escorted me to a cart. I was driven down to a lower level, then through an endless, dimly lit underground tunnel. A monotonous pattern of pale light-spots pulsed on the cart, the concrete floor, and the walls as we raced through. The clickity-clack and roar of a train shook the corridor as the passenger tram raced through nearby, carting travelers between terminals.

After several long minutes, the cart pulled up next to a steel door. The police ushered me out and opened the door. Brilliant white light blinded me. I squinted as a set of fingers shoved between my shoulder blades, sending me stumbling forward.

A pair of strong hands caught me, and I breathed the thrilling scent of woods and sunshine before I'd even finished blinking. Peering up into his face, I winced. His left cheek was reddened. He frowned at me with stern eyes and lowered brows.

"Do you really hate me this much?"

His tone scathed me, but then, I probably deserved it after everything I'd put him through.

"Please," I begged, "I need to do this. I need to make everything right, so you won't have to be compromised by me anymore."

I reached up, gently cupping my palm next to his cheekbone. He closed his eyes, sinking his head against my hand.

"Your bruise is warm," I murmured, upset that he'd sustained an injury because of me.

"Your cold fingers feel good," he mumbled with a half-smile.

I allowed my fingers to trail down his cheek as I removed my hand. He gazed down at me.

"You know, there are cameras everywhere at the office. When we realized you were gone, we watched that whole brain-processing scenario on your entirely-too-expressive, pretty little face: your whole guilt trip, followed by the part where you figured something out. We saw the footage of you leaving and getting into a cab. And from there, it was pretty easy to track when you booked a plane ticket."

"But I used cash?"

"And your real I.D., which I see you found back at my place."

"Oh."

"You seriously think you can go back there?"

"It would be crazy, right?"

"Yeah?"

"I'd have to have 'gone troppo' to try and do it, right? Like no one would ever suspect it, right?"

He took my chin between his thumb and forefinger. The remainder of the wall between us instantly dissolved; he was just the man I loved, and I wanted nothing more than to be able to melt into his embrace.

"Kells, whatever you're thinking of doing, it's suicide," he said gently. "You're not going."

I shook my head. "You don't understand. You have to let me go. I have to do this. And I thought of telling you first, but if I tell you what I know and what I figured out, you have to report it to your superiors, right?"

"Right."

"But I'm not bound by the same rules as you. I can go and not tell anyone."

"Go and do *what*?"

I took a deep breath. How much could I tell him before he had to choose between me and his job?

"I don't want to be the one holding the key anymore, but I won't let you be compromised because of me. I'm cleaning up the mess I've made. I'm throwing the key away."

"Sweetheart, first of all, it's not your mess, and second, *when* are you going to stop trying to protect me? That's *my* job!"

"Well, *babe*," I said, unable to suppress a grin at the rush of hearing him use the term of endearment with me, "I'll probably stop about the same time you do. I'm in this with you for as long as you want."

He closed his eyes and shook his head slowly. Then he opened them, studying me.

"What if I said I want forever?"

My heart electrified in my chest, filling me with wonder and hope. He brought his mouth down hard on mine, crushing me in his arms. I threw my arms around his neck. Was it possible we could get out of this Cad-2 crap and make it work on the other side? Our lips moved in rhythm. Panting, we pulled apart.

"What if I told you I had some latitude?" he asked.

"What kind of latitude?"

"I can act in the interest of my country without first notifying my superiors if there is imminent danger to human life."

I considered his words. "So, if I tell you what I'm up to, you'll come with me?"

"I'll decide whether or not I should go. *You're* not going." He shook his head firmly.

I cocked a brow. "Hey, cowboy, we are *not* going to play this game forever. I've made my decision. I'm going because I have to. Not because I want to, not because I have something to prove, and certainly not to torture you. You have to trust me. This time I really do know what I'm doing."

Durango scowled at me. Doubt, fear, and frustration clouded his features. His grip tightened on my waist, and he shifted his weight.

"Fine," he finally snorted. "Guess I'm going, too. What's the task?"

"I can neutralize the mine," I said.

His eyebrows shot up. "How did you come to that?"

But I shook my head again. "If you're coming, we have to go now. My plane's about to take off, and we have to get you a ticket."

"Don't need one. Come on."

His warm hand enveloped mine as he led me out a back door and into a hallway. We took an elevator up to ground level, down another corridor, and outside onto the tarmac toward a long, sleek jet. It looked like the one I'd taken on my flight from Guwahati.

He ushered me up the stairs ahead of him. Turning the corner into the cabin, I stopped abruptly. Officers Chip Van Diemen, Oscar Tindal, Gelen Coorabie, and Jim Powers were already seated in leather chairs. They nodded at me. Powers held an ice pack on his eye. A bandage was taped across the bridge of his nose.

"Okay, we're ready," Durango boomed to a flight crew. He put his hand on my shoulder. "Come on, let's take a seat. You can brief us once we're airborne."

"*Us?*" I stared at Powers and Coorabie. "Everyone here is coming? To China?"

"Sweetheart, if we're going to take on more assassin-monks, don't you at least want to have someone as pissed off as Jim on our side?"

Officer Powers grinned broadly under his ice pack and saluted. In disbelief, I followed Durango over to a sofa and took a seat next to him. The plane began to roll. As soon as the front wheels lifted, Tindal spoke.

"Okay, Trunk, before we leave our airspace, what's the game?"

"I'm going to let her tell you," Durango said.

The men turned their gazes expectantly on me. The responsibility of being right about all of my hunches suddenly scared me. What if I was wrong?

No, I thought, re-thinking my rationale, *I* know *I'm right.*

"We're going to neutralize the mine," I began. When all of their eyebrows shot up in skepticism, I backtracked nervously. "Maybe I should explain how I figured all of this out first?"

"Yes," Coorabie said dryly, "please do."

90

I took a deep breath to steady my nerves.

"There are many stories posted on the walls of the Zhuang Dian castle. I know this because I used to ditch my sculpture class most days and wander the halls. The stories were posted in several languages, including English, so I worked my way around the floors, reading them all. Until I was caught—but that's another story. Anyway, one of the stories on the walls is the legend of an angry, white fire dragon who lived in the area thousands of years ago, long before the castle was built.

"The soil in that area was extremely fertile, so over the years, people kept trying to build their villages and farms on that land. But each time, the fire dragon would come. Sometimes he would kill random individuals; other times, he would destroy the whole village. Eventually, people left the land—and the fire dragon—alone. The fire dragon became silent. Five hundred years passed. The legend was written off as an old tale, all but forgotten.

"Now, the land remained desirable, and it was eventually claimed by a new, fierce, and advanced clan. The clan built their flagship village, *Qiángshì*, on it. Over time, the city grew and prospered until it was a gleaming center of sprawling proportions. But then the fire dragon awoke. Furious that his land had been stolen, he belched forth a stream of such incendiary magnificence that the entire, huge city and everyone in it was destroyed. In fact, the fire dragon's eruption was so powerful and far-reaching that it roused the gods from their slumbers in the heavens.

"The gods, angered at having been disturbed, sent a silver water dragon to challenge the fire dragon. The dragons fought for ten hard years. Finally, the water dragon took the fire dragon around the neck and dragged him to a cave deep underground. There, using his own body, the water dragon pinned the fire dragon to the earth, silencing him forever."

I looked at the men. I couldn't read their expressions.

"You get it, right?" I asked. "The fire dragon is the Cad-2 mine, and the water dragon is a river?"

They eyed me dubiously.

"And there were two dragons, with the warrior-baby, on the door of the conference room? And on the puzzle box?"

Durango looked alarmed.

The air on the plane was too warm. I unzipped Peta's hoodie and shrugged out of it.

"Okay, maybe if I explain the other part, it will make more sense. Does anyone have the satellite photos?"

Jim Powers handed me the file, and I knelt on the floor of the cabin, spreading them out until they made one large picture. The officers leaned over from their seats to look.

"There was another class they offered once a week while I was at Zhuang Dian. It was a punishing, two-hour yoga class, and only like five or six people ever did it each time. No one took it more than once except for one or two total yogis. And me. Now, I'm no yogi. But when it was nice out, which was three out of the four weeks I was there, they did the class on the deck of the highest turret available to an outsider—which is the only reason I did the class: I liked the view. I liked it so much that I even stole a key so I could go out there on days when they didn't have the class." I pointed to the turret on the satellite image. "You could see the whole southwest mountain range during the session, and on days when I would sneak out to the turret on my own, I would always go over here to this wall. You could see *everything*. From the mountains down to the valley, through the *unbelievable* flora… here," I traced my finger down the image through what my line of vision had been, "all the way down to here." I indicated a spot on the ground beyond the edge of the turret.

"It was usually right around six o'clock when I was out there—just before dinner—and when I was looking, I would always see this little line of bedraggled workers. I *thought* they were leaving the monastery. Until I saw this photo today. The workers were going this way, and they were coming from over... here." I pointed at the three large boulders set into the hill. "I couldn't see it from the turret, but I always assumed there was more of the castle that spread out that way. But there's not."

"Maybe they were gardeners," Chip van Diemen suggested, no longer flirting but genuinely pondering my idea.

"In this section?" I shook my head. "No. It's beautiful, but this is all wild. This hill is fairly steep."

"Do you think this is where the mine entrance is?" Durango asked.

"Yes. And the bulk of the plume is underneath the castle."

"And the water dragon?" Oscar Tindal, the young, blond tech specialist, asked.

"Is that a dam over there?" Durango asked. He dropped to his knees and pointed at a spot west of the three-boulders hill. Suddenly all of the officers were kneeling around the image.

"Yup," I nodded. "And this is a sunken garden." I pointed below the dam.

"Oi, I bet if the dam didn't make the waterfall go down this hill here..." Jim Powers said as he jumped onto my train of thought.

"The river would flow right through those gardens," Gelen "Rob" Coorabie said, "but where would it come out?"

I backed away from the image so the men could see what I already understood. I eased onto the sofa, relieved to have my point of view validated. Oscar and Chip immediately began calling in for photo blowups of the dam, the gardens, and the topography around the base of the castle. Jim forgot about his ice pack as he dug through his briefcase for a timeline on Yat-sen Xun's takeover of the monastery. Rob jumped on the Internet to arrange our ground support upon arrival, and Durango drew all over the map, organizing a tactical operation. Fifteen minutes later, he plopped down next to me.

"Nice work, Morrison."

"Thanks," I grinned. "But there's something I don't get. Why would you have brought everyone to Sydney if you were just going to try and talk me out of going to China? What if I'd agreed?"

"Yeah, well, I wish you would have," he said, slinging his arm around my shoulders. "But you *are* the stubbornest person I've ever met."

"Second-most I've ever met," Chip commented. "She's perfect for you!"

"Besides," Rob grinned—the first time I'd ever seen that expression on his face, "it's not like he wouldn't have just turned the plane around. Maybe he would've taken us all to Fiji for dinner or something, eh?"

"Rob!" Durango said sharply. He gave Coorabie a quick glance, but not before my curiosity had been piqued.

"They let you do that with a government plane?" I asked.

"Sure," Durango answered, "it's full of government officers, isn't it?"

I whipped my head from Durango to the others in time to see both Rob and Oscar exchange loaded glances. I scooted out from under Durango's arm.

"You're shoveling again, aren't you?" I demanded in a low, hurt voice. "I thought we were past that."

"Look, sweetheart, remember when I said there was a lot we still needed to talk about?"

"Yes. You said you weren't going to have to leave me and go on yearlong missions and stuff, but you wanted to go back to your place first—?"

"And we never got to talk because of *this* whole thing."

"Yeah? So what's up?"

"Okay." He twisted his mouth around as though deciding what words he wanted to form.

"You know the company that my brother runs?"

"Beach Produce, right?"

"Yeah. Well, I'm a silent partner in the company."

I thought about it for a second before inspiration lit.

"Oh! I get it!" I smiled.

"You do?" He seemed skeptical.

"Sure! *Beach* Produce, and that picture of you and your brother at the beach. You named the company after a great memory the two of you had. That's adorable! I don't get what it has to do with Australian intelligence and your travel schedule, but it's still really sweet."

Durango's face was frozen in alarm. "Um...?"

"That's not why you called it that?"

"No, that part was right."

"Okay? What am I missing?"

"Um, sweetheart, my brother and I are equal partners in the company. Fifty-fifty."

"That's nice. Oh! Are you saying you're going to retire from spy work and go do the fruit company thing?"

"No, that's not…!" He raked his hand through his hair in frustration. "Kells, haven't you ever heard of Beach Produce?"

"No. Why?"

Durango twisted his mouth around some more. All four of the others had swiveled their chairs, riveted to the conversation. When Durango still hadn't answered, the others began to pipe up.

"Bris-Baked Chips, Sydney's Sugar Canes, Poppy-Pop Sodas," Oscar said.

"Bloomin' Fruit Juice," Chip added. "Bloomin' Fruit Cups, Bloomin' Fruit Pops."

"Veggie-Might Snack Stix, Tazzie Frozen Yogurt," Rob muttered.

Some of those product names were very familiar. The Bloomin' brand was in every grocery store in the U.S. My ad agency had recently tried to land the super-hot Tazzie account. But I'd had no idea there was a single company behind all of those brands. And if Durango and his brother *owned* the parent company, did that mean that Durango…?

"He's filthy, stinkin' rich!" Jim laughed.

I knitted my brows and frowned in confusion at Jim. Then I looked back at Durango. He shrugged with an embarrassed half-smile. My eyebrows shot skyward, and my jaw dropped. I sat up and stared into the distance, remembering things that suddenly made sense.

"So your apartment," I said slowly, "you *own* it, own it?"

"Yes," he nodded.

"But you're going to sell it and buy the house, to cover the cost, right? You said you were going to 'unload' it?"

"I, um, already bought the house."

"What? But we just looked at it today, and I've been with you the whole time. When could you possibly have closed on it? You mean you already…? But how could you have known that I would like that one?"

"I didn't. Back when you were in hospital in India, I sort of bought five houses that I thought you might like—"

"You *bought five houses?*" I frowned, trying to comprehend the amount of money involved, but I had no idea of the Australian real estate market. Then I thought of something else. "What about this jet?"

"Yes," he nodded.

"This is your company's jet?"

"Um, no. It's mine."

"It's... yours? You *own* this *jet*?"

"Yeah?"

Even though I'd had nothing to eat since breakfast, my stomach became extremely unsettled. I frowned, trying to reconcile this new bit of information with the Durango puzzle. My fingers found my bent nickel.

"Kells?" He scooted closer and put his hand on my shoulder. "Are you okay?"

"Not sure yet," I answered, not looking at him.

"Oi!" Rob scoffed under his breath. "Most women would be doing cartwheels to find out the guy they were dating was rich."

"Yeah, but when have you known *him* to 'date' anyone?" Chip retorted quietly. "Clearly, she's not 'most women.'"

"Yeah, well, Trunk was right about one thing," Jim smirked. "She *is* easy to read as a book. And to think, two months ago, he thought *she* was on the job! Ha!"

"*What?!*" I spun and stared straight at Durango. "You thought *I* was a *spy*?"

"Well, I'd pulled you off my roof with a backpack of Cad-2."

"I didn't know Li had taken the box, and I sure as heck didn't know what was in it! And how do *they* know you thought that?"

"I couldn't do *that* in-depth of a background check on you myself in the small amount of time I had. Not if you were CIA or something."

"*These guys* did an *in-depth* background check on me? How in-depth?"

No one said anything. The other men looked away, and Durango twisted his lips, embarrassed and apologetic. They may as well have just told me I'd been running around in the nude for the past two months in front of all five of them. Blood rushed to my cheeks.

"Never mind, I don't want to know," I squeaked. "Please excuse me."

I stood and walked through a door at the rear of the cabin that I assumed led to a restroom. Instead, I found a smaller room with a sofa and a chair. Sitting on the sofa, I hugged my knees to my chest. So, Durango had known all about me, pretty much the entire time I'd been trying to figure out who he was—or what he was. He was a mystery; I was an open book.

And this other revelation that he was rich. Not just well-off, but loaded enough to own a jet, a luxury apartment, five houses! That put him in a different level of lifestyle than I was able to comprehend.

I released my knees, dropped my feet to the floor, planted my elbows, and dug my fingers into my hair, shaking my head. My stomach churned. Who *was* this man, and how could he possibly love me? He was a gorgeous, billionaire intelligence agent, and I was a nobody with a failed career.

The door opened and closed softly. Durango sat down next to me.

"Are you okay?" he asked cautiously.

"I feel kind of exposed right now. Clueless and naked."

"Kells, I'm sorry. I was going to tell you everything. Truly I was."

"You know, I get that once I said I was working for terrorists, a background check was to be expected. But at some point, you could have let me in on the little nugget that you've *always* known *everything* about me, probably from the 'F' I got on my high school chemistry final to the last parking ticket I got. Or maybe it's worse than that? Maybe you've seen the horrible picture of me in braces and headgear when I was thirteen. Or the one Avi took of me on my twenty-first birthday. *Ugh.* Or the citation I got when I crashed my moped into a bike rack. Ha! My *parents* don't even know about those two. Or is it even worse? Have you seen the embarrassingly short list of all the guys I've ever slept with? Or my idiotic exercise in futility, wasting seven years of my life trying to move up in a company that only ever let me shift sideways after I'd moved halfway across the country just because some jerk flirted with me? I mean, seriously! The whole time I thought we were getting to know each other; it didn't really matter because you already knew everything!"

"It's not like that," he answered in a low voice. "No one was ever judging you. I certainly wasn't. We're professionals; this was part of our job. We were just looking to see if you were something other than what you appeared to be: a civilian. The only thing that triggered anything was the fact that you don't carry any debt. That's highly unusual, though commendable. Beyond that, once I knew you were exactly what you seemed, that's when I began to let my guard slip around you."

"The thing is, I never realized I was a 'job' to you. I thought I felt a real connection. I really thought I knew you."

"Kells, that *was* real. You do know the real me." He took my chin in his fingers, turning my head until I met his gaze. "No one has ever… *I* have never…."

Still too humiliated to look him in the eye, I turned my head away. "No. *You* may have known the real *me*. In fact, your whole department may have known the real me."

A chuckle laced with sarcasm huffed past my ribs, burning my eyes as it went. I clamped my molars on my tongue until the urge to cry subsided.

"Whatever research you've done could only have backed up what you saw with your own eyes," I muttered. "I was honest with you. I gave you everything that I am. But at some point between 'sure, I'll help you escape China,' and 'I love you,' *you* could have let *me* all the way in, too."

"Kelly," he insisted, cupping my cheeks in his hands, forcing me to look at him, "you *are* all the way in. It's been killing me that I haven't been able to communicate everything about my life to you because of what I do for a living. I *promise* you that the whole shoveling phase is over. I don't need to do that anymore. I *won't* do it anymore. And I'm sorry you had to find out about these things in this way."

His penitence, coupled with the fact that I really did understand—and admire—the loyalty that bound him to his job, started to weaken my sense of betrayal. He caressed my cheeks with his thumbs, the serious tenderness in his eyes matched by the gentle smile on his lips.

"You're one of the most interesting people I've ever met," he continued, "and definitely the most human in the way you experience things. Everything is so raw and in the present with you. I love seeing the world through your eyes, and I love seeing *me* through your eyes. You make me feel I've done something right, at least at some point in my life. I am more myself around you than I even remembered it was possible to be. You get who I am without all the facade, and I love your smile so much that I want to always be someone who gets to put it on your face. I want to spend every day with you, I want to take care of you, and I can't *wait* for it to start."

"Sometimes I look at you," I whispered, "I can see *you*, and I know everything I need to know. But then I learn these new things about you, and it changes what I thought I knew, and the puzzle pieces don't fit right."

"You and your puzzle!" he laughed softly. "Okay, let's finish it. What do you want to know? Ask me anything."

He took both of my hands in his and sat up, his eyes bright and expectant. Electricity coursed through my fingertips in his palms, but this time I was glad. As if he could sense it, he tightened his grasp.

"Okay. Start at the beginning. Tell me about yourself."

91

"Actually," he mused, "you already know the early years. The stuff I told you on the river was all true. I'm the youngest of four: Reg, Brenna, Tannie, and then me. I grew up in Mackay, Queensland, played footy through high school, then dual-majored in international relations and Indonesian at UQ, with a diploma in geographical science, or 'maps,' as you called it. Two months after graduation, my father was killed on assignment in Somalia."

"On assignment? I thought you said…?"

He saw her brows shoot up and understanding dawn in her eyes. He nodded.

"That's why your parents were in Spain when you were conceived," she said.

He laughed. "And why they were in Vietnam near the site of the Battle of Long Tan when my sister Tannie was. Dad did banana farming on the side, between assignments. We never knew the truth until after he was gone, and by then, I'd already enlisted in the military. I'd begun to lose interest in the agricultural lifestyle in my last year or two of schooling. I knew there was something else out there better suited to me, and Reg was running the family business just fine, practically on his own, anyway, before Dad passed. He didn't need me. Right after Dad's funeral, I left for basic training.

"I spent three years in the regular army before I applied and tested for the Special Forces training course. After completing it, I was assigned to the Fourth Battalion, Royal Australian Regiment, and I did that for another five years. As you know by now, that's how I met Sandy and Khin—during one of my deployments.

"Toward the end of my time with 4RAR, Mum died. And that came on the heels of a particularly tough assignment. Something changed inside me afterward, and part of me began to shut down. I looked at my siblings one day—all of them living 'regular' lives, married with kids—and suddenly nothing about that connected with me. I told myself then I'd never find someone or have a family. I didn't recognize it, but I was beginning to cut myself off from my own emotions by denying they existed."

"Because you were so upset about your mom?" she asked quietly.

For a fleeting moment, he considered explaining the mission in Cambodia, the one that had been the primary cause of his decision to leave the military and had also led to his recurring nightmare. He'd never told anyone, and something told him he should tell her. But the mission was classified, and the nightmare infrequently happened these days, so he skipped the details for now.

"My mum, coupled with that last assignment, was probably a lot of it. But there were other things, too. A year after Dad died, I'd given Reg my share of what Dad had left us, so Reg could turn the farm into what became Beach Produce. Flash-forward, by the time Mum died, six years later, the company was going gangbusters, and I had more money than I knew what to do with. I began to overindulge. Made some dumb decisions and came up empty—a lot. I only lasted a little while longer with the military before I knew I needed something different.

"The Service was a natural segue. Once in, it immediately felt right. I got to travel, it was mentally and physically challenging, and the only relationship I had to focus on was the one with my country. I buried myself in the job. I hid my financial assets—except from my immediate team, which was unavoidable—and, in the lifestyle I led, most of the time, no one knew who I was anymore. I could be whoever I invented. The contact I had with other people was mainly superficial—for business, pleasant camaraderie, or entertainment purposes—but that was the way I wanted it to be. Told myself it was in my blood because of Dad. The job was my life.

"Unfortunately, that also began to feel hollow over time, but it took me a while to realize I'd lost my sense of direction. By the time I started living in China, after seven years with the Service, I'd begun to wrestle with what I'd done with my life, wondering if any of it had been worthwhile.

"Yunnan was different from my other assignments. It was strange living in one place for so long. After a year, I was getting to know and like some of the locals, which I hadn't allowed myself to do in a very long time. I told myself it was fine because I was just going to turn around and leave them all anyway. The mission was a bust—waste of a year. But by then, I was beginning to recognize that I'd been going through the motions of life, but I wasn't sure if it meant anything anymore. Why did I even do this job? And then, just when I was ready to throw in the towel, the universe intervened."

"What happened?"

"I met you." He reached out and stroked her cheek. "You have no idea what you've done to me."

Kelly closed her eyes and leaned her head into the caress. Then she caught his fingers and kissed them, meeting his gaze with a gentle smile. He couldn't possibly be more smitten.

"But let me back up a second. You deserve to know all of this part: Two years ago, we heard a rumor that someone was working with large quantities of Cad-2 either in or around the Three Rivers Protected area of Yunnan. As unbelievable as it sounded, our source was credible, so we had to check it out. We began scoping out the region, posing as everything from researchers to tourists. My job was to embed with the locals. But after a year, we began to think we were chasing a ghost. The substance is, after all, notoriously difficult and costly to produce. Mass quantities of it were unheard of.

"But then we thought we'd had a lucky break. The night you and I met, I was supposed to have had a meeting in which I pretended to be a buyer."

He told her about the poker game and the messenger in the seedy bar on the same night she'd escaped from the monastery with Li.

"You were supposed to meet with Nathaniel Richardson?" she gasped.

"I never had a name before you gave it to me that day at the gas station, but it probably would have been him. He's been under surveillance by your government ever since.

"Anyway, at that point, I was the last one of us left in the area, and I thought the whole thing was just a scam. I was literally waiting to be sent back home. But then I got a knock on my second-story patio door just as I was coming out of the shower..."

He recounted his version of the events to her. It was hard for him to believe that night, a little over two months ago, he'd been prepared to kill her if necessary—this woman with whom, at some point during their present conversation, his fingers had become interlaced.

"By morning, when the reports came back negative on you, I knew you were going to be a key witness to a murder—and probably also to an arms deal—so I was going to help get you to safety, in addition to acquiring the box. That's when I saw you and Li on one of the security monitors picking up the car keys and sneaking out of the house. No part of the background check told me anything about how obstinate you could be. I made a dash for the parking lot and waited for you to show up. By the way, the look on your face when you realized you'd been caught was priceless." He winked. She shook her head and giggled.

He recounted their journey out of China.

"When you were almost strangled by the monk at the hotel, I knew you were just an ordinary civilian, but with an extraordinary sense of purpose. You had concrete ideas of right and wrong, coupled with that impossible stubborn streak—I was fascinated!

"Color began to seep back into my dreary, gray world, and I suddenly wanted to protect this beautiful creature who'd started to remind me why I did what I did for a living. I had to learn more about you, if for no reason other than to reinvigorate myself by understanding black and white again. I also still needed to get a closer look at the box. Fortunately, our second phase of travel gave me that opportunity. Though, if anyone had predicted what was in store for me, I'd never have believed them.

"That whole day on the river, the deeper we got into the wilderness, the more you relaxed into yourself, and I began to slip right along with you—little bits of me that I shared against what I thought was my better judgment. I watched the bafflement on your face as you saw me pulling back, clamming up, reigning myself in, though you had no idea why. Everything with you felt so disturbingly natural. Still, I had a job to do, and I had to keep that my priority."

He told her about the monks he'd come across on his "walkabout" the morning after they'd camped at Tingming Lake, finding the transmitter in the box, and his version of their trek through Burma.

"Through the years, I've met countless people of all shapes and sizes. I was convinced I'd seen it all, and everyone was the same. No matter what face they put on, they were all out for themselves. Whether it was for money, power, sex, or even because of a need to fulfill a sense of duty, most people only care about what's in it for them.

"Then I met you, and you refused to play games. You were exactly what you seemed. That immediately set you apart. Soon I realized your only thought was to protect everyone else around you, including me, whom you didn't even know. You carried a deadly secret, doggedly refusing to share it because you were afraid the knowledge would endanger other people. That was amazing, inspiring.

"And then, as I spent time with you, I enjoyed seeing things through your eyes. You lived in the present, fully experiencing each moment with whatever emotion it carried. I repeatedly lost myself in your vision of the world until I wanted to be the person you thought I was. You had good guys and bad guys, and I wanted to be one of your good guys."

"Durango, you already *were* one of the good guys when I met you."

"I love my country; I do what they ask of me," he replied. "But so much of what we do is governed by laws, rules, and regulations. It becomes a giant, confusing game of politics, one big blob of gray."

She shook her head. "I get what you mean about the political stuff, but if you hadn't done everything that you did, I wouldn't be alive right now. Neither would Qing or Li. And those children that you saved from the traffickers! None of it was part of your job, but you did it anyway. You put yourself on the line for us, and you made the decision to do it on your own. That came from here." She pressed her hand to his heart. "You are the best man I've ever known."

He closed his eyes and grabbed her wrist, holding her palm to his chest.

"This is what I mean," he breathed. "You keep making me feel that everything I've done with my life has been for a reason. You keep turning me back toward myself, and I actually like what I see, even though since meeting you, all of my decisions have been based on *you*."

He kissed her fingertips and continued.

"As Qing began to drive away from the bazaar—and I kept checking to see if you were breathing—it finally dawned in my head what my heart had been trying to tell me much earlier. It was as if my entire existence had led up to the point where our paths crossed—where the universe had literally dropped this incredible being into my arms—and if I could keep you safe, maybe I could keep you. This feeling of being so close to another human, of not just knowing you but understanding you, admiring you, *desiring* you, and knowing that you reciprocated—at least I was pretty sure you did—I could have that forever. All I had to do was be smart enough to see it and take it."

He recounted the car chase with the monks and their subsequent trek through the jungle into India.

"Your affinity for water slides is impressive," he grinned.

"Okay, once again, I didn't slip down that muddy mountain on purpose. I was focusing on where I was placing my feet, and I crashed into Li."

"Yeah, well, if you're this much fun when you don't mean to be, I can't wait to find out what you're like when you do!" He grinned and resisted the urge to kiss her again until her questions were done. He couldn't tell her *everything* yet, of course. Just enough to satisfy her and not scare her away. He did, however, grab her legs behind her knees and pull her closer to him on the sofa.

She giggled again. Then her gaze drifted back into reverie, and her smile faded.

"By the time we left Burma, Qing had started to question a lot of things about you," she said. "He was the one who asked me if it was enough to know *who* you were without knowing *what* you were."

"So that's what started the wheels in motion on you giving up on me?" Durango asked.

"It wasn't you I was giving up on. It was me. My life was like years of trying on all these different outfits, and none of them fit. Then finally I found the dream dress, made exactly for me, gloved perfectly to my body. But it was a Cinderella gown, and it was almost midnight. In fact, that's exactly what you said to me as we were getting in the cab, 'It's almost over.' And I didn't want it to be, but I didn't know how to make it go on. And when you dropped us off at the hotel and left, it felt… final."

"I was coming back."

"I didn't know that. I didn't hear from you all day, and I thought it was really over. I felt sad, frustrated, and empty."

"I had work to do. I went to the Australian embassy, called my office, briefed my superiors, requested reinforcements, and secured travel arrangements for you,

Li, and Qing. There was a lot of red tape involved. By the time I got back to the hotel, it was late. You were already—how did you put it—getting your girl on? Good thing I made it when I did. That limey bastard was already undressing you from across the room."

"The British guy who tried to rescue me from you?"

"Yeah, him."

"Don't be so hard on him. When I ducked into the club again, later, he helped me get away from MacAyers. The last time I saw him, I think he had a broken nose."

"Good." Durango smirked. "Maybe we can send him a medal or something."

"Speaking of medals, what were those medals in that box I found at your apartment?"

"They were from my time with the 4RAR. One was the Star of Gallantry; the other was the Victoria Cross for Australia."

"What were they for?"

"They just mean that I did my job really well a couple of times."

Kelly frowned and shook her head. "Why are you always so evasive when someone asks you about something good you've done?"

"I don't mean to be evasive. It's just how we were raised in my family. When you do something good, you get your satisfaction from the doing, not from calling attention to yourself afterward. That diminishes the deed. Plus, it gives you a big head."

She rolled her eyes. "So go on."

"Well, let me just say that I have never hated my job as much as I did at that moment in the hotel room when I realized you'd pulled away from me because you thought I wanted that box, not you. Simultaneously, I was overwhelmed when I figured out you were still trying to protect me from being hurt by you. I don't think anyone has ever cared about me like that.

"And then, just before we ran out the door to retrieve the Cad-2, which I still can't believe you stashed in the hotel refrigerator, you said you loved me. My entire *world* shifted with that, and it was all I could do not to take you in my arms and run away with you on the spot. But that's when I knew." He slid his hands up her arms to her neck, cupping her jaw.

"Knew what?" Her eyes were pools of golden-flecked chocolate, gazing at him with trust, warmth, and love.

"That I got to keep you."

"Yeah," she whispered.

This time he did kiss her. She responded by sliding her arms up his chest and around his neck, pulling him closer. His right hand drifted down her front and trailed back up under her shirt. Her breath quickened as his fingers caressed up the smooth skin on her belly. Gently, he felt his way up until he reached the raised scars below the left side of her ribcage.

Suddenly she pulled back and touched his arm, stopping him. *Oh, fuck!* He hoped he hadn't just hurt her. She pressed her forehead against his. The sweet taste of her lips lingered in his mouth.

"Is that where…?" he asked, not touching the scars but not taking his hand away. She nodded. "Does it hurt?"

"No."

Relief flooded him. She was just self-conscious. That, he could help with. His fingers touched the scars again. "I want to see it."

"What?"

"I want to see it," he repeated.

"They're icky." She crinkled her nose.

He raised an eyebrow and smirked. "I'll show you mine?"

"I've seen you without your shirt on," she scoffed. "Your body is perfect."

"Hardly," he snorted. "Nice to know you think that, though."

He sat back, unzipped his pants, and pulled down the waistband of his underwear. An uneven circle the size of a nickel and an embossed, four-inch line marred the flesh next to his left hip bone. She stared, seeming interested and not the least bit repulsed.

"What happened?"

"Sniper fire during a hostage recovery mission while I was with the 4RAR. Almost lost a kidney."

Tentatively, she reached her hand out as though asking permission. When he didn't stop her, she gently touched the old wounds, caressing the bumpy skin with two fingers while her other fingers rested on his abdomen.

"Where did it happen?"

"Melbourne."

"It happened in Australia? What exactly…?"

"A political extremist showed up at a diplomatic summit that was supposed to have been private and secret. After a few hours, we got the main guy, but as we were evacuating the twenty hostages, his buddies started popping off from the top of the atrium over the lobby. I got my sights on one of them just as he lined up with the Malaysian prime minister. I jumped, took him out, and blocked the shot."

"Wow! That's so cool!"

"Yeah, it sounds impressive when you talk about it, but all I remember about the time is that it hurt like a beehive up a bandicoot's arse. Got me right below my Kevlar. That's why they gave me the Star of Gallantry, though—the gold medal with the orange ribbon that you saw. None of this is public record, of course, since the summit was supposed to be a secret."

"Of course." She nodded in understanding, but her eyes shone with admiration.

"But I only saved one person that time, not two-and-a-half million." He arched a brow pointedly. Then he grinned and sat forward, reaching for the hem of her shirt. She grimaced and shrugged, then lifted her embroidered tank above the base of her ribs. He ran his finger lightly over the twin, half-inch, magenta scars where the thoracoscopy tube and fiber optic scope had been inserted to repair her pneumothorax. He remembered her body flying through the air and crashing down hard on the rooftop patio. It was amazing that those small marks were the only physical remnants of what she'd been through.

"My ribs didn't break just from the blast," she muttered. That got his attention.

"What do you mean?"

"Yat-sen Xun kicked me. Though, in his defense, I *had* just lit him on fire."

Durango felt his brows shoot up. She'd had to actually physically fight with Yat-sen Xun—not just words—and she'd still managed to get the fireworks lit? Also, she'd lit him on fire? He guessed that explained Yat-sen Xun's charred appearance after the blast, but he realized something else and frowned.

"You know, I don't think anyone's asked you about your encounter with him. What happened exactly?"

"When he kicked me, I felt *and* heard the bone crack. Landing on the ground after the blast just made it worse. But I was running *away*. It's not like I deliberately jumped in front of a bullet like you did. Yours is way cooler."

He ignored the compliment and focused on potential intelligence that he and his team might have overlooked. "What did he say to you?"

"Not much. Just your standard, megalomaniac diatribe: 'Who do you work for? How did you manage to find out about my secret plot to take over China and the world? I'm the true emperor, yada-yada-yada.' I think he called me a 'ding-a-ling,' too, or something that sounded like that. Then he did that ninja-choky thing, and that's when I Bic-flicked him." She explained how she'd managed to get the firework lit and continued to have to fight with Yat-sen Xun until the blast "saved" her.

"But *I* got something way better than a medal," she grinned. She trailed her hands up his shirtsleeves and laced her fingers behind his neck.

"Oh, really?"

"Yep."

A phone near the sofa rang. Durango felt a twinge of irritation. "Hold that thought." He picked up the receiver. "Oi." He listened. "No, not Kunming. See if you can get us straight into the one in Lijiang. Let me know." He turned back.

"Now, where were we?" He traced his fingers down her arm until they interlaced with hers. "What else haven't I told you?"

He was delaying what he really wanted to do with her at the moment, waiting for the phone to ring again, plus the rest of their circumstances were all wrong right now. She seemed to agree because she didn't seem put off.

"We got past MacAyers, the bomb, the hospital," she reflected. "When did you leave the hospital?"

"I was ordered to go home straight away, but I stayed until you were out of surgery and your parents arrived. I wasn't supposed to talk to you until they'd finished deposing you—a job you made unnecessarily impossible—but they couldn't even begin to do that until you were cleared to travel. I spent my free time trying to get ready for you down here."

"The houses?"

"Yeah. I narrowed it down to the five I thought you might like, bought those, and I also cleaned my apartment, had your stuff from the monastery shipped in, got a copy of your birth certificate, started researching architect and design firms for you to talk to—"

"Whoa—my birth certificate?" She jerked her head back in surprise.

"If you're going to be living here for any length of time," he said vaguely, hoping he hadn't said too much to put her off.

"Sounds like red-tape overkill. I'd have thought my passport would be good enough. And architects and designers? Why?"

"Well, obviously, I didn't know which house you were going to choose, but all of them need some sort of modification for upgraded security systems, at the very least. On the one you picked, we're probably going to want to make some structural changes. Maybe a new kitchen—we could knock down a wall and expand it to flow more from the front of the house. Then I was thinking we could expand the back end through the existing patio and do a pop-up second level, maybe move the bedrooms up there, and improve on closet space. Did you see how shallow the closets were?"

The shadow of a frown crossed her features.

"I thought the house was fine the way it was."

"Oh? Didn't you even want to renovate the kitchen?"

"I don't know… maybe? I mean, I hadn't really thought about it yet. Maybe just some paint?"

She seemed upset. Maybe she thought she thought they would have to do the renovations themselves, which would be a lot to take on, especially on the heels of her recovery from surgery. He should mention the contractor.

"I want you to at least meet with the designer as soon as possible, so we can get the contractor started on it before my next assignment." There. That should help.

"When does your next assignment start?"

"First, I have to finish this one. Then I was going to take a few weeks off. But the next time I go, I wanted to take you with me." He studied her, wondering if he should tell her the rest.

"You're allowed to bring civilians with you on assignments?"

"Certain types of civilians, yes. Those guys take their wives all the time." He nodded his head toward the forward cabin.

"Those guys are all married?"

"Well, Chip isn't. But the others are."

"*Jim Powers* is married?"

"Yeah," Durango laughed. "His wife is really nice, too. You'll like her."

Kelly raised her brows in doubt. "The woman must be a saint."

She tried to stifle another yawn. Then she shivered. "So, what's it like being rich?"

He automatically shifted, pulling her close and caressing her skin to warm her. She responded by pressing ever-so-slightly into his side, and then her muscles relaxed. He felt relief that at least it wasn't *him* she'd seemed jumpy about.

"Well, we didn't grow up rich, Dad being a 'banana farmer' and all. We always had food, shelter, decent educations, and whatnot. But we were never rich. My brother's company didn't start turning any serious profits until about ten or twelve years ago. In that time, I've learned that money really and truly can't buy you happiness. It can only get you some nice toys."

"Is that why you still work?"

"Pretty much. I enjoy what I do, and I'm good at it. Makes me feel like I'm helping people. Especially since my wake-up call two months ago." He squeezed her shoulder.

She smiled up at him but couldn't stop the next yawn. She pulled back, tucked her feet up to the side, scooted her hips away, and laid her head on his thigh. He was surprised for a moment, and it occurred to him that he'd never had anyone do that with him before. Yet here she was, doing it as though it was the most natural thing in the world: resting her head on his lap. He stroked her hair, marveling at its softness, and amazed at how, on the one hand, he wanted to take her to bed, but on the other, she was tired, and this just felt… nice.

The phone rang again. Durango picked up.

"Hey… Okay, good. What's our ETA? ... Okay, thanks." He hung up and had an idea, so he lifted her head off his lap. She pushed herself upright.

"Hang on a second." He stood and pushed a button.

The front cushions moved forward, and the back flattened down, converting the sofa into a bed. Opening a cabinet, he pulled out a plush blanket and a pair of pillows. Then, he climbed over her and lay down with his front pressed against her back, covering them both with the blanket. He slunk his arm around her chest, hugging her to him. She interlaced her fingers with his, snuggling even closer, and sighed. He kissed her neck.

"So that green SUV we wrecked in Burma," she asked sleepily, "I really don't have to pay you back for that?"

"No," he chuckled softly. "I don't even have to pay for it. It was a work-related expense."

"Whew!"

He felt her limbs relax deeply. A second later, her breathing became even. He stayed like that, holding her, for a very long time. It was more intimate than any relationship he'd ever had with a woman. He found it interesting that he could feel so fulfilled by another person.

Also that he could feel so protective of someone.

Which is why there had never really been any question in his mind about what was going to come next. Even though she wasn't going to like it.

92

Kells. Sweetheart, wake up."

His voice, a gentle, sonorous rumble, came from the wrong side of the makeshift bed. The sound was followed by his lips, soft on my cheek. I smiled into a full-bodied stretch, turning toward him as I blinked my eyes open. He was crouched next to the converted sofa.

"We'll be landing in a few minutes. You should eat something."

"What time is it?" I rubbed my eyes and sat up.

"Four a.m. in Canberra; one a.m. in Yunnan."

I'd been asleep for at least a few hours. Durango smoothed strands of hair off my face, and that's when I noticed he was wearing his black gear again. Reality, and the gravity of the mission, sank in. My smile faded.

"Did you sleep?"

"I was really comfortable for a *while*," he began.

"But?" I asked in alarm.

"Let's just say I'm not the only one in this relationship who smells good," he muttered.

Oh. That. I stood into his embrace and wrapped my arms around him.

"Sorry," I said in a tone suggesting I was anything but. "Let's go take care of business, and then we can go home and… take care of business."

I stood on tiptoes and kissed him. He kissed me back, but his tender expression became serious.

"Sweetheart, um?"

I raised my brows.

"I've been thinking it over, and you really don't need to come."

"I don't… what?" My ears began to pop as the jet descended.

"Well, you've explained your theories, and we've all studied the map and the data. There's really no reason for you to come. We can do it without you."

Still sluggish from sleep, my brain slowly began to process what he was saying: he didn't want me to come to the monastery. *But, wait a minute!* The overwhelming sense of urgency flooded back through me.

"What do you mean 'there's no reason' for me to come? This *whole thing* was my idea! I'm the one who *has* to do this because of everything I know! Plus, no one will ever suspect me to return here, and between the two of us, I'm the one who isn't bound by as many rules and regulations. You're only here because you followed me, and you could still run into your political-game trouble. If anyone has to go, it's me. This is *my* mission."

"No, Kells, you really *don't*, and this has been *my* actual assignment longer than it's been your self-imposed one."

I pulled away from him. The cabin shook as the wheels touched down, shaking me off-balance. Durango reached out to help stabilize me, but I righted myself and stepped away from him.

"I'm the *only one* who took that darned class so many times, and looked over the turret, and read the mythologies on the walls, and *also knew about the Cad-2!* Neutralizing the mine was *my* idea. I *want* to do this. I'm going."

"*No*." His icy blue stare and the hard set of his jaw might have intimidated me in the past, but no more. On top of that, his definitive tone made me see red.

"Whoa! *Not* asking permission!"

"*Americans!*" he muttered and looked away, raking his fingers into his hair. He took a deep breath, which didn't seem to calm him down much because his tone was still testy. "Alright, if you went and did things your way, what exactly would you do?"

"Well," I started slowly, "I hadn't got that far yet, but I'm thinking if I go into the mine, I can get a teensy amount of Cad-2, run it back to the top of the dam, then leave and wait for it to blow up the dam when the sun comes up and heats it."

"Hmm," Durango pretended to consider, "resourceful, organic, and… oh! Fatally unpredictable! You saw firsthand what a tiny sliver of that stuff did from far away. Even if you *managed* to extract a sample half that size—and assuming you *didn't* run into any Shaolin monks—you could still blow a hole straight down to the main plume and—"

"Chillax! It's just one idea! I'll figure it out once I get there. Besides, I'd be detonating it right next to a water source. Remember the dragon story? The main plume would be drenched before the… incendiary-ness… hit it."

Durango's frown deepened.

"Maybe I'm not making myself clear. I *don't want* you to go. I'm *requesting* that you choose to remove yourself from the mission. *We* know what we're doing, we have precision-target devices we've been trained to use, and as smart as you are, this isn't your area of expertise. You'll be in the way, and you'll be a distraction."

It felt like Percy Loomis all over again, telling me I wasn't good enough for the position—which was what had led to my *entire* trip to China in the first place. Which was how I wound up embroiled in this mess, to begin with—and suddenly, all of the anger and humiliation I felt about my own failures came out directed at Durango.

"How would *you* feel if someone took *your* project away from *you*?" I yelled.

"A lot better than if *you* got hurt or *killed* just because you were too stubborn to admit that I'm right about this!" he roared back.

I glared at him, fuming, my lower lip jutting out. Unfortunately, my proprietary feelings about the mission began to be usurped by an inkling that he was right and that he and his team were better suited to handle this task. Memories surfaced of my blind attempt to save the children in Burma, followed by his actual accomplishment of the deed. But there had been blood. Not his, but what about next time?

Thoughts of the danger *he* would be in, of *him* getting killed, plagued my vision. A quiver trembled my chin.

"Aw, sweetheart, please don't sulk," he cajoled. "I'm sorry I yelled."

"It's not that," I whispered. "I'm worried about you."

Any hardness left in his face melted away as he took a step forward and grasped my shoulders.

"When are you going to trust me, Kelly?" he asked softly.

"I—"

About to insist that I *did* trust him, I stopped myself. This was it. It wasn't about a power struggle. It was about really believing in him, letting go, and standing back, watching him walk into the fire. I knew we were both aware he might not make it back, but he was the one who was trained to do this between the two of us. And *this* was who he really was.

My eyes burned as I knew what I had to do. The lead balloon in my chest expanded until it squashed my churning stomach. On top of the premature sense of loss, terror prickled the hairs on the back of my neck. How could I let him go?

"Kells?"

Hot tears spilled down my cheeks. I closed my eyes and hung my head. Is this what it would always feel like every time he left? Then again, what other choice did I have? I loved him.

"How far can I go with you?" I whispered, meeting his gaze through my watered vision. He pulled me into his arms, and I choked back deeper sobs so that I could inhale his scent through stuttered breaths for what might be the last time.

"I didn't think I could love you any more than I already did," he murmured, sounding surprised. He kissed the top of my head and hugged me tighter. After a long minute, he pulled back, cupped my face in his hands, and stroked my wet cheeks with his thumbs. His expression was of love… and relief.

"Stay here. I'll be back before you know it." One more quick, passionate kiss, and he was through the door to the forward cabin.

He immediately blended in with the others, who had also changed into black-gear outfits. I hung back, watching the huge men as they grinned, electrified with the promise of action and stealth. They punched and shoved each other playfully and descended the stairs into the inky, whirring night.

And then the cabin was silent.

The purr of a car's engine floated in from outside the plane. I walked up the aisle, arriving at the hatch in time to watch the last of them, Oscar, as he climbed into the back seat of a black car that pulled away from the tarmac even as he was shutting the door. My heart sank as I watched the scarlet taillights fade away.

93

Rob Coorabie drove. They headed north toward Lijiang from the airport, then skirted the city, heading west, to get on the national highway that paralleled the Yangtze. Their intermittent conversation was mostly meaningless banter and off-color jokes. Stuff to get their minds off the pre-mission tension. They'd all been here before, the others as tourists, Durango as the guide.

It felt strange to be back so soon after he'd spent most of the previous year wanting to leave. Barely ten weeks had gone by, but he was a different person now, he thought. He'd changed. Although, he reflected, his relief at her not being there was only partly because she'd have been a distraction. There was something else they needed to do, and he didn't want her there for it. So maybe he wasn't completely a different person. Maybe some things never changed.

The highway curved east, following the river. Given that it was the middle of the night, in the middle of the week, and a less touristy season, they made good time. Within two hours, they turned onto the rutted, old road. The castle loomed high on the steppe, a dark shadow against the hulking mountain that continued to rise above it. The moon was about to set, and its light was already hidden by the mountains to their west. Aware that the sound of the tires crunching on gravel would carry, they stopped a half-klick downhill from the gates. Rob executed a harrowing five-point turn on the precipitous road and parked next to a tree.

They got out and walked silently uphill. A strong breeze stirred the treetops, indicating an incoming storm. Soon thunder echoed low in the distance.

They reached the top. The gates sat closed and chained, the monastery beyond completely dark. Oscar Tindal opened a large duffle bag and handed a bolt cutter to Jim Powers. Chip held the chain steady to reduce noise, and Jim made the snip, timing it with another roll of thunder. They waited. Nothing stirred in the castle.

Chip, Jim, and Rob carefully unwound the chain. Durango and Oscar applied lube to the gate's hinges on one side. They opened that side of the gate and waited again. Again, nothing stirred.

All five men slipped through the opening and entered the monastery's grounds.

They split up.

Each did what he needed to do.

Ten minutes later, there was another noise. This time it was undeniably louder than the thunder, and the ground shook.

This time the castle did stir.

And all hell broke loose.

94

It had been five hours. I couldn't wait around anymore. I had cash in my pocket, and I needed a rental car. The flight crew was resting, so I'd found the control to lower the stairs on my own, and now every muscle in my legs, thighs, ankles, and feet flexed and contracted as I hurtled myself forward against the doom to which I'd condemned him.

I knew I'd told him I would stay put with the plane. But I'd spent five hours staying-put, which was an hour too long for it to take for them to be back by my best guess.

And it was all my fault.

I shouldn't have told him my idea. I shouldn't have told them what I knew or what I'd figured out. I should've clammed up, said nothing, and let him take us all to dinner in Fiji. Or even let myself go to jail if that's what it would've taken. But now he was out there, facing off against who knew how many ninja assassin monks, and it was all my fault.

I'd heard the November storm start up in the distance hours ago. As it grew, it reminded me of the storm that had been raging when I'd escaped the castle with Li two months ago. The trigger was too much, and the lightning and thunder were now in full force as I headed for the terminal. Hard rain drove sideways, hitting me square in the face. I could barely see. My arms churned forward through the squall toward the first reference light, which was low to the ground.

I was about to veer past it when a pair of powerful arms shot out of the blackness, catching me around my waist. My legs, still in motion, went flying forward. The arms swung me around, so I landed on both feet.

"Kelly! Where are you going?"

I gasped. And then I threw my arms around Durango' neck, crying against his warm skin. I'd been so blinded by fear and rain that I hadn't recognized the "reference light" had been their vehicle's headlights.

"I thought… The storm!" I blubbered. Pushing wet hair out of my eyes, I searched his face. "Are you okay?"

"I'm fine. We're all fine," he answered. Relief surged through me at those words. He handed the rental car keys to an airport employee who'd apparently been standing there, getting wet and watching me make a fool out of myself. The employee hopped in the car and drove it away. "Come on. We have to get a move on."

More relief as he ushered me back to the plane and up the stairs in front of him. The jet's engine began to whine. One of the flight attendants closed the hatch behind us. Rob exited the forward lavatory, having already changed back into his other clothes. Oscar had already changed as well. I must have passed by them while I was running. Rob grinned and nodded at me, passing Jim, who entered the bathroom next.

"What were you doing out there?" Durango asked, tossing me a fluffy, white towel. "Thought I told you to stay on the plane?"

"Thanks." The engine's whine picked up, and the plane started to roll. I removed the damp hoodie and wrapped the towel around my shoulders. "You said 'with,' not 'on.' And I *tried* to stay put for as long as I could, but then the rain started, and there was rain *that night* when I left the monastery, and I freaked out, and…" I shrugged.

Then I caught sight of Chip, still in his black gear, his arm drooped at a funny angle. In fact, Oscar and Rob seemed a bit bedraggled as well. I frowned.

"What happened?" I asked.

Jim exited the restroom. He was the only one who looked the same as before, with a black eye and tape across his nose. He grinned, punching Chip's shoulder as he plopped into a nearby chair.

"Oi!" Chip protested, glaring at Jim.

I whirled back to Durango. A fine red line beaded up on his cheek through his previous bruise. I gasped.

"I thought you said you were all fine?" I demanded, whipping my towel from my shoulders and gently pressing it to the cut on his cheek. The plane lifted off the ground. I staggered to the side, but he caught me around the waist, steadying me. He kissed me.

"We *are* fine," he insisted gently. "Let me go change."

He kissed me again then went into the lavatory. Placing my towel down so I wouldn't ruin the sofa leather, I took a seat.

"What happened to your arm?" I asked Chip.

"He dislocated his shoulder in a three-on-one," Oscar said.

"Would've been seven if you and Trunk hadn't stolen the others from me!" Chip complained.

Jim nodded at Rob and Oscar, who got up. Oscar grabbed Chip's legs, and Rob held his good arm.

"Ready, mate?" Jim asked Chip.

"Get on with it," Chip nodded.

Jim yanked Chip's arm, twisting it. A crunch-pop sounded, and Chip roared, exploding out of Rob and Oscar's grasps. Durango exited the bathroom. Chip jumped to his feet and took a swing at Jim, who ducked just in time. Durango caught Chip's fist with one hand and punched him in the face with his other. Chip shook his head.

"All right, then?" Durango asked.

Chip grinned and sat back down.

"Thanks, mate," he said.

I stared at the five men.

"Sheesh," I finally muttered, "I'd hate to see the other guy."

Rob smirked; Oscar chuckled.

Durango pulled out a blanket and draped it over me. Sitting down on the sofa, he slung his arm around my shoulders and stretched his feet out in front of him, closing his eyes. The other men settled back into their chairs. The cabin became quiet.

I grew impatient.

"So, did it work?" I demanded finally.

"Did what work?" Durango asked without opening his eyes.

"The mission!" I replied incredulously, sitting up, letting the blanket fall down. "Breaking the dam! Neutralizing the Cad-2 mine! Preventing one of the most combustible substances on earth from being unleashed on the innocent populace! The whole reason we came to China!"

"Oi," Rob called over, "what's she talking about?"

"Yeah," Jim yawned, "Anyone here been to China?"

"Not in a long time," Oscar said, shutting his lids.

"Mmm," Chip agreed, his eyes already shut.

I stared in disbelief. "Are you *kidding* me? After the past week and a half I've spent with you guys, now you're going to pull the Fraternal Order of James Bond on me?"

"Bond's a pussy," Jim slurred as he fell asleep.

"Sweetheart, come here. You're wet and cold," Durango said.

"*Et tu?*" I cocked a brow. He didn't respond.

"Fine," I muttered, "since no one else has been there, I guess I'm just going to have to make a trip myself to take care of some business."

In a blur, I suddenly found myself on my back on the sofa, looking up into his intense blue eyes.

"Or," he said, his expression serious, "you could just trust me to protect you."

"But I did!" I protested though I kept my voice down since some of the guys were already out. "I let you *go*, and for *hours*—!"

"From the truth," he cut in. "From having to know any more than you already do. Can you let me do that?"

Exhaustion lined his face, despite the passion in his gaze. In addition to whatever it was he'd just done, he also hadn't slept on the flight over.

"You're asking a lot," I grumbled.

He nuzzled my neck. I gasped in delight, arching my chest toward him.

"Oh, no," I whispered, pushing him up and off of me, "we can play hardball later after you've slept."

"Okay," he agreed, pulling me up with him, "but you should get some too. You have a doctor's appointment at five tomorrow."

"A doctor appointment? Is that part of that whole Australian-overkill thing, like my birth certificate?"

"Yeah, it's this weird thing we do after people have cracked ribs and punctured lungs. It's called a checkup."

"Oh. One of those." I sighed and snuggled into his chest, surprised at how quickly I was able to get comfortable. It was almost as if his exhaustion drained into me. His breathing became deep and even, and within a few seconds, so did mine.

95

Fortunately, the late afternoon in Canberra was warm and sunny because my hoodie was still damp. With the time difference, we hadn't been able to go home for a shower and change after the flight. We drove straight to the doctor's office on the west side of town. It bothered me that he still hadn't even given me a hint about whether he and his team had been able to successfully neutralize the mine, even if I sort of understood why. It felt like something was off between us, but I didn't want to start an argument, so I didn't bring it up. Besides, there was something else on my mind.

"I should probably make another doctor appointment after this one," I mumbled as the car careened along on the "wrong" side of the road, which was still slightly unnerving.

"Oh? Why's that?"

"You know. Girl stuff."

"Oh, you mean because you're not on birth control?" he asked.

"How did you…?" I puzzled. Then it hit me. "Oh, *no way*. My medical records, too?"

Durango shrugged. "Sorry. Should I have pretended not to know?"

"No," I agreed after thinking about it. "But wait a minute, you've known all this since the beginning. So back in India, at the hotel?"

"Why do you think I stopped and asked if you were sure? I mean, I had protection with me if you'd wanted to go that route. At first, I thought that's why *you'd* stopped, but I couldn't figure out why you were apologizing."

I considered this for a moment.

"But what if I'd said yes?"

We turned into the hospital parking lot, and he gave my palm a squeeze before turning off the ignition and turning toward me.

"Sweetheart," he reached for my hand, "I've known since Burma that I was ready to do forever with you. And anything and everything that goes with it."

He leaned in and kissed me, a kiss that was sweet, sincere, and full of love. My heart simultaneously exploded with joy and froze in fear. I'd had no idea he'd had feelings this big for me all the way back since Burma, and that part was wonderful. But I didn't know how to respond to the other part. I mean, I knew I wanted children *someday*, but he'd already been thinking this way for two months! Part of me was ecstatic; the other part was terrified. I was silent as we entered the building.

My appointment was with a cardiothoracic surgeon, Dr. Walyunga, who kept an office on the second floor of a medical office building next to a hospital. It was two minutes past five when I checked in at the desk. The receptionist was standing and had her purse on her arm.

"Well, Miss Morrison, you're his last patient of the day," she said cheerfully. "Dr. Walyunga is just finishing his notes from surgery. I'm going home now, but the nurse will come and get you when the room is ready." She handed me a clipboard with a few pages to fill out. Then she left, and I went to sit with Durango in the small, empty waiting area. When I finished the paperwork, he reached for my hand again.

"You know, we were supposed to meet with the designer next week," he said, bringing up the topic of the house again, "but I could probably pull some strings and have her meet with you tomorrow if you're up for it."

"Oh, you don't have to do that," I said, feeling my nerves go jittery again. "I would hate to ask her to drop other clients, and—"

"No worries! She's already excited to meet you. I'll take care of it. It's not a problem."

I took a deep breath.

"Why does it have to be so fast?" I said in a rush.

"I thought I explained all of that, about my next assignment, and, er… oh! Are you having second thoughts about the house? Or about… us?" His voice was cautious, bordering on dejected.

"I love you, cowboy," I said quietly, "but yesterday morning, I woke up thinking that you were a fugitive, that I would never see you again, and that I was going to prison. In the past thirty-six hours—give or take a time change—I got you back in my life in the *best way*, only to have to let go of you last night, so you could go on an impossibly dangerous mission. Do you have any idea how that feels?"

He didn't say anything. I played with his fingers.

"You've had time with this," I continued in hushed tones. "You've understood more of everything that's been going on for the past two months, while I've had to blindly guess for most of it. It feels like I've made this giant leap of faith, but I don't know that you have."

He jerked his head back as though I'd slapped him.

"You want me to prove that I love you in some other way? Is that it?"

"No. I *know* that you love me. But," I searched for the right words, "you just don't trust me the way that I trust you. There's a piece missing."

"You and your damn puzzle! If I'd have let you come and risk your life, would that have been trust?"

"No, I agreed that you were right about—"

"Or if I tell you everything that happened? You know why I can't do that!"

"No! I *don't* want you to compromise yourself!" My voice rose.

"Then what?"

"I can't… I don't know! Maybe I just need to process everything that's been thrown at me in the last day and a half before we start… playing house!"

"Miss Morrison?" The nurse entered the room as though she hadn't heard my last, rather loud, testy statement.

I rolled my eyes miserably at Durango then got up to follow the nurse into the exam room. She left for a moment while I undressed from the waist up, donning a hideous, paisley hospital gown that wrapped closed in the front. When the nurse returned, she took my vitals, reviewed the paperwork, took me to a side room for new X-rays, led me back to the first room, told me to have a seat on the exam table, and left again.

The fluorescent lights overhead did nothing to help the two-tone vanilla and maroon walls. Magazine-less, sitting on the crinkly tissue paper, I occupied myself for a while by studying the tacked-up human anatomy images detailing skeletal, circulatory, and pulmonary systems. The left lung. That's the one that had been punctured.

I opened up my paisley gown and touched the small, twin, dark pink scars beneath my ribs where the chest tube and scope had been inserted. If I'd managed to stay put that night in India, maybe this wouldn't have happened. Maybe Durango would have been able to tell me the truth about himself that much sooner, and I wouldn't have had to spend two months away, not knowing what had become of him.

Then again, if I'd known the truth and had stayed put, maybe I wouldn't have gotten to the Cad-2 in time, and he and Qing and Li and I—and everyone in Guwahati—would have been reduced to vapor. So maybe it was supposed to have worked out this way.

I didn't like what I'd had to go through today, letting go of him like that. It felt like a piece of me died when he'd walked off the plane. But as horribly sick as I'd felt in the pit of my stomach, I knew at that moment that I would put up with it every time he left, for as long as he wanted to have this profession. So maybe I was just being foolish, delaying happiness for both of us by hedging on going forward with him.

But there was the other issue, niggling the back of my mind, that I couldn't quite put my finger on.

Over and over, he'd saved my life, deliberately throwing himself in harm's way to protect me. He never allowed me to risk my own life, not on purpose. It was chivalrous of him, noble. And it wasn't that I didn't want to live.

But it was almost as though he didn't think I was capable of succeeding. Like he thought I'd fail if I tried, and he had to protect me from disappointment.

I certainly knew about failure, having experienced it repeatedly for the past several years. But I knew how to get back up, too. I *did* have strengths and the courage to attempt new things, and I needed to know that he could stand back so I could at least *try*. I needed to know that he could see I had value, that I could accomplish something, and that I wasn't some porcelain doll about to shatter.

The door opened. I closed my gown as the doctor walked in. With his name embroidered on the pocket in red letters, his white lab coat seemed too short, flapping at his hips, and his face was buried behind my charts, studying my history.

The door clicked shut behind him.

"So, Miss Morrison, I see you're from the United States, and you're here for a follow-up to injuries you sustained in… India? Is that right?" My hospital records from Guwahati had been transferred here, so there was no hiding that part. From behind the file, his voice sounded vaguely familiar. I shrugged. It would get easier to distinguish everyone once I'd lived here longer.

"Yes, Dr. Walyunga," I answered, probably botching the pronunciation of his name.

"Interesting," he said. He held up one of my X-rays, keeping it level with the file, and seemed to be considering something. His fingernails looked dirty, which struck me as weird for a doctor. Or maybe it was a reflection from the X-ray. "What brings you to Australia?"

Given my circumstances, I hadn't been asked that question yet, and I didn't know how I was supposed to answer. But "your country's intelligence agents needed to question me because I'm a witness to an illegal international arms deal" probably wasn't it. I went with another part of the truth.

"My boyfriend lives here," I explained.

"Does he, now?" he chaffed. His tone made me frown.

The doctor lowered the X-ray and the file, and for the first time, I saw his face. His blond hair was disheveled, and a weeks-old shaggy beard shadowed his jaw. A crazed gleam beetled in his eye. It wasn't a doctor. It was Colin MacAyers.

96

My heart stopped. If MacAyers was wearing the doctor's lab coat, where was the doctor? And Durango, sitting in the waiting room—was Durango okay?

"Where is Dr. Walyunga?" I managed through a dry mouth. If MacAyers didn't know Durango was out there, I wasn't going to be the one to tell him.

"The cardiothoracicist had a myocardial infarction, if you can believe it," MacAyers said, pulling an empty syringe out of the lab coat's pocket. "I've always wanted to say that, by the way."

Laughing, he tossed the syringe at me. I threw my hands up to avoid touching it; it bounced off my chest and landed in my lap. A translucent plastic cap covered the needle, but I could still see blood beaded up inside. I recoiled but didn't touch it, too stunned and scared to move.

"What do you want?' I asked, afraid of the answer.

He held up his hand to silence me and cocked his ear toward the door. "*Wait* for it!"

I strained to listen. A long minute ticked by, and then a woman shrieked. Another minute and footsteps hurried down the hall toward my room.

MacAyers ducked behind the door. He pulled out a pistol and put a finger to his lips.

The door pushed open. The nurse popped her head into the room. Tears of panic reddened her eyes.

"I'm sorry, Miss Morrison," the nurse hurried through my words, "but we've had an accident, and Dr. Walyunga is going to be unavailable to see you today. Will you be okay to see yourself out?"

More footsteps in the hallway. The sound of a gurney rattling down the corridor. Voices. An emergency response team from the hospital was rushing to take care of Dr. Walyunga.

The nurse turned her head back to the hallway to watch the team. I gulped and glanced quickly into MacAyers's cold, steel gaze. From behind the door, he leveled the pistol even with the nurse's head. If I said nothing, I'd be alone in the office with MacAyers. If I said something, the nurse would be dead and maybe also the hospital response team.

"Sure," I answered.

I was probably dead either way. But was Durango okay?

"Thank you," the nurse replied hastily, not even looking back at me. She shut the door, and I locked my gaze on MacAyers.

His lip curled up slightly. From the hall, the nurse spoke to the team. Her voice and the sounds of the gurney diminished away out of the office. Silence settled on the room.

"Okay, they're gone. We're the only ones left," I said. "What do you want from me?"

How long could I keep Durango out of this?

"You know, I've heard of sheilas like you," MacAyers said, "but I really didn't believe it until I saw it with my own eyes back in India. How many times are you going to throw yourself on the tracks for him?"

Shallow breathing took over. MacAyers knew Durango was here. A knock sounded at the door.

"Kells? Are you still in there? Are you getting dressed?"

A surge of relief that he was alive mixed with desperation to get him out of here. MacAyers moved away from the door, positioning himself behind the exam table. He nudged my head with the pistol.

"Go on," he whispered. "Invite him to the party."

"I'm mad at you!" I yelled at the door. "I scheduled an uber, and I'm leaving! Just go away!"

"Aw, sweetheart, I apologize. I shouldn't have pushed you like that. If you want to wait, we can wait. We'll go at your pace, whenever you're ready. Can I come in?"

"No! Just go away! I'm going back to America!"

MacAyers swatted a stinging blow to the side of my head with the muzzle, then walked around the exam table and crossed the room. He glared at me and aimed the pistol at the door. Durango was on the other side of the door. My heart began pounding against my ribs.

"Sweetheart, can't we just talk about this?"

"Do it!" MacAyers whispered furiously. He slid his thumb across the back of the gun, unlocking the safety.

"No!" I screamed in desperate response to both men.

"Aw, shit, I'll do it myself," MacAyers hissed. "Come on in, Trunk!" he boomed.

The door opened slowly. Then Durango entered quickly, his own pistol preceding him.

MacAyers retreated behind me. The circular barrel of his muzzle felt cold against the back of my skull by the time Durango had fully entered.

I bit my lip and tried to convey unfathomable apologies to him in the millisecond glance he gave me. All of his attention focused on MacAyers.

"Colin." Durango nodded as if they were meeting casually in the street. His aim stayed with MacAyers's head.

"No. Down," MacAyers said.

Durango hesitated. MacAyers's barrel pushed hard against my head, and I winced. Durango held his hands up and set his gun on the counter. The pressure on my head released.

MacAyers emerged on the right side of the table, motioning Durango to the left, away from his pistol.

"How do you do it, Trunk?" he asked bitterly. "Your whole life, they just fall all over themselves for you. And this one's a real piece of work. She was ready to go to prison for you before, and now she's ready to take a bullet? Nice. Wouldn't have pegged you to hide behind a woman, but it wouldn't be the first time I was wrong about someone, would it?"

"Leave her out of it, Colin. This is about me, not her." He placed his hands on his hips.

"Hands *up*! I know where your spare is! And yes, it sort of is about this little seppo bitch who bilked me out of fees with both the monks and the Arabs with her fireworks stunt. Besides, I understand congratulations are in order. You're a couple now. So, what do you say to turnabout as fair play?" MacAyers pushed the muzzle into my right shoulder.

"Meaning what?" Durango asked. For the first time, a glimmer of fear flashed behind his eyes.

"Well, you did my wife just before we got married," MacAyers pointed out.

The muzzle slid across the front of my hospital robe and down the V of my exposed skin. I clutched at the robe. MacAyers forced the muzzle down between the folds of fabric until the cold circle pressed against the bare flesh between my breasts. My breathing became very shallow, and I felt my pulse hammering in my neck.

"Don't you think it's only fair that I 'do' your girlfriend?"

I gulped. He didn't mean "do" as in "have sex." He was going to kill me, right here, while Durango watched.

Durango took a quick step toward MacAyers's arm. MacAyers whipped his gun off me and pointed it at Durango. Instantly, Durango inserted himself between MacAyers and me.

"You're going to have to kill me first, Colin." Durango eased his hands toward his back.

"Hands *up*!" MacAyers screamed. "In fact, turn around! I don't want her reaching for it, either!"

Durango slowly raised his hands and turned, facing me. I knew that look. His mind was racing, calculating his next move. He glanced down, then raised a brow in question. I followed his gaze to the empty syringe in my lap.

"You know, it didn't have to come to this, Trunk," MacAyers announced. "I was willing to let you leave here. Wounded, of course, but alive. Professional courtesy."

An idea hit. From MacAyers's position, he couldn't fully see me behind Durango. In slow, careful motion, I slid my hands onto my lap. Grasping the syringe, I removed the bloody, translucent needle cap. The size and weight of the syringe in the fingers of my right hand felt familiar. I could do this.

I glanced up at Durango. He knit his brows in confusion.

Work with me, I thought.

But Durango had no idea what I was thinking. I glanced down to the right.

Just move over. I can do this!

He looked alarmed as if to say, *You're nuts if you think I'm giving him a clear shot at you.*

MacAyers continued babbling. "You know, if you're bent on death, I could just go right through you, Trunk. But it will probably make it more painful for her since we don't know what part of her will get hit first. If you move, I promise she'll only feel it for a second. The point, though, is that you get to watch. Now step aside."

Yes! I willed my thoughts into his blue eyes. *Step aside!* I glanced to the right again.

No! He frowned firmly back at me.

Yes. You have to trust me this time.

Kells, I can't! Don't ask me to do this!

Trust me.

I countered the agony on his face with a calm resolution of my own. Ripping my eyes from his gaze, I focused beyond Durango, willing myself to see through him, on the spot where MacAyers would be standing once Durango moved. Taking slow, measured breaths, I raised my arm, fingers gripping the syringe like a pencil.

Or a dart.

"Fine, Trunk," MacAyers grunted. "Have it your way."

I reached out with my left hand, trying to push Durango to the side. To my surprise, he exhaled a tortured huff and pivoted to the right of his own accord.

Time slowed down. MacAyers paused for a fraction of a second, seeming surprised that Durango had actually moved. In the last instant, my right arm was exposed. I flicked the syringe with expert precision at my target: MacAyers's right eye.

The dart found its home.

Durango lunged at MacAyers, and the gun went off. MacAyers shrieked.

Durango knocked MacAyers to the ground. The pistol clattered on the linoleum. A mixture of red and clear fluids began to pool on the floor under MacAyers's face. Kneeling on MacAyers's back, Durango grabbed MacAyers's head and wrenched it to the side. A pop and a crack echoed off the walls. MacAyers's body slumped lifelessly. My ear burned.

I met his cobalt gaze, and then his arms were around me. I hugged him back as if I could absorb his life force. Nothing else mattered.

"Don't ever do that to me again," he breathed.

I inhaled his wonderful scent. He was alive. He pulled back and cradled my face in his hands, lifting my head. His eyes burned with desperation.

"If this is what it does to you when I leave, I can quit. I don't want you to have to go through this, either. We can take our time, get to know each other for as long as you want."

"No," I shook my head. "I don't need to wait anymore. I'm ready *now*. I want you—who you are, the way you are. I love you, Durango Archibald Trunk, and I want to spend forever with you and anything and everything that goes with it!"

An expression of overwhelming love crossed his face. Still holding my chin, he closed his eyes and lowered his warm lips to mine. When we pulled apart, he pressed our foreheads together.

Suddenly he frowned and pulled his hand away from my left cheek. A crimson line stained his fingers. I reached up and touched my ear. It felt intact, but the top was wet.

"Am I hideous?" I crinkled my nose.

He smiled. "Never. But if you're worried, it's just a superficial wound. Here."

He found gauze in the cabinets and cleaned my injury. Shaking his head as he stopped the bleeding with a tiny bandage, he muttered, "Darts champ, huh? Very impressive." Then he crouched down and began to wipe off the syringe that was still sticking out of MacAyers's ocular cavity.

"What are you doing?" I asked.

"Keeping you as much out of this as possible," he answered. He was removing my fingerprints.

"Stop," I requested. Jumping to my feet, I crossed the room and put my hand on his shoulder. "You don't need to protect me from everything."

He stopped, then sagged and leaned his head against my leg.

"I will always want to," he sighed.

I raked my fingers through his hair.

"And sometimes I'll let you," I murmured.

97

He had to call the event into his office. It was another three hours before we were able to leave. Fortunately, it was only a ten-minute drive back to his apartment.

"You exhausted?" he asked, his arm around my shoulder as we rode the elevator up.

"Not really. I slept on both plane rides. You?"

"No, just hungry."

"Yeah, food sounds good," I agreed. We walked down the hall. "But what I really want is to burn these clothes and take a hot shower."

"Knock yourself out," he laughed, opening the door for me.

We crossed the slate floor, passed through the living room, and veered left through the dining room to the hallway. He flicked on a light switch. The blank white hall led to doors on the left and the right.

"My room is that way," he pointed to the right, "but I didn't want to be presumptuous, so I had that room set up for you." He pointed left.

"Oh," I said in surprise, trying to hide my dismay. "That was very… gentlemanly of you. Thanks," I added as he retreated toward the kitchen.

I turned left down the hall. A delicate floral aroma filled the air. Entering the room, I felt around, located the switch, then gasped in delight.

A square, black headboard against a white wall met my eyes. The queen-sized bed was made up with white sheets and a cream-colored comforter, accented with pink throw pillows and a pink throw blanket—glossy black lamps with white shades perched on black nightstands. Two dozen red roses burst from a vase on one and two dozen pink ones on the other. A creamy armchair sat in one corner next to a black table that held more roses. Beneath my feet, a plush ebony and eggshell area rug covered most of the tile.

To my left, the closet door was open, and I saw that all of my clothes from the hotel had been brought in and hung up, as well as my things from the monastery. My suitcases were tucked neatly on a shelf. A giant window was covered in floor-to-ceiling white drapes with a black accent stripe.

I rounded a corner to find a large, white bathroom with black granite countertops, a huge multi-head shower with a broad, built-in shelf for shampoo and conditioner, a neat stockpile of fluffy, white towels, and even more roses.

Grinning broadly, I turned on the shower and stripped off my clothes, carefully placing my bent nickel necklace on the counter. The water pulsated from amazing angles. In ten minutes, I'd washed my hair, shaved my legs, and lathered and rinsed my entire body.

I got out and grabbed a fluffy, white towel from the rack, only to discover it was a heated rack, and the towel was warm. Wrapping myself in the delicious sensation, I bent my head upside down and began a quick blow-dry. When my hair was down to ten percent damp, I whipped my head upright, flinging my hair back to finish the blow-dry, and was startled to find I wasn't alone in the bathroom.

I met his gaze in the mirror. He stood, arms crossed, leaning against the wall, his lips in a smile, but his gaze intense. Like me, he wore nothing but a towel. I took in his delicious, Adonis-like figure. He noticed my admiration, and his smile became a mischievous, self-satisfied grin curling one side of his mouth.

He pushed off the wall and stalked toward me. I watched him in the mirror. Butterflies of anticipation fluttered in my stomach. He came up behind me, curled his palm around my right hand, which had frozen in midair, took the blow-dryer from me, turned it off, and set it down. At the same time, he wrapped his other arm around my belly.

"Okay, now I'm being presumptuous," he growled.

"I'm really good with that," I whispered.

He grazed his teeth down my neck, which sent mini-shivers of pleasure through my body. I gasped. Then I twisted around and massaged my palms up his hard, broad chest, the same chest I'd accidentally braced my hand on the night he'd pulled me off his roof. I'd dreamed of touching him like this for real and couldn't believe it was finally happening—and how much better it was because of everything we'd been through and how well I knew him now. I moved my hands up, exploring, and he dipped his head, crushing his lips to mine, pulling me tight to his chest. One of my hands went into his damp hair. The other clutched his strong shoulder. His tongue caressed into my mouth, and I arched against him, causing my towel to fall down to my waist. He pulled back and began to kiss his way to my chin, neck, and chest, then lowered his lips to my left breast, slowly teasing the other with his thumb. Waves of pleasure radiated from my nipples straight to my groin. I exhaled a sound of delight, and in one swift movement, he discarded both of our towels, locked his lips back on mine, and picked me up.

We were kissing frantically and never made it to the bed that he'd had set up for me because he brought us through that room, down the hall, and directly to his own room. By the time we'd made it the short distance there, we were crazy. I'd already maneuvered around in his grasp, getting my legs around his waist, and had wriggled down onto the tip of his erection. Our tongues thrust desperately into each other's mouths. He lowered me onto his king-sized bed and immediately finished entering me. We made love hard and fast, climaxing together within seconds.

We panted, catching our breaths, gazing at each other in wonder. Durango was still inside of me, and I relished the sensation. Then, looking deeply into my eyes, he began to move again, slowly. I responded gently but was surprised when the wave started to build again, higher… higher… He balanced his upper body on his forearms so that our chests rubbed lightly against each other, increasing the pleasurable friction in my breasts. My calves were still twined around his powerful thighs. He looked me in the eyes once more.

"I love you," he said. And then he kissed me deeply.

I felt the shudder start between my legs. It built and built, and grew and grew until my entire body literally rocked with wave after wave of the most intense detonation ever. The waves kept coming, and I heard his breath go short, and then he, too, groaned. He quivered hard against me, sending the wave up to a place I didn't know was possible. I think I actually screamed.

He collapsed on me, spent and grinning. I was still dazed, riding the most delicious aftershocks. Then he rolled to the side, pulling me with him into his arms.

"I love you, too," I managed to sigh, just before we fell asleep.

When we woke an hour later, it turned out we weren't done.

We alternately slept and made love for hours. We took a break to eat at one point but ended up feeding each other food and then christening his kitchen island. Then one of the dining room chairs. (I *know* I screamed that time.)

By sunrise, we were back in his bed—again—tangled, exhausted, and delirious. I collapsed on his chest, breathing hard for a few seconds, and then moved my arms to rest my chin on the back of my hands. My legs still straddled his hips, and I experienced a sensation of possession: *This man is mine.* He stroked a lock of hair out of my eyes, and I knew my sensation was right. He belonged to me, and I to him.

I grinned up at him, still catching my breath.

"You're *beautiful*," he murmured, with an incredulous tone, like he was seeing me for the first time. I loved him even more for that because I knew I must look a mess after all of our tumbling around, but he meant it. Then he said something else:

"Marry me, Kelly."

I felt my grin being replaced by shock and lifted my chin off my hands. I stared at him, but he continued to hold my gaze evenly.

"*What?*" I breathed.

He sat up, taking me with him, until I was kneeling, with my thighs hugging his legs. I couldn't read his expression. He kissed my nose, then scooted out from under me. I scrambled to the side and suddenly felt the need to cover up with the sheet, even though we'd just spent the last several hours getting to know every inch of each other's bodies.

He trotted across the room to his dresser, and returned carrying a small, black velvet box. He knelt on the bed next to me.

"Marry me, Kelly," he repeated. He opened the box.

I looked down at a large, round diamond flanked by four smaller diamonds positioned like compass points, all set into an exquisite platinum band. I blinked and gasped.

"Oh, Durango! It's beautiful! When did you…?"

"As soon as I got back here from India."

My jaw dropped open. "As soon as…?" He'd already been planning this since *then*?

"Sweetheart," he said tenderly, cupping my cheek with his free hand, "I told you: I've known since Burma that I was in love with you. You're it, for me."

My heart expanded against my ribs. My vision went watery.

"Kelly Morrison, will you be my w—?"

"*Yes!*" I cut in. "Yes, Durango Trunk, yes! I love you." I said the last three words with everything in my heart and tears spilling down. I threw my arms around his neck. He kissed me sweetly, through a smile which he couldn't seem to stop. Then he took my left hand. His fingers trembled as he slid the ring on my fourth finger. He pointed at one of the smaller stones, the one in the "east" position.

"This one was my mother's."

Fresh tears started in my eyes. We'd met in the Far East. I clapped my right hand to my mouth.

Unable to speak for a moment, I finally whispered, "*Thank you!*"

He stroked away my tears. "No, Kells, thank *you*," he said huskily. "All those times you said I saved you, really it was you saving *me*. You've given me the world in a way I never knew it existed. You've given me a life. I love you."

"I love you."

He kissed my head, my cheek, my neck. I let myself fall backward underneath him once again. I knew there were things I didn't yet know—things he hadn't told me about himself, and maybe some other things he needed to tell me, too. We'd get to those, in time. But after all of this, after all my searching and feeling lost, I'd finally found where *I* belonged. Right here, with him.

Acknowledgements

Some people disappear for weeks or months at a time while they are writing. I disappeared for years at a time. To my surprise, some people decided it was okay to keep me in their lives. The following are folks without whom I would not have made it this far:

To my writing coach, Lori DeBoer; my editor, Kate Seeger; and the excellent team at Grimweir.

To my writer friends, some of whom read this story in very early stages, and who kept encouraging me to write, especially Brenda Moffat, Jen Daly, Ginny Shepard, Monica Fritch, Brenda Clarke, and the rest of the Independence Inklings. To Doug Clifton, Judy Rose, JT Evans, Brenda Laartz, Gavin Ehringer, Jean Rosecrans, Michael Renier, and Dom Nozzi.

To my friends, who kept the other parts of me sustained (and also kept encouraging me to write), especially Annie White, Sheri Herkimer, Patricia Arguelles, and Rosemarie Harrington.

To my family members, who always believed in me, especially Matt, Tim, Joy, Maureen, Kathleen, Kevin, Martha, Uncle Bernie, Aunt Hilde, and Rick.

And to my children, who didn't care if I never wrote a single word.

Thank you!

www.ingramcontent.com/pod-product-compliance
Lightning Source LLC
Chambersburg PA
CBHW060542310726
48982CB00009B/1351/J

* 9 7 8 1 7 3 7 6 0 8 7 1 4 *